PHOENIX FLAMES

A CONSPIRACY OF RAVENS BOOK TWO

SHELBY LEE

table of contents

author's note

Phoenix Flames is a dark, romantic suspense novel that contains triggering situations. It is a why choose novel, meaning our heroine does not ever have to choose between our three heroes. This book is intended for mature audiences 18+ and contains the word 'fuck' probably far too many times.

For a full content warning list, please visit:
https://linktr.ee/authorshelbylee

*To all of my smutty humans who just want someone to
dominate them from time to time.*

raven

The world is silent following Pierce's confession, except for the pounding of my heart and the rushing of blood through my ears. My hands are shaking, and my chest is heaving with the breaths I'm struggling to take. My gaze flits back and forth between his eyes in a panic.

He leans in closer, holding my hands tightly in his to keep me from flying away from this moment.

I may have broken our relationship, and he may have crushed us further into oblivion, but I know in the end, we're on the same journey back to the soul-crushing love we had before.

I look up at the boy—no, the man—who stole my heart. The one who's owned it since the moment we met. The way he's looking at me? It's like he's been waiting for this moment much longer than he's aware of.

Inhale.

Exhale.

"Pierce," a voice startles us both from the moment, and Pierce's jaw tics in anger when he looks over my shoulder, glaring at the voice's owner. "Sorry, but we gotta go or we'll be late."

"Coulda fuckin' waited two point five goddamn seconds or some shit, Nix," Pierce grits out, exhaling loudly before meeting my eyes again.

My pulse is still pounding in my ears, but I'm glad Phoenix interrupted. I'm not sure what my answer would have been, whether I would have said I loved him back or torn him a new asshole for the bullshit he's put me through recently.

With Phoenix's presence invading the room and reminding us of our meeting with Maxwell, neither one of us will get an answer anytime soon.

"Hey all you cool cats and kittens, are we going or what?" River yells out from the garage.

I roll my eyes at his annoyingly adorable antics and slide off the bar stool, schooling my features and fixing the leather jacket to my body.

"You ready, Red?" Phoenix asks, bringing his hand to my lower back right as we step into the garage.

We've all decided to take the bikes today, and I'm apparently riding with Pierce.

I didn't get a choice, of course.

Something I'll be glad to plan revenge for later.

"Red?" Phoenix pulls me from my thoughts, halting my movements when we reach Pierce's bike. He tilts my chin up with a finger, forcing our eyes to meet. I shake my head.

I am not in the mood to talk about it right now.

Any of it.

"Fuck off, Nix," Pierce says, shouldering past Phoenix to place my helmet onto my head. "I'll be careful, little bird. I promise."

I huff out a breath in response.

"Seriously. Trust me a little, please?" he begs. His hands tighten on the bottom of the helmet to keep me from turning away.

We stand there for a moment staring at each other, but when I don't respond in any fashion, he sighs and releases me, placing his own helmet on his head.

All the guys climb onto their bikes, and I wrap myself tightly around Pierce's body. We take off slowly out of the garage, one after the other.

Phoenix and River ride ahead, opening the gate and waiting outside for Pierce to shut the garage door. When we pass them after locking up, they take off side by side behind us on the road.

As all three bikes roar through the trees, I can't help but wonder if we're leaving one lion's den and heading into one far worse.

The ride ends before I can get used to being this close to Pierce on a death machine again. Luckily, it's also before I can reminisce too much about the last time we were on a bike together, boundless and free.

"Stick fucking close to me," he says after we all take our helmets off. He wraps his arm around my shoulders, tugging me tight into his side as the other two step up beside us.

River grabs my hand and holds it in his as we make our way toward the front doors of the Cobalt University admin building. "You'll be okay with us, come Hell or high water, RaeRae."

His words comfort me, sure, but the loss of his hand when we step inside does the opposite.

I sometimes wonder what others think of our relationship, since it's anything but conventional. They all probably think I'm a slut, or we're all simply seeking the sexual side of things.

They'd be wrong, of course.

"Ah, Mr. Jackson," a woman speaks up from behind the front desk. Her long brown hair is straight, and she's wearing a black pencil skirt and a white blouse. The desk is so tidy, I wonder if she even uses it. "Mr. Langston is waiting for you with Mr. Perkins in his office." She pauses for a moment, taking in our group, narrowing her eyes at me briefly before meeting his gaze again. "Shall I escort you in?"

"Got it, thanks," Pierce grits out, moving past her toward the closed door which displays Maxwell's name on it.

I don't know what I was thinking of doing when I saw Maxwell after finding out he's my father, but I know for a fact it wasn't to stand as frozen as I am right now. My feet refuse to move past the threshold while I take in all of our similarities.

Our blue eyes.

The way our skin matches, even with the deep tan I'd gotten this last summer.

An errant curl that hangs from the center of our hairline.

I swallow roughly, battling the tears threatening to

giveaway my inner turmoil.

Why did he have to be the way he is?

"Pierce, my boy!" Maxwell bellows out, his arms stretched wide, a cigar in one hand and a glass of amber liquid in the other. "Come, give me good news about Ms. Hill! I hope she's helping build our reputation back to its glory days."

"She's doing just fine," Pierce says, calmly walking toward the desk. He places his hand on top of my shoulder and pushes gently, urging me to sit down after everyone else does.

I do, if only to keep my knees from buckling under me.

"Ah, good, good." Maxwell says, taking a puff from his cigar before putting it out in a black ceramic ashtray on his desk. Leaning back, he swirls the liquid around Once.

Twice.

Three times.

Then looks me directly in the eyes.

The room falls silent enough to take in the differences in everyone's breathing. I keep mine as steady as I can, but I'm certain my nervous pulse is echoing around us.

"Maxwell is putting me up to VP of Alpha Mu, PJ," Jimmy says from behind the man himself.

He'd been silent, and we'd all been trying to ignore him standing there.

"Bullshit," Phoenix snarks at the same time River lets out a loud, incredulous laugh.

"I must have misheard you, Jim-boy," Pierce grits out, glaring at him with an incredible amount of vitriol. "Say it again. Slower this time."

"I. Said. Maxw–" Jimmy says sternly.

"Boys!" Maxwell admonishes, laughing as he slams his glass on the table. We all jump, but he doesn't care, continuing on. "Jimmy is stepping up to take some of the work off of you. Gives you three time to do the job I've asked of you. Ms. Hill," he says, turning his eyes toward me now, "how have things been for you? Do you need anything?"

Keeping my back straight and my gaze impassive yet polite, I shake my head. I hold a small smile on my face to stop him from sensing that I know something.

"Alright then. If you wouldn't mind stepping out for a few minutes. There's some secret fraternity business I need to talk about with the boys. Miss Tricia can grab you a glass of water when you step out." Maxwell waves his hand toward the door and I nod sharply as I rise to my feet.

I need to get out of here.

Every male voice in Maxwell's office pipes up into loud chatter the second the door closes behind me. I'm half-tempted to walk back in there, stomp my foot, and wait them out until they include me in the conversation. The other part of me is aware of how much I don't want to be in there with my father and Jimmy.

Breathing becomes harder and harder for me, forcing me to sit down on a leather couch on the wall opposite the front desk. I bring both of my feet up onto the black material, folding my legs and wrapping my arms around my knees as I place my head between them.

I'm so over Jimmy Perkins.

But he's never gonna be over me...

I MOVE BACK *against the wall the second I hear the rustling of the curtains. Drawing my blankets up over my nose, I only expose the top of my head.*

The creaking of the floorboards followed by footsteps alerts me to his presence.

He sighs.

"Well, I'd hoped you'd be asleep for this one, sugar," Jimmy says. His drawl is a little thicker, and I can smell the alcohol stench from all the way across the room.

I don't remember if I locked the window, or if I was foolish enough to leave it open.

Again.

Trauma tends to fuck with my head that way, ensuring I forget all of the important things I should be doing.

I reach for my phone on my nightstand, intending to call 911 and get someone over here, but Jimmy rushes me and knocks it to the floor.

"Tsk, tsk, Raven," he chuckles darkly, shaking his head. Reaching toward me, he yanks the blankets down, revealing me to him.

I feel so exposed, even in sweatpants, a hoodie, and fuzzy socks.

Barely any skin is showing, yet he looks at me as if I'm already naked for him.

"Fuck, you look so delicious for me, Raven." Jimmy's lips tilt up in a wicked grin, raising those blue eyes to meet my gaze. Red rims his. What did he get into tonight? His drinking is the biggest part of our problems.

I blink back tears as he trails his hands down my body, digging in too hard, scratching me with his rough nails. Attempting to save my dignity, I pull up swiftly, curling in on myself. I manage to knee Jimmy in the balls, and he tilts to the side, unable to catch himself before he falls to the floor with a loud thud.

Too bad no one else is here to hear it.

Scrambling as quickly as my shaking body will take me, I grab my phone from where it fell, avoiding Jimmy's writhing form. I pull up a new message and text 911, telling them what's going on and where I'm at.

Jimmy manages to get himself up, but I avoid him entirely as I rush toward my closet, shutting and locking the door.

I installed the chain the last time he attempted this, and it's coming in handy now. Even as it rattles from how hard Jimmy hits the door, it never breaks.

Too bad I do.

I curl into myself and cry and cry and cry; hating the silence of it all, aside from my sniffling.

By the time the cops arrive, Jimmy has already left, and I spend an hour relaying information through a text message with a very frustrated officer.

"This is the fifth time this month, Ms. Hill. How are we supposed to trust you at this point? False reporting is illegal and a misuse of police resources. Maybe you should go back to Stangler. They would be able to help you more than we ever could. You need to learn how to communicate faster, anyway. Texting isn't going to save you in a life or death situation." The cop rolls his eyes before he stands up, sighing when he sees my dumbstruck expression. "I'm sorry we can't do more for you, Miss Hill. I truly am. Please refrain from

making any more false calls, otherwise we'll be forced to charge you."

Both cops step out the front door, but the second one pauses, looking at me solemnly. "Have a better night, Miss Hill."

They both leave, and I lock myself back in the closet to fake a sense of safety in a world where my voice means nothing in any form.

"SHE'S BEEN like this since she came out here. I truly do not know what happened, I swear it!"

"Yeah, well, maybe you should have knocked on the damn door and asked for one of us. Even your precious sugar daddy would have understood."

"Mr. Jackson, you should watch your tone before–"

"Before what, Ms. Tricia?"

"Pierce. She's coming to."

I open my eyes slowly, though I'd rather keep them shut to avoid the look of absolute stress and anguish on Phoenix, River, and Pierce's faces.

The latter looks downright pissed as he glares at the lady from across her desk.

River is standing between the other two, arms crossed as he stares down at me with worry disturbing his normally happy demeanor.

Phoenix kneels at my side, his hand running through the hair at the top of my head. His brown eyes are warm and inviting, comforting. I drown in them for a few moments, matching my breathing to his as I come down from whatever attack just happened.

"Flashbacks getting worse?" Phoenix asks, leaning over to place a soft kiss on my forehead. Pretty sure he does it to comfort himself at this point. It does little to ease me.

I nod in response, meeting River's gray eyes and smiling softly. The tension in his shoulders loosens, and he lets out a long breath of relief before turning to look at Pierce and his rigid posture.

Those green eyes drag from top to bottom and back again for good measure. He nods sharply and looks at the woman once more.

"See? She's fine," she snarks. I wonder if she'd be crossing her arms over her chest right now if she didn't fear it'd pop those suckers out of her shirt. Maybe stomping her Mary Jane's into the ground for good measure.

I huff out a silent laugh and meet Phoenix's gaze again, finding the humor there, too. I sit up slowly, but he stops me with a hand on my shoulder.

"Let's go back out to the bikes and get you some fresh air, hmm?" he asks.

Placing his hand on my lower back, he escorts me out of the admin building, down the stairs, and over to a bench which lines the sidewalk in front of the parking lot. He pulls me down to sit next to him, wrapping an arm around me and drawing me in tight.

The sun is shining brighter than it was when we got here, though it's battling the winter storm clouds which have rolled in over recent days. More leaves are falling, mimicking their own version of colorful rain while they cascade to the ground. It's gorgeous and brutal watching nature fall to its death only for it to feed new life in a few months.

Much like healing, the world has to hurt sometimes for us to appreciate its beauty when it thrives.

"Feeling better, Red?" Phoenix asks as he places his hand on my thigh, squeezing it gently.

Looking over to him, I smile and nod, and he smiles softly in return.

We're both being fake as fuck right now, and I wonder who will crack first.

I'd like to be the last this time around.

"Alright dudes and dudette," River shouts as he bounds down the stairs from the admin building, Pierce on his heels looking angrier than normal by like a two. "Time to get the show on the road!"

"And by the road," Pierce says, reaching out to grab my hand and pull me to my feet, "he means we have a bit of a drive ahead of us today. I need to meet with a contact and I don't want you out of my sight."

"So, after the attack she just had, you're going to take her out of her comfort zone more? To a meeting you could take River to?" Phoenix raises his brow, folding his arms in frustration.

I look up between both of them, sighing when I see neither of them backing down. I reach into my pocket and grab my phone, quickly sending a text to the group chat.

It'll be fine. Change of scenery can be good for me after these attacks.

Everyone takes a second to read the message. Phoenix steps toward me, grabbing my jaw gently to keep me from shying away. "You tell me if you've had enough then, okay Red? I don't want to see you blackout on the back of his damn bike and fall off. Got it?"

"Yes, Daddy, she's got it," Pierce snarks, yanking me from in front of Phoenix and grunting when he earns a slap to the back of his head. "Fuckin' ass," he whispers.

"I'd kill you if she didn't love you so damn much, *PJ*," Phoenix says. He climbs onto the bike, and I don't miss the cocky smile on his face before he pulls his helmet over his head.

Phoenix has been an enigma to me most of the time I've known him. He'll do whatever Pierce says and be angry as hell about it, then find me and fix me back up. I should be pissed he follows Pierce's orders...but so do I, so what does it say about me if I lash out about it now?

I sigh.

These men will be the death of me.

CHAPTER TWO

phoenix

I swear to every deity ever, I *will* murder Pierce Jackson by the end of today.

After seeing Raven have yet another panic attack, something that's been happening more frequently over the past few weeks, he still insists on taking us on his little trip to meet his contact.

I don't understand how he can love her and treat her like shit at the same time.

I shake my head, kick up my kickstand, and squeeze the throttle hard, using the roar of my bike to drown out my growl of frustration.

I sure as shit do know how. I did the same shit to Lexi at the end.

We tear out of the parking lot like our asses are on fire. They probably are, since Maxwell is breathing so closely down our necks now. He has to know we told Raven everything by now, but he made no mention of it, and didn't treat her any differently than the first week she was at school.

Our ride to this meeting lasts a solid hour, and I know Raven has to be sore. She never relaxes on the bikes, so her entire frame is stiff when gets off the back of Pierce's bike.

We all watch, entranced, as she stretches her limbs out and pure pleasure takes over her face.

I'm not the only one adjusting his dick when we all finally manage to look away. We gather near the shitty, run-down apartment building Pierce parked in front of.

"He's on the third floor, third door on the left." Pierce grabs Raven's hand in his, and I glare at the back of his head. He really needs to stop touching her without permission, or I'm going to blow a fucking gasket. My anger comes out of the blue, but I've always been a slow-to-boil type.

Just so happens I've had the burner on for too long this time around.

"So, Nixy," River says, his voice jovial as he bounces towards the front lobby of the building.

"What do you want, River?" I raise a brow, but don't bother to look at him.

"Why so angry today? What's up?" He knocks my shoulder with his own and I clench my jaw. We stop right inside the building behind Pierce and Raven as they ascend the stairs.

Her gaze meets mine when they turn to head up the second set, and I smile for her, waving her on before turning toward River. When I set my glare on him, he rightfully flinches, and I bite back my grin.

"I'm over Pierce's overlord shit. Aren't you?" I fold my arms across my chest, taking in the fading tattoos along my forearms and making a note to see my artist soon.

"What do you mean?" River questions, though he sounds like he knows exactly what I mean.

I swallow before taking a deep breath and meeting his eyes. "I mean, I'm over him running the ship the way he does. Running the ship at all, actually. He's abusive as shit and Red doesn't deserve an ounce of it. Doesn't matter if she believes she does. She doesn't."

River nods along and chews on his lip once I finish talking, his gaze flitting up toward the staircase and back to me a few times. "What do we do about it?"

I groan, wiping my hands across my face. "That's the bullshit thing, Riv. We can't do much about it. Maxwell has us in a chokehold. Pierce has enough shit on us to either put us in the ground or in prison." I place my hand on River's shoulder and look at him seriously. "I'd rather stay out and above ground with Red. Wouldn't you?"

He nods and pats my hand before removing it from his shoulder. He takes a leisurely fucking stroll up the stairs with his hands in his pockets. "RaeRae will blow soon, Nixy boy. Just you wait." His voice echoes eerily in the stairwell. Goosebumps rise along my skin while a shiver flows through my body.

Pierce graces us both with a deadly glare when we finally crest the top of the stairs on the third floor landing. One of his arms wraps around Raven's shoulders, and he lifts the other before knocking five times on the door they're standing in front of.

"Code," a voice full of gravel barks through the wood.

"Souls," Pierce responds in monotone.

"Backs up against the wall, hands off any weapons."

We all move up against the opposite wall and free our hands, standing stock-still while the sound of locks disengaging and chains echo from the other side.

The person who steps out looks mean as hell. Tattoos line his exposed chest and arms, his ratty jeans showing grease stains from long ago, and cover the tops of boots which have seen better days. His graying hair sticks out in every direction, and a cigarette hangs between his lips, the end still lit, ashes falling onto the floor while he takes us all in.

After a moment of deadly silence, while he rakes his dark eyes across us all, he sighs and pulls the cigarette from his mouth, flicking more ashes off the end before gesturing us inside.

"Jackson. I have what you want, but you need to get the fuck outta here, boy. I told you half a decade ago to leave. The fuck you doin', huh?" The guy grunts in dissatisfaction as he closes the door. Placing the cigarette back between his lips, he shakes his head and mumbles to himself about stupid fucking kids and their penchant for trouble.

"With all due respect, Sarge, I've stayed to protect my girl," Pierce grits out, his arm still around Raven's shoulders.

We all stand right inside the door, watching as the older man struggles with his tanned and worn fingers to flick through paperwork in an old, used trunk. He's still grumbling, shaking his head, when he finds what he needs and spins around to hand a stack of papers to Pierce.

"Boy, I ain't got time for your shit anymore. Stop bringin' trouble to my door. Got enough of it next door, anyway. Hayes is headed for prison soon enough, he keeps allowin' that Sommers girl to manipulate his sorry ass." Sarge scoffs before a coughing fit overtakes him.

As he waves us all out, his words penetrate through my brain and I freeze. River slams into my back and we both grunt. I look Sarge directly in the eyes and ask, "Sommers? Sommers girl?"

His coughing fit finally subsides and he nods. "Yep. Sure is pretty, that'n, but she's sneaky and her daddy watches her like a hawk. She don't think he does, of course. He's sneakier. Slimier, too."

I twist my head around and meet Pierce's wide-eyed gaze before looking at Sarge again. "Which apartment is his?"

"Enough questions. Don't like stalkers or slimy dicks 'round me more'n necessary." He ushers me out with a firm hand on mine and River's shoulders.

"But—" I say, only to be met with another shove. I stumble out of the apartment but quickly recover, attempting to lodge myself back into his apartment.

"See ya never, boys. Be careful." Sarge slams the door in our faces before I can manage another thought.

"She's out?" Pierce barks, gripping my arm and twisting me around.

"Fuck if I know! I thought she was in for at least five—"

"An egregious fucking sentence for her shit, if you ask me," Pierce says.

"I—" I stop mid-sentence, looking around the hall and toward the other three doors.

Hayes. Sommers...

"I've gotta find out," I say to no one in particular, eyes drifting from one door to the other.

"And what are you going to ask the fine folks who live here, hmm? 'Hi. My name is Phoenix West, and I'm searching for my psycho ex-girlfriend who killed my family and would like to *talk* to her'? Get your shit together, Nix. We'll talk about it when we get back to Junk. Let's go." Pierce rolls his eyes when I glare at him, and I make a point to flip him off when he turns away.

I stare around the hallway a bit longer and sigh.

She shouldn't be out this early...

"LEXI!" *I shout, sneaking up behind her and tapping her shoulders.*

I succeed in scaring the hell out of her, and she shrieks, spinning toward me, holding her arm out as if to slap me.

"Phoenix, you jerk!" She squeals when I pick her up and twirl her in my arms, her legs wrapping around my waist.

I pull back from our embrace long enough to stare into those pretty storm gray eyes. My heart leaps in my chest, attempting to escape, and I slam my lips to hers.

"That's enough of that now, both of you," Lexi's father snaps out.

I'd only meant to be passing by the church, but after seeing her standing alone on the sidewalk, I had to say some-

thing. I had to touch her. It's been weeks since we've seen each other.

"Lexi, get off that heathen. You've already forced my hand to cleanse you before you marry Carter. He's thankfully agreed to marry a sullen woman." Whitaker shakes his head, narrowing his eyes at me over Lexi's shoulder.

I glare back for a few seconds before schooling my features and smiling sadly at Lexi. "I'll see you later at the club, yeah?" I whisper into her ear. She nods, and I place a soft kiss on her cheek. Reluctantly, I release her.

She swallows and wipes away a stray tear before turning toward her father and walking to his side.

"Best stay away, boy. She's too good for you."

I grit my teeth, spin on my heel, and walk away.

We'll see who's too good for who, Pastor Sommers.

We'll see.

"YOU OKAY, NIX?" Pierce asks.

We've been back at Junk for a good hour, and I've spent the entire time cleaning. The place is immaculate, and it shines and sparkles just the way I like it. I sigh when Pierce sets his drink down on the countertop without a coaster underneath it, leaving watermarks behind.

Grabbing a round cork board coaster, I pick his strawberry soda up and raise a brow at him while I place it down on top. He shrugs, and I chuckle softly. He's so helplessly in love with Raven.

I clear my throat and meet his gaze. "I'll be fine. Just wish I knew why the fuck she's out...and where she is..."

"Fuck that. Fuck her. Fuck them, Nix. Forget it all and move on already." Pierce rolls his eyes and grabs his drink, chugging the rest of it.

Before I can shove the bottle down his throat and pray he chokes on it, Raven walks in and looks between us as she makes her way toward the fridge, grabbing her own bottle of the strawberry soda. She slides into the seat furthest from Pierce, and he grinds his jaw, glaring at her.

"Hey, Red. Doin' okay?" I ask her.

She nods and sips her soda, keeping her gaze on the countertop.

"Blue—" Pierce says, his voice pained and pleading.

Raven shakes her head, her unruly red hair bouncing around her face. She swallows and points at the pile of papers Sarge gave us.

Pierce stares at Raven for an uncomfortably long time before sighing, his posture deflating as he reaches out for the papers. He picks through a few of them, pulls out what looks like a report of some sort and starts to read it. Of course he reads it to himself instead of out loud, so we're forced to wait for him to finish.

Taking the time to make dinner, I walk around the kitchen and grab what I need to cook spaghetti. Noodles from the pantry, bread from the counter, and a mix of ingredients to make sauce. Add butter and garlic for the bread. The water in the pot is already boiling by the time Raven sneaks her way between me and the stove.

I look down at her, raising a brow when she shrugs and grabs the noodles, snapping them in half and placing them in the water carefully so as not to burn us. My hands land on her shoulders and I massage the muscles there, hoping to ease some of her tension.

Leaning down until my lips are near her ear, I whisper, "What's he done now to piss you off, Red?"

She shrugs, and I dig into those muscles a little more, her body melting against mine. Her head leans back until it's resting on my shoulder, her eyes shut and lips twisted between pleasure and pain.

Her thoughts and her body are warring right now.

I let her body win by drifting my hands down her arms, satisfied when goosebumps rise along her flesh. My dick swells, and she attempts to sneakily grind against me, but I place my hands on her hips and stop her.

When she glares up at me, I kiss her lips softly, slowly, until she's putty beneath me. I luxuriate in her and am about to take this to an entirely different room when Pierce curses loudly, startling Raven and I out of our moment.

"Son of a bitch!" he roars, tossing the papers on the countertop, rough enough they smack against his drink, cracking the glass and spilling it across the counter and onto the floor.

He thankfully saves the papers from their demise as I hastily throw a towel over the red liquid.

"Care to fucking share the reason for your tantrum?" I grit out. I'd rather march over to him and punch him in the nose than clean up his mess. Again.

"Just," he groans, "this shit doesn't look good, Nix. It's lethal."

"What's lethal? My good looks, right?" River asks as

he enters the room. He kisses Raven's cheek when she silently laughs at his bad joke. I have to stop from rolling my eyes.

Whatever makes her smile right now.

"Rapture is a killer. Five people died in the first trial, but from the research done on this...and with the way Maxwell uses the cheapest shit to make the biggest profit..." Pierce sighs, grabbing his hair and pacing around the room. When he stops right in front of Raven, his eyes are almost soulless with how empty they are. "This could kill dozens...hundreds, if it's done the way Maxwell does everything else."

Raven flinches and wraps her arms around herself. Those blue eyes seek me out, and I open my arms, grateful when she rushes to nestle into me. Pierce glares, of course he does, because I've become her comfort in the absence of his.

Did it to yourself, dumbass.

"So, I'll be the one to ask the dumb question." River leans his back against the island counter, his eyes drifting from where Raven is toward Pierce. "What the fuck can we do about it?"

"That's the bullshit thing, Riv," Pierce says, shutting his eyes long enough to take a deep breath and compose himself. "Nothing. We have to give this to Maxwell. His threats in there earlier—"

"Were bullshit and you know it's because he's scared," I interrupt, raising a brow when Pierce's glare lands back on me.

Raven moves from my arms and leans over the

counter where her notebook and pen have made their permanent home. She writes a note down before holding the paper out to me, and I hide my smug grin.

I like being her go-to person. Seems I've done something right in my life.

Ruby taught me well.

"Send it to him," I read from the paper, lifting my gaze to the others who look shocked to say the least. "We can find an antidote, surely?" I sigh and rake my free hand across my face before meeting her gaze sadly. "Red–"

"We could. There's an opposite to everything, right?" River interrupts, looking between us all, then shoves away from the counter. He moves toward the large book-shelf lining the wall near the door to the garage. Reaching up, he trails his fingers along book spine after book spine until he finds what he's looking for. He pulls it out and walks back to us, slapping it down on the countertop. "Surely science is on our side, yeah boys?"

"I'm tired," Pierce says, his eyes latched onto Raven.

She's still standing near her notepad, chewing on her lower lip in contemplation. When Pierce sighs, she looks up to see the defeat wash over his features just before he turns and heads up the stairs of the loft. She shifts those pretty eyes toward River who grins at her, placing a kiss on her forehead and squeezing her hand. He whispers something I can't hear into her ear, and she nods slowly. Their eyes meet for a tense moment, and I look away.

"I'll finish getting dinner ready, then. Shouldn't be too long."

"Got it, Nixy," River says. His tone is solemn.

Will we ever get to enjoy Raven and her sweet smile for longer than a split second?

The slamming of the upstairs bathroom door signifies the one person causing the most grief. Removing him from this situation might be the best course of action.

TO: UPINFLAMES@MYEMAIL.COM
FROM: RMHILL@MYEMAIL.COM
SUBJECT: MYSTERY MAIL

Hi. Salutations. Greetings?

How are we supposed to start an email to a stranger, exactly? I don't even know who you are, yet I'm sitting in the day service room (known as the common room, because it sounds fancier, and I need to feel a bit fancy for a change, okay?) writing an email to a mystery person.

Probably shouldn't reveal too much, but I'm using the email they gave me when I got here, as I didn't want to make one up myself.

Great idea that was, because now you know my last name, but alas, I digress. Do people even talk like that? Whatever.

You said on your sticky note that you wanted me to have a place to talk freely, since it's clearly hard for me to get anything across in group.

You'd be fucking right about that, Flames. You'd be absolutely fucking right.

I'm tired. I can't speak, and I did a LOT of speaking before I suddenly couldn't anymore. Fate and karma are working hard against me for some reason.

Tell me a bit about you in your reply, and I'll tell you all about me and how this shit happened.

Kindest regards,

RM Hill

PS: What's with the pineapple sticker on your note? It

might behoove you to know that I absolutely loathe pineapple pizza. (I'll be surprised if I get an email back after this.)

raven

Monday morning rolls around after a long weekend where the guys simply plowed through science textbooks. They tried to reverse engineer Rapture with numbers and symbols all over pages. Since Phoenix is getting a biochem degree, he led the charge on that particular task.

I, on the other hand, did not comprehend half of it.

Which is fine, because I spent the weekend studying for things I do understand. It's finals week for this semester of classes.

Studying with the guys was...in many ways, exciting, but over the weekend I made sure to keep myself bundled up and in places where cuddling was more difficult.

No way in hell would I fail my first semester here because of dick. Or dicks, plural.

Phoenix convinced Pierce to take the Jeep to classes this week, stating it was far too fucking cold for bike riding. He was mostly concerned about me, though.

Pierce insists I always ride on the back of *his* bike, wrapped around *him* and following *him* around. His head has grown bigger than the sun itself, and he acts like we revolve around him, too.

River opens the back door for me and I slide out, smiling sweetly at him when he wraps his arm across my waist, pulling me close to his side.

"She should be on my side, so we don't confuse the fucking school about who she's with," Pierce grits out. Grabbing River's bicep, he pulls me into his own hold, arm wrapping around my shoulders.

"Fuck what people think, Pierce. When the hell did you start caring?" River snarks, glaring daggers at his best friend.

"Since Maxwell threatened her safety by putting Jimmy in the game. She's mine. Period." Pierce's grip on me tightens when River steps toward us. Stuck between both of them, in their war over me, the tension only rises. Pierce loosens his hold when River angrily throws his hands up and turns, marching off to his own class without a word.

The class directly across from my own.

I shake my head, giving Phoenix a slight wave after he kisses my cheek, walking toward his own class without a word.

"Jesus they're up in arms lately, huh, Blue?" Pierce scoffs as we begin walking. He slides his palm along my shoulder to keep me warm, though the red leather jacket they got for me, paired with my long sleeves, leggings, jeans and boots are already doing the trick.

By the time we're standing in front of my class, I'm

seething mad at Pierce for flaunting me around campus when he knows damn well I belong to all three of them. He was the one who said it on my first day here, in front of the entire fucking Alpha Mu house.

"I'll be back to get you as soon as class is over. Don't wander off. I don't know what else Maxwell could be up to." Pierce lifts my chin to meet his gaze, but when he finds nothing but contempt in my eyes he sighs and presses his lips to mine. While it's a sweet gesture, I almost feel numb from his kiss. I'm too angry, too stressed, too disappointed in him to be able to even like his touch at this point.

He finally releases me and takes a few steps backward with devastation marring his face.

We have a silent conversation in that hallway, and I'm not sure either of us truly understands what the other is saying anymore.

TUESDAY ARRIVES and the overall feeling around the house is a mix between exhaustion and bitterness.

Toward Maxwell.

Toward our pasts.

Toward each other.

Phoenix and Pierce stopped talking to each other last night after a massive fight over a stupid math equation. I've been bouncing between the loft with Pierce and River and the lounge with Phoenix.

No one has touched me, and I don't particularly want them to, either.

I was elated when I was learning to ride the bike last week, but this week?

This week feels like a turning point I didn't know I was heading toward.

Someone in this house is going to snap, and I suspect it will be me.

"Raven!" Pierce yells, startling me from my thoughts and my comfortable position curled up in Phoenix's arms.

Phoenix passed out a while ago with his arm across the top of my chest, my body resting between his legs and my head on his shoulder. His steady breathing lulled me into a trance, and I'm sure I'd have fallen asleep if it weren't for the notes on my own lap.

Turning my head, I take in his peacefully sleeping form and smile softly before kissing his chest right where his heart beats steadily. I sigh and sit up, moving my notes back onto the coffee table.

"Raven! Get your ass up here!" Pierce yells again, and I flip him off in response, though he can't see it from my position directly below the loft.

I stretch my arms out, wiggling my body to get the blood to flow back into all of my limbs properly. Once I can feel everything again, I cross my arms over my t-shirt clad chest–Phoenix's t-shirt–and walk to the stairs. My socks mask my footsteps, so Pierce appears at the top of them about to yell for me again when I hit the last few steps. He exhales heavily and waves me up.

"Fucking finally. The hell you doing down there, anyway? Not a single soul is still studying. We're all winging it at this point. Right, Riv?" Pierce questions the other, who looks up from a notebook guiltily before tossing it behind him on the bed.

He clears his throat and nods, offering a blinding smile to me as I make my way to him. "Right," he says to Pierce.

"Whatever. I'm not here for a damn degree anyway. Maxwell fucked my whole future. Not sure what the hell to do for a job once we take his ass down." Pierce pulls me from between River's legs, turns me around, and lays me back on the bed.

My heart rate spikes, but not in arousal as it has recently. I thought I was okay with all of this, but with the number of PTSD attacks I've had, and all of the surfacing memories...

I sniff back tears and place my hand on Pierce's chest as he descends on me, pushing against him to get my point across.

He pauses, his brows furrowing for a moment before he grins cockily. "C'mon, Rae. We all need to blow off some steam right now." He leans down and places a gentle kiss to the side of my neck, and my body betrays me.

River's face appears when I turn my head, and he presses a sweet kiss to my lips, which I reciprocate.

Kissing River is always light and fun. It's never been a challenge to be with him, though lately, we've been too focused on school, too focused on Maxwell and his threats.

"Fuck, keep kissing her just like that, Riv. She loves it." Pierce's voice is husky, coated in lust as he commands his best friend. His hands travel along the oversized shirt I'm wearing until he reaches the hem, pulling the material up my thighs and exposing my underwear and stomach.

I try not to think about who's touching me right now.

Pierce is right about one thing; we all need a release right now. The tension is too thick.

Orgasms are a girl's best friend, after all.

Whoever said it was diamonds was materialistic.

This?

This feeling of being loved, cherished, *worshiped*?

This is what we all want in life.

Everyone wants to feel the tingling in their spine from a simple touch.

The way mine does when Pierce's tongue traces the skin above my underwear.

The way my heart thrashes in my chest when River nibbles on my lower lip like it's his favorite snack. How my nipples harden impossibly when his warm hand lands on my breast, massaging it until my back tries to arch and my toes want to curl.

"Fuck, you're so wet for us, little bird," Pierce growls out. He presses his nose and mouth against me, inhaling deeply. His groan of pleasure shouldn't satisfy me, but it does, so I arch into him until he has to hold me down with his hands on my hips, forcing me further into the bed.

River breaks from our kiss, his lips swollen and eyes dark with arousal. His dirty blonde hair is disheveled, and I reach up to slide my fingers through it, tucking back a strand hanging in front of his eyes. The gray storm inside of them pulls me in and holds me there. Pierce manipulates my body, pulling down my underwear and positioning my legs wide before diving in like a man starved.

My back arches, and I shut my eyes against the onslaught of pleasure his mouth brings me. I try to remember this is my best friend, the guy I first fell in love with, but it's difficult to reconcile that with the man who doesn't ask for consent when he'd spend hours pleading for *me* to slow down.

River places his cheek against mine, his mouth near my ear. A tear escapes me and trails between us, and he removes his hand from me instantly. "You have the control, Rae. Do you want us off of you?" he whispers.

My body and mind war with me for a few seconds before I nod frantically, clenching my hand in River's hair and holding him to me as Pierce stays the course, not noticing or caring about my responses.

With a parting kiss to my cheek, River removes my hand from his hair and sits up, smacking Pierce in the back of the head. "Off," he commands.

His tone is so brutal, so different from his normal playfulness, Pierce doesn't retaliate against the smack in the back of his head. They both simply stare at each other; River with a mask of anger and Pierce a full look of astonishment on his face.

"What the fuck, Riv?" he asks after a long pause.

"She's crying. She doesn't want you on her. She doesn't want *you* at all right now. Get off. Go take a cold shower." River's tone brokers no argument, and he folds his arms across his chest, waiting.

Pierce's green eyes meet mine and my vision instantly blurs with a thousand unshed tears.

I don't move.

I don't attempt to communicate.

I simply lay there, splayed open in front of my childhood best friend, at his mercy if he so wishes.

I watch as his expression morphs from confusion to pain then, predictably, anger.

"Fuck this," he grits out, pushing away from the bed hard enough to make himself stumble backward a few steps. He marches to the bathroom and slams the door shut so hard it feels like the whole loft trembles with me.

I can't hold my tears back anymore. They pour down my cheeks as I pull my underwear back on and use Phoenix's shirt to cover myself. I breathe in his rainforest scent and calm down after a few moments.

"Go back down to Nixy boy before he comes up here," River orders me calmly as he rubs my back. "I've got Pierce. You focus on you right now." He shoves up from the bed and walks toward the bathroom, waiting outside the door as I make my way to the stairs.

When I look back at him, he smiles and waves me away. I walk down the stairs with my heart in my throat and confusion clouding my brain.

How do we get past this?

I thought I'd forgiven and forgotten what they'd done to me months ago, but Pierce's commands and River's compliance are constantly replaying in my brain lately, flashbacks bringing the entire drunken assault to the front and center.

Then there's Jimmy's bullshit from the end of senior year, after I came back from therapy.

The way the cops ignored my every statement, thinking it was trauma fogging my thoughts.

Phoenix appears at the bottom of the stairs looking angry but adorable with how rumpled he is. His black hair sticking out from his bun and his tattooed chest on full display.

I need to take the time to decipher his artwork soon.

"You okay there, Red?" he asks. His voice is husky and warm.

I nod in response as I reach the bottom of the stairs, looking up at him for a brief moment before remembering my tears. I look away and step toward the kitchen, but he pulls me back gently by the arm and tilts my chin up with a finger.

Our gazes clash and my heart pounds in my chest while butterflies and bumblebees fight for dominance in my stomach.

"I'm going to kill him. I swear I will." Phoenix sighs and kisses my forehead, and I force a smile, shaking my head at him.

Pierce may be pissing us all off, but he's still the first boy ever to steal my heart.

He crushed it into a million pieces, and I plan to make him pick up every single one and put them back together again.

WEDNESDAY IS MUCH THE SAME.

We all wake up, eat our chosen breakfasts, head to

class, take our exams, come back for lunch, and study for the next one.

All day, Pierce was silent. He didn't touch me. Didn't kiss me. Didn't reach for me at all.

I should be relieved, but I'm confused as hell. And hurt.

I want him to want me, but I want it to be on my terms.

I sigh and place my mug of hot cocoa down on the coffee table, staring out at where he's attempting to fully winterize the garden.

The guys brought out a modular greenhouse to place around the dirt plots and have been working almost nonstop on it since we finished lunch earlier. They didn't want my help, of course.

Leave the woman out of the manual labor.

Shaking my head, I curl back up in my blanket with my study notes for tomorrow, flipping up the hood of River's sweatshirt I stole this morning when he wasn't looking.

At least Pierce is using his hands for something good today.

THURSDAY...

It's too silent.

Too still.

Are we crumbling before we've had a chance to stand?

"THE FUCK IS GOING on with the damn coffee maker?" Pierce shouts, throwing his hands up in frustration. "Fuckin' need this shit to get through this last damn final." He continues to mutter to himself as I shovel another spoonful of cocoa puffs into my mouth.

"Maybe it would help if you plugged it in, PJ," River supplies helpfully from beside me. His arm is over my shoulders, and he's stealing bites of cereal.

Well, I guess it's not stealing if I'm feeding him. And I have been feeding him *a lot* this morning.

Hence the reason the box is out and I've had to refill the bowl twice already.

"What do you mean fucking plug it in? Do I look like a fucking idiot to you, *RJ*?" Pierce snarls the nickname River hates the most, glaring at the man in question.

The only sound in the room is Phoenix's soft footsteps as he pads through the kitchen to the coffee maker and plugs it in.

"Shut the fuck up, please. It's Friday." Phoenix says. "Last day of finals. Get your shit together, and let's get a move on."

River and I both hide our grins with more bites of cereal.

Don't know how we ended up sharing, but he sat down fifteen minutes ago, leaned close and opened his mouth.

I simply obliged and fed the beast.

"You two are too fucking cozy," Pierce bites out when

he turns back around with hot coffee in hand. "Cute fuckin' couple, huh, Nix?"

"Pierce," Phoenix sighs, rubbing the bridge of his nose in frustration. "Just drink your coffee. You two," he points at me and River, "hurry up and get dressed. Classes start in twenty minutes." He walks out of the kitchen and heads upstairs.

River and I hurriedly finish our third bowl of cereal together, and he surprises me by taking it to the sink and cleaning it. He nudges me up the stairs with the cutest grin on his face, staying behind to deal with Pierce's wrath in my place.

I swear those two are opposites in every way.

Rushing up the stairs, I bump into Phoenix at the top and wrap my arms around him to avoid falling back down.

He chuckles and steadies me with his hands on my shoulders, turning me to face the closet. "Hurry up, Red."

I rush to get dressed. With my boots zipped and my black beanie hat covering half of my red curls, I amble toward the garage and hop into the back of the jeep beside River.

"I swear to god, Nix, I can't keep doing this shit. She's shut me out. I've shut her out. I don't know how to fucking come back from any of this, much less that night at the frat house. I feel like shit but–"

Phoenix clears his throat and nods toward me in the backseat, sitting with my eyes wide showing both my panic and curiosity.

I meet Phoenix's brown eyes in the rearview mirror

and glare, which only serves to make him chuckle deviously.

"Last day of class for the winter!" River yells from beside me, and Pierce takes that as his cue to drive us out of Junk and back to class.

Whatever he was saying is clearly not important enough for him to say to my face, so he hides it behind his permanent scowl.

School that day is...too easy.

I studied enough for the exam, making the time in class fly by.

But once class is over, none of the guys are waiting outside like normal.

I walk toward the parking lot all alone with my body on high alert as I look around for them. They wouldn't leave me here intentionally, would they?

Pierce might.

I sigh in relief when I see the jeep, though no one is in or around it, so I keep my guard up as I lean against the driver side door.

"Hey there, sugar."

Jumping a mile in the air, I cover my racing heart with my hand and whirl around. Jimmy Perkins steps near the front of the jeep, a cocksure grin on his face and two Alpha Mu boys on either side of him. His blue eyes almost sparkle in triumph at my fright.

"Where are your boyfriends? Hmm?" he muses, biting down on his lip while he takes me in from head to toe.

I shiver and cross my arms over my chest, trying to hide my rapid breathing.

I cannot black out here.

Not in front of him.

"You see, you're supposed to be at the frat house doing something special for us right about now, and the Prez ain't there. Neither are his golden boys, so I was just wonderin' if you'd seen 'em, since they seem to follow you wherever you go." Jimmy laughs and shoves his hands in his pockets as he closes in on me.

Predator, screams my brain.

I shake my head when he gets too close, holding out my hand to get him to stop.

He steps forward, of course, until his chest is to my palm and my skin burns on impact.

"Aw, sugar. Scared of little ol' me? Can't see why." He leans down until his face is in front of mine, lips tilting in a half-grin before he licks them. Our eyes meet. "We had so much *fun* together, didn't we?"

"Get. The. Fuck. Away from her!" Pierce shouts.

Jimmy's body flies backwards, landing on a patch of concrete. He yells out, clutching at his back and glaring up at Pierce. "Not like you were here to protect her, PJ. She'd be safer at the frat than out here all alone. Right boys?" Jimmy looks up at the two frat boys standing on the sidewalk, awkwardly shuffling as they realize their mistake of standing against their president. "Fucking...right?" Jimmy yells up at them.

A few of the guys look around uncomfortably, but most of them nod. Jimmy grins smugly when he gets the reaction he wants from them.

"I'll always fucking protect her,. You know that more than anyone. Get your ass out of here before I run you the fuck over." Pierce glares at the three men until Jimmy stands, adjusts his clothing, and leaves with the other two.

"Let's go grab some food and get the fuck home. I'm exhausted," Pierce says, giving me a quick once over as he climbs into the jeep.

I shouldn't feel a warming in my heart for him, but when his actions show how much he actually cares, I can't help it.

The door slams shut, and I flinch. River wraps me up in a tight hug, comforting me as best he can. "It'll be okay, Rae. Everything will eventually cool off, or Pierce will burn the world down trying to make it that way. I hope you know that."

When I nod against River's chest, he kisses the crown of my head and releases me. We climb into the back of the jeep and I keep my gaze trained out of the window the whole way back, refusing to look at any of them and risk them seeing the uncertainty on my face.

"Boys, get out," Pierce says the second he has the jeep parked in the garage.

I meet his gaze in the rearview mirror as I move toward the door. Surely he's not barking commands at me after being silent for the last two days.

"Raven, stay."

Clearly, he's delusional.

I shake my head, palm the door handle and try to open it, but Pierce presses the child lock the split second before I can get out.

"I said stay," he grits out.

Phoenix and River look at Pierce, then me, before getting out of the jeep.

"I'll be right–" Phoenix says, but is quickly interrupted.

"Go!" Pierce yells.

Phoenix flinches, wide-eyed as he backs away, nodding slowly.

I wish he'd stand up more for me when it really fucking mattered.

These boys need to sort out their priorities.

The second the doors to the jeep close, Pierce presses down on the lock button again. The sound of silence envelops us, louder than the blood rushing in my ears.

"Raven," he whispers, his gaze meeting mine in the rearview mirror again. Pain is all I see, and it saddens and infuriates me.

All he has to do is pay attention, and he'd see the damage he causes.

Instead, he's blind to it all.

Pierce clenches his jaw before turning and climbing into the backseat beside me.

I reward his efforts by sliding against the opposite door, curling in on myself and keeping my eyes downcast.

He can't sway me with words anymore.

He can't use our past to fix our present.

"Stop shutting me out and just listen. I'm doing all of this shit *for* you. You see that right? Tell me you fucking see that?" He uses his finger to tilt my chin up, his green eyes penetrating my blues all the way to my soul.

My heart clenches, but I rip my head away from his hold and shake it back and forth.

"What the hell do I have to do to show you I mean

what I say, huh?" he asks. He leans forward and pulls me into him.

Manhandling me again.

Nice.

"Please, just let me love you. Let me protect you," he whispers into my hair.

A tear falls from my lashes and I wipe it away quickly. I push off Pierce and crawl to the front seat of the jeep. I'm almost able to press the button to unlock us from this hell when he pulls me back by the hips, slamming my ass down onto his lap. I whip around and glare at him. He responds by kissing me angrily.

It's rough.

I tear at his hair. I tug. I pull. I scratch.

He responds with groans. Bites to my lip. Fingers digging in further.

I try to push away, and he follows me until I'm laying back on the seat, my legs around his hips and his growing erection digging in with delicious friction.

"Fuck," he groans, pulling away from my lips to attack my neck with nips and sucks, distracting me from my anger.

I shut my eyes and dig my nails into his biceps, using as much force as possible to push him away. It's abrupt and painful enough for Pierce to stop in his onslaught and sit back on his haunches.

He looks up, finally reacting to the painfully loud wrapping on the windows and angry shouts from Phoenix. Pierce only glares back at him, flipping him off before looking back down at me.

The jeep fills with the sound of our silence and heavy

breathing, and I struggle to stop the tears which threaten to overflow.

"Inside?" he asks, and I scoff, rolling my eyes. "What the fuck, then, Raven? What the fuck do you want from me?"

I angrily point toward the door, jerking my head at it to add as much emphasis as I can.

"Fine, get the fuck out." He leans into the front seat and unlocks the jeep.

The door opens immediately and Phoenix is there, helping me out while glaring at Pierce.

"You're on a thin fucking line, Jackson."

"Get the fuck out of my way, Nix. Let her go. She wants to fight. Let's fucking fight. Yeah, little bird?" Pierce shoves forward, and I flinch backward, my back hitting Phoenix's chest.

His arms wrap around me, and I relax.

It's premature, however, because Pierce only steps further toward us and wraps his hand around my throat. His nose presses close to mine, squishing it painfully. I wince, but it doesn't stop his next words.

"Fucking fight me, Raven. Get it out. Then we can move the fuck on and you can chill the fuck out."

I square my shoulders.

The corner of his lips tilt up into a half-smile, and he releases my throat. He takes a step back, holding his arms out wide. "C'mon then, little bird."

"Pierce," River grits out, his panicked gaze flitting between us both.

"Nah, let her at me. Well deserved, I think. I've only spent half our fucking lives protecting her. She's ungrateful as shit and doesn't see how I've given up everythi–"

I launch myself forward.

If I had my voice, I'd be screaming at him.

If I had my voice, I'd be landing each punch against his pretty fucking face with a curse.

My hands ache as I slap and punch at him. My nails tear as I scratch his skin until it breaks and bleeds. I kick and shove and silently scream, tears trailing down my face and sweat mixing as it slides down my chin and neck.

I abuse the hell out of his body in ways he won't soon fucking forget.

He's on the ground before I realize I've put him there, and I straddle him, my fists landing on the side of his face, near his temples.

I'd kill him if I didn't still fucking love him.

He'd be ready for a shallow grave if I didn't nearly pass out and come back to myself when Phoenix rips me away.

Away from my best friend who's laying on the floor of the garage.

Beaten.

Bloodied.

Groaning.

Defeat shining in his eyes as he gapes at me.

I lean forward, though Phoenix holds both of my biceps to keep me from descending on Pierce again, and spit directly onto his face.

"Enough, Red. He's had enough," Phoenix whispers.

pierce

The room is so deadly silent.

My heart feels like it's been crushed.

My body hurts like a motherfucker, and I'm shocked my little bird managed it.

I taught her how to fight, but I didn't teach her how to scrap like *that*.

Groaning, I look over at River. "Help," I croak out. I need help to my feet, and he provides it, allowing me to slump my body against his side as he holds me upright.

Raven is still jerking in Phoenix's hold, attempting to come at me again, I'm sure.

I'd let her.

Hell, she can kill me if she wants to.

I swallow and wince at the pain in my throat, bringing my hand up to run along the scratch marks she left there. Pulling my hand away, I shake my head when I see the amount of blood drawn.

"Blue," I say softly, walking toward her but stopping barely out of her reach. "How do I fix this, baby?" I ask.

Her tears stream down her face, landing in a puddle on the ground. She shakes her head a few times, looking me up and down, wincing when she takes in the damage she dealt.

I sigh and look up at Phoenix, then River at my side. Shifting my gaze back toward Raven, I take in how absolutely lethal she looks. She's gorgeous right now. A gorgeous warrior sent to destroy me, I'm sure of it.

"Do I need to get down on my knees and beg you, little bird?" I ask, stumbling forward a step, out of River's protective hold. "Do I need to kiss your feet? Clean them for you daily?"

When I meet those pretty blue eyes, she shakes her head firmly again, inhaling shakily as she takes me in.

She doubles over when I fall to my knees in front of her, tears flowing harder now. I watch as her chest heaves with her silent sobs, grateful I can't hear her. Frustrated because the memories of her cries echo in my brain anyway.

From my spot on the ground, I lay my hands palm up on my thighs and stare up at her, tears threatening my own eyes as I lay my heart out for her again.

"Tell me how to fix it, Raven. Tell me how to gain your trust again. Please," I beg, voice cracking.

She shakes her head frantically, wiping away her tears so she can see me, but she doesn't find a way to answer me right away.

I stay there on my knees for what seems like a complete

century before she reaches into her pocket for her phone. She types into it with shaking fingers, leaning against Phoenix to keep her balance as she fights her trembling frame.

She shows me the phone when she's done, and my heart nearly evaporates into ashes at what I read.

RAVEN

Don't touch me again. Not until I ask
you to.

"Blue, I—"

She shoves the phone closer to my face, and I raise my hands.

"I get it," I whisper. I look up into those furious blue eyes and nod once, cementing my fate.

She inhales deeply and spins on her heel, stomping inside the loft like her ass is on fire.

"Good fucking luck," Phoenix says, trying to contain his grin.

"Shut the hell up. Go watch over her. She hurt her hand when she landed the first punch. Wouldn't be surprised if she sprained her thumb or some shit." I sigh and drop my head back on my shoulders, shutting my eyes to avoid seeing River's face above me.

It's silent again for a while and I take the time to reassess my life choices.

Surely she won't hold out too long.

FUCK, I hate being wrong.

Rae didn't look at me for the entire weekend.

Not when we were all on the couch watching a movie while she read whatever book she's into.

Not when I made her favorite brand of hot chocolate with extra large marshmallows.

Not when I brought her a new hardback copy of a book she recently five starred on Goodreads.

She didn't look at me, reach for me, nothing.

And my soul is crushed.

This punishment is the worst I've ever endured, and the rest of the house is getting a goddamn kick out of it.

"Hey, Rae, come cuddle?" River asks her, holding his arms out wide from his perch on the other end of the couch.

Phoenix is upstairs, lost in his laptop, probably looking up Lexi's file and trying to find out when she was released from the hospital.

I watch, livid, as Raven stands up and makes her way over to River, bringing her blanket and Kindle with her. She sits her ass right on his lap and curls up into his side as he pulls the blanket around them both.

He meets my gaze and winks, and I flip him off before standing and walking toward the garage.

Fuck this shit.

I can adhere to her rules.

I can avoid touching her.

But I can't watch her give affection to everyone else in the house.

"Pierce," Phoenix says as I pass the staircase.

Turning in his direction, I raise a brow and fold my arms, waving a hand for him to speak.

"She's been out for five fucking months."

"Wait," I laugh incredulously. I walk up the stairs toward him and lean against the railing beside his computer desk. "There's no way she's been out this long and we haven't seen her."

"Take a look for yourself, dickhead." Phoenix sighs and shoves his chair away from the desk, running his hands through his hair as I lean down to take a look.

Sure fucking enough it says Lexi Sommers was released on *good behavior* in July.

I laugh, loudly, and look at Phoenix. "Since when has she ever been good?"

Eyes narrowing, he meets my gaze. "The world fucking destroyed her and you know it. I told you everything, and you know none of this was actually her fault."

"Jesus Christ you're delusional when it comes to her." I back up, avoiding his swinging palm as I look out the window behind his desk. "Let's hope she doesn't fucking come for you, or she'll see the barrel of my fucking gun instead of a quick jaunt to a hospital. Bet her daddy had something to do with her getting out, too."

Phoenix says nothing for a while, tapping away at his laptop hard enough I wonder what it ever did to him. When he finishes, he slams it shut and pushes to a stand. "I just hope she leaves Red out of whatever plans she comes up with next." He sighs and walks toward the bathroom.

Have to give him credit, though.

He's clearly no longer pining after his psycho ex-girlfriend.

My phone buzzes in my pocket and I groan before

pulling it out, only to regret the choice when I see Maxwell's name on the screen. I sit down on the edge of the desk and answer it. "What?"

"Respect, boy. That's all I've ever asked from you."

"Yeah well, excuse me if all the other things you've asked from me were irrelevant. The fuck do you want, Langston?" I grit out, closing my eyes to imagine I'm anywhere else but in *his* town.

"The frat needs to do something for Christmas, and since my daughter–"

"It's too damn late to plan anything, and you know it."

"Well, Jackson, I have connections and I plan to use them to ship packages to the base in Washington, D.C. alongside a hefty donation to the President. Need to get my name in lights up there." Maxwell chortles, the click of a lighter echoing into the line. He inhales deeply, and I'm grateful I can't smell his nasty cigar through the phone.

"We'll get on it tonight, then." I tell him, instantly regretting having to tell Raven to do anything, much less taking her to the frat house to do it.

"Good, good. I already told Jimmy you were on your way. You have ten minutes."

The line goes dead.

"What will we get on?" Phoenix questions from the bathroom, his arms folded across his chest as he leans against the door frame.

"We need to go to Alpha Mu. Packages for the base in D.C. or something."

"It's too fucking late for that, Pierce. What the hell?"

"Yeah, told him that. He has *connections* though." I roll

my eyes and walk toward the edge of the loft, looking down at Raven and River in their happy little bubble downstairs.

What a shame I have to pop it.

Not.

"Hey, get your asses up. We gotta go to the house for a bit. Maxwell says ten minutes."

They both look up at me then back at each other before standing and walking up the stairs. The second they cross the threshold, I bolt downstairs, into the garage and wait in the jeep.

Who the hell knows if I can restrain myself while I watch her change.

Avoidance is key right now.

I don't wait for them to buckle themselves in before I tear out of the garage, past the gate, and toward the frat house.

The last time we were here, I was pretty certain I'd kill Jimmy for breathing in the same room as me.

This time?

My temper is higher than it's ever been and I have no one else to lose it on, so he'd better watch his back.

We pull into the driveway of the house, and I have to park at the end behind a line of cars. My irritation only rises when I see Jimmy pull a blonde out of a red sports car, yanking her into his body and palming her ass for the whole world to see.

Classy.

I scoff and turn the engine off. "Alright," I say, "let's get this shit done as quick as possible and get the fuck back home."

"Aye, aye, captain!" River says, saluting me. He grins wildly when I glare at him in the rearview mirror.

I can feel Raven's eyes tracking my movements, but I avoid them at all costs, swinging the door open hard enough for the hinges to squeak dangerously.

Great. Another thing I have to fix.

"Jackson!" Jimmy yells, waving me over. The blonde stays under his arm, spending a few seconds eyeing us all up.

Raven moves to Phoenix's side, grabbing hold of his hand in a show of ownership. River slides up beside her, staking his claim simply by being near her.

I clench my jaw and step in front of them, placing my hands in my pockets to hide my fists.

"Took you guys long enough. We're just about to start." Jimmy grins and raises a brow. "Well...this situation looks cozy."

"Shut the hell up, Perkins," I tell him, clapping him painfully on the shoulder and steering him toward the house.

"Aw, such sweet words, PJ! Didn't know you loved me that much." He laughs at his statement, a few of the frat guys following suit. The blonde lets out an obnoxious giggle, and I'm pretty sure my ears bleed for a second.

Walking into the frat house is a task in itself.

When I first got here in January, I was absorbed in myself and had the task of getting revenge on Raven. Or at least losing myself in doing whatever Maxwell wanted me to do. It was his way or the highway anyway, so I threw myself into working with him, did anything the old president asked of me, and zoned out.

One day I was questioning the shit I was doing...the next I was being named the new president while the other was being carted off on a hefty prison sentence.

I was forced into a life I didn't want to be living, leading guys I loathed, wondering if Maxwell would ever let me go, even after I graduated college. Though I might never graduate since I'm certain I failed half of my exams in the last week.

"Let's get this show on the road, boys!" Jimmy yells, pulling away from me. He walks to the center of the large living room.

Everything which once took over the room is nowhere to be seen. Long folding tables are set up in three lines, and boxes—both empty and full of random shit—are everywhere. Every person I see is wearing their winter hats, but their coats are thrown in a pile in an untouched corner.

They're all smiling.

I look over to Raven, who's smiling shyly as she takes in the scene.

"Did you do this?" I ask her.

When she looks up at me, she shrugs and takes her bottom lip between her teeth. Looking up at Phoenix, she pokes his shoulder then points to me.

"Yeah. She got an email from Maxwell during finals to get something planned. This is what he suggested and, well, she was able to deliver in a short time frame. Pretty proud of her, actually," he says. His grin grows when Raven's cheeks redden and she scurries away from us all.

"I didn't know Maxwell contacted her," I grit out, shoving my shoulder into his as I pass by him. "Tell me next time. I need to know."

"You don't need to know everything, Pierce," he replies. His tone pisses me off.

"Whatever. Let's get this shit packed up."

For the next three hours, we stuff random shit into the care packages for the military. I guess Rae did her research and I can admit she put everything together really well. There are checklists and stations for each item. She's turned my chaotic frat house into a well-oiled machine who joke around and wear Santa hats, for fuck's sake.

She's standing at the end of the final table, looking painfully beautiful in her black winter coat and boots, her hair falling over her shoulders every single time she leans forward.

I wish I could hug her, kiss her, tell her how fucking proud I am of her.

River bumps into my shoulder and chuckles when I glare at him. "You have the last box, boss-man."

"Huh?"

"Drop the razor in the box, Pierce," he says, his voice taking on an air of command.

Pretty sure I should be angry about it, but I'm also sure I should get the hell out of this frat house before I have the compulsion to actually fix shit for them. I have more important shit to deal with.

River's hand lands over mine, forcing my fingers apart slowly until I'm able to pull myself to drop the razor into the box of care items. He pushes the box down the line and wraps his arm around my shoulders, pulling me out of the main room and into the hallway. "Are we still heading to Rae's for Christmas?"

My back hits the wall as I slump over, folding my arms

and nodding. "Yeah. We should probably leave the day before Christmas Eve. Might be best to celebrate then so they can grieve on Christmas Day."

"Look at you," he grins. "You *are* capable of caring for others, PJ!"

I reach out and smack him on the back of the head. He laughs it off and pulls me toward our coats, which we hung up at the front hall. "What about the other two?"

"They're going to finish up the last box and come right out. I already made sure of it," he quickly says the last part when I look up at him in question. "Don't worry."

"I always fucking worry," I grumble, folding my arms once I have my winter coat on. It's a leather jacket with wool lining the inside. I toss on my hat to cover my unruly hair and step out alongside River, keeping close enough to him our shoulders bump along the way.

When we're outside, the silence is a breath of fresh air for me. There's not a single soul out here to disturb the fucking peace. It's also—

"Snow! Fuck yes!" River shouts, sticking his tongue out predictably and catching a few flakes instantly.

I meet his gaze and roll my eyes, walking toward the car, trying to ignore the smile threatening my lips.

"Wait!" he shouts, and I turn to look at him.

My mouth drops open when he pulls out a kitchen knife and walks toward Jimmy's car. "The fuck, Riv?"

He shrugs, looking back at me and winking. Idiot.

I laugh under my breath and cover it with a cough. "He's going to know we did it, dumbass."

"I don't give a shit. He knows we've done a lot of shit, but we also know he knows we know a lot."

His sentence confuses the fuck out of me and I tilt my head. "What?"

"You know." River grins and hunches toward the front left tire, puncturing it with ease.

I hover behind him, hiding his body from any passersby as he does the same to the rest of the tires on Jimmy's piece of shit car. When we're done, River impales the knife onto the last tire and I lift him up by his shirt.

His shocked face makes me grin, and I push him back against the passenger door, pressing my lips roughly to his. We both groan as our warmth contradicts the cold all around us. I grip the back of his head with one hand, leaving the other in his shirt to hold him right where I want him.

Fuck if anyone sees.

Fuck everyone at this point.

River places his hands on my pecs, grinning into our kiss when he feels how fast my heart is racing. He rocks his growing erection against mine and I push right back, clutching his hair in my fist to the point of pain.

He lets out this breathless moan and I grin, biting his lower lip before pulling it into my mouth to soothe the sting with my tongue.

We break away after a few minutes, and I love how kiss-bitten his lips look, how red his face is. How fucking delicious his heavy breathing sounds to my ears.

"The hell," River says, softly laughing as he runs his fingers through his messy hair, "was that for?"

I shrug and step toward the jeep, hands stuffed in my pockets.

"You're going to finish what you started, Piercey Jackson," River calls after me. "Mark my fucking words! Gah! I hate having my dick hard in the cold. It's weird."

He follows me to the jeep and I laugh when I see his faux anger. My laugh makes him raise both brows before he follows suit.

Raven and Phoenix come out a few minutes later, finding River and I sharing a joint like we aren't on campus with eyes all over us.

We both shrug when Phoenix raises a brow, and he rolls his eyes before he lets Raven inside the jeep, following her into the back.

"Hey!" River says, rushing to the door, barely missing his finger being smashed to bits when it closes. "Fucker took my spot," he grumbles, marching toward the front passenger seat.

"I got a spot for you, Riv," I tell him.

When he whips around and looks at me wide-eyed, I shrug and finish the last of the joint before opening the car door and sliding in.

"Off we fucking go then, hmm?" I say mostly to myself as I crank the engine.

TO: RMHILL@MYEMAIL.COM FROM: UPINFLAMES@MYEMAIL.COM SUBJECT: RE: MYSTERY MAIL

Hi. Hello. Salutations.

It's a unique start to an email, and I don't blame you for being unsure about what to say. I gave you nothing about me, and I clearly know who you are. I simply wanted you to have a space where you didn't feel judged.

So even while my eyes are on you, Red, I don't want you to think I'm judging you. I have a feeling you're the type to overthink and overanalyze, and make up bad shit without even trying. Am I right?

A bit about me, to make you feel better:

- I showed up here at the beginning of January. Tried to 'unalive' myself. Since I won't talk about it, the docs just keep pushing back my 'release date'. It's fantastic! /sarcasm

- I used to be in a band. Last show I played? Christmas Eve. Showed up at 1am on Christmas Day to see my house burnt, family inside. Dark shit, yeah?

- I don't remember the last time I smiled, but when I saw you walking down the hallway this morning in those bright purple leggings, fuzzy socks on your feet which were stuffed in those slippers, and the black hoodie hiding your body? I'm sure my lips twitched at least a little.

Tell me, Red. Tell me everything.

Flames (as you've dubbed me, so I shall be)

PS: I don't mind pineapple on pizza, but I don't particularly love it either. Shame about your best friend. I don't judge anyone for their tastes.

raven

The smell of chocolate overwhelms my senses, stirring me from the deepest sleep I've managed in months.

I guess I really was on high alert around Pierce.

We came back to Junk to pack up and hopefully snag a good night's sleep before our trip back to our hometown. River and Pierce slept downstairs, as usual, and when Phoenix asked if he could join me in bed, I happily obliged and spent the night soaking up his body heat.

"Wake up, sweet girl, it's time to go," Phoenix says.

Opening my eyes, I'm met with his warm gaze and the sweetest grin on his face. I smile as I sit up, reaching for the hot chocolate only to frown when he pulls it away, pointing toward his cheek. Leaning forward, I plant a soft kiss where he told me to, and am rewarded with my morning drink. I bring it to my lips and sip slowly, closing my eyes as I savor the warm chocolate sliding down my throat. I sigh, and Phoenix chuckles.

"We're all packed up. Figure you wanted to pick something to wear before I toss your bag in the car." Tattoos peek out from under his black sweater as he stands and stretches his arms above his head and I sip more of my hot chocolate to try to cover my blush. There's not a doubt in my mind all of these boys are hot as hell, and I'm rewarded daily with shirtless men sauntering through the loft.

It'd be a travesty if I never touched any of them again.

I place my hot chocolate on the nightstand and pat the bed beside me once. It's enough to snag Phoenix's attention; he sits next to me, worry already taking over his features. I shake my head, hoping to wave off his concern and smile softly as I place my hands on either side of his face. His skin is rough against my palms from his day-old stubble, and I delight in the friction when I rub my thumbs across it.

"What are you doing?" Phoenix asks. He leans into my touch, looking at me with the warmest expression of adoration. My heart skips a beat when he reaches his hand up and covers my palm with his, pushing his fingers between mine to hold me there. "You're beautiful, Red. Strong, too. You know that, right?" he asks.

I nod, because if there's anything Phoenix has taught me recently, it's to be confident in myself and my feelings. No doubt allowed. It doesn't shine through at all when he looks at me this way, and I hope he knows that. I lean toward him, climbing to my knees so my face is level with him, and place my lips softly against his.

A sweet kiss for my sweetest protector.

Phoenix moves my palm from his face to his shoulder

and leans into me, placing his other hand on my cheek. He parts his lips, forcing mine apart as he slowly thrusts his tongue inside of my mouth.

It's a slow and sensual dance we perform. Caressing the other with hands and tongues as we luxuriate in a brief minute of reprieve.

My heart gallops in my chest when he pulls away, breathless but smiling almost boyishly. He licks his lips as he looks at me, no doubt taking in my own flushed face which matches his.

Pulling back, he pushes a stray hair behind my ear. "I think we'll be okay this Christmas, after all."

I sigh and nod, looking down at the blankets as I sift my fingers through them.

"Hey," he says, lifting my chin, "we will be. We've got each other this year, and that's better than the alternative."

"Time to go!" Pierce yells, his voice echoing against the walls and making me jump.

I place my hand to my heart and shake my head, meeting Phoenix's gaze and seeing anger there for a brief second before it dissipates.

With a soft smile for me, and a kiss on my forehead, he stands and points toward my hot chocolate. "Finish up, get dressed, and we'll go."

He disappears down the stairs, and I force myself to ignore the angry whispers from all three men as I put my clothes on.

The hot chocolate has long been cold by the time I manage to make my way down to the living room, almost bumping into a pacing Pierce when I round the corner.

He avoids touching me by hopping backward dramatically, holding his hands up, and smacking his head against a picture frame.

My heart hurts for him, but I'm determined to keep him waiting. I need to see him keep this new promise and learn boundaries...for once.

"Here's a new mug, Red," Phoenix says, handing over a travel mug of fresh hot chocolate. I look at him sheepishly. He's well aware by now that I forget all about my drink if I have something else to do in the morning.

"Bags are all in the trunk. Blankets secured. Pillows at the ready. Snack," River grins, pulling me into his side, nearly making me drop my mug, "in my current possession. So hands off, Nixy boy and ask for permission first!" He looks down at me and winks.

I roll my eyes and swat at him playfully, hiding my smile behind my new mug. Looking around at all of my guys, I take in their jeans and hoodie combos, glad I decided on the same, only a little peeved at not having warm enough leggings for this weather.

It dropped to far below freezing last night, and the frost on the ground outside rivals what's on the windows. There's a light dusting of snow, but most of it is melting as soon as it touches down.

By the time we all climb into the jeep and the heat blasts out, I'm toasty warm and comfortable leaning against River's side.

Pierce's eyes lock with mine in the rearview mirror and I ignore the pain I see there in favor of meeting Phoenix's gaze, blushing when I find him staring, too.

He's been intense with me ever since we got back

from the encounter with Maxwell. Watching over me, helping me with more things than necessary. Touching me often, just to tell himself I'm here and safe.

The gates groan when they close back up behind us, and I reach for my phone, sending a text to the group chat, which River immediately reads over my shoulder.

"Rae's wondering if we need to fix up the gate. The groaning made her uneasy."

Phoenix looks at me and smiles. "Already on it. We have a guy coming when we get back."

"What did Maxwell say about the recipe, Pierce?" River asks. He pulls my tense frame into him, rubbing his hand along my shoulder, attempting to calm me.

"The fucker was so excited. He has a team working on it already." Pierce rolls his eyes. He turns us onto the highway, settling himself into the seat and switching on the cruise control the second it's safe to do so.

"What's our plan, then?" River asks.

"Find an antidote...anything to help get it out of people's systems until we can find a way to take him down. I don't have any other ideas."

"What about Jimmy?" Phoenix asks, his gaze hardening on Pierce who grits his jaw before responding.

"Fuck him. We'll take him down with Maxwell. I've got enough shit on him. Sure I can find more." Pierce leans forward and switches on the radio. "Enough of this. Let me focus on driving. Roads are slick."

He turns the music up, killing any chance of conversation, and I settle in for the long drive to my mom's house.

Fewer fireworks are expected this trip, I hope.

"GOOD MORNING EVERYONE," *the doctor says. Her voice is soothing, but her white coat has me feeling the opposite.*

"Morning," mumbles the rest of the group.

Except for me and one other.

He's sitting in the farthest corner away from me, his legs stretched out in front of him, feet crossed at the ankles and his arms over his chest. His dark eyes are hooded, almost as if he's trying hard to keep himself awake. Stick straight black hair is falling haphazardly from a man-bun at the crown of his skull, and for some reason it makes me weak in the knees every single time I see him.

I don't know what it is about this guy, but I've been drawn to him for weeks now.

I wonder what Flames would say in response to my little obsession.

Curling my legs up in my chair, I pull my lower lip between my teeth to keep myself from smiling and giving away my thoughts.

I bet he'd be jealous. He seems like the jealous type.

"Miss Hill?" the doctor pipes up.

Looking up at her, I shake my head and point toward the next person.

We've spent the last month attempting to help me talk, and I have come to the sad conclusion I just can't. I'll be damned if it didn't have them trying harder. They think my mutism is selective, my choosing, but I truly haven't been able to make a single sound since the day my mother died.

I was sitting next to her bed, lamenting about ruining my relationship with my best friend, when the doctors came in and said I had to pull the plug on her support machines. She was simply hanging on by a thread, suffering for no other reason than my comfort in having her alive and in front of me.

So I told them to take her off the machines.

I took a few moments, and finally said "Goodbye, mom."

When they declared her dead...

I was numb.

When they were asking me question after question about her arrangements...

I suddenly could no longer make a noise.

I panicked. I tried to scream. I cried. I begged in my head for Pierce to come barging in like he used to before I ruined us.

I needed him to fix this for me.

But he never came. My crying was silent. My scream didn't shatter every window the way I wanted it to. My panicking only sent me to my own hospital room where they had to sedate me, so I wouldn't cause harm to myself or the rest of the building.

When I made it home two days later, I had an even bigger meltdown and destroyed every medical item inside of my mom's house. It didn't do her a lick of good, and it wasn't going to be doing me any favors either.

"Phoenix?" the doctor asks, and my gaze snaps up, meeting those brown eyes across the room.

"Pass," he says. His voice is low, husky.

"You've hardly spoken a word in group. Dr. Hartmann is always asking if you've finally chosen to share with the group. It would do you so much good, Mr. West." While this woman is sweet as candy, she gives Phoenix a chastising

glare before shaking her head and furiously writing notes down.

"I, uh," he says. Clearing his throat, he looks around and rolls his eyes when he sees all eight patients staring at him. "I still struggle daily with the dark thoughts in my head, and I'm really hoping to win the battle against them soon. The world doesn't mean for us to struggle this much, but we struggle nonetheless, and let it beat us down until we're stuck in a place like this. With people looking down on us, studying us, psycho-analyzing our choices." His voice grows more confident, and he sits up, leaning over his knees and folding his hands together. His eyes bore into mine and my spine snaps straight as my body fights the urge to squirm under his stare. "But what if their choice to hold us here is only prolonging our suffering?"

His warm stare feels like it's probing my deepest thoughts, and I swallow, looking down at my lap while I pick at my fingernails.

"Well, that couldn't possibly be true. We're here to help you beat back the dark thoughts, Mr. West. We only want the be—"

"The best for us? Yeah," he kicks back into his relaxed position, placing his arms behind his head, "so I've heard."

"HEY, RAERAE," River says softly. His arm wraps around my shoulders, and he uses his other to pry me off his chest. "Let's get inside, sweet girl. It'd be a travesty if I froze my nuts off out here."

I grin sleepily at his comment, shaking my head and

cringing when I touch the drool caked on my cheek. I use my shirt to wipe it clean, a blush heating my face.

River chuckles and plasters a noisy kiss right on the spot. "A little spit never deterred me, baby girl, don't worry."

Our eyes meet, and I try to glare at him, but lose the battle when he makes a goofy face. Shaking my head, I sit up fully and wait as he opens the door. He holds out his hand and I grab it, using it to pull myself out of the jeep. The second my feet hit the ground, I stretch my arms out, shivering when my shirt rides up and exposes my stomach, inviting every bit of cold to brutally kiss my skin.

"Hungry?" River asks as he slides his arm around my shoulders again, tugging me toward the front door.

I shrug and rest my head against him, wrapping my arm across his lower back to steal some of his warmth.

"Phoenix is making hot ham and cheese, I think. Better get your ass in there and eat like a good girl for him, Rae." River lets go of me when I step into the house. "I'll bring your bag up to the master, 'kay?"

Smiling sweetly at him, I nod and watch as he saunters backwards precariously down the stairs. He spins at the last minute to avoid falling on a slab of black ice, and I huff out a breath of air, folding my arms over my chest.

River has been sweet and doting on me lately. He apologized profusely about that drunken night, and has done so many times now. I've forgiven him. He was only following Pierce's orders, and it's not like I hated *everything* happening, after all.

My body and mind still war with each other about it.

"Red?" Phoenix calls from the kitchen, and I spin to

find him in yet another apron, this one his own he brought from home.

I don't remember the moment I began calling Junk my home, but the last few days have definitely felt more domestic. The kitchen smells divine, and I peek at the packaging to try and figure out how Phoenix managed to make a hot ham and cheese sandwich look so good. He tosses any evidence back in the fridge or into the trash can, and I playfully scowl at him, only to be rewarded with a soft smack to my ass in retribution.

"Let me do what I do best, and you stop being nosy. Got it?" He kisses my forehead softly and nudges me toward the island counter.

After I sit down, River enters the room and plops onto the stool next to me, placing his forearm on the top of my chair. He grins widely when I lean into him. "Did you make some for me, Nixy?" he asks.

"No, actually," Phoenix deadpans, "I was hoping you'd starve and die."

"Awww," River coos, looking at me with faux admiration. "Ya hear that, Rae? He says he loves me!"

"Jesus," Phoenix groans, shooting me a glare when I hide my laughter behind my hand. "Someone needs a lesson around here."

River hops off the chair and rounds the counter, bending over to present his ass to Phoenix, and the tears I was holding back fall as I laugh harder. "Spank me. C'mon. Someone needed to teach me manners *years* ago."

"The fuck?" Pierce barks, and we all freeze, staring wide-eyed at each other before turning toward him, the mood sobering considerably.

When we all fall silent, Pierce rolls his eyes and stomps to the stove, grabbing his own sandwich from the plate Phoenix had been stacking up.

The sound of our combined silence is deafening.

"I'll just," Pierce says, pointing toward the dining room. Without anyone answering him, he nods to himself and steps out of the kitchen. No more words spoken.

"Fuck. This tension is too thick, sweet girl. I'm gonna go sit with him, 'kay?" River asks me and I nod. "Can I have a kiss?" He looks almost shy.

I lick my lips and smile sweetly at him, grateful he sought permission.

"Sweet," he grins, and places a soft and too quick kiss on my lips. "I've got him. We have some prep to do for our early Christmas, anyway. You eat up."

Phoenix sits down next to me with sandwiches and chips for us both, sliding my plate in front of me. "Eat up, Red. It's gonna be a long few days."

I nod and eagerly bite into the hot ham and cheese he made, tossing my head back when the flavor explodes in my mouth. My eyes close of their own accord but snap open when Phoenix's hand rests on my thigh. My blood warms from the contact and I slowly chew my food as I take in his heated stare.

Usually I avoid watching people while they eat, but Phoenix is devouring his sandwich in much the same way as he devours me.

"Dirty girl," he mutters. He points to my food. "Finish your sandwich. I'll be back."

I nod and take another bite, watching his every move.

He walks around the kitchen, cleaning up the mess

he's made, throwing trash away and washing the dishes. When he's done, he opens the fridge and writes a grocery list of things we'll need for the next two days. River and Pierce have demanded we do a normal Christmas dinner, so we'll spend most of tonight prepping the food.

A task I thoroughly enjoy doing with Phoenix.

"Hey," Pierce calls from the doorway.

I look over my shoulder at him and tilt my head in question.

"We're going to check out the Christmas market before it closes. Do you guys want to go?" he asks. His usual confident tone is nowhere to be found. In its place is an unease I can't help but feel guilty for putting there.

"I have to get the rest of the groceries, but take Rae," Phoenix says, meeting my gaze. "If she's okay with it, that is."

I take a moment to think, but ultimately decide walking through the market won't be so bad. Especially with River there to constantly beat back any tension. Looking at Pierce, I nod in response.

"Okay. You might want to dress warmer. It's colder here, and it's supposed to start snowing again." He clears his throat and stuffs his hands in his pockets. "If you want to, of course."

Phoenix snorts, but coughs to cover it up. When I look back at him, he shrugs and turns toward the fridge and his task at hand.

"I'll go warm up the car," Pierce says as he steps out of the room. "Take your time," he calls back.

I slide off the stool and walk toward Phoenix, placing

my hands on my hips and glaring down at him where he sits on the floor.

"What?" he asks innocently.

Grabbing the notepad and pen from the counter next to his head, I write out a note. When I'm done, I thrust it at him.

Stop making fun of him. He's trying, and he's sad.

Phoenix rolls his eyes and raises a brow at me. "You give him too much credit, Red. He's not sad, he's a wounded puppy and he still won't take no for an answer. Watch yourself around him."

"I've got her, Nixy," River says as he slides up behind me, wrapping me in his arms. "It's just a fun little date, and I promise to be the meat in this sandwich today."

"There shouldn't even be a sandwich, River. She runs this ship now, and Pierce needs to get the hell on board or walk the plank." Phoenix grunts as he stands, shutting the fridge and leaning against the counter.

"Like I said, I've got her," River grits out. He spins me and smiles brightly. "Go get changed, Rae. We'll meet you out in the car when you're ready."

I look between both men for a moment, nod and do exactly that.

I guess we're going on a date to the Christmas market.

river

"She getting dressed?" Pierce asks me not even a millisecond after my ass hits the passenger seat.

"Yeah."

He nods and stares out of the windshield at the garage door for a moment. The joint in his hand threatens to singe his fingers, so I take it from him and inhale deeply, groaning and resting my head against the seat.

"I don't know how to act around her if I can't touch her, Riv," he says quietly.

I hand him the joint back, meeting his eyes and watching them fill with pain. "That's the problem, bro. You need to learn how to enjoy her without touch. You'll need her," I say when he tries to object, "but you have to restrain yourself." I laugh and he rolls his eyes.

"Might as well get some rope while we're out. This shit is harder than I thought. I've always needed to be near her. Always needed to touch her. She never objected before–"

"Before we got drunk and assaulted her?" I lean back against the seat, watching the front door of the house for Raven. "I've done a lot of groveling already. I've finally earned her trust, but I still ask her permission nine times out of ten."

"When the fuck have you done your groveling? I haven't seen it." Pierce grits his teeth and puts the last of the joint out in the console ashtray.

"Not everything has to be seen or approved by you, PJ."

"Shit was easier before she showed up," he grumbles, tossing his head back and closing his eyes.

"Yeah, but it wasn't as fun." I grin when his eyes pop open to glare at me. "Maybe you aren't having fun right now, but in the end, you know you'll earn her trust back."

"And I'll be eighty by the time that shit happens," he says.

Raven steps out of the house looking like a fallen angel dressed in all black. She's wearing tight as sin jeans, boots that reach her knees, a puffy coat and the gloves and hat Phoenix insisted she buy on our way out of town this morning.

I move to slide out of the car, but Pierce puts his hand up to stop me. I pause and stay where I am, watching closely as he climbs out of the jeep and walks toward the back door, opening it for her.

"Your chariot awaits, little bird," Pierce says. He's gentlemanly about it; doesn't touch or ogle her. He simply holds the door, waits for her to climb in, then closes it behind her. Back in the front seat, he meets my eyes and his lips lift at the corner for a second.

"See? You can do this. Just leave the douchebaggery behind and you'll be fine." I pat him on the shoulder, ducking when he tries to hit me.

"Fuck off," he grunts, though I see a true smile shine for the split second he thinks no one is looking.

As he pulls out of the driveway and drives us toward town, I turn in my seat to peer back at Raven. "Hey, sweet girl. You look delicious, by the way. Sure we can't make it purr in here?"

"What?" Pierce says, and I laugh, winking when Raven looks at me questioningly.

"Make it purr. You know? PRR. Pierce, River, Raven. I'm in the middle, for obvious reasons." I sit back in my seat, grinning at Pierce when he glares at me from the corner of his eye.

"Don't see how that could work," he grumbles.

The clicking of the turn signal instantly irritates me, but I take a breath and force a smile. "You aren't creative enough with this dynamic yet, Piercey Jackson. You'll get it, eventually." I pat his shoulder patronizingly and catch Raven giggling behind her hand. "But since you can't touch her...hmm," I sigh and flail my arms in the air. "What's a guy to do?"

"You're insufferable," Pierce grits out.

"Yeah, but you like me that way," I retort.

My phone buzzes in my pocket and I nearly die on the spot at the text Raven sent.

RAE

He could watch. Or...direct?

"Raven Hill!" I gasp, covering my heart with my hand.

"You dirty girl! That's just...," I shake my head as I grin at her, "fucking perfect. We definitely have to test it out."

"Test what?" Pierce asks, attempting to grab his phone from his pocket, despite the fact he's driving.

I swat at his hand. "Hands off your phone while you're driving."

Rolling his eyes, Pierce mock salutes me with his middle finger, then makes a show of putting both of his hands onto the correct spots on the wheel. "Yes, sir."

"Fucking careful," I tell him, my voice quiet enough Rae can't hear.

"Yes, sir," Pierce whispers, a grin already on his delicious fucking lips.

"I'm going to die and it'll be both of you at fault," I groan.

RAE

Death by orgasms sounds delightful though.

I look back at her and raise a brow, and she huffs out a cute little laugh which brings a bigger smile to my face. The first month with Raven around taught me a lot about her mutism, and when I found out it was due to trauma, I looked up a lot of shit. Like how her brain can one day decide to heal or not, but there's really not much of a cure.

Therapy could work, but nothing is guaranteed.

So for now, I'll take her silence and watch her body language closely to make sure I don't fuck up again.

Pierce may have steered the ship that night, but I still went along with it—drunk or not.

"Alright," Pierce says, breaking me free from my

thoughts and obvious staring at our girl. "Stick close. I don't think he will be, but Jimmy could be in town, and since we busted all of his tires...well..." he sighs and turns off the engine.

"Let's avoid a Christmas Eve Eve fight. Got it." I open my door and slam it closed as I wait for Pierce to help Raven out of the jeep. I'll let him be the chivalrous one today, make myself hold back so he can show her he's the same guy she fell for in the first place.

Pretty sure she fell for him before Maxwell's bullshit, so maybe he isn't the same guy.

"I think everyone has their gifts already, so we can walk around for a bit. Check it out like we used to." Pierce grins at Raven, and I can practically see the way his skin is crawling to touch her, hold her.

She smiles softly up at him, nodding a few times before looking toward the market, a wistful expression claiming those beautiful blue eyes.

It's not much, since we *are* in a small town, but what you can see is magical all on its own.

Trees wrap around the entire property, and a Christmas tree farm is at the back of the large lot, drawing many last minute decorators and couples in. Vendors of all sorts meticulously line the lot, both known and unknown brands, and shops showcasing their winter and holiday themed items. It smells fucking amazing, too. Roasted peanuts, actual chestnuts being cooked over a fire, a myriad of pies, and hot chocolate in a multitude of flavors.

Wrapping my arm around both Raven and Pierce's shoulders, I tug them in close to me and walk us all toward the hot cocoa stand, skipping the line because I don't have time for that shit. I grin at the shopkeeper and order three mugs full, then point out the flavor bar to Raven. "That's where the good shit is, huh?"

She grins and nods happily, moving toward the woman doling out liquid and powdered flavoring. She waits for us to bring the mugs over, and picks mixtures for us all.

Pierce ends up with peppermint, and he scowls at her, but takes his like a good boy.

I get some mocha mix which smells and tastes better than the best damn coffee I've ever had.

Rae orders herself a caramel and double chocolate flavoring, adding on marshmallows and whipped cream.

"Good choices," I praise her, and she blushes.

"She's been giving me this peppermint shit since we were kids, and I still fucking hate it," Pierce grits out, raising a brow in challenge at Rae who simply hides her silent giggles behind her whipped cream.

After a long drink, she lifts the mug from her face only to show off a massive white and sugary mustache.

I burst into laughter, and she tries to wipe it off. Reaching out, I grab her wrist and grin. "Allow me?" I ask.

She shrugs and nods, her eyes flitting toward Pierce who suddenly *loves* his peppermint cocoa.

Leaning forward, I move my hand from her wrist and place it on the side of her face. The closer I step to her, the more my body warms, and I grin when her eyes finally lock onto mine. "Can I kiss you?" I ask her in a whisper.

She nods, and I lean forward to bring her into a sweet kiss, trapping her top lip and cleaning off the cream.

Sugary and addicting, like Rae. After a few seconds, I peck her lips once, twice, three times before backing away, grinning like an asshole when I see how flushed her cheeks are.

"Do we need a tree?" Pierce asks, clearing his throat as he begins to walk toward the back anyway.

Rae shakes her head and reaches into her pocket for her phone. Growing frustrated, she holds her hot cocoa out for me to grab, but I back away so Pierce has to instead.

I shrug when he raises a brow at me.

RAE

Phoenix has a tree being delivered sometime tonight. We need decorations, though. I...destroyed all of them last year.

She inhales deeply as a look of shame washes over her face, and I wrap my arm around her shoulders again.

"Out with the old, in with the new, that's what I always say!" I smile broadly, ignoring the pang in my chest for my girl and all she went through last year.

"You say a lot of shit, Riv. Hard to keep up some-times." Pierce hands Rae back her hot cocoa and sips his own. He steps to the other side of me, avoiding even an accidental touch with her.

We walk down the aisles of vendors until we reach the Christmas trees. When we cross the threshold, Rae's eyes light up as she takes in their beauty. I watch her as she looks around at everything, my heart skipping a beat when she glances back at me; she has a massive amount of happiness shining in her gaze.

I don't miss the way her eyes flash toward Pierce, her smile dimming as they no doubt remember their previous trips here.

The trees around here are massive pines, growing larger as we meander toward the back, where less people have ventured and our footprints become the only ones to disturb the frosty grass. There's mistletoe a few feet ahead, and when I point it out to Pierce, he groans and rolls his eyes. Wiggling my brows, I carefully tug Rae forward until we're directly underneath it.

"Hey RaeRae," I catch her eyes, and she tilts her head to the side, finishing up another sip of her cocoa. "We seem to have found ourselves in a predicament." I point at the mistletoe and she looks up, tilting her head back so she can see it. I capture her chin between my thumb and forefinger, bringing her face toward me. "Can I kiss you again?"

"Jesus, I'll meet you two at the front," Pierce grits out, spinning around and storming out of the trees.

Rae sighs and places her palm on my chest for a moment, watching him leave us.

He has to get over his jealousy, or this shit will never work long term. And I really want it to.

"You don't have to say yes, you know," I tell her softly, though the pang in my chest proves how much I want her to say yes.

Looking back at me, her eyes light up before she leans up on her toes and presses a kiss on my cheek.

Not exactly what I was going for, but I'll take any and every way she deems to put those pretty lips on me.

She grabs my hand and tugs me toward the front of the Christmas trees, and I take the chance to lace our fingers together, hiding my grin behind my mug.

Pierce is standing in front of a booth full of snow globes, staring at them with a look of contemplation on his face which morphs to annoyance when he sees us coming. He places the one from his hand back down, and I rush forward, grabbing it to see what had him thinking so loud.

I nudge him with my shoulder and grin while I inspect it. "Really, dude?"

The snow globe he was looking at holds a tiny tropical island inside of it with a palm tree. A couple is kissing near it, dressed to impress for the beach. Tilting it upside down, I snort out a laugh when I bring it back upright and watch, amused as hell, as tiny pineapples mixed with glitter fall all around the couple.

"Hands down this will get you castrated, but I say buy it and give it to her." I pat him on the shoulder before handing the globe back to him.

Rae has lost herself in a sea of chocolates at a booth a few down from us, and I take the time to watch her.

From our trip so far, Raven's hair is peeking out of the black beanie hat she shoved on her head, strands falling out and laying across her neck. She looks fucking gorgeous as always, her ass is phenomenal, and she's got this badass vibe about her in all that black.

I'd gladly let her trap my throat beneath those boots, too.

"She likes the chocolates with marshmallows inside," Pierce says as he steps up to my side. He's holding a red cloth bag with the snow globe company's branding on it, and I look back toward Rae to not spook him with *feelings*.

"Go get her some, then." I fold my arms and watch her as she reaches for a sample cup given by someone she clearly knows. Her face lights up in a bright smile as she tastes a few different bite-sized pieces, then writes her thoughts down to show the business owner. "She handles all of this shit like a boss, honestly," I mutter.

"That's because you struggle to shut up and couldn't imagine a moment of silence if it bit you in the ass."

"I should be offended," I grit out, fighting my smile.

"But?" Pierce asks, raising a brow at me when our gazes meet.

"You're not wrong. Plus, that was funny as fuck." I hold out my fist, he rolls his eyes before bumping his to mine. "Go get our girl some chocolate. And don't be a dick about it!"

"Wouldn't dream of it," he mutters under his breath as he makes his way over to the booth.

I follow, sit down on an empty bench across from the booth, and watch.

He avoids touching her at all costs, like he has been since she demanded it of him, and it's impressive how he does it. Their hands almost brush, but he pulls his fingers back in time.

She's not as careful around him, and anyone watching would think she's coming on to him.

I mean, she is, but she's doing it to deliberately fuck with him.

She leans in, he leans back.

She reaches for a candy at the same time as him, he quickly snags a different one.

She's playing a push and pull game with him that's far too entertaining.

I take a video and send it to Phoenix.

> This shouldn't be that funny, but she's fucking with him and I don't even think she knows it.

My phone buzzes after a few minutes of watching the train wreck in front of me. I ignore it for a few seconds, chuckling when Rae attempts to feed Pierce a piece of chocolate. He pretends to have a coughing fit, stepping out of the booth to escape. He glares at me when he sees me laughing. I shrug before looking down at my phone.

NIXY

I'd rather she chopped his balls off.

I chuckle.

> Nah. She enjoys them, and you won't make her sad, ever.

NIXY

How do you know that?

> You don't keep secrets from her like the rest of us do.

NIXY

As far as you know.

My brows jump to my hairline. I'm about to call him

when Rae walks up to me, a bright smile on her face. I shove my phone back into my jeans pocket and spread my legs, hoping she takes the invitation.

She falters for a second before stepping between my knees and holding up the little bag of chocolates she scored. The light in her eyes makes my heart skip more beats than normal when I'm around her.

I hesitantly reach my hands out toward her hips, meeting her gaze in question. When she nods, I waste no time in pulling her to me until she has no choice but to steady herself on my shoulders. I anchor her in place and smile up at her, hoping she can't hear how erratically my heart is beating.

I may have done my groveling through hundreds of texts and memes, but I still don't feel redeemed enough.

Could be the religious trauma.

Could be I'm turning into a decent human.

The world will never know.

"Get what you wanted, sweet girl?"

She grins and nods, reaching into the bag and grabbing what looks like a mini peanut butter cup wrapped in clear plastic. After unwrapping it, she holds the candy out and I lean forward, using my tongue to pull it into my mouth, dragging it along her fingers as I move back.

Rae blushes a bright red which threatens to match her hair, and I grin.

Marshmallow and caramel explode onto my tongue as I bite into the dark chocolate and I swear I enter heaven before I realize I've died at all. I shut my eyes and groan, tightening my hands on Rae's waist to ground myself.

I swear she picked the best flavors just for me, and the

thought makes me pause, nearly choking when I swallow the thing without fully chewing it. Coughing, I beat at my chest a few times, holding my hand up to stop Rae from worrying.

"I'm fine," I choke out when I'm able to breathe again. "Did you get that for me, sweet girl?"

Our eyes meet, and her blush deepens, creeping down her cheeks and throat until it gets lost beneath her jacket. She shrugs and moves backwards out of my arms, pointing toward the front of the market.

"You want to leave?" I tilt my head to the side as I furrow my brows. "We've only been here–"

"An hour and a half. We can leave if she wants," Pierce says. He shrugs when I look at him. "What the lady wants, the lady gets, right?"

I struggle to determine if he's being sarcastic or not.

"Besides, we should stop by the store and get the rest of the decorations." Pierce gestures toward the front of the market, his eyes glued to Rae, waiting for her to move.

Once she straightens her spine and walks ahead of us, we both follow behind her, side by side and nearly in step with the other. We look like bodyguards, and anyone who would assume such a thing wouldn't be wrong.

We'll all protect her until the end, of this I'm sure.

"Hangin' in there, Piercey Jackson?"

"I swear to all that is unholy, River Jacobs, I will murder you if you keep calling me stupid shit."

I grin for a split second before biting my lip to keep it at bay. Schooling the rest of my features, I shove my hands in my coat pocket and steal a glance at him. "What would you rather me call you?"

Pierce stiffens for a moment, falling out of step with me and nearly tripping over his own two feet. He grunts and shoves me in the arm, forcing me to stumble a little. I can't help but chuckle and skip ahead, trying to catch up with Rae.

"Hey RaeRae!" She looks back at me and I point to Pierce. "Pretty sure PJ wants me to call him Master or Sir now. Should I?"

Rae freezes, then cracks a wide smile, her eyes lighting up dangerously.

"I hate you both," Pierce says as he passes by me, walking ahead of Rae. "I really, truly, hate you both."

"Nah, bro, you love us. Doesn't he, RaeRae?" I wrap my arms around her shaking shoulders and walk with her to the car.

The tension may be broken for now, but I have a feeling Pierce is going to bring it back any minute now.

TO: UPINFLAMES@MYEMAIL.COM
FROM: RMHILL@MYEMAIL.COM
SUBJECT: VALENTINE'S DAY

This would have been the first Valentine's Day with my childhood sweetheart, best friend, love of my life.

Joke's on me... I ruined it all.

Anyway, good afternoon.

Did you get a red rose, too?

I don't know who sent mine to me, and I'm close to burning it, because I'd rather celebrate Anti-Valentine's Day like I used to with *him*.

Y'know, back when we denied every single look that was charged with this sexual tension and took it out on video games instead?

I always sound so grumpy in these emails to you, Flames. I'm sorry.

Do you think love is real...or is it a social construct made to condition us to falsely tie ourself to someone, buy stupid shit for one day (have you seen the prices of wedding dresses? Stupid!), then buy houses, have babies, spend more on them, rinse and repeat until eventually humanity just...ceases to exist and we spent our time simply....following 'the plan'?

Now I sound like Leonard from group...sigh...

Till next time,

RM Hill

PS: I hope you got a rose, Flames. I'd have got you one, but you won't tell me who you are...so...

raven

"Honey, we're home!" River calls as we enter the front door, bags in tow.

We spent an hour and a half at the market, and I thought we'd spend less time at the department store. Buying decorations shouldn't be that hard, right?

Wrong.

So. So. Wrong.

River had to try on over half of the Santa hats he came in contact with, and he kept putting them on me as well. It was both delightful and a nightmare because all eyes were on us.

Anyone who knew about me and Pierce last year kept side-eyeing me every time River would lay his hands on me intimately.

Those who knew about my mutism kept waiting with bated breath to see if I'd speak, make a sound, anything.

Those we knew in high school who knew what Jimmy

was doing at the end of the year were watching me to see if I'd break.

It was the most annoying trip to a store I've ever experienced, and I didn't get to be as playful as I would have liked to with River.

I tried to float away instead, barely recognizing what I was doing.

I did get a kick out of seeing Patty Gardner working the cash register, a rather large baby belly protruding from her shirt, and a jealous look marring her pretty features.

She could have gone somewhere, but she let Jimmy ruin her reputation. She also didn't care to help me when she knew what he was doing, so...I simply killed her with kindness by smiling at her brightly and clutching River's hand hard enough to make both of our knuckles white.

I'd have grabbed Pierce's hand...but he's absolutely still in the doghouse, so I let him carry all the bags.

When I step into the house, the smell of Christmas greets me. Pine trees, cinnamon, nutmeg, vanilla. It's overwhelming, warm, inviting.

Full of memories.

Phoenix has clearly been doing a lot of work while we were gone, and my gut twists with guilt.

"This tree is fuckin' amazing, bro," River says, pulling me from my thoughts.

"Probably cost a fuck ton, too," Pierce grumbles as he sets down the rest of the bags right on the coffee table in front of the couch. He puts his hands on his hips and stares at the tree, inspecting it like he's trying to find something wrong, so he can admonish Phoenix about it.

He doesn't, which angers him to the point he bends down and starts taking things out of the bags.

"Let's start with the lights," Phoenix says as he sees box after box being taken out.

"I'll go grab a ladder and some tools," River announces, moving toward the doorway.

"I have something else in mind." Phoenix attempts to hold back his grin, but fails, and we all freeze.

The last time he had a smile like that, I ended up stuffed more than the Thanksgiving turkey.

My body heats, and my panties get wet.

"I can't touch her," Pierce says, pain lacing his tone. "What the fuck am I supposed to do if I can't touch her?"

"Fuck if I care," Phoenix grits out. He glares at Pierce while grabbing a box of the lights. "Upstairs, Red. Naked and on your bed. Two minutes."

I'm frozen, thinking about all of the things he's clearly been planning.

"Now," he commands, jolting me out of my lust filled stupor and sending me practically flying upstairs.

Heart racing a million miles a second, blood rushing through my ears, I undress in record time and try to tamp down my excitement about what he wants to do to me.

It's been sexless around here.

While I almost gave in and let myself go with Pierce and River the other day, this is the first time Phoenix has initiated. He also seems to have an idea about how to include Pierce without *including Pierce.*

Watching him suffer is becoming a new favorite hobby, even if it does make me feel guilty.

Boundaries are necessary.

I can hear the boys' muttered conversation as they ascend the stairs and walk through the hallway, but it cuts off when they enter the room and see me in all of my naked glory.

"Fuck," Pierce grits out, scrubbing a hand along his face.

"So pretty like that, Rae," River says as he saunters into the room.

Phoenix thrusts his hand out, stopping River in his tracks. "Is this okay, Red?"

I nod, licking my lips and squirming, trying to get friction between my legs.

"Three taps, got it?" His voice is the deep, husky, rumbling tone which sends goosebumps through my *soul*.

I nod again, moving to close my legs out of pure vulnerability now.

"Don't be shy now, pretty vixen," River says, his voice no longer playful. His eyes follow me, heating me up, and I squirm again.

Cold air assaults my pussy as I open my legs, showing the guys how wet I am for them.

All of them.

The thought of Pierce being forced to stay back, only allowed to watch, gives me this feeling of dominance I never thought I could feel.

I'm empowered.

Especially when he groans and pulls the computer chair out before sitting down in it, crossing his arms over his chest.

Phoenix walks toward the bed with a strand of the

new Christmas lights in his hands. "I'm going to tie you up now, Red. That okay?"

Consent is so fucking sexy.

I nod frantically, my heart speeding up the closer he gets. When he leans down and grabs my wrist, I exhale loudly, tossing my head back on the pillow. He pulls my hand to the edge of the bed, splays it open, then drags his fingers so gently back toward me. Goosebumps rise in his wake, and I shut my eyes to the onslaught of heavy lidded stares drinking in my every reaction.

"Eyes," Pierce croaks out.

Phoenix pauses in his feather-light onslaught of my senses and I open my eyes. He looks at Pierce, arching a brow. "Who said you were in charge?"

"Fucking...please?" He meets Phoenix's gaze before drifting his eyes to meet mine. "Please, Blue."

"Don't let him manipulate you," Phoenix whispers.

I look up toward him, meeting his eyes and trying to find out whatever he's not saying. After a few seconds I take a deep breath and bring my free hand up in the air, signing *It's okay.*

This placates Phoenix. He nods once before exhaling slowly, breath cascading across my cooling skin.

River moves along the other side of the bed and mimics Phoenix's movements; pulling my hand to the edge of the bed, trailing his fingers up my arm. It's intoxicating how they work together to work me over.

"Spread those pretty legs wider for us, little vixen," River says in my ear before kissing the skin behind it.

My back arches and I struggle to follow his command, too lost in Phoenix doing the same on the other side.

Their free hands trail down to either one of my thighs and pull until I'm the most exposed I've ever been in front of them.

At their mercy.

Phoenix moves away from me, and I meet his gaze as he wraps my left leg in the string of LEDs. He nods toward River, who quickly works on doing the same.

The light bulbs are cold on my skin, and I fight back the urge to scramble away. As they continue to tie my body up, I look to where Pierce is sitting, his knuckles white from the force he's holding himself together with. His eyes dart from where River has tied my foot to the end of the bed, and his jaw clenches when he meets my gaze.

I keep my eyes locked with his as his friends tease my body and tie me up with no intention of inviting him to play.

"Does it get you hot, Red?" Phoenix whispers in my ear. "Does it make you feel powerful, knowing he can't come over here and fuck your pretty little cunt like River and I are about to do?"

His dirty words have their desired effect on me, and my breathing becomes heavy and ragged. I bite my lip when River places soft kisses along my rib cage, his hot mouth contrasting the cold air in the room. His teeth nip at my nipple and my whole body shivers.

He chuckles.

"Tie her hands to the headboard," Phoenix commands as he pulls away from me, standing up and adjusting himself in his dark jeans. "Tap the wall if you need out, Red. We're paying attention, I promise." He grins smugly when he catches me staring at the bulge in his jeans and crooks his finger, bringing my gaze up to meet his. "Dirty girl. See something you like, hmm?"

My fingers clench the slats in the headboard when River ties them together, and I nod in response to Phoenix's question.

"Do you feel too exposed right now, Red? Too...open?"

I swallow audibly as his words wash over me, nodding enough times, all of my boys chuckle at my expense.

River finishes tying me up and takes a minute to slide his fingers along his handiwork.

"You're not plugging those in, are you?" Pierce asks.

"They won't get too hot, and the bulb type I told you to get won't burn her skin. She's fine." Phoenix leans over to the nightstand, plugging the lights in. "Lights off," he orders.

Pierce surprisingly obeys, standing and walking toward the wall where the light switch is.

The second he flicks it off, Phoenix turns on the string lights and my body becomes a colorful target on the mattress.

"Holy–" River says, but Pierce interrupts him.

"Beautiful," he whispers in awe.

"Down, boy," River tells him, chuckling lightly when he's rewarded with a smack in the back of his head.

"She's so pretty lit up like that. All those colors on her body." Phoenix grins as he undoes his jeans, and it grows when he notices me watching him. Shaking his head, he changes direction and reveals his tattooed, muscular glory by taking off his shirt. "You'd look better with my handprints all over you though, wouldn't you, Red?"

All I can do is nod. No thoughts are in my head, except 'Please, fuck me' and 'Please, spank me'.

Because yes, I would absolutely look better with his handprints all over me.

"Open your mouth for me," Phoenix says as he walks toward the bed.

My mouth parts without me telling it to.

"Good girl," he praises. He leans onto the bed with one knee and brings his hand up, trailing his fingers lightly along my cheek until they reach my open mouth. Slowly, with much torturous purpose, he shoves his fingers in my mouth, threatening to gag me. His eyes are full of warning as he begins to coat himself in my saliva.

Satisfied, he pulls them from my mouth and replaces them with his tongue as he kisses me. He trails his fingers down my chin, my throat, circling each nipple, before descending to meet my aching pussy.

I buck my hips, seeking the friction he's denying me, and earn a soft and quick slap to my thigh for my efforts.

"Nix!" Pierce barks, voice strained with arousal and anger.

"Don't worry, PJ," River says, his own tone just as frustrated. "She'll tap out if she wants or needs to. Ain't that right, Rae?"

I break away from Phoenix's kiss and nod, meeting Pierce's gaze across the room.

He looks so strained, and the bulge in his jeans seems as painful as the one in River's. Both adjust themselves at the same time, and I bite my lip, drifting my gaze between the two.

"Want me to touch him, little vixen? Get him off so he

doesn't burn the house down?" River looks at us, and he looks ready to bust when I nod.

Relief flashes through Pierce's gaze and I wonder if I should have denied him an orgasm this time. That thought is forgotten when Phoenix nips at my neck and thrusts his fingers inside of me.

"Watch them, and don't come until I tell you to," he growls into my ear.

His thumb rubs my clit as he moves inside of me, the strings from the lights digging into my skin enough to keep me from grinding my hips against his hand.

It's not enough.

I watch, entranced, as River—in typical River style—strips his clothes off and tosses them on the floor.

"You need some tact, man," Pierce says, voice wavering as he watches his other best friend step toward him.

River says nothing, dropping to his knees in front of Pierce so quickly the sound of him hitting the floor makes me wince in sympathy.

Phoenix's fingers are doing magical things to me, and my attention splits between him and the other two. With nowhere to fully focus on, I take it all in together, my senses becoming overwhelmed. My eyes roll to the back of my head when those skilled fingers rub against my g-spot.

"Don't come yet. Watch," Phoenix says in my ear, using his free hand to grip my jaw and hold my head to the side, forcing my gaze onto the spectacle they're putting on for me.

River reaches forward and undoes the button of

Pierce's jeans, making a show of looking up at him while lowering the zipper. "Lift," he commands, voice low and raspy.

Pierce's face blanches, and he glances back at me, our gazes clashing as we have a silent conversation.

This is the first time they'll be doing something like this in front of me. I'm not sure who told him I wasn't okay with them being together, but they were wrong.

My pussy floods when he lifts his hips and shoves his pants down with River's help, exposing his hard cock. I watch as River instantly grabs for it, squeezing and twisting his hand upward until he can drag his thumb along the slit.

"Fuck, she's clamping my fingers like a vise. Keep doing whatever you're doing," Phoenix tells them.

I try to look at him, but with his firm hold on my jaw, all I can manage is watching him out of the corner of my eye.

His lust is evident on his face, and he does nothing about it, simply pumping his fingers in and out of me like a machine.

A slow...

Meticulous...

Fucking machine.

The sound of Pierce's groan draws my eyes back to the other two. River has his dick so far down his throat I'd be concerned for him if I didn't see him pumping his own so furiously. Pierce tosses his head back, heavy-lidded eyes peering at me across the room as his hands push down on River's skull, controlling his movements.

"If watching River suck Pierce's dick gets you this wet,

Red, I might make them do it more often." Phoenix nips at my ear before lifting away from me, drawing his fingers up toward my mouth and shoving them inside. "Suck like the pretty little whore you know you are."

"Jesus," Pierce grunts. From Phoenix's words or River's mouth, I don't know.

Obeying, I use my tongue to clean my own juices off Phoenix's thick fingers, shutting my eyes and exhaling heavily when it makes me hotter.

Satisfied, he pulls them from my mouth and pushes his pants and boxers down before using the fingers I sucked to coat his dick in my saliva. His free hand to yank his shirt over his head.

My breathing picks up.

Pierce groans.

River gags.

Phoenix exhales loudly.

The sounds and smells of sex are so potent, it's all I can focus on.

"So pretty, Raven. So, so fucking pretty," Phoenix grunts as he continues to tug on his dick. He moves toward the bed, trailing his gaze along my body until he meets my eyes. "Can I fuck you?"

I nod frantically, and he and Pierce chuckle at the same time.

Phoenix's gaze snaps up to meet Pierce's, anger taking over his features before he schools them and leans over to the nightstand. He grabs a condom from the top drawer and rips it open with his teeth. I watch, enchanted, as he rolls the latex onto his dick. He gives himself a few more pumps, then climbs on the bed and hovers over me.

Phoenix rests his forearm next to my head and slides his fingers through my hair gently. He uses his other hand to notch himself inside of me with just the tip.

Just that is enough to make him groan.

"I want you to watch River gag on Pierce's dick while I fuck you slowly. I want you to get so fucking hot for it your pussy chokes my dick." Phoenix grips my chin and forces me to meet his gaze, his brown eyes burning with desire. "You gonna do that for me, Red?"

I nod.

"Good fucking girl," he says, leaning down to give me a kiss so intoxicating my head swims. It doesn't last long, and he grips my chin to make me watch the other two. Phoenix pulls back to untangle the lights from my legs, then takes one of my ankles over his shoulder. He thrusts inside of me in one smooth move, pulling my pelvis up off the bed to find a deeper angle.

It's hard as hell to watch one act while another is being performed on my body. Pierce's gaze traps me as he continues to face fuck River like he's done it many a time before.

And maybe he has.

River tightens his hold on Pierce's thigh after a particularly hard thrust, and my pussy does exactly what Phoenix wanted it to; it clenches until it chokes his dick.

All three guys groan at once, and my eyes flutter closed to the onslaught.

"Eyes, Blue," Pierce barks out, earning a sexy as sin growl from Phoenix.

I open my eyes, meeting those lust-filled green ones I've loved for far too long.

River pulls away to catch his breath and turns to watch Phoenix thrust into me in a slow and torturous pace, giving me everything and nothing at all. "Shit," he says, "she's so fucking pretty while she's getting fucked."

"I wasn't fucking done, Riv," Pierce tells him, gripping River's hair. He stands, and I watch his cock as it bobs between them.

I lick my lips, my breath stuttering as he shoves his dick roughly into River's mouth and down his throat until he gags, loudly. My toes curl when Phoenix drags his dick along that perfect spot inside of me, and I toss my head back, struggling to keep the eye contact Pierce is begging me for.

River is using one hand to tug at Pierce's balls and the other to jack himself off.

Pierce has all of his fingers in River's hair, but both eyes are on me.

Phoenix reaches between us and begins to meticulously rub my clit. "Are you going to come for us, Red? We don't get off until you do. Do you know why?"

I look up and meet his gaze, shaking my head.

"Because," he grunts as he thrusts into me a tad harder, more frantic, "you are the queen. You sail this ship. We," he says against my neck, groaning when I clench around him after hearing River gag again, "are yours. Understand?"

When I nod, he bites into my skin and drags his dick along my g-spot. Sweat builds on his brow, and I breathe out heavily when his fingers rub faster at my clit, my back arching until my stomach presses up into his, my nipples rubbing friction against his heated skin.

"Fucking come for us, beautiful," he commands, pinching my clit with his fingers and biting at my neck again.

White floods my vision, my body tenses, a silent scream bleeds into the air, and I'm close to losing consciousness.

Pierce and River's twin groans of release echo through the room as Phoenix picks up his pace, prolonging the aftershocks of my orgasm as long as he can before he stills. His dick throbs inside of me and my clit nearly reignites with his skin grinding against me.

"Holy shit," Pierce says as he flops his naked ass onto the desk chair, his hair mussed up with sweat.

River cleans his sticky hand up with a discarded shirt, then leans his head on Pierce's thigh.

"One of you go get a towel," Phoenix commands as he pulls out of me, shuddering with his own aftershocks.

"For what?" Pierce questions, raising a brow.

"Aftercare," River says matter-of-factly.

Phoenix nods, confirming his words, before leaning down to kiss me gently. Slowly.

Pierce growls and the sound of the chair hitting the wall startles me enough to pull back, my heart breaking in my chest.

"Nope," River says as he stands and moves toward me.

Pierce walks into the master bathroom and I meet River's gaze.

"Let him throw his tantrums. He's earned the punishment, sweet girl. Don't feel bad for setting boundaries." River grins and leans down to kiss me soft and slow, the taste of Pierce overtaking my senses.

"Shit," Phoenix says, his hands reaching for my wrists. "This was a dumb idea."

River pulls back from kissing me and furrows his brow, though he places a hand in my hair to brush it from my face. "We didn't get it that tight, I thought."

"Yeah, well, she squirms," Phoenix grins and shakes his head, pinching my side in admonishment.

I can feel my cheeks heating with a blush as I shrug.

It takes a few minutes for them to untangle me, but when they do, they each claim half of me and begin massaging all the circulation back into my limbs.

River sits up against the headboard with my back to his chest, gently rubbing my wrists and forearms, while Phoenix sits cross-legged at the end of the bed and does the same to my legs.

Pierce walks in, seemingly having composed himself, and stops briefly before moving toward the bed. He looks between the other two, then blows out a long breath and hands the towel to Phoenix, who nods at him as he backs away and starts getting dressed.

I sigh and shut my eyes, settling into the sensations of River rubbing soothing circles in my skin as Phoenix cleans me up with the warm, wet towel.

Boundaries are hard to set, but they are so incredibly necessary.

A tear falls from my eye before I know it's formed, and River uses his thumb to quickly swipe it away. I look up and watch as he follows Pierce with his gaze, a sadness lingering there for him.

"You sore, Red?" Phoenix asks, tossing the towel toward the pile of dirty clothes. When I shrug, he shakes his head and grins almost boyishly before tugging me up from the bed and into his arms. "You need a shower and some cream on these marks."

I nod, briefly locking eyes with Pierce when we pass by him.

The ache in his gaze hurts me, but not enough for me to give in.

pierce

Christmas Eve morning sucks.

My mom's not here.

Rae's mom's not here.

And Rae still won't let up with her bullshit punishment.

I spent all day yesterday avoiding her touch, and when we were all up in her room?

I'd have preferred death to that scenario.

Probably the fucking point.

"Do you think I could wake her up with my face between her thighs?" River grins from the doorway, rubbing his hands together as he summons that scene up in his head.

"Nope," I say, popping the P obnoxiously. "She hates anything sexual being done to her in her sleep. I tried once," I flinch when I remember *that* particular punch to my junk, covering it with my hands.

"Wasn't pretty, was it?" River winces in sympathy.

I shake my head and lean against the door frame, folding my arms as I watch her sleep, a peaceful smile on her face and her hair fanning out behind her.

None of us slept with her last night.

We left her to herself, as she requested, and no one said a thing when we heard her sniffling late at night.

We knew she would be a broken mess, and Phoenix is no better.

He'd have been up by now, but I have a feeling he might be ignoring the dates creeping up on us as much as Rae is.

"We need to wake them both up, though. For gifts," River says.

I look over and see a wide smile stretching his face and my heart clenches at how attracted to him I am. Never would have thought his sunshine personality would be what brought me from the brink of devastation last year, but here we are. Wrapping an arm around his shoulders, I turn us both and step down the hall toward the stairs. "Let's get the cinnamon rolls out of the oven, then we can wake Phoenix up, who can help us wake Rae up."

"Sounds like a plan, Stan!" River grins when I roll my eyes and shuffle him toward the stairs.

It doesn't take long for us to have the cinnamon rolls made and plated. We head up to wake Phoenix, who grumbles quite a bit but perks up and fixes himself the second we mention Rae.

He has it bad for her, like the rest of us.

If only he'd join "Team Pierce" and stop glaring at me for simply existing, that'd be great.

"Should we sing a song to wake her up?" River asks, earning a smack to the back of the head from me and an eye roll from Phoenix. "Take that as a no then," he grumbles.

Phoenix steps past both of us and sits next to her on the bed. Leaning down, he stretches his arm out and places his hand on her cheek, brushing her hair from her face as he whispers softly to her.

Jealousy burns in my gut as I watch them.

I miss touching her.

I miss being the one she goes to for everything.

I'd take a fucking hug at this point, but that won't happen for a while, it seems.

A lone tear falls down my cheek as I watch her remain comfortable under someone else's touch.

"Hey," River whispers from my side, wrapping his arm around my shoulders and tugging me to him.

I quickly swipe away the tear and straighten my spine, hoping like hell he didn't catch it.

"Keep up the consensual shit. Keep asking. Keep listening. It's not as nice as yanking her into your arms whenever you want, but she's finally learning how to set her boundaries and keep them. This is making *her* stronger, bro. It's beautiful."

I blow out a breath and look back to see Phoenix as he leans down to place a gentle kiss on Rae's lips.

She runs her fingers through his hair for a second, then freezes, eyes opening wide when she notices me and River standing in her doorway.

Phoenix leans away from her, stroking her cheek once more before gesturing to us. "They brought cinnamon rolls. Wanna eat in here, or the kitchen?"

Rae's eyes lock with mine as she points downstairs.

Like the good little boys we all are now, we walk out of her room and back down the stairs again. River sets the dish of cinnamon rolls onto the counter, then grabs plates for everyone to use. Phoenix grins when he sees the coffee and hot chocolate is already made, quickly filling mugs and setting them near the food.

By the time Rae is downstairs, I'm sitting on one end of the island, River beside me, her spot is still empty, and Phoenix has taken his place at the other end.

It's become normal for us to sit in this arrangement.

Before my...*punishment*, River and I would be swapped. I'm the furthest from her now, yet my skin still lights up, my breath still catches in my throat, and my heart still skips beats when she sits down and smiles at all of us.

She signs *Thank you* before diving into her cinnamon roll.

"All the gifts are under the tree and ready to be shared as soon as we're done eating," River says after swallowing a large mouthful of his food.

"There's a few surprises for later, too," Phoenix's lips twitch, attempting to hide his grin behind his coffee mug.

"I gotta get a box out of the jeep," I tell them. I finish the last bite of my cinnamon roll and head into the garage.

My gifts aren't much at all, but I'm hoping this solidifies the seriousness in which I take us all. This relationship may be unconventional to some, but it works for us, and that's all that matters.

River is holding the door open when I turn around, and I smile at him in thanks as I pass by. He smacks me on the ass and I spin quickly to glare at him. The asshat shrugs and saunters away like nothing happened.

And now my dick is hard.

River's always been so fucking playful, taking shots at me whenever he has a chance and riling me up just to see what fucking happens.

I sigh as I place the box down near the tree, sitting on the coffee table and bringing my hands up to rub my fingers across my temples.

It took him less than a month to make me snap...

"WHAT'S UP WITH YOU, DUDE?" *the Alpha Mu president snaps out. He's glaring at me like I've kicked his puppy or some shit.*

"Nothing," I snap back, narrowing my eyes when he takes a step toward me.

"Fuck, go get laid." He laughs.

Yeah, not happening.

I've been here for a month, and I don't even remember why the fuck I agreed to this shit. Other than to get away from Raven fucking Hill.

"Yooooo!"

Oh, fuck.

I look up.

River Jacobs, one of the other Alpha Mu pledges. He's been here for a little longer than me, having started at the beginning of the school year instead of halfway through. His dirty blonde hair nearly reaches his shoulders and looks like someone's been digging their fingers into it.

He also always looks freshly fucked.

"What's up?" I ask him, voice devoid of any emotion.

"Awe, bro, no need to sound so excited to see me!" He plops down on the couch next to me, wrapping his arm around my shoulders and tugging me into his side like he's done a million and one times in the past week or so.

If he keeps touching me, he's going to find himself splayed out on the floor.

Getting fucked.

Wait, no.

"What do you want?" I ask him, pulling away from his hold and sitting on the other end of the couch.

I truly have no qualms with him, but after many a long talk about our lives and where we want to go after school, he's become increasingly annoying with his questions about the girl who broke my heart. All he knows right now is the basics: a girl broke my heart and I'm pissed about it. I refuse to tell him more.

"What don't I want is the real question." He grins when I narrow my eyes at him. "The answer, Piercey Jackson, is fucking crabs. Got tested. I'm all clean, and now I'm down to fuck again!"

"Why are you telling me this?" I ask, folding my arms over my chest.

He shrugs and bites his lip, and I hate that I notice how plump and wet they look right now.

It's not that I'm against fucking guys.

It's that I'm still holding out for Raven for some fucking reason.

"Hey, so I'm pretty sure our lock is broken and I wanna fix it. Come help?" He sounds sincere enough that I shrug and follow him up the stairs and down the hall.

We enter our room, and before I can look at the doorknob, he has my face pressed into the wood, his body firmly against mine, and I hear the distinct click of the door locking.

What. The. Fuck!

I can't speak with my face smashed, and my dick aches as it makes contact, too.

I can't move.

I can barely fucking breathe.

"You keep holding onto whatever you're holding onto back home, bro, and you'll shatter before the year's out," River says. His breath bathes the back of my neck in warmth as his hand tightens in my hair. "Some advice? Holding onto the past does absolutely fucking nothing."

"What—" I try to speak, but my jaw clenches when all I manage is to drool on the wood.

River presses my face further into the door and leans in until his lips brush my ear. "I'm going to make a deal with you. I'll let you use me as your little toy to get off, but you gotta share your shit with me."

I tense, then push off of the door with my hands. River stumbles backwards, nearly falling into the wood of our bunk. I twist around and collar his throat, shoving him against the bed. "I don't share anything with anyone, bro." I spit out.

He grins and raises a brow. "I know. You need to, though. I saw you with Mr. Langston yesterday. What're you—"

I cover his mouth with mine in an attempt to shut him up, earning a pained and lust-filled groan from both of us.

No one needs to know my secrets.

Our hips collide as I settle myself against him, and I place one hand in his hair, keeping his head still as I devour his mouth with my tongue. My other hand catches his wrist which tries to undo my jeans. Breaking away, I glare at him. "You saw fucking nothing. Now get on your knees. You can suck my dick like a good little fuck toy."

He doesn't hesitate, dropping to the floor so quickly, I can feel it when he lands at my feet. I unbutton my jeans and unzip them before sliding them off just enough for my dick to be released. Tossing my head back in painful relief, I pump myself a few times, looking down and locking onto River's storm gray eyes. "Open your mouth," I command him. He does. "Tap my thigh if you need me to stop. Other than that?" I shove my dick between his lips and groan, loudly. "Suck."

He thought he was topping me?

Fucking laughable.

The sweet sound of him gagging on my dick nearly brings me to my knees, and when I move back, he clenches onto my thighs and pulls me further down his throat. He's not shy about his skill around a dick, and I find myself the beneficiary of one of the best fucking blowjobs of my life.

Sorry, Rae.

I lean forward and brace myself on the bunk bed, clenching onto the wood as I look down at River. Our eyes lock when he reaches up and grips my balls in his hand, and my breath stutters when he tugs gently. "F-Fuck," I moan, breathing heavily when he does it again. "Touch yourself," I tell him, "make yourself come with me."

He takes his sweet ass time pulling his dick out, still keeping his mouth full of mine, swirling his tongue around my head. His spit drips down and lands on the tip of his the moment it's free, and the sight nearly makes me bust.

"Hurry the fuck up." I slide one of my hands into his hair and thrust a few times in his mouth, slowly, coating myself in more of his spit.

He pumps his hand over his own dick, before bringing his free one up to play with my balls again, rolling them in his palm with a firmness I've only managed on my own. Strands of hair fall into his face and I find myself moving them back to lock eyes with him again.

I wonder what kind of storm is hiding there.

"Do you like choking on dick, River?" I ask him as I push to the back of his throat, knees shaking when he gags again, panic shining in his eyes.

He nods.

"Fuck," I breathe, pulling away and thrusting back in. I pick up my pace, watching as he handles me and his own dick in tandem. It's a fucking sinful sight, and the sounds of our mixed groans and heavy breathing take over our little room.

He does something particularly impressive with his tongue along the vein on the underside of my dick, and I smack the wood with my hand.

"Shit. Come!" I shout at him, unloading heavily down his throat with a strangled moan.

He hums around my cock as he pumps his quicker, the wet sound making me twitch with aftershocks. Stilling, his eyes meet mine as he lets out a ragged moan as he spurts all over himself, his shirt catching the majority of his cum. Pulling away slowly, he licks the rest of the cum off my dick and leans his head against the bed as he sits back on his ass. "Damn," he says, voice hoarse from the throat fucking he endured.

I pull my pants up to cover my ass and sit down beside him, resting my head back on the bed next to his. "Pretty fucking much," I say.

We both laugh, and the tension fizzles out of my body like a live wire's been cut.

I spend the rest of the night getting him up to date on everything I've done for Maxwell Langston, my split with my ex-best friend, and all the things I plan to do about both.

"YOU OKAY?" River asks as he sits next to me on the coffee table, the old wood creaking precariously.

I shrug and look up to meet his eyes, wondering what the fuck made him stay besides the secrets we both hold onto for each other.

"Be happy for a change, bro. Just today, at least," he whispers the last part before perking up and grabbing a Santa hat from his other side. He places it on my head, a grin splitting his face when he puts a matching one on his.

"Nix get one, too?"

"Abso-fucking-lutely he did!"

"Not happy about it," Nix says as he enters the room

behind Raven, who is dressed in fuzzy Christmas socks and some flannel pajamas.

How she looks hot like that, I'll never fucking understand.

Pretty sure it's just because it's her.

"Okay, present time!" River says, clapping his hands together and standing. He moves toward the tree and points around at all the presents one by one as if he's struggling to pick which one to start with.

"Oh my God," I groan, wiping a hand down my face. I stand up and move to sit in the recliner, crossing my ankle over my knee as I wait for River to make a damn decision.

"Alright, I feel like our queen should go first," he says.

"Obviously," Phoenix replies, annoyed.

Rae sits on the center of the leather couch, pulling her knees up until she's cross-legged. Her hands lace together in her lap and she watches River with amusement shining in her pretty blue eyes.

"Man, my gift is too sentimental. It sets the bar high, bros, real high." River spins around with a small box in his hand, and my heart threatens to give out.

"Absolutely not," I grit out, tempted to stand up and pummel him.

"Chill," he says, rolling his eyes at me. Stepping toward Rae, he sits on the coffee table in front of her and holds the tiny black box out for her to take.

Hand shaking with nerves, she grabs the box, her gaze flitting quickly around the room to all of us in confusion and, dare I say, fear. She manages to open the box, and lets out a heavy breath before taking a small, silver band out.

"It, um," River stutters, swallowing harshly before grabbing the ring and pointing toward Rae's thumb. "It's my old purity ring. I want you to wear it. A promise from me to you. I'll keep true to you, and listen to all of your wishes." His voice shakes as he asks, "May I?"

A serious River is rare enough that the whole room is captured in the moment when he slides the ring over her thumb. It fits perfectly, because of course it fucking does. She examines it for a few seconds with tears in her eyes before throwing herself at River and hugging him so tightly my chest aches for one just like it.

I meet Phoenix's gaze over their shoulders, and he shrugs, a small smile playing on his lips.

Of course he'd be okay with something as serious as gifting her a goddamn ring.

I think back to the one I'd had burning a hole in my pocket last year and am reminded of everything which went wrong to put us in this scenario instead.

"Alright," River says, kissing Rae on the forehead before he pulls away. "Who's next?"

"Just, uhm, let her give you yours," I say. I'm not ready to share yet.

Rae looks to Phoenix and he shakes his head. "I'll wait until last. My gift is a little more encompassing."

"Dirty bastard," I say, grinning but masking it quickly so no one sees.

Rae steps around the coffee table and leans over to grab a box. She comes back around to sit again, thrusting the box at River.

He shakes the box next to his ear, and she huffs out a

laugh we all crack smiles for. "Wait! Christmas music! What the hell, guys?!"

I lean forward to press a button on one of the remotes and classic Christmas tunes play softly through the sound system. "Happy?" I ask, brow raised.

"Yes!" He grins and looks back at Rae as he opens his gift. Paper goes flying everywhere and when he tears into the box to get a peek inside, he barks out a loud laugh. Reaching in, he pulls out a stack of books. "You little minx," he tells her, meeting her gaze for a second before looking back down at the covers.

"What are they?" I ask.

"Books," Phoenix retorts.

"No shit," I growl out, glaring at him.

"I asked her to let me read some of her favorite dirty books. She said she wouldn't let me touch her copies with a ten foot pole, so she'd get me my own." He grins at her after flipping through some of the titles. "Thank you, sweet girl. I have lots of studying to do now." Leaning forward, he kisses her gently for a moment before pulling away and placing the books back in the box. "Who's next?"

Rae turns to look at me and I shrug. "Alright, you asked for it." I stand up from the chair and walk toward the massive box near the tree. "Riv, a little help?"

"Sure thing," he says as he stands up and makes his way over to me. With his shoulder brushing mine, he looks down at the box. "Don't tell me you got her a puppy, dude."

"The box would have holes for it to breathe, numb-nuts. Also, we have too much shit going on for a puppy." I kneel next to the box and break open the tape. "Here goes nothing," I whisper.

One at a time, I pull out three black leather jackets and hand them over to River. When I reach the bottom of the box I take a deep breath and pick up the last one, white knuckling it as I rise to my feet again. The red is the same as the one we got her a few months ago, but the design on the back is different. New. Packed with meaning.

"So, I, uh," I stutter, clear my throat, "had these made. For all of us. Thinking the same thing as River. This is a promise, I guess." My voice is shaky, and I curse it for making me sound emotional. I don't get emotional. "Don't look yet," I say quickly when River starts turning the jacket around. "Put them on. Everyone has one."

I walk over to Rae and hold the jacket out. "Can I help you into it? Minimal touching, I promise."

She nods and rises to her feet. Her lip stays between her teeth as she watches me, skepticism shining in her eyes. Blowing out a breath, she turns around and holds out her arms.

Carefully, so as not to touch her, I slide each side of the jacket onto her arms, and adjust the collar as best I can. Deciding to chance fate, I whisper, "Can I move your hair?"

She freezes but nods, her own breath stuttering out of her when I gently lift her strands with my hand. I move them from underneath the jacket and place them over her shoulder so that the design on the back is fully visible.

"Beautiful," I whisper, watching as goosebumps rise along the back of her neck. With great difficulty, I move away and grab the last jacket, shoving my arms into it roughly as I try to tamp down my frustration.

"Holy shit, this is epic, Pierce," River says in awe.

I look over to see him taking in the design on the back of my jacket, Phoenix staring at River's. Shrugging, I smile genuinely for the first time in what feels like forever. "Had a little help, obviously."

"Did you go through our usual place?" Phoenix asks.

"Nah, somewhere new. Gave 'em the specs and told them to make something that would last."

"Top fucking tier material, Pierce."

The compliment hits me square in the chest, and I wave him off, turning back toward Rae to see what she thinks.

Tears are flooding her eyes, and I so badly want to wrap her in my arms and protect her from the world. But she also needs protecting from me, so I don't move a muscle as I watch her. She turns toward all of us and River spins so she can see the back of his jacket.

A Raven with wings spread wide, its beak pointed skyward, opened in a scream, hovers above a collection of three skulls. At the top of the design is a long, white ribbon which says "A Conspiracy" and matching that on the bottom is text which reads "of Ravens".

She smiles brightly when she sees it, tilting her head this way and that as she takes in all the subtle differences in each jacket.

Mine has green stitching, River's has blue, and Phoenix's has a burnt orange. Each color matching the under glow for our bikes.

We all chuckle when she takes her own jacket off to

see the back. Her design matches ours, except the Raven has a crown on its head.

She turns back around as she puts it on again, and those tears finally fall. She rushes toward me, I'm helpless to stop her from wrapping her arms around me for the first time in what feels like ages.

I painfully keep my hands to myself, allowing her to hug me to her tightly for a few more seconds. When she pulls back, she signs and mouths *Thank you*, and in good faith, I sign and mouth back *You're welcome*, which only succeeds in making her cry again.

"You did good, dude," River says, patting me on the back as everyone moves back to the couch, grinning as he sits next to Rae.

"Alright," Phoenix says as he plops down on the other side, "Time for Pierce to get his gifts. You all know what I'm getting you, so I think River should go first."

"Yes!" River shouts, standing up quickly and jostling Rae in the process. She falls into Phoenix and I can see her shoulders shaking with silent laughter. "Sorry, RaeRae."

She shakes her head, waving him off and pointing at the tree.

He follows her silent command, walking toward the tree and grabbing a box barely bigger than the one he gave to Rae. Sitting down on the arm of the recliner, he chuckles when I raise a questioning brow. "I'm not ready to marry your salty ass yet, Pierce. Calm down."

"How do you know my ass is salty?"

"Strip and let's find out," he retorts.

"Alright, let's get a move on," Phoenix barks out,

laughing when both River and I look over at him like wounded puppies. "I have plans. You're stalling."

River opens the box and shows me a bracelet with what look to be pearl sized white beads lining the whole thing. "This looks cool, Riv, thank you." I reach inside and pull it out, running my fingers along the different textured beads and grinning.

River's shoulders are shaking with silent laughter and I look up at him as I place it on my wrist. "Didn't think you were into bracelets, but I thought it'd look hot, so." He shrugs and snorts another laugh, quickly covering it with his hand before looking at the other two. "Last gifts!" he calls.

Rae looks nervous as she stands and steps toward the tree, grabbing her last two gifts. She goes to Phoenix first, because of fucking course she does, and hands him a small envelope. A blush creeps its way along her cheeks and descends until it gets lost beneath the jacket and her pajamas.

My dick grows hard as I imagine just how far that blush goes, and I have to rub my hand over it to get some relief.

"Want some help?" River asks in a whisper.

"Fuck off," I tell him, though the idea doesn't sound so bad.

"Fuck, Red," Phoenix says, wrapping her up under his arm and placing a kiss on her head. "I'll definitely be using this, and soon." He grins wickedly down at her before twisting his hand around to show us the card she got him for the sex shop down the street from CU.

Rae smiles up at him and places a kiss on his cheek.

She grabs the little gift bag from beside her and brings it over to me, hesitating before placing it on my lap. She looks guilty.

"What'd you do?" I ask her, raising a brow as I watch her fidget with her hands.

She shrugs and bites her lip, looking up to meet River's gaze. They both share a silent conversation and struggle to maintain their composure.

"What the fuck?" I snap as I pull out a bottle of my favorite whiskey. It'd be a great fucking gift, actually, if my little bird's handwriting wasn't front and center on the label. "For when times get hard?" I read, raising a brow at her and glaring. My lips twitch with an impending laugh, and I struggle to sound angry. "You're a little shit. Both of you, actually." I shove River off the chair, and he busts out into laughter, Rae laughing silently but just as hard as he is.

I open the whiskey and take a big swig to deal with their bullshit. Capping the bottle, I place it on the table beside me. "Fucking troublemakers, both of you."

"Yeah, but you love us anyway," River says as he gets to his feet, tugging Rae into his side to stand in front of me.

"Yeah," I say softly, "Yeah, I do." I meet Rae's gaze, hoping I sound as genuinely in love with her as I feel. Her features cool considerably before she audibly swallows and retreats back to the comfort of Phoenix West like he's the end all be all of her happiness.

"Okay, what's your plans, Nixy boy?" River asks.

"Food first. We need our girl fed and hydrated for what I have planned." He grins wickedly and the glint in his eyes when he looks toward me instantly has my defenses rising.

"Thanksgiving part two?" River asks, bouncing on his feet, once, twice, a third time as he rubs his palms together.

"Thanksgiving part two," Phoenix confirms.

I'm the only one getting soft at the prospect.

TO: RMHILL@MYEMAIL.COM FROM: UPINFLAMES@MYEMAIL.COM SUBJECT: RE: VALENTINE'S DAY

Hey there, Red.

I hope your day went better after that email. Did you get to stuff your face full of chocolate? I hope you did, and that it perked you up a bit.

FYI, I ended up with too many roses and I'm entirely uncomfortable about it.

I may have been in a band, but I really don't like attention being on me like that, like this.

There's too much pressure from society to do this, do that, be perfect or get shafted.

But love?

No, it's not a social construct.

Valentine's Day absolutely is, but love is the byproduct of magic, I'm sure of it.

My parents were so in love. I got to watch the manifestation of true love every single day until they died.

So...no, I don't believe love is made up. I do believe it's abused by our capitalistic society, though.

Question, if you could travel anywhere in the world, where would you go?

Till next time,

Flames

raven

Christmas music blares in the kitchen as Phoenix finishes making the dinner he's been working on for the past three hours.

My stomach grumbles and River stops our dancing, grabs a deviled egg, and holds it in front of my mouth. I part my lips and sigh contentedly when the different flavors flood my taste buds.

I gave Phoenix a book with all of my favorite recipes, and he'd shooed me away, diligently working to put this all together by himself. Pierce has been playing various video games in the living room while River has kept me entertained. We've danced, cuddled, read from one of the books I gave him, and occasionally joined Pierce in his gaming marathon.

Aside from Phoenix, who's using cooking to distract himself from his feelings, we've all been relaxing and taking a collective breath today.

The jackets Pierce bought us all are hanging on the

coat rack, mine on top of all of theirs, and I smile as I think about the hard work which went into the design. He may not have made it, but it was his idea, and he made sure it was done justice.

"What's going on in your head there, little vixen?" River asks, twirling me again once I've finally swallowed the food in my mouth.

I shrug and lean my head against his chest, closing my eyes and just *feeling*.

His arms wrap around my body until his hands rest on the spot right above my ass, and he keeps them there respectfully. A new song comes on, and he begins a slow dance with me, leading me while also allowing me to have control.

It's sensual and comfortable.

I might be in love with him.

I grin and pull back to look up at him, my hands landing on his shoulders. Leaning up on my toes, I place a soft kiss to his lips, inviting him into a slow and languid moment.

"Food's ready," Phoenix says, snapping a towel out and swatting me on the ass with it.

I break apart from River and glare at him, rubbing the sensitive spot he no doubt left marks on.

"Get over it. You'll have time to play soon, I promise." He grins and points at the food as he meets River's gaze. "Grab Pierce and help with this. Rae, go sit. Head of the table, where the Queen belongs." He winks, and I shake my head.

The dramatics of these boys.

Once seated at the table, still in my flannel pajamas

because they wouldn't let me change a damn thing from this morning, I watch as they work together to bring all the food in. Sure, they were friends before I came into town, but seeing them like this is magical.

Smelling all the deliciousness Phoenix cooked up has nothing on the sight of it lining the table like this. He went extra hard on this lineup of food, and when I see the fake grin on his face from across the room, I sigh.

It's all a distraction for himself.

"This is a lot to clean up later, Nixy," River says as he plops down on my left.

Phoenix sits on my right and shrugs. "Cleaning will work some of the food off before we have dessert."

"Should I leave?" Pierce asks as he takes his spot next to River.

"Absolutely not. I have plans for you, too." Phoenix chuckles darkly and begins to fill my plate, asking how much of each item I want.

He makes me use sign language to answer, because he's in the mindset that the more we use ASL, the easier it will get.

Practice, practice, practice.

Once everyone has food on their plates, we dig in.

No one here prays. Praying hasn't done anything for any of us before.

"Swear you haven't taken cooking classes before, Nixy?" River asks around a mouthful of food. He swallows when Phoenix glares at him.

"No. I spent a lot of time learning to cook back when—" Phoenix clears his throat and shakes his head.

"Just spent a lot of time learning to cook is all. It frees my mind of the clutter most days."

All three boys have a silent conversation and Phoenix sighs, slouching back in his seat for a change and dragging a hand down his face. "My Domme taught me, okay?"

I have a feeling this is for my benefit, seeing as no one but me is surprised. No one would look at or hear Phoenix and think *he* was a sub. Not a soul. When I sign *What the fuck?* He laughs and takes a sip of water.

"I was involved in a kink club. The best way to learn to be a Dominant is to experience everything a sub would under your care." He shrugs and takes a bite of ham, meeting my gaze as I process that.

"So, you see, Nixy boy is a *certified Dom*," River grins and takes a bite of his own food, winking at me when I gape at them all.

"There's not a certified anything, River. I'm just trained. I didn't want to hurt Le—" Phoenix clears his throat awkwardly again and groans. "I wanted to do things properly without hurting anyone, that's all. Now, eat, drink, be merry. I'd like to bend our Queen over the table, or the couch, and make her lose her mind."

No one speaks after that, digging into the food and surprisingly keeping the table itself void of mess as they clean their plates.

Not thirty minutes later, everyone is sitting back, sipping at the wine Phoenix broke out to pair with the food. It's definitely working to loosen my muscles, if not my inhibitions, if my eye-fucking of Pierce is anything to go by. Exhaling loudly, I sip the rest of my wine before setting it down and reaching for my glass of water, chugging it all at once.

"Good girl," Phoenix says, and I feel my cheeks heat at his praise. "Boys, table," he commands.

They stand and do as they're told, clearing the table within five minutes. I swallow as I watch Phoenix look around, almost as if he's contemplating the best course of action. He grins after a minute, then turns toward me and slides my chair toward his until he's forced to spread his legs, trapping mine between them. Meeting my eyes, he slides his hands up my trembling thighs and hooks his fingers in the waistband of my pants. "How many taps?" he asks.

I hold up the number three.

"Show me."

Reaching out, I tap his bicep three times, firm and in quick succession.

"Can I have control?"

I swallow nervously and nod, anticipation thrumming through my veins.

"Stand," he commands, his voice low and in that dominant tone I now know he was trained to use.

The thought has me clenching my thighs together briefly in search of friction before I finally stand. I stumble, catching myself on Phoenix's shoulders.

"River," Phoenix calls out.

"Yeah?" River asks upon entering the room.

"Her shirt. Take it off of her." Phoenix commands. "Slowly," he says with a pointed glare toward the other.

"Got it," River says.

Both men near me like this has me squirming, wet

and uncomfortable under their torturous touches and ragged breaths.

Phoenix grins up at me and leans in to place a kiss on my belly button the second it's revealed to the room. River drags my shirt up my body slowly, fingertips ghosting over every inch of my skin he can manage.

"Gorgeous," Phoenix says before tugging my pants down as slowly as humanly possible, fingers dragging across my thighs. His gaze stays locked with mine, and I struggle to keep contact when my nipples pebble painfully against the cold air. "Steady, my Queen," he grins, and places an open-mouthed kiss to my stomach before lowering his face and doing the same to my left hip, then the right.

"You're trembling, little vixen," River says, pulling my shirt off and tossing it to the side. He leans in, placing his hands over my breasts, and tweaks both of my nipples at the same time. My back arches, and he nips at my earlobe, pulling it between his teeth and groaning when my ass rubs against his erection. "Fuck. You're such a vision like this."

Pierce's pained groan comes from my side and my eyes snap to meet his, my head lolling back on River's shoulder. I exhale heavily when I see him leaning against the wall, hands clenched into fists to hold himself off.

"Don't worry about him, Red," Phoenix says. He pulls my pants and underwear off my feet and tosses them toward my shirt. "He'll be fine."

I look down at him and raise a brow in question, earning me a soft smack to the hip.

"Don't doubt me," Phoenix admonishes.

Nodding, I bite my lip and let my head fall onto River's shoulder again. Phoenix runs a finger through my folds, dragging the wetness to my clit and circling it before diving right back into me.

"Eyes. Blue, please," Pierce begs from his stance, and I oblige him.

I shouldn't, and I know that, but my heart doesn't know how to be a bitch like my head wants me to.

Our eyes meet, and my pulse quickens.

Fuck, he has such gorgeous eyes.

Gorgeous everything, actually.

"I think Pierce deserves to sit down and be a good boy for once, don't you, River?" Phoenix asks, drawing back and sticking his fingers into his mouth, licking them one by one as I watch him with heavy-lidded eyes and squirming thighs.

"What I wouldn't give for him to be *my* good boy for a night," River says. He massages my breasts for a few more seconds, but lets them go in favor of dragging his palms down my sides and toward my ass. He grasps my cheeks in his hands and hums in appreciation as he takes in the view. "One day, one of us will have this pretty little ass, Rae."

I tense.

Phoenix stands and captures my chin between his fingers, forcing my gaze to his. "Only with your consent, Red. You are the one with the power. Got it?"

I nod.

"Sign it," he commands.

I do.

"Good girl," he praises. "Now, Pierce, she may be

punishing you, but I have my own punishment. Sit your ass on the chair."

"My ass will get cold!" Pierce says. But he still walks toward the chair Phoenix pulls out.

"Ah, here's the part of my punishment you'll kick me in the dick for later." Phoenix grins and walks into the living room, coming back with a small suitcase. He places it on the table and begins rifling through it for a few seconds before pulling out handcuffs and a blindfold. "Now, Pierce, tell me," he turns around, sliding the blindfold through his hands while the handcuffs hang off one of his fingers, "Who's in charge?"

"You?" Pierce questions, his eyes locked onto the items in Phoenix's hands.

River makes a buzzer sound from behind me, and I turn my head to meet his gaze in question. He shakes his head and points toward the others.

Did he and Phoenix talk about this already?

Clearly I wasn't invited to *that* particular tea party.

"Try again," Phoenix tells him, anger now lacing his words.

"Rae?" Pierce says it like a question again.

"Ding, ding, ding!" River says.

"I don't understand how she's in charge when you're the one bossing us all around right now, Nix," Pierce folds his arms over his chest.

"I'm going to teach you all about this shit one day, since you're finally open to listening. For tonight, however, you're keeping your hands to yourself. Place them on your thighs, palm up. Legs spread."

"Nix what the–" Pierce barks out.

"Fucking do it," River interrupts, gaining a smug smile from Phoenix.

"Fucking...fine," Pierce says. He sighs before doing what's asked of him, spreading his legs and placing his hands on his thighs, palm up. "What now?"

Phoenix walks around the chair a few times, his gaze traveling up and down Pierce's body before he stops in front of him. He snaps a handcuff on one of his wrists, followed by the other. Gaze shifting toward the suitcase, he asks, "Rope please, River?"

"Got it," River says. He grabs a few coils of colorful rope and holds them out to Phoenix.

"Jesus," Pierce grits out.

"She gave me control for this scene, and this is what I really wanted for Christmas." Phoenix falls to his knees in front of Pierce and my breath catches. He looks back at me and raises a brow. "Not happening. The only thing ever going in my mouth is your needy cunt, sweetheart."

I squirm for a moment, and River hands the rope over to Phoenix, taking pity on me by sitting on the chair at the head of the table and pulling me into his lap.

"This is going to be great," he whispers in my ear as he wraps his arms around my waist.

Phoenix meticulously ties Pierce's forearms to his thighs with a red rope. All I can see is his back as he continues to tie knot after knot. Once done, he tests their stretch before grabbing a black one and tying his calves to the chair legs. He turns to the side, and I see a look of smug concentration on his face, which makes my heart gallop in my chest.

What the fuck is happening, and why am I more

turned on now than when two men were playing my body like a fiddle?

"This is dumb," Pierce grits out when Phoenix stands.

"So are all of the bullshit things you pull with Raven, but you don't see us insulting your intelligence." Phoenix walks back toward me. He turns his head to the side, so he can see Pierce out of the corner of his eye. "Much."

"Seriously? What's the point here, Nix?" Pierce asks.

"To keep your hands to yourself. Don't make me shove a gag in your mouth, too." Phoenix grabs the blindfold he had put on the table and slides it through his fingers. "Let me test his willpower, hmm, Red?"

I blink up at him, confused for a moment until he leans toward me and wraps the silk black material over my eyes. My senses are both underwhelmed and overloaded the second he ties it behind my head.

All I can do is hear and feel at the moment.

Cold glass touches my lips and River's fingers gently tilt my chin up. I open my mouth to take the drink of water offered to me, my arousal only growing at these two men caring for me.

"Good girl," Phoenix praises once I've swallowed. He replaces the glass with his lips and kisses me long and slow, taking my breath away. "Now," he says after he pulls back, "he can't see those pretty eyes. You can't see anything, and you're forced to *listen* and *feel*. Doing okay, Red?"

I nod, and he taps my cheek lightly.

"Sign it," he commands.

Lifting my trembling hands, I sign *I'm okay*.

Satisfied, he kisses me once more before cold air replaces his warmth in front of me.

No one says or does anything for what feels like forever, until River spreads his legs and tosses my ankles over his thighs. I am as far open as I can be, unable to move, unable to see.

I hear a chair scrape across the floor. *Did they move Pierce?*

"Little vixen, are you soaking for us?" River asks. He slides his hand down from my stomach and cups my pussy, squeezing enough for the friction to drive me wild. He chuckles when I try to squirm, rubbing my ass all over the hard ridge in his jeans. "Keep going on like that and I won't even have to get naked. It'd be a shame."

I let a grin stretch my lips...and do it again.

He groans and squeezes my pussy harder. "There are plans tonight. Let Phoenix do his Dom shit."

The air around me heats, and warm hands caress my ankles, calves, and thighs.

"So beautiful splayed open like this," Phoenix croons. His lips land in an open-mouthed kiss on each of my thighs. "I'm going to make you a sobbing mess by the end of the night. That okay, sweetheart?"

I don't respond for a moment. Too long, if Phoenix's pinch to my thigh is any indication. Bringing my hand up, I sign *Yes, Sir* and he growls his approval, biting into the thickest part of my thigh.

"River, put those thick fingers inside of her and tell me how wet she is," he commands.

River does exactly as he's told, quickly thrusting two of his fingers inside of me as far as they can go. He pulls them out roughly, then shoves them back in again a few times, groaning, rocking his hips against my ass. "Fuck," he whispers. He pulls them from me fully, and drags them up along my thigh, creating a delicious sensation when the cold air connects with the wetness on my heated skin. "She's drenched."

"Red, I'm going to give you as many orgasms as you think you can handle tonight, then I'm going to give you as many as *I* know you can handle. Good?" Phoenix asks.

Good, I sign.

He rewards me with a slow kiss on my thigh, trailing upwards until his lips land over my pussy.

My head falls back on River's shoulder again, my ear resting against his pulse point. I listen to the heady *thump thump* as Phoenix seals his lips over me and flicks his tongue around my clit.

Friction from River's jeans heats my skin when I squirm. His dick rubbing on my ass has me debating whether or not we could play *that way* yet. The smell of my arousal invades the air.

I'm dreaming.

I have to be.

Phoenix thrusts his own fingers into me, curling them against my g-spot as he sucks my clit into his mouth, massaging it with his tongue.

My back arches and River clamps his hands down onto my hips to keep me still.

Everyone's heavy breathing is louder than freight trains to me right now, and I try to tune into Pierce's, but I can't.

Not when Phoenix uses his teeth to scrape at my clit

and thrusts his fingers deeper inside me. He moves them quickly, rough enough to shove my hips back against River.

I'm shaking. Trembling. Aching.

He uses his other hand to prod at my untouched hole, and it shocks me how wet I become. His finger breaches my entrance, and I soar with the strength of my climax.

River holds me down as Phoenix continues thrusting his fingers and tongue inside of me, riding me through every ebb and flow of my orgasm.

My breathing slows, but instead of moving back, Phoenix doubles down, reigniting the flames I was sure would slow.

The day-old stubble on his cheeks rubs against my inner thighs. River pulls his hands off my hips and reaches up, massaging my breasts and tugging my nipples in between his fingers. They harden to the stiffest of peaks and River only uses the opportunity to play with them more. He leans down and kisses my neck before pulling skin between his teeth and sucking.

Phoenix moves his fingers away from me, and my hips chase him. He chuckles and places his hands on my thighs. "As much as I'd love to die between your thighs, sweetheart, I don't want to die *just* yet."

That gets a laugh from all the guys.

I bite my lip and try to stay still as River continues to place little love bites all over my neck and shoulders. The air grows warmer as Phoenix leans toward me, and I nearly jump a foot in the air when River moves his hand from one of my nipples, only to be replaced by Phoenix's mouth.

He bites and sucks at each of my breasts, and River thrusts his fingers inside of me. One hand rubs furiously at my clit and the beginnings of a second orgasm race toward me. He doesn't let up, thrusting those fingers hard and fast. The wet noises should be embarrassing, but they only spur me on.

I grind, he grinds, and both guys groan when I stiffen and let out a silent scream, stolen by Phoenix's mouth when he kisses the remaining breath from me.

Slowly, as if afraid to let the fire die, River pulls his fingers from my pussy. I hear him hum and can only assume he's sucking my arousal from his own fingers.

Why is that so hot?

Phoenix pulls away from our kiss, tugging my lower lip in between his teeth for a second as he does. Once he frees me, his hand brushes hairs from my forehead and I sigh, leaning into his touch.

I'm suddenly sleepy, and *extremely* aware of River's cock digging into my ass.

"You did so good for us, sweetheart. Here, drink some water," Phoenix says. He brings another glass to my lips and I obligingly sip at the drink.

"Nix," River grits out.

"Sorry," Phoenix says. He pulls the glass from me after I've had a good drink. Lifting my boneless body into his arms in a bridal carry he starts to move me somewhere. "You doin' okay, Red?"

I sleepily nod and rest my head against his shoulder, curling into his warmth.

"Don't sleep yet. We aren't done with you." He chuckles when my body tenses.

Warmth caresses my back when he lays me down, and I wish I could see what they've done around me, or if I'm still in the dining room. A pillow is pushed under my head, someone grabs my ankles, massaging them gently. The guys are whispering.

I'll just take a nap.

"You good, Red?" Phoenix checking in on me has to be the hottest and cutest thing.

I sign *Perfect. Sleepy.*

I hear him and River chuckle.

"No sleep yet, little vixen. That was only two. You can handle more than that," River states matter-of-factly. Like he hasn't come twice and been laid out on a warm and fuzzy blanket.

Phoenix's rainforest scent takes over before he presses his lips to mine, kissing me upside down, his chin pressing against my nose. He brackets my face with his hands, trails them down until they cover both of my breasts.

My body lights up again, but I can't squirm because River's warm skin brushes against my ankles.

Did he strip?

"I want you to suck my dick like the good little slut you are while River fucks your sweet little pussy and Pierce watches helplessly."

"Jesus," Pierce grunts, and I hear the chair rattle.

"Take what you can get. Be glad I didn't blindfold and gag you," Phoenix says. "Slide her down, Riv."

River slides me across the table until my ass is hanging off it and his cock is brushing against me. He groans and squeezes my thigh. "Hold on, little vixen."

I hear the faint rustling of clothes and ripping of plastic. That small warmth grows into a roaring fire.

I don't know how the guys managed to get me this worked up three times in a row, but surely one can die from too many orgasms, right?

"We're gonna have to work your tolerance up," Phoenix says playfully. He kisses me, massaging my breasts and tweaking my nipples into hard buds until I'm writhing beneath him. "There we go. Open those pretty lips for me."

As always with Phoenix, I oblige.

He takes a finger and pulls my mouth open as wide as he wants it, then nudges his dick inside slowly. His groan is delicious, and River's forced to hold my thighs open as I attempt to rub them together for friction again.

"I got you, little vixen." River slides his hands up toward my hips and reaches underneath until he has a handful of my ass. He lifts me up and notches his dick inside of me. His breath stutters out when he asks Phoenix, "Ready?"

I don't hear anything, but they both thrust inside of me in unison. I'd gag if I could, because Phoenix's dick is long and thick, and I'll be sore as hell tomorrow.

River pulls out of me until he's barely in. Phoenix does the same.

They thrust back in together.

Their twin groans force me to grip the blanket beneath me, white-knuckling it as my body is pinned between them.

After a few slow thrusts like this, they begin to alternate, and my body has no idea how to deal with the sensations.

I let myself go.

I don't think.

I just feel.

Phoenix grips my chin and tilts my head back until it's precariously sliding off the table with each of River's thrusts.

I dig my feet into River's ass the next time he bottoms out, breathing out heavily when he brings his hand to my clit, rubbing it as furiously as he was before.

The pressure, the sensation of being this full, only gets worse when I hear Pierce's heavy breathing.

How close he is to us now. How much can he see?

Is he watching this with anger or lust in his gaze?

"Focus on us, Red," Phoenix growls out, thrusting inside of my mouth and wrapping his hand along my throat. "Focus on how full of dick you are. How hard you'll come this time. I want you to soak River like the little slut you are. Got it?"

I don't have the ability to nod, so I lift my hand and sign *Got it.*

"Good. Fuck-fucking good girl," he says, his hips stuttering with him.

Phoenix losing control could be a bad thing.

Or a deliciously good one.

"Fuck, I need you to come for us, little vixen," River moans with his next thrust, his chin landing on my knee and his heavy breath falling across my skin. He tilts his dick just so and drags it along that magic spot inside of me, making my legs shake. "Fuck yes," he groans. "Just like that. Squeeze me."

I squeeze around him and run my tongue around the head of Phoenix's cock. River drags his dick along my sweet spot again as Phoenix leans down to take a nipple in his mouth and another in his hand.

I float. I swear I do.

The back of my eyelids light up white. My soul leaves my body.

I'm hardly aware of either one of them finishing. I swallow Phoenix's cum like he tells me to, and River's hips slam against mine a few times before he stills inside of me.

The world fades in and out.

I start to cry.

Shaking, trembling, quiet sobs as both guys finish.

"What the hell?" Pierce barks out, and the chair rattles again.

"It's fine," Phoenix tells him.

Slowly, ever so carefully, the blindfold slides from my eyes. The harsh lights of the dining room are gone, replaced by the dim setting, so I'm not blinded by them. Phoenix's concerned face is mere inches from mine as he soothes my body.

I barely feel River pulling out of me.

"You got her?" he asks.

Phoenix nods and begins twisting the blanket around until he can lift me into his arms. "You got him?"

"Yeah," River responds. He walks toward us and kisses me sweetly, even as I continue to cry. "You'll be okay?"

I shrug, and he chuckles as he kisses me on the cheek.

Phoenix carries me up the stairs and into the master bathroom, placing me on top of a towel which is on the counter. He brushes a few strands of hair from my face, and leans in to kiss me. Those few seconds help to slow my heart rate back down to normal, and stop my crying, at least a little. When he pulls back, he smiles almost boyishly and walks toward the bath, turning on the water.

He's either helped me bathe or bathed with me at least twice a week since the night River and Pierce got drunk and pulled their shit.

How I've forgiven them, I don't understand.

"You're thinking so loudly, Raven," Phoenix mutters as he steps toward me. Placing his hands on my thighs, he meets my gaze. "Tonight was supposed to be about letting your thoughts go, sweetheart." He lifts a hand between us and signs *What's going on?*

Biting my lip, I sigh and bring my own up, struggling to think of the hand movements, but roughly I try to tell him about my conflicting thoughts on forgiveness. Once I'm done, I flop both of my hands onto my thighs and blink furiously to tamp down my tears.

"Neither the world, nor our feelings, are black and white." Phoenix lifts me from the counter and pulls me with him into the bath. He settles his thighs on either side of me and tilts me backward until my back rests on his chest with my head on his shoulder. "You don't have to forgive them or give them anything. Your feelings are valid. Your thoughts are valid. Your body is yours and yours alone. If you never let them fuck you again, they'd understand. I won't make excuses for them, either."

Sighing, he uses a cup to wet my hair, then massages my strawberry soda scented shampoo onto my scalp. I close my eyes and lose myself in his touch for a while. He speaks up again when my hair is fully rinsed out.

"I was there, Red. I was there and I did nothing."

I shrug and sit up, picking at my fingernails.

"Why forgive me and let me become your safe space?"

Spinning around in the tub, I cross my legs and lift my hands. *I should blame you for not stopping them, but I know Pierce has something over your head, just like River's. I don't know what you're afraid of, Phoenix, but I at least know you are afraid.*

He's smiling now, and I raise a brow at him, flipping him off when he tries to grab for me.

What? I sign, putting a little oomph into my hand movements.

"Your ASL is getting so good, Raven. Those classes are exhausting, but you're learning so fast." He shrugs and pulls me back into his arms. "You're amazing, Raven. You don't have to forgive any of us, and yet you have. I lo—" he clears his throat, "I like that about you, a lot. You're giving us grace when the world hasn't deemed us worthy of it."

I scoff and pull back. *What have you done that hasn't been worthy of grace?*

Phoenix's eyes darken as he looks off to the side. He shakes his head, brings his gaze back to me and signs, *What I haven't done would be an easier list.*

I slump into his arms, resting my forehead on the center of his chest as I breathe him in.

These boys need to tell me more of their secrets before I resort to digging for all the answers myself.

Raven's fast asleep next to me on the bed, curled up on her side with an arm and a leg thrown over my body.

River never surfaced upstairs last night. Neither did Pierce.

Who knows what they got up to, but I do remember hearing raised voices, something breaking, then silence.

Leaning down, I kiss Raven's forehead gently before I climb out of the bed and get dressed. Jeans and a plain t-shirt will suffice today.

Death anniversaries suck.

I lean against the window and watch as heavy snow continues to fall onto the ground, wondering if it'll be safe for us to travel today.

No one wants to travel on Christmas, but I wanted to see my old home, or what's left of it, for a few minutes today. Since it's half an hour from campus and Junk, we decided to cut our trip short.

We can spend the few days between Christmas and New Year's formulating a plan of attack for when Rapture hits the streets of CU.

Fucking Maxwell Langston...

Scrubbing a hand down my face, I lean my head against the window sill and sigh.

"RUBY, *I can't leave you. You're all I've got left.*" *I panic when she brings her hands to my face, backing away.*

"Phoenix, you are not in a healthy headspace. I need you to focus on you for just a moment. A day. A week. A month. Whatever it takes." She sighs when I drop to my knees in front of her, wrapping my arms around her thighs like a begging, pleading child.

I am that, though.

I'm alone and terrified and depressed, and I won't survive if I don't have her.

"Ruby, please," I beg her in a whisper. Tears well up in my eyes when I search her green ones. "I don't have anyone left."

"I know, my sweet Phoenix." She places a hand in my hair and runs her fingers along my scalp. Sighing, she tugs my hair until our gazes meet again. Her features harden. "I can't be this for you anymore. You'll get attached to me, and you know I'm only your teacher, hon."

"I know," I whisper. My voice cracks and I look down, tearing my head away from her hold. Tears fall onto the ground finally, and I release her, curling in on myself. "I know."

"Let me get you outside to your car. Dave is going to follow you. Make sure you get back to the hotel safely, okay?"

She helps lift me up off the ground, then wraps her arm around my waist as we walk toward the exit.

Her husband is there, a concerned look on his face. "You need anything, you let us know, got it?"

I shrug, and he stops me in my tracks as I step toward my car. My gaze snaps to meet his brown eyes.

"Not a request, son." He tightens his hold on my bicep. "You call us if you need anything."

"I fucking did that," I snap.

"This lifestyle won't work for you when you're all in your head. Get yourself right, do you hear me? Let us take you to doctor's appointments or whatever you need."

I pause for a moment and take a deep breath, then nod. "Got it. I start grief therapy next week."

"Let us drive you," Ruby says as she slides under her husband's arm and leans against him. "Give us a call before your next appointment, and we'll take you."

"Okay," I say reluctantly.

When they both look at me sternly, I sigh.

"Okay, yeah." I nod a few times before turning back toward my car.

I get in and drive around for a few hours, only to crash head first into a guard rail on the highway, lucky to get away with not a scratch on me.

Unlucky enough to get put in Stangler Med Center for my failed suicide attempt.

I SWIPE the tears from my cheeks, then clear my throat and straighten my spine.

Fuck the memories.

Pierce and River are cleaning off the car outside now, and my heart threatens to stop beating when I meet River's eyes through the window.

I wave away the concern I see and turn back to the bed, on a mission to wake Raven up and feed her before we leave.

"Hey, sweet girl," I croon as I lean down. I place a soft kiss on her forehead, nose, and both cheeks before she stirs even once. I smile when her lips pull into a gorgeous sleepy grin. "Time to get up and eat. We have some traveling to do today, remember?"

She nods, and one of her eyes pops open, only to shut again. Grabbing the blankets, she pulls them up and over her head, and I fight with her to tug it back down. She glares at me for a second before breaking out into a grin.

"There she is. I'll make you the last bowl of cocoa puffs while you get dressed. Make sure you dress warm, there's an assload of snow outside." I smack her ass playfully when she turns over to hide her face again, and laugh when she looks back at me with a shocked expression. "I don't know why you think River is the only playful one. I just lost myself for a bit."

Her face grows solemn, and I smack her ass again, faking a grin for her benefit. "C'mon. Up and at 'em, Red."

I walk out of the room and down the stairs, quickly making her a bowl of cereal but leaving the milk out. The girl will take her time in the morning if we let her, and I'm not in too much of a hurry to go see my family's death site. I lean against the counter and fold my arms as I watch the snow fall outside.

"Holy shit, my nuts have shrunk and frozen," River says as he enters the house, knocking snow off his boots. Pierce follows, shoving him forward until he stumbles.

He doesn't look as pissed off as I thought he would this morning.

I glance at River and he grins smugly.

Here I was hoping Pierce would have blue balls today.

"She up?" Pierce asks as he sits down on a stool at the island. He looks over and sees the cereal, raising a brow. "I knew we had them. You guys have been hiding them, haven't you?"

River and I meet each other's gazes and laugh, shrugging it off.

"Fuckers," Pierce says, though it's lost its venom.

Wonder if he's learning his lesson, finally.

Raven steps into the room in black sweatpants and a thick white sweater, hair in a messy bun on top of her head, and, of course, she's wearing her favorite purple fuzzy socks.

"Morning, Blue," Pierce says.

Everyone freezes, because his voice is warmer to her than it has been, almost ever, and he's smiling at her like he fell in love all over again.

She hesitantly signs *Good morning* before walking toward the counter and sitting on her stool.

I grab the milk out of the fridge and pour some into her cereal.

Thank you, she signs.

Welcome, I sign back.

"I really need to pay more attention in that class," Pierce grumbles, grabbing his coffee and sipping it.

"Obviously she told you to fuck off, told Phoenix she's gonna blow him for all these cocoa puffs he's provided her, and he just told her she can suck him off in the car on the way home." River says all of this with such a serious look on his face, it's hard *not* to believe him.

"Or she told you good morning, thanked Phoenix for breakfast, and he said she's welcome." He shrugs and sits down between Pierce and Raven, slapping a sloppy kiss on her cheek before she can get food in her mouth.

"You're strange," I tell him. I slide Raven's hot cocoa to her in a travel mug.

"Ah, yes, trauma does do that to a person," River snarks, earning a raised brow from a full-mouthed Raven.

Raven leans back as she chews and signs *I'm sorry*.

He shrugs and signs back, *I'm good*.

"What?" Pierce asks.

"Pay attention in class next time," I tell him.

He sighs and scrubs a hand over his face before taking a long drink from his coffee. His eyes dart between River and Raven, who are now having a full conversation in sign language.

That class has been the best investment I've ever made.

When Raven finishes eating and the kitchen is clean, we pack up the perishables to bring back home with us and load ourselves into the jeep. Pierce is driving while Raven and River get comfortable in the backseat, and I sit in the front passenger seat.

"Rae, do you want to go see your mom?" Pierce asks quietly, almost as if he's nervous.

She chews her lip and looks between us all for a moment before nodding. *I think I need to* she signs.

"You probably should," I tell her. "We can visit every Christmas. Bring her some flowers or something."

Raven meets my gaze and smiles softly, nodding.

"Stop by the store on the way, then."

"What were her favorite flowers?" River asks as we pull into the store not five minutes later. "I'll grab them, so you can stay in the warmth."

Raven looks lost in thought for a moment before she reaches for her phone and pulls up a picture of poinsettias.

"Got it." He kisses her temple and climbs out of the jeep, nearly slipping on his ass as he rushes inside the small grocery store.

"You wanna grab anything for your family, Nix?" Pierce asks.

I shake my head and settle into the seat, pulling up my phone. "No need."

River comes back a few minutes later with the flowers Raven asked for, and her face lights up when he hands them to her before closing the door.

I watch from the rearview mirror as her smile slowly dims the closer we get to the cemetery.

"Want someone to go with you?" Pierce asks her after he parks off to the side near a row of tombstones.

She shakes her head and climbs out of the car, taking the bouquet with her.

We all watch as she walks with those flowers toward her mother's grave.

With her back to us, we don't get to see if she laughs or cries, but we watch her shoulders shake. The jeep is quiet. Our bodies are tense. And not a soul knows what we should do.

"I want to fucking hold her so bad right now," Pierce says. His hand clenches tightly around the door handle, poised and ready.

"She'll come around," River says.

Pierce whips his head around and glares at him, "You say that every single fucking day and she hasn't done much."

"She hugged you yesterday," I remind him.

"I couldn't hug her back," he says. He releases his door handle when Raven walks back toward us, a wistful and sad smile on her lips.

"That was too quick," I say. "I'm worried."

"I think she's numb," River points out. He opens the door when she makes it to the jeep and grins wide at her. "Welcome back, gorgeous! You doin' okay?"

She shrugs as she slides into the seat, that same smile still stretching her lips. She uses her hands to sign *Let's get going*.

"As you wish," River says with a douchey wink.

"No one let him ever watch that movie again," Pierce says before turning on the car and driving us out of the cemetery.

THE CAR RIDE was louder than I thought it would be, made longer by the music blasting through the cab, River singing, and Raven's silent but audible huffs of laughter.

She would interrupt the music to switch to a new one nearly every ten minutes, and with a five-hour drive? That's a lot of song changes.

I have a migraine at this point, from a mix of stress and sensory overload.

"Take a right here, then continue until you're at the end of the street," I direct Pierce. "You'll fucking see it," I tell him.

Half a block away, my family's house is still an empty lot, burned and decrepit and lonely.

"Nix—" Pierce whispers, but I hold up a hand to shut him up.

I haven't been here since closing shit up with insurance the day after New Year's.

I don't remember it being this bad.

I don't remember much from that time, apparently.

I climb out of the jeep before it fully stops, slamming the door behind me. A few feet from the front of where the porch steps used to be, I simply sit my ass down on the cold and ice covered sidewalk. I rest my elbows on my knees and...stare.

They didn't have a fucking chance.

The sound of footsteps in snow alerts me to someone having followed me, and I look up to see Raven moving my way. The guys intelligently stayed inside the jeep.

"Get back in the car where it's warm," I tell her.

Looking back at where the house used to be, I exhale a heavy breath.

Raven doesn't listen, because of course she doesn't, and sits down next to me. Her leggings will soak right through. She meets my gaze with a challenging brow lifted, then points to the lot. *What the hell happened? You haven't told me anything, Phoenix*, she signs.

I sigh. "Can I tell you when we get back to Junk? When it's warm?"

She shakes her head harshly and stands up. *No. Tell me now.*

Scrubbing both hands down my face, I contemplate how much I should unload on her during an already difficult day for us both. When I hear her footsteps retreat, I call out, "Stop. Stay."

I meet her eyes and wave her over, but instead of having her sit on the ground next to me, I pull her onto my lap, so she doesn't get too cold. Wrapping my arms around her middle, I rest my head on her shoulder and inhale deeply, letting out a long breath which fans across her, drawing goosebumps to the surface of her skin.

"I had a girlfriend. Lexi. I've told you a little about her. We were...madly in lust, I'd say. I may have loved her, but I loved playing with her body more. We were inexperienced, bored, and attracted to each other." I huff out a laugh, shaking my head. "She was attracted to the idea of me more than anything. I was in a band, and she'd come to all of my practices, my shows, everything. The biggest fan and the biggest hardship. She wouldn't leave me alone for anything, even to sign autographs at garage shows."

Raven shakes her head but doesn't interrupt.

"Well, last Christmas Eve, I told her enough was enough. We broke up an hour before my show, I told a buddy she was barred from entering, and she flipped her shit entirely. I was kind of a prick about it, though." I shake my head and rest my forehead against Raven's shoulder, sighing heavily before kissing her there and placing my chin back where it started. "I flipped her off every single time I passed by the door. My buddies made fun of her. It wasn't me. That wasn't me at all. I was so tired of her shit. Her dad's shit–Whitaker Sommers is grade A material for federal prison, by the way."

She turns her head and raises a questioning brow, signing *Does he abuse her?*

I nod, and she makes a face before turning back to look at the lot. "Yeah. He does a lot of shit he shouldn't, and he lives barely ten minutes from here. I'd love to burn *his* fucking house down."

Is he the one who burned yours down? Raven signs.

"Nope," I say, popping the P. "Lexi did it." I hold Raven close when she tenses in my arms. "I wasn't home. She left about midway through that show and came here. Burned the whole place to the ground." My voice cracks and I have to clear my throat. "Whole family was inside. Mom, dad, brother and two younger sisters." I fidget with the zipper of Raven's coat, licking my lips as I contemplate the next words. "She went to jail for two nights, then got put in a mental health facility. I thought she'd be there for a few years at least…"

But? Raven asks.

"She got out this past summer. After six fucking

months." I growl and grab a rock, tossing it toward the lot. Had the house been there, I'd have broken a window.

She's not going to come do anything to you, is she? Raven signs.

I shake my head before resting my chin on her shoulder again. "No. I have a permanent protection order against her. She'd be stupid to try. Though I have a feeling Whitaker could get her out of jail if he really wanted to. She fucking...she...*broke* me." I force back the tears of anger, frustration, devastation.

We sit there for I don't know how long. Raven curled up in my lap, my arms wrapped around her. I tell her a few stories of dumb shit my siblings and I used to do, how they'd embarrass the fuck out of me at shows. How mom and dad would buy me a new guitar and microphone every Christmas since I was ten. I tell her about my little sisters wanting to be professional dancers, so we'd have dance classes two or three times a week and half a dozen recitals. A functioning, happy, supportive family unit.

Burned alive.

Raven's shoulders tense and I snap my gaze toward her. Someone is walking toward us.

Tiny, bundled up, all alone.

"What the fuck?" I ask, standing and helping Raven to her feet as well. "Get in the car, Red," I command her, pointing toward the jeep.

Raven looks between me and the quickly approaching figure. *Is that her? Do I need to call the cops?*

I shake my head. "No. Don't call the cops. Get in the car and lock the doors." When she doesn't move, I meet her eyes and narrow mine. "Now, Raven."

She scrambles to do as I tell her, fighting herself as she climbs in the back with River. She locks the doors, I hear them click, but keeps those pretty blues on me for as long as I watch her.

"Phoenix?" Lexi asks, her voice small and trembling.

"Alexis," I grit out, folding my arms over my chest as I stare her down.

She looks a goddamn mess. Her hair is in disarray under the hood shadowing her face, and there are bags under her harsh gray eyes. She's twitching, almost like she was when I caught her using drugs the first time.

Not her first time doing them.

My first time catching her.

"You, uh, you look good," she says, bringing her thumbnail between her teeth as she looks anywhere but at me.

"Can't say the same for you. Why are you here?" I sound like a prick right now, but she fucking deserves it.

"Trying to find a way forward, I guess," she says so quietly I almost don't hear her.

"You aren't supposed to be within a hundred feet of me. I could call the cops right now."

"Please don't." She looks up and meets my gaze, hers filling with tears. "Can't you lift that? I... I've been good...to you, at least."

I snort and shake my head. "To me? Who's your latest murder victim, Lex? Old Manny down the street?" I point toward the brick house barely out of view. "Or are you here to finish me off now? Huh?"

"No one!" she shouts. She whimpers and shrinks in on

herself, looking at the empty lot again. "No one. I still love you, you know?"

"Jesus, Alexis. Get a fucking grip. We've been over since far before last Christmas Eve and you know it." I step toward the jeep, wanting to get far away from her, but she grabs the back of my jacket with enough force to make me stumble backward and nearly slip on the ice.

"Please, PhePhe..." she whispers. She looks up at me under her lashes, tears falling from them. "Please."

"Get the fuck out of town, Alexis." I pull my jacket from her grasp and turn back around, quickly hopping into the car, but not before I hear her next words.

"Not until I fix us."

"You okay?" Pierce asks.

"Go," I bark, keeping my gaze on the side mirror.

Pierce drives away, and I watch as Lexi crumbles to the ground, only to be caught by a male figure I hadn't seen previously. He pulls her up into his arms and turns to look toward me.

I meet his gaze when we pull up to the stop sign, the ice blue of them catching in the light. The death glare he settles on me sends alarms blaring in my head, unease roaring in my gut.

TO: UPINFLAMES@MYEMAIL.COM
FROM: RMHILL@MYEMAIL.COM
SUBJECT: RE: RE: RE: CONSEQUENCES

Afternoon, Flames.

Listen (or read, whatever strikes your fancy lol), I don't think your last email told me enough about what happened.

I get it, you had a crazy ex who killed your family, but really, Flames?

You blame yourself?

That should be the reason they keep you in here, because there's no way someone like that is your responsibility. You're young - fuck that, we're still young!

We should only have to face the consequences of our own actions, and just because you split up with her...that doesn't mean you deserved all of this, Flames.

Cheer the fuck up.

At least you didn't lie when you left her.

I feel like the world's biggest fraud.

I'm grieving something I could have, but I'm the one pushing it away.

Not like I've heard from him since before my mom died anyway...

Sigh...

RM Hill

PS: Seriously, stop apologizing for shit that isn't your fault!

raven

"You should have called the cops, Nix," Pierce says the second we enter the loft.

The tension on the way home from Phoenix's burned house was...too much.

I still can't breathe.

"Yeah, well, they wouldn't do fuck all in that town and you know it," Phoenix says.

I pass by everyone after taking off my boots and coat, then lay down in the corner of the sectional. Bringing my blanket over my body, I curl up and try to even my breathing. It's difficult to think about all the things Phoenix went through last year. How he didn't talk about *any* of them in therapy.

I wonder if he knew the guy from my email—

Shoving off the couch quick enough to draw the guys' attention, I stride right up to Phoenix and glare at him.

"What the hell, Red?" he asks, confusion lining his face.

You were the one emailing me? The whole time? So you know everything and more? Why not tell him, I point toward Pierce, *when you knew I was mute? You knew what caused it. Phoenix, you knew it all, and you didn't tell him!*

Tears flood my vision and I angrily swipe them away.

Phoenix, for the first time since I've known him–outside therapy–is unable to remedy a situation. He stares at me, dumbfounded. I know he understood what I signed, because we've been studying ten times more than the other two. His eyes darken as he clears his throat, but before he can get a single word out, I slap my open palm across his cheek hard enough to leave an instant handprint.

Satisfied, but truly hurt, betrayed, and feeling kind of dumb for not realizing it sooner, I spin on my heel and stomp toward the stairs. I pass by River on the way and shake my head when he asks if he can follow me up.

I don't need any of these fucking men if they're all hiding secrets.

Pierce still holds them close.

Phoenix struggles to tell anyone anything for fear of looking weak.

And River's secrets are just as loud and clear as his attempts to hide with humor.

With the eerie silence, I build a nest of blankets and pillows on the big bed as a 'fuck you' to every one of them. Warmth envelops me as I wrap myself up in as many comfort items as I can, and shut my brain off, finding the escape of sleep for the night.

"MISS HILL, *you've been told your mutism is trauma induced, correct?" asks the doctor.*

We're in a group session, and she knows how much I hate these, especially when she singles me out.

My silence does that for me most days, thanks.

"I dare say you may be able to pull yourself out of this, then," she continues on, "and tell that pesky sadness inside of you that you are in charge. You have control of your mind."

"Some of us don't actually have control though, Doc," says a voice across the room.

Her head snaps toward him, and I bite my lip to hide my grin.

This guy.

"Well, Mr. West, the entire point of being here is to get it under control, is it not?"

He shrugs. "I'm here under duress, Doc. Excuse me if I'm not thrilled at learning how to control my emotions."

The doctor sighs and rubs at the bridge of her nose. "Very well then. Miss Hill," she looks back toward me, "what have you tried to do with your voice?"

I pick up my pen and paper, fighting the will to draw a middle finger on it to get that particular point across, and begin to write.

The entire room is far too silent as they watch me for what feels like an eternity. After finishing the last letter I hand it to the girl next to me who's been reading my notes aloud for the past two months.

"Miss Hill says she's tried screaming at the top of her

lungs, tried singing in the shower again, tried to curse all of the Gods and prayed to the Devils, yet not a thing has brought back her voice, so why would her own will do a damn thing?" The girl hands me the note, her blush intensifying. She hates cussing, she hates defying the doctors.

I hate the doctors at this point.

They haven't fixed me. They've only told me what they want to believe, and there hasn't been access to sign language classes like I was promised a week and a half ago. I've been sneaking in learning it through the emails from Flames, and that's pretty much it.

This has not been helpful for me one bit.

It's only kept me from ending things the way I see fit.

"Well," the doctor says, clearly flustered, "perhaps we should get you into some sign language classes. It would help in the, um, meantime." She clears her throat and turns her body toward the person next to her. "Riley, how are you today?"

I drown out the monotone voice of everyone else, meeting Phoenix West's gaze and blushing when I see his eyes on me, watching, calculating.

I WAKE the next morning with the smell and warmth of hot chocolate precariously close to my nose. Popping one eye open, I'm met with River's sheepish grin.

"Morning, sweet girl. Thought someone should wake you so you don't sleep *all* day." He sets the tray of food down on the nightstand before waving toward it. "Hot cocoa, and some warm oatmeal. I hope it's okay..." he trails off.

I sit up and pat the bed next to me, smiling when he climbs on top of the mountain of pillows and blankets I used to keep them all out. Reaching over, I grab my mug of hot cocoa and grin when I see the amount of marshmallows in there–looks like the whole bag.

River dares to speak again once I've taken the first sip, but his voice sounds scared, like he'll be the next one in the dog house. "The guys are meeting with Maxwell this morning. Trying to convince him not to release Rapture this early after development and without tests." He sighs and runs a hand down his face before meeting my gaze. "They're going to come back black and blue, probably."

Nodding, I take another sip of liquid then put the mug back on the tray. I grab my bowl of oatmeal and take a few bites as I think about what to do.

Putting out fliers warning people *away* from a party is a surefire way to get them to go *to* the party.

Calling the cops is useless. Both Cobalt University and Blue Lake cops are paid off by corrupt individuals.

Telling everyone about a new drug on campus will only excite over half of the fucking population here.

I sigh and lean my head back on the headboard, meeting River's gaze before shrugging.

"Yeah," he says, "I don't have a single idea, either. We're going to have to set up around the party and monitor what switches hands. You think we could pay people for them? Maxwell pays us all pretty well for doing his dirty work...it'd be pretty fucking funny if we paid people to *dispose* of his drugs with his own money."

Oatmeal gets stuck in the back of my throat when I laugh, and I have to pound my chest a few times to get myself right again.

He's right. Using Maxwell's own money to dispose of his lifelong project would be a glorious way to fight back.

"We've got five days before this party, and all I am is worried," he says solemnly. "I'm proud of you, you know?"

I tilt my head to the side and place my oatmeal down on the tray, signing *Why?*

He shrugs, then groans. "Fuck. We've kept you in the dark on a lot of shit. Mostly so you didn't think any different of us. We're all so big and strong for the most part, and knowing we're weak? You'd definitely find a group of some other assholes to keep you entertained."

Shaking my head before he finishes speaking, I grab both of his hands in mine and bring them in my lap. Looking up, I steel myself for what comes next, then sign *Tell me everything.*

"May I?" he asks, gesturing toward the headboard.

I nod and he moves to sit beside me, stretching his long legs out in front of himself. He grabs one of my hands in his and twists our fingers together as he takes a deep breath.

"This is the fucked up story about a boy who wanted to die since the age of eight when he learned God wasn't going to save him, his friends, or his mother." He looks at me for a second. "You sure you wanna hear that?"

I take a deep breath before nodding firmly, hoping my calm spreads to him for what I'm positive is going to be a rough story-telling session.

"Okay, so," he says as he leans his head back against the headboard, his eyes glossing over as they look up to the ceiling. "Dad's a preacher, big name, too. Mom's been by his side since college. They actually went here," he grins and shakes his head, "with Maxwell Langston. Dad was real buddy buddy with Langston. They had so many plans to take over this town, make it their own, yada yada." River scoffs, a look of disgust marring his beautiful face.

"Well," he draws the word out, "the big falling out happened because of the five deaths in the eighties. My parents stayed where they were, which is only about a forty minute drive, by the way. Just in the opposite direction of Phoenix's town. Anyway, they were strained for a while, since Maxwell apparently went insane when you and the drug recipe were taken. After a few years, my dad and Maxwell reconnected, and now they get up to some stupid shit all the time together. Sketchy, illegal, one thousand percent unethical. They're disgusting pigs in so many ways. Since Maxwell owns the cops around here, though, it doesn't matter. He supplies them with their bumps of coke to stay awake on night shifts, they turn the other cheek."

I move my hand from River's and grab my oatmeal, using the opportunity to piece my own thoughts together. What the living hell are all of these men doing this shit for? Can't they just live a happy life with their wives and kids?

Fuck, leave other people alone, it's not that hard.

"My dad's an abusive shit," River says as he laughs, "and that's a story I really do not want to get into. Let's just say there's a reason I'm so openly sexual with anyone. I've been exposed to too much shit, and it's ironic because I listened to my dad spout about purity bullshit at least once a month." He looks down at me. "Can I keep that extra shit to myself for a while? I've already unloaded a fuck ton on you."

I shrug and nod, knowing this has to be painful enough already.

"Well, my mom's been addicted to any and all Maxwell Langston drugs since they were in high school, and it's to the point she'd die from withdrawal within a day. So Maxwell keeps them supplied if they keep their mouths shut about the deaths they caused and a slew of other shit. When I was seventeen, he told my dad I had a spot here for free so long as I helped him run his drug business. So," he tosses his hands out, gesturing to the loft, "here the fuck I am."

Swallowing the last bite of my oatmeal, I put the bowl back on the nightstand and sit up, turning toward him. *What's keeping you here, then?*

His gray eyes pierce into my soul for a moment, then he grins. "Well, initially it was the threat of Maxwell banning my mom from the drugs, which would kill her. Now?" He reaches for me, pausing for a second to wait for my nod, before he pulls me into his lap and wraps his arms around me. He sighs in contentment when he rests his head on top of mine. "I'm stuck here for you. And the guys, of course."

I snuggle into him and smile softly. *Thank you* I sign, making sure he sees it.

"You're welcome, sweet girl. I promise I'll stop keeping secrets from you. Or I'll die trying."

We sit like that for a while, and it's not until I hear the roaring of the bike engines that I realize we both dozed off. Sitting up, I nearly bust my head into River's nose with how quickly I move.

"Hey, they're okay. You don't have to–"

He stops talking the second I bound down the stairs to check on them.

"Rush," he finishes.

I don't want him to be right about Maxwell having hurt Pierce and Phoenix, but I have a bad feeling in my gut, and I don't ignore that, ever.

"Jesus Christ, I'm going to look like I have purple face-paint on at this fucking party," Pierce says as he walks inside. He looks back at Phoenix, not seeing me, and sighs. "This is going to make her more worried about us. We need to keep her here on New Year's Eve. She won't like it but–"

He stops mid-sentence when he sees me standing there, arms folded across my chest and foot tapping.

I probably look like the crazy girlfriend right now, but I don't care. How dare they think they could leave me here? As if I can't help them? As if my own plans haven't worked for us before? I keep glaring at him until Phoenix enters the room, nearly looking as bad as Pierce.

They're both covered in bruises, scrapes, and blood, at least on their faces. I can't imagine what the rest of their bodies look like.

Deciding to ignore the tension in the room, I point

toward the kitchen, hoping my glare keeps them in place for a few minutes, at least.

"Rae–" Pierce says, but I stomp my foot and point again.

What I wouldn't give to scream at him right now.

Phoenix pushes past Pierce, avoids any contact with me when he pauses, and a stool scraping against the floor sounds seconds later.

Pierce simply stares at me for a moment more before his shoulders drop, and he sighs. He walks the same path as Phoenix and I hear another scrape of a stool.

River is standing on the bottom stair, grinning at me. "That was hot, little vixen. Take charge more often, it gets my dick hard."

I bite back my smile, roll my eyes, and walk into the bathroom to grab the first aid kit.

Within the next half hour, I have both men cleaned up as best I can, and am tending to the worst of Phoenix's wounds. Pierce says absolutely nothing about me touching him, but I can tell the tension in his muscles is from holding himself back from touching me.

"Fuck!" Phoenix shouts when I get peroxide in a particularly large cut. "Easy, Red, please."

I glare at him and River chuckles from the other end of the bar.

Phoenix glares at him. "Hope you spilled your secrets, too, or I'm about to have a long speech to give."

I slap the side of Phoenix's cheek lightly to turn his head, and he levels a glare on me. I'm sure it would result in a rougher treatment if our circumstances were different. Running my finger through some antibiotic ointment, I begin placing it over the worst parts of his face, wincing in sympathy when I reach the largest one on his temple.

"I gave you Flames to give you freedom, Red," he tells me.

I meet his gaze and press my finger in a little harder on the next scrape. He winces and I bite my lip to hold back my smile. If this is the only way to torture these men, then I'll keep doing it until they've decided I can hold my own. Not a damsel in distress, not a little girl who needs protecting. I'm a woman beaten down by shitty life circumstances over and over again, and I'm fucking over it all.

Next step: knee one of them in the nuts. Probably Pierce, but he's been good lately, so maybe not.

"Whatever devious thoughts you're thinking, Red, put them on the back burner. Let us recover from this bullshit first. Please?" Phoenix's eyes look tired, so I take pity on him and wrap his largest scrapes up in medical bandages and start throwing everything away.

"I've got it," he says as he stands. He grabs all the wrappers and other waste and tosses them in the trash can.

"What'd Maxwell say?" River asks.

"We need to stop questioning him, that's what," Pierce grits out. He reaches across the counter for an apple and takes a big bite.

"Well, that's unfortunate," River says.

"What's more unfortunate is how many deaths will come from this shit," Phoenix tells him.

What about your idea from earlier, River? I sign.

"Oh yeah! How about we take our last paychecks, cash 'em out, and buy the pills back from people? We all hate using Maxwell's dirty money, so let's recycle it for good use." River shrugs, a blush crawling up his cheeks when Pierce and Phoenix gape at him. "You guys really need to stop thinking I'm the stupid one here."

Phoenix looks between us and nods slowly. "What do we do with the pills we acquire?"

"I want to send them off to a lab or something. Get an anti-drug or antidote made...whatever it's called. I want us to be safe more than anything. If we find something that works?" Pierce shrugs as he takes another bite.

"We could mass produce and save the whole town," Phoenix says. "Alright. Who the fuck is going to take four college kids seriously, though? And that shit would cost more money than we have, and you know it." Phoenix looks pointedly at Pierce, who simply shrugs and bites into his apple again.

"Well, now that's out of the way," River walks toward the fridge and opens it, sticking his head in. "I'm fucking starving."

phoenix

Snow swirls around Raven as she walks ahead of us toward the frat house. Her hair is cascading in beautiful red waves down the center of her back, barely reaching her ass, and her black leather dress accentuates every fucking curve on her body. She's tall enough in those heels for her chin to meet River's shoulder, too. Proven when he steps up beside her, his hand on the small of her back.

He's the only one *not* in the doghouse right now.

She still hasn't forgiven me, and I'm at a loss for the second time in my life.

The first was when my whole family died.

"Stop fucking moping," Pierce grits out, bumping his shoulder to mine.

"I'd rather mope than throw tantrums like you do," I snap.

"Yeah, well, at least she's touched you recently."

"She fucking slapped the hell out of me, brutally tended to my wounds, and slapped me again for good measure. The last two with a *smile* on her face!" I toss my hands out and glare at him, raising a brow in challenge when he smiles.

"Man, I don't know why you didn't admit who you were while you were in the hospital together."

"I wanted her to have a safe place. She didn't fucking have one."

"But now she knows you know all of her internal thoughts, and how she felt about every little thing. Hell, didn't you say she talked to you about...well...*you* in one of those emails?" He laughs and smacks me on the back a few times when we step up to the front door. "You have a lot of groveling to do. Do it quickly before she won't let you touch her."

"Shut the fuck up, PJ," I grit out, shoving past him through the door so I don't lose River and Raven. Those two getting lost in a house party together is dangerous, but this one in particular?

Deadly.

"Ah, look! The Prez and his lackeys are here with their girl!" Jimmy shouts above the noise. He's standing on top of a coffee table, which looks precariously close to buckling.

"Hey, look! There's the idiot who thinks he owns this house when he knows I have a ton of shit over his head. Get the fuck off that table before you break it, dumbass." Pierce shoves past the bodies in his way and grabs the bottle of whiskey from Jimmy's hand, quickly taking his own sip of it. His face twists up and I can't help but laugh at his stupidity. "Shut up, Nix," he grits out when he passes by me to walk toward the kitchen.

"Fuck, I'm so tired of this place," I tell him as I follow behind.

"I was tired of it before I got here. Maxwell's had me by the balls for too long, man."

I hum my agreement and look over to see River grabbing Raven a bottle of water, staring down at her sternly while he talks. My eyes take in her stance, her nearness to him and how her shoulders are relaxed.

"Fuck," Pierce snaps out, pulling me from my thoughts. When I meet his gaze, he nods his head toward the side door a group of guys recently came through.

"Holy shit," I say.

They're all dressed in full black tuxes, with faces every person here is going to be drawn to, and bodies which match the swagger they walk in with.

"Did he hire Chippendales to sell drugs at a college party?" I ask, eyes wide as I look at every single one of their pockets. I don't notice anything out of the ordinary until one of them opens his jacket and pulls out a bag, swapping it quickly for some cash a girl hands him. "Jesus. Did they advertise ahead of time?"

"I'm going to go introduce myself, find out who the fuck they think they are. You go buy that off the girl before she takes it. Riv's got Rae, so I'm not worried about them at the moment." Pierce sighs heavily and squeezes my shoulder for a second before moving toward the group of guys.

I walk over to the girl who bought from them, adjusting my own suit jacket as I step into her space. Grinning, I meet her eyes, hoping like hell she's not already high on something else. She's too pretty for this shit. "Hey there. I saw you buy something, but I want to pay you for it. I'm kind of... collecting those pills tonight."

"Holy shit!" she squeaks out, and I groan internally. "You're Phoenix West! I was *such* a big fan of your band. *Such* a big fan. The Flaming Eyes, right?"

"The Flaming Blue Eyes, actually," I correct her, holding the smile painfully on my face.

"Yes. Sorry, I may have had a little something before coming here." She grins and holds up the bag. "I wanted to try this new thing they're putting out. Are you collecting them all for yourself, Phoenix?" She wiggles her eyebrows and giggles obnoxiously.

"Nope," I pop the P and lean down into her space more, "just want to keep pretty little girls like you safe and sound. Heard this one could be a killer."

"Killer, you say? Why would I give it back to you if it's going to be that amazing?" She opens the bag and pulls a pill out, but I snatch it from her wrist. "What the fuck?" she yells. "Get off of me!"

"I'm saving your life. Thank me later," I tell her. I switch the bag for two hundred dollar bills and put the pill back inside, sealing it shut before placing it in my pocket.

A familiar female walks past me with a bag in her hand and I snatch it from her, sighing. "Sorry, Kendall," I say when she looks about ready to kill me.

It's going to be a long fucking night.

"Hey Nixy, what do you want us to do? I'm too fucking nervous to let RaeRae out of my damn sight, man." He proves his point by tugging her into his side until it looks like they might become one person if he pulls a little more.

"Pierce is dealing with the crew that popped in. I'm looking for bags to buy off people. You guys...enjoy yourselves, I guess." I shrug, quickly meeting Raven's eyes before looking away. It pains me that I lost the spot as her comfort person.

"Alright, well," River lets go of her, then bows and extends his hand for her. "Care to dance, m'lady? I believe the world moves forward another year at the stroke of midnight, and it could crumble to dust at our feet."

Raven shakes her head, silently giggling as she places her hand in his.

He stands up straight and escorts her onto the dance floor, tossing a wink back at me.

He's got her. She'll be fine.

"But will I?" I mutter to myself. Clearly, I don't have a clue what to do if I'm not taking care of her, and she made it clear I should back the hell up.

"We have three hours of this shit?" Pierce says when he passes by me.

"More, if the amount of baggies being handed out is any indication."

"Why aren't they taking them yet?" He folds his arms across his chest and looks around at the crowd mingling.

Enough people are already drunk that I'm worried

about another infraction from the school board. I recognize quite a few cops here tonight, though.

Maxwell's a goddamn scumbag.

"Heeyyy," Jimmy yells as he walks up to us both, throwing his arms over our shoulders. "You guys gonna get one of those and take 'em at midnight? Or are you gonna be party poopers like you have been since your bitch showed up?"

"Watch your fucking mouth, Jimmy," Pierce grits out, struggling to get out of his arms. "You're a disrespectful shit."

"Eh, from what I've heard, so are you. That makes us brothers now?" Jimmy grins and ruffles Pierce's hair, turning it into a damn nightmare.

"Absolutely not. Even if we shared blood, or shared parents, you'd never have been a brother to me. Get off me," Pierce grunts when he finally pushes Jimmy away, brushing off his suit jacket and glaring at him.

"Be kind, or I'll tell Maxwell what I saw your boy here doing a few minutes ago," Jimmy says, lips tilting into a cocky smile when Pierce's face pales. "I'm not an idiot, so don't treat me like one. Now, go have a fun fucking time. I can't wait for midnight!" he shouts, riling the crowd up before losing himself in it.

"Breathe," I tell Pierce, holding onto his shoulder so he can't chase after him. "Not worth it. Not worth what we can save by taking Maxwell down, and you know that."

Pierce nods a few times, takes a deep breath, then exhales slowly. Tension leaves his shoulders, and he grabs an unopened bottle of beer from a passing tray.

"Even closed, you shouldn't trust it," I tell him.

"Fuck it. Can't trust much around here." He opens the bottle with his teeth, spits the cap out onto the ground, then chugs the whole beer in one go.

"You're a dumbass sometimes, ya know that, right?"

"Yeah, it should be on my headstone when I die. Which will probably be tonight."

"Let's go try and save these idiots. We'll meet up with the other two, say, around eleven forty-five?" I adjust my suit jacket and let my eyes wander, searching for the next person to buy a pill from.

"Sure. If they're popping these at midnight, we should have enough time to minimize the damage. Good luck," he tells me with a slap on the back.

I grunt and nod, zoning in on my next target.

It takes considerable effort not to yank the bags from people's hands, but by the time eleven forty rolls around, I have about two dozen pills in my possession, and I've doled out nearly four thousand dollars of Maxwell's dirty drug money. The irony is why we did it this way. I shove the pills into a bag in the back of the jeep, wait for Pierce to do the same, then we shut the door and head back inside to meet up with our girl.

Whether we get a kiss at the stroke of midnight is up to her entirely.

"You think she'll come close to me?" Pierce asks as we shove through the people at the front door.

"Anything's possible right now, Pierce."

We find the other two, and I fail to hide my smile when I see how utterly *spent* she is, and sober to boot. She's gorgeous with her skin sweaty, pupils dilated from lust and heady excitement. River's kept her entertained all night by himself, and she's either really good at masking her happiness, or she really is this genuinely elated right now.

"Hey broskis! How are we doing the kiss at midnight? No offense, Nixy boy, but you scare the shit out of me and I don't wanna kiss you." River cackles when I knock him upside the head, and Raven's shoulders shake with her laugh.

"I'd say you're the only one not in the doghouse, so she's probably gonna kiss you. Fuckin' enjoy it," Pierce grits out.

Raven turns in River's hold and glares at Pierce, quickly signing *That won't get you out of the doghouse, dumbass.*

River and I bark out a quick laugh when we see Pierce's confused face.

"Pay attention and learn ASL, you'll thank yourself later." I chuckle when he points his glare at me.

We bullshit for the next few minutes, drawing closer to Raven until we're all revolving around her like she's our sun, moon, and stars. Our collective silence is met with the heavy looks we all share with her, and the scent of her arousal becomes thick between us.

"I don't know what dirty thoughts you're thinking, Red, but keep doing it and one of us will have to dive in to get a taste of you."

She swallows audibly, and I watch as her pupils constrict and her eyes darken.

"Five," the crowd shouts together.

Raven's gaze flits between all three of us.

"Four."

Those with Rapture pills are happily pulling them out of their bags.

"Three."

Raven leans back against River, clutching his arms around her waist as she frantically looks between me and Pierce , frustration lining all of her pretty features.

"Two."

Pills are lifted, people tap them against others'.

We didn't fool anyone, because those who I took pills from now have new ones ready to pop.

"One."

I meet Pierce's gaze, and his eyes are wide with the same panic I'm now feeling.

"Happy New Year!" the crowd yells.

They pop the pills and yell some more.

Couples kiss.

Raven looks between us all. I see her decision coming a mile away, as does Pierce.

She bolts out of River's arms, rushing toward the door.

We all yell for her, because it's not safe.

It was never safe.

She crosses the threshold.

Maxwell appears in the doorway.

He's angry.

So, so fucking angry.

"Boys," he greets us.

Sound plays in the background, people cheering, dancing to the loud music, but for the three of us? Bags are thrown over our heads, and something hits me in the temple.

I collapse.

ICE-COLD LIQUID SLUICES down my body and I gasp loudly, only to inhale the material of the bag which is over my head. I groan after spitting it out, leaning back against a hard and cold surface.

"Ah, good job. You're all awake now. Take off the bags."

My head is yanked at a weird angle when the bag is pulled off, and a white light blinds my irises. I try to escape it, but only manage to smack my head against the surface behind me.

"Now, boys," Maxwell says, anger and amusement mixing in his tone. "I know I told you merely days ago to leave the Rapture business alone. I mean, I think I did. Jimmy?"

"Sure did," he snarks, "and I helped you rearrange their brains to make sure it stuck in there." He grins, twisting a baseball bat around in his hands as he looks down on us.

"Put it away, Jim," Maxwell orders him. He sighs, rubbing the bridge of his nose as he looks between us. "I'm putting Jimmy in charge of the frat."

"What the fuck?" Pierce shouts, spit flying in front of him. It's tinged red, and I wonder how hard he was hit to end up with blood in his mouth. He turns to look at me with worry on his face, and I see a nasty bruise forming on his jaw.

"You've barely been active. You're defying my orders. You're spending most of your time *fucking my daughter*." Maxwell gets right up in Pierce's face with the last words, gripping his jaw in his short, thick fingers. "I told you to keep your hands off of her, yet you defied the one thing I really needed you to do."

"Why, so you could sell her off to the highest bidder so long as she had her virginity intact?" Pierce growls, yanking his chin to try and escape Maxwell's hold.

"No, boy, so Jimmy here would marry her. He doesn't want your filthy fucking group of friends to dirty up what's his." Maxwell makes a sound in the back of his throat before smacking Pierce on the cheek and rising to his feet. "You've done it now, but I suppose he'll have to handle her how she is. Speaking of," he turns toward Jimmy, "she's in the other room. You can go talk to her."

"Isn't he her brother?" River spits out.

I've only seen him angry like this once before, and it didn't turn out pretty for the guy who's still in a medically induced coma.

"Only half, Mr. Jacobs. All will be fine." Maxwell waves him off, and the three of us share a look of pure disgust toward this man.

"She'll bite his fucking dick off if he touches her again, watch." Pierce lets out a maniacal laugh, but I hear his panic.

"Eh, so be it." Maxwell grins as he steps toward the door. "Mr. West, I have someone who has paid top dollar to have a meeting with you. Call me utterly surprised when it just so happened I needed someone with his talents tonight." He twists the knob, opens the door, and speaks quietly to the person behind it.

"Who the fuck?" Pierce whispers.

"No idea," I reply.

I nearly puke when the guy I saw holding Lexi on Christmas pops through the door.

His ice blue eyes are angry, his face is red, and his fists are decorated with brass knuckles.

Surely she didn't send him.

But why the hell would he want to hurt me like this? Or work with Maxwell?

Shit's not making sense, and I'm blaming the knock on the head.

"Xavier Hayes, I don't believe you've formally met Mr. West. Phoenix, Xavier is a very good friend of Alexis Sommers. Says you're the reason she's not doing so well." He clicks his tongue a few times before leaning back on the wall, crossing one ankle over the other and shoving his hands in his pockets.

"What the fuck, Maxwell?" Pierce asks, venom lacing every word. "You can't–"

"Mr. Jackson, at what point have I ever allowed you to tell me what I can or cannot do?"

Pierce snaps his jaw shut and Maxwell grins.

"Mr. Hayes, I'll give you the floor for ten minutes. Don't kill them, because they still have jobs to do." Maxwell casually lifts his phone and presses a few buttons. "Ah, and don't forget your payment for this, Mr. Hayes. I'll have my insurance policy right in my pocket, just in case. I'm sure you understand."

Xavier looks toward Maxwell, grunts out something like 'We'll see about that', then turns to glare at us. He shakes his hands out and grins wickedly at me, and I wonder if he's going to kill me anyway.

"Alexis Sommers is not worth whatever price you're paying," I tell him. I sound scared, and I hate it.

"Alexis Sommers is worth more than the world to me because the world is worth nothing to either of us. You," he barks out a laugh as he takes a few more steps toward me. The zip-ties on my wrists grow tighter as I try to pop out of them to no avail. "You are worth nothing, but she sees you as everything. So I'm here to rearrange your everything until it is nothing. She deserves that much."

"She deserves the fucking electric chair!" Pierce yells at him.

"Shut the fuck up. I only came here to teach him a lesson, but I paid enough to beat the fuck out of you and the other shit stain, too!" Xavier turns his gaze back toward me and brings his hands up. He glares down at me once he's barely a foot from me, and I hate that I have to look up at him. "I'd give a bigger speech, sound like a real man or some shit, but I really don't like how she idolizes someone who could leave her out in the cold like that, so," he shrugs.

"The fuck are you—" I don't get another word out.

Heat and pain twist my face up the second those brass knuckles collide with my skull. I briefly hear Pierce and River shouting curses and pleas.

I know my ribs break, and I know I cry about it.

What I don't know until I'm close to blacking out, however, is that Jimmy has been holding a trembling

Raven in the corner, forcing her to watch as another man takes down one of hers.

It's brutal.

Unforgiving.

And for the second time in the new year, I fall to the floor and black out.

TO: RMHILL@MYEMAIL.COM FROM: UPINFLAMES@MYEMAIL.COM SUBJECT: RE: RE: RE: RE: CONSEQUENCES

Before you chastise me again...

I get it.

I shouldn't be taking on her problems as my own. I shouldn't be allowing myself to drown in the sorrow that is *her life* when she stole mine and my family's in a stupid split second decision.

But the world hurt her so bad, and I can't help but think that if I'd held out for *that much longer* she'd have gotten the help she needed, and I'd have been able to quietly slip away without these major consequences looming over us all.

Fuck.

I hope she gets help, and maybe one day, when she's ready, and the world is ready, she can find love with someone who understands her more than I ever did.

I know I fucked things up along the way, I'm sure I did.

Maybe I was a coward by not wanting to go to her family dinners every Sunday?

Who knows...

Till next time,

Flames

raven

"Let me fucking see him!" Lexi screeches from the hallway.

Again.

For the third time in the last hour, but the millionth in the past week.

I lean my head back against the window and look over at Phoenix, my heart clenching in my chest for him.

I hate that we weren't on good terms when this happened.

I feel responsible.

"Hey there, RaeRae, I got you some of the good cocoa from down the street." River hands over a piping hot styrofoam cup of the sweetest hot chocolate I've ever had.

I sign *Thank you* before taking it.

He nods as he sits down on the hard plastic chair.

"Someone get her the fuck out of here," Pierce barks out as he enters the room. He turns back to glare outside at Lexi, who's still wailing about her true love and how she never meant for him to get hurt. "Shut the hell up. You're lucky the cops here are as crooked as the ones your daddy owns, or we'd call to report you breaking the PO." He slams the door shut in her screaming, crying face and leans against it with a groan.

"I thought she sent Xavier, honestly," River laughs ironically before sipping from his own cup. "Shit, this is good hot chocolate. Good call, Rae." He grins at me, and I frown when I notice how tired he really is.

Bags are forming under all of our eyes, and I know the problem is Lexi more than it is Phoenix.

Not to mention the gunshot to my heart when I found out Jimmy is my half-brother. I still haven't been able to come to terms with it. Nor have I brought it up to the guys.

They knew about it and never told me.

More secrets. More lies. More shit to be mad about.

But now is not the time.

Phoenix has been in a medically induced coma for six days now. They say it's to help his ribs and other bones which needed time to heal. He could have done that without being forced into a coma, and at home.

I would have taken good care of him, even if I was still mad at him.

A knock at the door startles us all, and Pierce turns around to open it. One of the security guards he recently hired pokes his head in. "We'll take care of her. How's he doing?"

"They should be taking him off the drugs today. Hopefully, he'll be released into our care tomorrow."

Pierce leans against the door, folding his arms. "What do you have for me Trip?"

"It's not looking good. I'm sorry. You guys might do better to get out of dodge. Get yourself as far from this shit as possible." He runs his hand through his brown hair, then glances back into the hallway. "I've gotta get her out of here before you all get kicked out. I'll see you all back at your place in a few days." He holds his fist out to bump Pierce's, then leaves with a scowl on his face.

"I like that guy," River says.

I nod my agreement.

"Yeah, Trip's a decent dude. He's got a kid. She's, I *think*, five now." Pierce steps toward the bed and sits in the plastic chair, leaning his elbows on the mattress. "Nix, dude, we gotta get your sorry ass outta here before more people come knocking." He sighs and rests his head on the bed.

I watch as his back rises and falls with a heavy breath, then take a sip of my hot cocoa. Now would be the perfect time to break down my own boundaries, but I don't. I simply move to sit next to River on the little visitor's couch and lean my head against his shoulders, closing my eyes as we wait, and wait, and wait.

"MS. HILL?"

I wake with a start, shifting into a more comfortable position on the couch in my mom's hospital room. Wiping drool from my face, I cringe and shake my hair out until it looks decent.

The nurse laughs as she comes in, smiling kindly. "Don't worry about looking good in here, sweetheart. Not a soul on this floor ever cares what anyone else looks like. How are you doing?"

I shrug, then grab my hoodie and pull it over my head. "How's she doing? Any changes?"

After taking down the stats she sees on the machine my mom is hooked up to, she frowns and looks toward me. "I think I'm going to go get the doctor. Let him know what's going on." She walks past me, squeezing my shoulder as she does, and I don't miss the tear falling down her cheek.

Moving into the uncomfortable plastic chair near my mom's bed, I grasp her hand in mine, as a tear escapes past her lashes. "Hey, mom. I know you know I haven't left. I'm still here. Still hangin' on, just like you. I don't know how much longer either of us has though, mom. I can only hang on for so long before I lose it." I inhale a shaky breath, a hiccup leaving me as I let the tears finally fall. "I got no one right now, mom. I need you to be okay. You don't get to leave me. Pierce is gone, or he's at least gone from school. I watched him clean his locker out yesterday." I lean down and rest my forehead against her stomach. "He hates me so much, and I hope he hates me forever. I don't want him to come back and find me a mess like this. It's why I told him to leave. Why I lied."

Tossing my head back, I swallow and use the bright lights in the room to burn the tears away. It doesn't work, and I curl up in the chair, still holding my arms out so I can grab my mom's cold hands. "I don't think I want to be here if he's gone and you leave me. I brought this on myself, at least where he's

concerned. But you? What did I do to deserve you going, too?"
Exhaling a deep and shaky breath, I look up and see her
sleeping face. Her eyes are taped shut, there's tubes and wires
everywhere. It's unsettling to know those machines are what's
keeping her alive.

A knock on the door catches my attention, and I sit up
straight, wiping my face off on my hoodie. "Come in," I
call out.

Dr. Thomas walks in, a frown stretching his lips. "Ms. Hill,
I'm sorry to—"

"She's dying, huh?" I interrupt him, because I can't listen
to the words he wants to say. I've always wondered if doctors
really meant what they said. "What do we need to do?"

"Well," he clears his throat and looks at the nurse, then
back to me. "Since you started funeral preparations two weeks
ago...all that's left is to..."

"Pull the plug? Wouldn't that be me killing her?" I snap,
glaring at the doctor through the tears pouring down my
cheeks. "I have to be the one to tell her to leave me? To say
goodbye? How's that even fucking fair?"

"Ms. Hill, she's not going to get any better. You're the next
of kin. You're the only one who can make the decision. I'd
advise—"

"Do it."

"V-very well then. Do you want a few minutes?" He looks
so uncomfortable right now, I feel guilty for being such a brat.

"Nope. Do it now before I chicken out. Please." My voice
cracks and I allow the sobs to wrack my body as I watch him
walk to the wall of wires and tubes and life-giving things.

Slowly, meticulously, flawlessly, he unhooks objects I didn't
know existed, until there's no sound in the room anymore.

No beeping.

No whirring from the breathing machine.

He solemnly calls time of death on Evelyn Hill, squeezes my shoulder, and steps out with the nurse to give me some time to grieve.

I lean on her chest, crying, and crying, and crying.

When she takes her last breath, I whisper "Goodbye, mom," and finally allow myself to break into a million more pieces.

When the doctor comes back to ask for my signature, I suddenly can't speak.

I panic.

I scratch at my throat.

I try to scream but nothing comes out.

I look at the nice nurse, begging her with my eyes, my soul, my whole being to fix it.

I nearly trash the hospital room before they inject me with a sedative and put me in my own room for the night.

Words like 'trauma-induced', 'selective', 'mutism', get thrown around.

Suicide is the only one running through my brain.

I'm so fucking grateful Pierce didn't ever have to see me this broken.

I hope that boy goes on to do great things.

Because I won't be here to do them with him anymore.

"RAVEN?" River whispers, shaking my shoulder. "Hey, you okay? You're crying, sweet girl."

I sit up straight, nearly smacking my head against River's chin. I sign *I'm sorry* before attempting to wipe away more of my tears.

"Hey, no, don't apologize." He pulls me into his side again and kisses the top of my head. "This can't be easy for you, can it?"

I shake my head and curl up into his side, sighing when Pierce wraps a blanket around me, carefully avoiding touching me. I meet his sad eyes with my own, guilt rising in my chest.

He'd have been so good to me when mom was in the hospital, but I broke us instead.

Fuck.

"Knock, knock," the doctor calls before entering. "Hey there. How are you guys doing today?" His eyes search mine before looking between the guys, clearly wondering who upset me. He clears his throat, shakes his head, and shuffles toward Phoenix's side.

I clench River's hand so hard both of our knuckles turn white.

After taking what feels like a century to assess Phoenix and all of his wounds, the doctor spins around and grins at the three of us. "He looks really good. I'm going to take him off of the medication which has him in the coma. Should come right out of it in a few hours."

"When can we take him home?" Pierce asks impatiently.

The doctor grins as he looks between the three of us. Surely this guy is not about to judge our relationship? "If we can get him walking in the morning, he can leave then. But that's the soonest I can promise, and I don't even want to promise that. He was badly beaten up, and you all were none the better, Mr. Jackson. I believe we treated a head injury for you?"

Pierce shrugs and sits back in the chair. "I'm fine. Head doesn't hurt even a little."

"I do hope you press charges against whoever did this to you." The doctor sighs and writes a few more notes down then walks toward the door. Looking back, he levels his gaze on me. "Keep these three safe for a few days, at least." He winks, swings the door open, and walks out into the hallway, shutting it quietly as he leaves.

"Well," Pierce says, leaning forward and settling a glare on Phoenix. "You hear that, Nix? He took you off the shit making you sleep like the dead. So now you gotta wake up. Our girl needs all of us right now." Looking up at me, he smiles and shrugs before leaning back in the chair.

"Guess we're playing the waiting game," River says. He groans, lifts my hand to his mouth, and kisses my knuckles gently. Meeting my gaze, his playfulness turns serious. "He'll be fine, sweet girl. How are you, though? That dream you were having had you crying."

Pulling my hand from his, I fix my hair before signing: *It was a flashback to when my mom was in the hospital. When she died.*

"Shit," he says, wrapping an arm around me and pulling me to sit on his lap. "I'm sorry. Here, finish your hot chocolate and we can go get some lunch."

I do as he says, meeting Pierce's eyes. The look of longing on his face makes me shift uncomfortably for a few minutes before I'm forced to look away.

I can't fucking break just yet.

"VERY GOOD, MR. WEST!" the nurse cheers, clapping her hands a few times despite the glare Phoenix has trained on her. "Ah, cheer up. You're going to break out of here in no time!"

"It better be in the next five seconds or I'm walking out by myself," he snaps. His voice is rough, cracking on some syllables. When he was attacked, his throat was stepped on, nearly crushing his whole windpipe. He's lucky to be alive.

"Aw, c'mon Nixy!" River croons, chuckling when that glare is laid into him. "We'll make sure to take *extra* good care of you. Right, Rae?"

I smile sweetly and nod a few times. Surely Phoenix can't get mad at us for tending to him back home. He nearly freaking *died* in front of us all. I'll never get the sight of that guy beating the living hell out of my men like that. Brass knuckles bashing into their bones and breaking skin with each punch thrown.

It was horrible.

"No one is tending to–*FUCK*!" he shouts before tumbling forward, nearly falling to the ground if Pierce wasn't tasked with standing in front of him for this very reason. "I've got it, I've got it."

"No, actually, you don't," Pierce snaps at him.

"I'll be fucking fine if everyone would stop watching me like I'm in a circus." There's that glare again, settled on me and River.

"I'm gonna take Rae to get some snacks," River

announces. He grabs my hand and we step out of the room, the sound of Phoenix's curses echoing into the hallway.

We move silently through the halls, and toward the elevator which leads to the cafeteria. I lean my head against River's shoulder and reach for his hand.

He grabs hold and runs his thumb along the outside of mine, a soft smile on his face. "Nixy's gonna be crabby as hell the next few days. You ready for that?" He looks down at me and chuckles.

I shrug against him.

"I'm sure there's a few ways to alleviate his crabbiness."

Yanking myself away from River in faux anger–because yes I've thought of this a few times now–I smack his shoulder, fold my arms, and glare.

His laughter echoes in the hallway.

We reach the elevator and when it opens, he slides his arms around me, tugging me inside and pressing the button to close the doors early. A few seconds after it starts moving, he presses the emergency stop button, and crowds me into the corner.

"I should have asked before I did that," he whispers, pressing his body into mine anyway. "I'm sorry."

I meet his gaze and shrug, licking my lips in anticipation.

"Can I kiss you?" he asks.

Before I finish a full nod, he leans in and slams his lips against mine.

My heart skips too many beats, and I become light-headed in seconds. I slide my arms up until my hands clench around his biceps.

He grins into our kiss, his lips caressing mine so gently yet rough at the same time.

The contradiction that is River Jacobs.

Hesitantly, as if wondering how much he's allowed to do with me, he moves his hands down and around to my ass, squeezing until I rock my hips into his.

He groans, and I dig my nails into his skin, pulling him closer.

With the gentleness only a lover can provide, he lifts me until my ass is precariously leaning on the railing of the elevator. One hand slides out and pulls my leg open so he can slide between my thighs. He grinds into my center and I break our kiss, letting out a heavy breath when I meet his lust-filled gaze.

"You're so fucking stunning. I love...the way your body feels against mine, sweet girl." His harsh breath fans my skin when he leans in to place soft kisses on my neck.

Was he going to tell me he loved me?

Would I be able to tell him I feel the same way?

Ignoring all emotional talk, I wrap my legs around his waist and tug him into me, grinding against him until we're both a panting mess. I tug at his hair, pressing my lips to his when he pulls his head back. I tug his lower lip between my teeth and tug, hard, before soothing the ache away with my tongue.

He reaches around and palms my lower back, pushing in until our stomachs are flat against the other's and I can feel the hard ridges of his abs through his shirt. My nipples pebble in my bra and I clench my thighs around him harder, his dick throbbing against me in response.

We don't come up for air until a buzzer sounds and a throat clears over the intercom. "Uh, as much as I hate to stop this...bonding time between you two, we need this elevator, and no one wants to clean it."

River tosses his head back and groans, a blush creeping along his cheeks and neck. "Got it," he replies to the voice. "Give me like...two seconds, and I'll start it up again."

The voice chuckles. "I feel you, brother. Go get a hotel or something. Crazy kids," he says before another buzz sounds and the elevator goes quiet.

I meet River's gaze, embarrassment taking its full hold on me.

After a few seconds, we both burst into a fit of laughter.

He adjusts himself, then helps me down from the railing, placing a kiss on my lips one last time. Leaning over, he presses the emergency button and the elevator moves again. "I guess I'll have to pick a different snack." He sighs, before groaning. "Never can have any fun these days. How dare some motherfucker beat the living daylights out of us." Shaking his head, he clicks his tongue a few times, then smiles down at me warmly.

But with the reminder of why we're in the hospital, my mood sours and I wish I could go back to grinding on his dick instead of worrying about what tomorrow brings.

When the elevator opens to the cafeteria, we're met with Trip's panicked expression, his phone held up to his ear, foot tapping impatiently. The second his hazel eyes land on us, he hangs up and clears his throat, shutting all emotions off on his face. "We got a problem."

"YOU WHAT?" Pierce yells at Trip the second he's had a chance to explain our new situation.

"Listen, Jackson–" he tries to say, but Pierce holds up a hand.

"Let me get this fucking straight. You followed them both, knew where they were headed even, but when you got there, they weren't in the car?" Pierce laughs, scraping a hand down his face. "Damnit, Trip. You followed the wrong fucking car?"

"I honestly don't know how it happened. I'm sorry, man. I must be distracted. My daughter's sick and–"

"I do not give a flying fuck about your kid, Trip. Not right now," Pierce snaps.

I stomp my foot to get Pierce's attention and fold my arms, glaring at him.

He only glares back.

"Listen, I know where he lives. I'll go stake the place out tonight. Maybe get a few other guys to watch the other entrances. I'm sorry, really I am." Trip looks guilty as hell, but also stressed out.

I rip a piece of paper off the table near the bed, while still glaring at Pierce, then write a note.

How can we help with your daughter? Do you need a babysitter?

"I couldn't impose on you like that, Ms. Hill. You'd get whatever she has, and Mr. West doesn't need to get sick shortly after all this shit." He waves his hand toward Phoenix, who's surprisingly still sleeping. "Let me get some other guys on the hospital," he looks at Pierce, "then I'll go set up and find them."

"You fucking better, Trip, or I'll lose my fucking mind."

Slapping the paper onto the table, I run a hand through my hair and fix the bun it's been in for most of the week. I don't remember the last time I showered, and I hardly feel like I've slept. The nightmares are the only indication I've shut my eyes at all.

"I swear we should take them out in the woods and kill them," Pierce says. He sits down in the plastic chair and leans his elbows on his knees. Putting his face in his hands, I watch as his back rises and falls with a deep breath.

"I want to know what Maxwell has on him. Wonder if we could twist that back around and use it to our advantage?" River sighs and lays down on the couch, eyelids drooping with exhaustion. "Wake me up when we need to do something useful, please." He looks up at me and opens his arms. "Take a nap with me, sweet girl?"

I shake my head and sit down on the bed next to Phoenix. Carefully, I bring my legs up onto the mattress and curl into his side, my cheek resting on his shoulder.

Sleep takes me within minutes.

phoenix

"I can fucking do it!" I yell at River, who keeps reaching for me like I'm some overgrown fucking toddler.

No. Fucking. Thank you.

I stumble on the crutches half a dozen times, trying to get through the loft and into the living room, but I'd rather have it that way than anyone else help me. I've already upset Raven by yelling at her for trying to help me in the car.

I'm a grade A prick today, and I hate it.

"You can take another two of the pain pills. Want me to grab them?" Pierce asks. His voice is devoid of emotion, clinical.

"Sure," I grit out. Finally, making it to the couch, I drop the crutches and let myself fall onto the soft leather. My bones practically rattle inside of me with how busted up they are, but I simply grit my teeth and lean my head back, shutting my eyes.

"Here." Pierce is holding out a glass of water and two hydrocodone.

I thank him with a bob of my head and take the pills, popping them into my mouth before grabbing the glass of water and chugging it down. I wish I felt the instant relief the morphine drip at the hospital gave me, but I'm rewarded only with the same dull pain I've been in since I woke up this morning.

"Alright." I adjust myself until I'm semi-comfortable, avoiding Raven's hurt gaze from the other side of the couch. "Spill. I need to know what's happening out there."

"Nix, I don't think it's—"

"Pierce, you've said it's not the right time since I woke up. It's never the right time, so tell me now and get it over with. I need to know so I can make a decision about damage control."

"When the hell did everyone stop listening to me?" he asks, tossing his hands in the air before sitting down in the recliner. "Fine. You wanna know? I've got a team already out trying to get this shit off the streets, and they're failing. Shit's popping up everywhere, and the casualties are higher than I thought they'd be."

"How many?" I ask.

"Enough to alert the FBI, if they were paying attention to Cobalt Springs at all."

"How. Many?" I grit out.

"Twelve dead. Twenty-five hospitalized."

"What the fuck?" I try to stand to my feet, wincing as I fall back to the couch. "Getting that shit off the streets is crucial, and we're gonna sit around here for how long? We've already wasted a week!"

Raven tosses my phone at me, opened to a message she sent.

RAE

We haven't wasted a single second by being at your bedside. Stop being an asshole. Heal. Pierce has enough guys on it.

"Red, I–" I try to apologize, but she stands up and rushes toward the stairs, disappearing as she ascends them.

I don't miss the tears she tries to swipe away.

"Fuck," I groan.

"Yeah. You need to let your body chill. Lay down, catch some z's, watch some shitty TV. We've got the outside shit handled." Pierce leans over and pats me on the knee, meeting my gaze. "She hardly left that room, Nix. Don't tell her she wasted her time." He stands up and walks toward the garage, grabbing River by the arm on the way out. "We're gonna go do some maintenance. Make sure everything's ready to go if we need to get out of here."

"Got it," I call back to him. I struggle to get my entire body up onto the couch, but when I do finally get to lay down on something that's not a stiff hospital mattress, I let out a long breath and shut my eyes.

Maybe sleep is what I really do need.

"PHOENIX, YOU HAVE TO LET GO," *Ruby croons in my ear.*

I shake my head, tears falling.

My cock aches, my muscles are too tense, everything hurts.

I don't know if I like it or want to safe word my way out of the rest of this session.

"Do I need to edge you again?" she asks, wrapping her hand around my cock. The ring around the base of it vibrates again as she presses the button and I yell out, eyes wide.

"No ma'am. Please," I beg her. For more, for less, to stop, to keep going. I don't know.

"Please won't get you anywhere if you don't let go. I'm here to show you what submissives can feel, Phoenix. If you can't let go of the control, how do you expect your own future submissives to do so? Hmm?" She twists her fingers around the head of my cock, then slides her hand back down until she can grasp my balls. Rolling them between her fingers, she hums in my ear. "Will you let go, Phoenix? Or will I?" She removes her hands from my body and I cry out.

"Please, please, please," I sob. I'm not above begging her anymore.

I've been coming to her to learn all things necessary to be a good Dom. It started as me wanting to learn for Lexi, but I've become addicted to many things about Ruby and the club.

Such as the way I can express myself fully.

The way Ruby listens to me more often than anyone else.

Hell, I'm even addicted to how quiet my mind becomes

when I submit to her, though she says the same can happen as a Dominant after a scene as well. During a scene, I'd have to be fully in control of my own mind, but as a submissive? Subspace is glorious and torturous all at once.

"Are you letting go?" I nod and she smacks my naked ass again. "No, you aren't. Your shoulders are tense. Breathe," she says.

I take a deep breath and let it out on a long exhale, groaning when she wraps her hands around my dick again.

"Good boy. Again," she orders.

Another long breath. Another glorious stroke down my shaft.

"One more and I'll let you come," she whispers in my ear.

I inhale shakily before letting a deep breath out, my whole body going lax finally as I allow my mind to go blank.

"Good," she says again. She picks up the speed of her hand, ensuring to caress the head of my dick with such expertise I nearly always have to fight back blowing too early. She bites into the junction of my neck and shoulder, moving her hand faster still, and growls out, "Come for me."

Fuck do I come.

She's been edging me for the last fucking hour, and the amount of cum that lands beneath us is potentially record-breaking.

I shout, my body tenses, and I cry harder.

I both hate and love it.

This is the only place on earth I feel safe enough to let my tears flow.

I'm so tired of handling everyone else's shit.

Taking care of Lexi after a particularly rough night with her dad or the church.

Driving my younger siblings everywhere.

Making sure the band has shows to play and our instruments are in good shape.

Filing for college classes.

Deciding if I even want to go to college.

I'm just so fucking tired.

Ruby unties me from the cross and coaxes me to the bed on the other side of the room. She begins rubbing her hands along my skin, bringing circulation fully back in where I'd tugged my wrists too hard. Uncapping a bottle of cream, she begins spreading it along the red marks and I sigh into the mattress.

She chuckles, her hair brushing across my back. "You're going to be extra tired tomorrow. Do you have work?"

I shake my head and turn, I'm laying on my back, my head in her lap as she massages my wrists with expert care. "No. I have to take Ruben and the girls to school, then take dad to a doctor's appointment. Mom works at the café for twelve hours, and I have to drive her to and from, too." I sigh and shut my eyes to hide the pity from Ruby's gaze. "Can we not talk about this, please?"

"I'm simply worried about you, Phoenix. Part of my job is checking in. Are you sure you won't take the car Dave's offering? Even one more vehicle will help your family a ton." She finishes with my wrists and places a soft kiss on my palm.

"You know I can't take from you guys."

"Very well," she says sternly. She shakes her head but leans down and kisses my forehead. "Go shower, then go home and get some rest. You'll need it."

I do as she says.

As I exit the club at three in the morning, she grabs hold of my bicep before I can enter my car. "Take care of yourself, too, Phoenix."

I shrug and half-grin in her direction. "That's what the club is for, Ruby." I wave off the rest of her concern and place a kiss on her cheek. After I get in the beat up family car, I wave toward her husband as he opens her door.

I don't truly know what compelled them to open this club, but I'm grateful for it every single fucking day.

Fuck sleep, I'll do that when I'm dead.

I WAKE to a warm body laying on top of mine. When I see Raven's red hair splayed out across my naked chest, I wrap my arms around her and breathe her in. "I'm sorry," I whisper.

She props her chin up on my sternum and shakes her head. Pulling her hands from between us, she gives me a slight half-smile and signs *You're in pain and cranky. But this is your only free pass.*

"Understood," I tell her. "I wasn't only talking about today, though. I mean all of it. The emails, the hiding, the stalking."

She raises a brow.

"I followed you around those halls and really shouldn't have. Probably should have gotten kicked out for it, but I was good." I grin when her shoulders shake with her silent laughter, then wrap my arms tighter around her. "I couldn't imagine you hating me for it, Red. I have no excuse for acting that way, I know. Forgive me?"

She places a finger on her chin and taps it a few times, looking up at the ceiling as she thinks about it. After a few seconds, she looks back at me and grins, nodding.

I blow out a breath. "Thank fuck," I whisper. "Can you grab me some of those pain pills?"

Nodding, she places a kiss on my cheek before carefully sliding off my body and walking into the bathroom. She comes back barely a minute later with another glass of water and two pills.

I take them both and chug, then set the glass down and hold my arms out for her. "Cuddle with me? You keep me warmer than any blanket's ever dared to."

A blush creeps along her skin as she climbs back onto the couch, wiggling enough to make my dick take notice as she tries to get comfortable.

I pinch her ass and she glares up at me. "Stop trying to get me hard, Red. I'm supposed to be recovering."

She hides her shit-eating grin by laying her head back on my chest.

"Red," I say in a warning tone.

She wiggles her hips again, this time in a slow, grinding fashion.

I groan. "Fuck, you're a temptress."

Shrugging, she lays her hand over my heart and trails her other along my arm.

I fucking love this woman.

I obviously won't tell her that, but I do.

Placing my hand in her hair, I run my fingers along her scalp and down her back until her own movements become sluggish, sleep threatening us both.

Or so I think.

She slides her hand down from my arm and in between us until she's able to palm my dick outside my pants. It grows impossibly hard at her touch, and she squeezes before sliding down my body, her ass up in the air. Looking up at me beneath her lashes, I can't help but thrust my hips toward her face lightly. She grins.

"Better finish what you started, Red."

She doesn't bother to sign this time, simply mouthing *Or what?* before pulling my sweatpants and boxers down in one.

I toss my head back and squeeze my eyes shut. "Red, you're going to pay for this."

She licks a line across the vein on the underside of my shaft, and I grip the couch.

"Eventually," I grit out.

I look down at her and watch as she drags her nails up my thigh until she reaches my dick. She grabs it in her hand and squeezes firmly. I nearly die when she lets a line of spit fall from that pretty mouth and land on the head, trailing down toward her fist. She moves her hand over me, coating me entirely in her saliva, and raises a brow when I shift my hips in her direction.

"Fuck, Red." I move my hand toward her head, but quickly take it back. "Can I put my hand in your hair?"

She pauses briefly, meeting my gaze, then nods. Frustration lines her features before she pulls back, wiping her hand off before she grabs for her phone.

"The fuck?" I ask, grabbing the blanket I'd used earlier and covering myself with it. "I don't want pictures of my beaten and battered body, Red."

Rolling her eyes, she taps away on her phone. After a few seconds, she turns it toward me so I can read the message.

RAE

I trust you. I'll tap out if I need to.

I look up at her as she sets her phone down on the coffee table.

She signs *I promise*.

"I don't deserve your trust, Red," I tell her honestly.

She rolls her eyes and positions herself back between my thighs, using her feet to push my pants and boxers the rest of the way off. With her ass up in the air like before, she grabs my dick and slides her mouth down on it so quickly, I see stars in seconds.

"Fuck yes, like that," I praise her. I grip her hair in my fist, using my other to move the remaining strands from in front of her. I watch her bring herself to tears with the need to breathe before she lifts her head up, gasps for that breath, and moves back down again. "Oh my god," I moan.

She trails her free hand to my balls and tugs on them gently, sending my hips soaring toward her face until her nose presses against my pelvic bone. Her tongue drags along the vein on the underside of my dick, then explores around the head before she dives back down until her nose touches my skin again.

Thank god she doesn't have a gag reflex, because I'm powerless. I thrust my dick further down her throat until I can feel the back of it, then push some more.

She swallows and her throat squeezes me.

"You're such a good little cocksucker, Red. So fucking good," I groan when she swallows again, tightening my hand in her hair and using my other hand to caress her cheek as I watch her. "So fucking beautiful with a dick in your mouth. Exactly where you're supposed to be."

I pull her off me when her face changes colors, caressing her cheek as she breathes, wiping the tears away. With my eyes locked on hers, I lick her tears from my fingers and grin when her eyes darken.

After I know she's gotten enough oxygen, I use both hands in her hair and push her back down until she swallows me again. I hold her face as I thrust up into her, falling more in love with her when she slackens her jaw and stills herself. She simply allows me to fuck her face the way I've wanted to for months.

The familiar sparks of electricity climb from the base of my spine, and I push her down until her nose is crushed against me. "Swallow," I order. She does, and I come down her throat with a long, drawn out moan. My hips grind into her as I ride wave after wave until I'm spent for the next fucking century.

Once I've released her head, Raven rests her cheek against my thigh, catching her breath. Her eyes flutter closed as I run my fingers along her scalp, and I chuckle, bringing her gaze back toward me.

"Sucking cock make you that tired, baby girl?"

Her blush only makes me grin wider.

"C'mon, call one of the guys and we'll take a bath before heading to bed. I think you've almost managed to kill me." I nudge her up from me and sit up, though my body screams in pain.

She looks over at me in worry, then signs *Too soon*.

I only shake my head and pull my pants back on while I call out for the other guys.

TO: UPINFLAMES@MYEMAIL.COM
FROM: RMHILL@MYEMAIL.COM
SUBJECT: FOOD

Quick, what's your favorite food in the whole world? And what does it say about your sex life?

Pizza–says you're lazy AF in bed

Nachos–dirty, dirty sex. Filthy. Messes everywhere ;)

Steak–powerful. Raw. Primal. Toss her up against the wall type

Caviar–missionary. (boring. NEXT!)

Sushi–exotic. Like...try new things. New positions. Toys. Fun shit.

Chocolate–romantic, feel good, 'make love'. (ha)

I really need to get out of here so I can freshen up my own food life.

I'm bored, and desperate...sorry.

'Til next time,

RM Hill

PS: What's your favorite food from that list, Flames? Hmm?

raven

The smell of barbecue makes my stomach grumble, and Phoenix chuckles from beside me.

"I thought you were full from earlier, Red?"

I smack his arm, and he barks out a loud laugh.

A very un-Phoenix-like loud laugh.

Between the blowjob I gave him and his medication, he's high as fuck right now.

"Someone's off in happy land today," River says. He grins as he steps into the living room with plates for me and Phoenix. "BBQ pulled pork sandwiches with beans and chips cause I was too damn lazy to make fries." He sets the plates down and leans toward me, pointing to his cheek. "Kiss the chef, for good luck."

"That's usually for before you cook. Or is this one good luck to her for daring to eat it?" Pierce asks as he sits down in the recliner, his own plate in hand.

I quickly kiss River's cheek and grin wide when I grab my plate, tearing into the sandwich instantly. Curling up into my corner of the couch–yes, it's mine now–I look out the window and watch as the snow falls.

"You know, now I won't let you kiss me and we'll see which one of you survives the night." River walks back into the kitchen and grabs his food. A satisfied groan escapes him as he plops down on the floor next to the coffee table.

We sit and eat in companionable silence, watching the windows frost up, the thick snowflakes fall, the night creep in. It's both beautiful and eerie.

Pierce's phone blares out a warning noise, and we all pause to stare at him as he answers it. Swallowing his last bite of food, his features harden as he barks out, "The fuck, Maxwell?"

I don't know what's said from over here, but anyone within ten feet would be able to hear the shouting on the other line. I meet River's gaze and see he's quickly trying to finish his food, shoveling it into his mouth.

"S'okay, RaeRae," he says to me the second he's done. He stands and gathers up the plates. "Need anything, Nixy?"

"Yeah," Phoenix replies, pointing toward Pierce, "That phone call to be on fucking speakerphone."

"Not a chance in hell," River says. "You're supposed to be relaxing. Here," he grabs my Kindle from the table and hands it over. "Read with our girl. It'll either get your dick hard or put you to sleep. Maybe both." He kisses my head and walks into the kitchen.

I don't miss the worried look he tosses over his shoulder.

Pierce doesn't say a word at first, simply staring out

into the yard while Maxwell continues to scream. After a few minutes of this, he stomps inside the garage, slamming the door hard enough the windows rattle.

"I feel so fucking useless right now," Phoenix says as I curl up into his side. He wraps his arm around my shoulders and rests his cheek on top of my head. "Let's escape together, hmm? What have you been reading?"

For the next thirty minutes, I use my favorite escape; a dirty book. Well...it'll eventually be dirty. In the next book. Hopefully.

Pierce walks back inside, fuming mad. He scrubs his hand through his hair, then arches a brow when he sees the anger on my own face. Though mine is for fictional characters this time. "The fuck is wrong with her?" He points toward me, looking between Phoenix and River like it's their fault.

"She's reading one of those slow burns again, even though it pisses her off. Last I read, one of the guys kissed the main girl's hand and Rae's heartbeat sped up." Phoenix chuckles when I glare at him and toss the e-reader onto the couch cushion.

"Awe, Blue, do you want me to kiss your hand?" Pierce asks, wiggling his eyebrows.

It's tempting, but *boundaries*, so I shake my head.

"Fair enough." He shrugs his shoulders, sadness shining through his eyes. "River!" he shouts, and I jump. He looks at me apologetically, but I wave him off.

PTSD sucks.

"What's up?" River says as he walks into the living room, drying his hands off on a towel.

"We need to go see Maxwell," Pierce says warily.

I jump to my feet, already shaking my head. I sign *Absolutely not. No. Fuck no.*

Pierce looks to River, who steps forward and grabs my shoulders, leaning down until our eyes meet. "Maxwell says jump, we say how high, remember?"

I shake my head again, tears of frustration threatening to fall. *It's not safe*, I sign.

"We know, sweet girl. We've got more security hired right now than we ever have. We'll be fine. So will you two." He leans in and presses a soft kiss on the end of my nose and pulls back with a grin. "You keep taking care of Phoenix, and we'll take care of the other stuff. We'll take the car, leave you the jeep in case somethin' happens with Happy over there." He snorts a laugh and I peer over my shoulder to catch Phoenix fully engrossed in my e-reader, reading ahead.

I shake my head and sigh, looking back to meet his and Pierce's gazes. *Keep me updated. Text me often. Please.*

"You got it, sweet girl." He wraps me up in a tight hug, lifting me off my feet and making me smile when he squeezes. "You better grab that from him before he starts spoiling it for you." He sets me down and slaps me on the ass to get me moving.

I playfully glare at him. Not a soul in hell will ever know I love when they do that to me. And no, I have no idea why.

"Holy shit," Phoenix says, looking up at me with wide eyes, "she does WHAT? HOW IS THERE MORE BOOK AFTER THIS?" he yells, showing me a page well ahead of what we were reading earlier. Did he even read the pages he flipped through?

I sit between his legs like I have been, yank the e-reader out of his hands, and go back to the page we left off on.

"We'll be back, little bird," Pierce says as he steps through the garage door.

Our eyes meet and my heart clenches with worry for them both.

He holds up his hand and signs *I love you, Blue* before leaving.

A tear falls from my lashes and I curl further into Phoenix's arms, using the book as a coping mechanism again.

"MS. HILL," *the therapist calls, and I shift my gaze up toward hers. "I was just saying how you could possibly work closely with Mr. West for a while. He says he's been wanting to learn sign language as well, so you'd have a partner." Her smile is as wide as it is fake, but she keeps it steady as I peek across the room to Phoenix.*

I raise a brow at him and he chuckles, shrugging. Looking back toward the therapist, I nod once and go back to drawing on the notepad I've resorted to carrying around this damn place.

"Very well then. Great job group!" She starts to clap, encouraging everyone to do the same.

If we all clap at the end of a session, we magically feel like we've done something great here. The happy emotions flood us, we smile and everything is perfectly fine after.

That's what she thinks.

Load of shit, if you ask me.

"Hey," Phoenix calls from across the room as I rise.

I look at him and wait for him to speak again.

He walks toward me and extends a hand. "Raven, right?"

A spark of electricity travels up my arm as I shake his hand. I nod, lifting my lips in a small smile.

"My brother was mute, but we never got around to taking classes to help him. Figured now's a good time to learn." He shrugs and shoves his hands in his pockets.

It's awkwardly quiet for a few seconds before he clears his throat.

"Want to head to the dayroom? They gave me a book for beginners, we could start there. Maybe they'll let us use the internet for this if we make our way through it." He shakes his head and laughs humorously. "That'd be something, wouldn't it? Access to the outside world?"

I roll my eyes and let out the small huff of air which passes as my laughter.

"Hey, that's a pretty smile."

My skin heats with a blush and I shake my head, keeping my gaze on the ground as we walk out of the conference room. I flinch when he places his hand on the small of my back, but he pulls away quickly.

"Sorry," he whispers. "Should have asked."

I shrug but don't even try to comment.

I shouldn't be surprised when a man recognizes consent is important.

I GASP, sitting up straight and wiping drool from my face. Looking down at Phoenix, I brush a hair from in front of his mouth and sigh.

A thud sounds from outside and I jump again, twisting my head this way and that, trying to make out whatever it is in the dark.

"Hmm?" Phoenix murmurs as I shake his shoulders, attempting to wake him. "It's late, Red. Back to sleep."

He grabs for me, trying to tug me down, but I hear another thud from the kitchen window. I jump to my feet, nearly falling over the coffee table we pulled closer to the couch hours ago. Phoenix sits up and rubs the sleep from his eyes, brows furrowed as he looks me up and down. "What's going on, Red?"

I point toward where I heard the sound last, frustration slowing my ability to remember the signs for the words I want to tell him. Tossing my head back and pleading to every deity ever, I sigh and reach for my phone, quickly typing out a message before showing it to him.

> I heard a sound, a few times. Different places. Where are the guns?

Phoenix sighs and reaches for me, pulling me between his open thighs. "Red, the guns are locked up. It's most likely an animal or something. Let's go up to bed, yeah? You're probably as exhausted as the rest of us. Stressed, too."

I stay there for a moment, listening for any other potential sounds, grateful Phoenix doesn't say a word as I do. My shoulders sag when I hear nothing else, so I nod, grabbing his hand and helping him to his feet.

We walk up the stairs, and I jump when I think I see a shadow in my peripheral vision, but chalk it up to exhaustion as well.

"C'mon," Phoenix says as he plops down on the bed. He opens the blankets for me and I climb right in, curling my body around his carefully so as not to disturb his ribs. "Get some sleep, Raven. The guys'll be back before we know it." He kisses my forehead and wraps his arms around me, using one of his hands to rub at my scalp, attempting to lull me into a deep sleep.

The unfortunate thing about going through seemingly endless amounts of trauma?

I continue to hear echoes of thuds throughout the night and dream up scenarios about people breaking in and hurting us. Maybe they'll hurt Phoenix and leave me all alone. Or maybe they'll hurt me and leave him to fend for himself in this state.

No one warns you the echoes of trauma are worse than the trauma itself most days.

My heartbeat finally settles from pure exhaustion an hour after Phoenix starts snoring, but as I close my eyes, I swear I see a shadow creeping around us.

Fuck it. It's just bullshit in my head.

pierce

"Shh," I tell River.

His feet are pounding in the garage, I can't imagine them being this loud when we get inside the loft.

"I am shh," he replies, chuckling when I glare. "I swear, I'm coming down from an adrenaline high, dude. I thought we were toast."

"Yeah, well, don't relax yet. We have a lot to do now." I run my hand over my face as I step inside. Darkness and silence greet me. Passing by the couch, I lean over and turn off the e-reader, wondering how long ago they went to bed for it to still be on.

Something is off, though.

Rae's favorite blanket is down here, and she never sleeps without it wrapped around her.

"Think Phoenix can handle a group snuggle up there?" River asks, grinning when I glare. "Man, I think you'll be out of the doghouse sooner than you think."

I exhale loudly, ignoring him as I quietly make my way up the stairs to check on the other two.

I've spent the last month and a half being as good as I can for Rae. Listening. Watching. Asking for consent for things I never thought needed consent in the first place. It's exhausting, but I've watched her slowly warm up to me again, and she no longer flinches every second I'm around her.

The benefit of not being able to touch her is that I have all this time to watch her, and her body language toward me is changing, little by little, day by day.

"I give it till Valentine's Day. If she hasn't touched you yet, I'll start hinting at–"

"What the fuck?" I bellow. There's a figure on the bed, arms raised.

Light reflects off the knife raised above Raven's chest, and the figure turns.

"Lexi?" River asks, shocked.

My heart rate skyrockets as I rush toward her, unsure what I even intend to do.

Unfortunately for me, she hastily crawls off the bed and drops the knife to the ground, the sound clattering louder than any gunshot I've ever heard.

"Lexi Sommers!" I bellow, wincing when Rae shoots up in a panic. I point toward her. "Stay still, Raven," I command her, my tone biting. She does, and I look back at Lexi who's in a stand-off with River, attempting to slide past him to the stairs.

He fakes one way, she tries the other.

All I hear is the blood rushing too fast in my ears.

Her body tenses.

River pauses, furrowing his brow.

She grins, squeaking as she barely manages to pass by him and barrels down the stairs.

River nearly falls down them as he tries to catch her when she passes. He rushes after her, and I hear him shout out toward her before something slams shut, glass clattering loudly through the loft. "Shit, she used the downstairs window. Back of the house. Call–"

"On it," I bark out, smacking Phoenix in the thigh where I know he isn't as hurt. "Get clothes on. Cops are on their way."

Raven is curled up against him, shaking, eyes wide... I hate it. I hate the fear in her eyes. It reminds me of the same fear I saw in them when I assaulted her months ago.

I hate myself.

"Trip," I bark into the line, "get the fuck over here. Inside. Call some boys to search the grounds. No questions. Now."

"What's going on?" Phoenix asks, confused, though his whole body is tense.

The sleep meds they gave him are not good for nights where an ex-girlfriend tries to murder your new one.

"You nearly died, that's fucking what," I spit, leaning over him and glaring into his eyes. "You both could have been killed. I knew it was a bad fucking idea to leave you two here."

"Because taking us to meet with Maxwell would have been better?" he snaps.

I growl before backing up and gesturing toward my body. "I'm fine, aren't I? Plus, we have a fucking plan. But right now, you two need to get in warm clothes so we can go outside."

Raven shuffles toward the closet and begins putting clothes on. She still looks so scared, eyes wide with panic.

I want to wrap my arms around her and tell her she's okay, but I'm stuck so far in this doghouse I might as well call it my permanent residence. When River comes up the stairs again, I point from him to Raven, and he moves to do what I want to. Turning back toward Nix, I take pity on him and help him into his winter gear. I grab him a few more pain pills, grateful these don't make him pass the fuck out.

"Hello?" Trip calls from downstairs as he enters from the back door. "You need to be out of here for the heat sigs to properly work, Jackson. Hurry up."

I lean over the railing and meet his gaze with narrowed eyes. "Who the fuck pays who, Trip?"

"I've got a team searching for her out back, man, but we want to check the house at the same time. Make sure she isn't hiding in a closet or some shit." He looks apologetic, but stands his ground.

Scraping a hand across my face, I turn back toward my own crew and wave them all down the stairs. "Get in the jeep and get it warmed up. We could be waiting for a while."

"Got it," River says. He grabs hold of Raven's hand and escorts her into the garage.

I follow behind Phoenix, making sure he doesn't take a quicker path down the stairs than necessary.

"Alright," Trip says when the rest of the crew is in the

jeep. "I've got about ten guys here. Six in the woods, the other four surrounding the house."

"I want you to kill her," I tell him seriously.

His eyes widen and he clears his throat, shaking his head. "Not what I do, Jackson. You know that. You may work for a guy like Maxwell, but I only work for you because I was desperate when I got back into the states. Don't take advantage." He pulls a heat signature reader from his pocket and turns toward the loft. "Sit tight. We'll find her."

"What are they doing?" River asks from the backseat. Raven curls herself up across his lap, eyes still wide with panic I saw a few minutes ago, her breathing too quick to be calm.

"Six guys in the woods searching, four guys plus Trip inside searching with heat sigs." I so badly want to run my hand along Raven's face and calm her. Instead, I meet her gaze and dig my fingers into my thighs. "It'll be okay, Blue. We'll get her, I promise."

"I shouldn't fucking be here. I should go somewhere else if she's going to attack–" Phoenix says quickly, panic fully taking hold of him.

"Shut your fucking mouth, Nix. You're part of the crew. You belong here as much as the rest of us." I sigh when I meet his tired gaze. "Listen, we'll lay low for a few days after they find her. Maybe try to file charges–"

"She killed my whole fucking family and got out with a slap on the wrist and a 'do better' from her sadistic fucking father. Charges won't do a damn thing and you know it!" he yells, startling everyone. His voice cracks as he leans forward, pressing his forehead into the dash. "I should have stayed with her and tried to keep the fucking peace. She was on a downward spiral for so fucking long..."

"Staying with a person to keep the peace in your life is only prolonging the torture you're subjecting yourself to," River tells him. He reaches forward and places a hand on one of Phoenix's shaking shoulders and meets my eyes. "No need to torture ourselves in the pursuit of someone else's happiness."

I rest my head back on my seat and close my eyes.

If all else fails, I'll kill her myself.

Trip can keep his high and mighty morals.

KNOCKING on the window stirs me, and I groan as I wipe the sleep from my face. Turning my head, I meet Trip's eyes and take a deep breath before sliding out of the jeep. I cross my arms and lean back against the door, waiting.

"Good news and bad news, man," he says, sighing and reaching for a cigarette. He lights it up and inhales deeply before blowing it out with frustration. "We got them both..."

"Okay, what's the bad news?" I ask.

He takes another hit and shakes his head. "Her dad's already bailed her out, and is trying to pin the entire thing on Hayes."

"Hayes nearly killed Phoenix, Trip, so I don't give a shit." I snatch a cigarette when he offers it, hiding it from Raven's line of sight in case she wakes up. After lighting it and taking a hit I say, "Still say they deserve to die but..."

"They're wayward kids, just like you four. Don't deny it."

"We aren't kids anymore, Trip. We're grown ass—"

"Young adults who still need guidance but have no one to provide it to you." He shakes his head and runs a hand through his hair. "Listen, I'm calling an attorney I know, who might work with Hayes, get him a deal for information on Maxwell. But," he raises a brow when I stand up straight, "you need to call the guy from the FBI."

I try to object, because that shit will get the rest of us in a lot of trouble, too.

"I know he gave you a deal for amnesty if you shared your shit. You need to at least think on it, man. Give your-self a few days. Talk it over." He finishes his smoke and claps me on the shoulder. "There's a right and a wrong way to go about a lot of shit, Pierce, and I think calling him would be the right way this time around."

I reluctantly nod and finish my own cigarette, tossing it out into the snow as I follow him out of the garage. "Hey, Trip?" I call out right as he reaches his car.

"Yeah?" he calls back, pausing with his door open.

"Keep yourself safe, too. Maxwell is bigger than Cobalt University."

His lips lift in a half-grin and he nods. "I'm well aware. I've got my crew, you've got yours. We'll take him down, eventually." He slides into his car and I watch as he leaves, snow already falling and sticking where he parked.

I stand there for I don't know how long before turning back and facing my own crew, sleeping in the warm jeep. Safe.

What the fuck are we tied up in, and how do we get out?

TOO MANY FUCKING people are surrounding my home right now.

Inside.

In the yard.

Outside the gates.

I feel exposed.

River comes up beside me where I'm watching a whole slew of strangers put up a new security system all across Junk. He wraps his arm around my shoulders and squeezes hard enough that I blow out a breath. "This'll work out. You know it will."

I shake my head and sip my coffee, cringing at the cold liquid. "I don't know. For the first fucking time, I don't feel like the protector. I feel like the one who's scrambling to pick up broken pieces."

River hums a mild agreement before letting me go and turning toward the room. "Nix is getting better. We should go back to school on Monday. Lots of people around, so we'd all be at least a bit safer."

"Under Maxwell's eyes, though," I tell him.

He shrugs, his bare shoulders brushing mine and creating goosebumps with the friction. His gaze flicks down to my hardening nipples and I cross my arms. He grins.

"It's cold. Shut up."

"Okay."

"Shut up," I say again, narrowing my eyes at him.

He holds up his hands and laughs. "I said okay."

I nod once and look back out toward the yard. "Too many fucking people, man."

Sighing, he walks into the kitchen and grabs his own coffee. "It's only going to annoy you more to know Trip plans to keep watch dogs on the gate twenty four seven."

"What?" I whirl around so fast I spill my drink on the wood floors.

Nodding, River holds up my phone. "Just texted you to tell you he feels better doing it this way. Lexi's apparently gone MIA and Hayes was bailed out this morning by some anonymous dickhead."

"I thought Trip was getting him an attorney?"

"Yeah, she showed up this morning to find his holding cell empty." River brings over a towel and helps me clean up the mess I made. When he rises, he shoots his cocky grin in my direction. "How you holding up?"

"I'm fine. I'm worried more about her safety than anything else at this point. Plus," I grin as I lift my coffee back to my lips, "I've got you to keep my dick wet in the meantime."

He barks out a laugh and shakes his head before stepping back into the kitchen. "I'll get shit ready for lunch, but we should talk to the other two about going back."

"Going back where?" Phoenix says as he bounds down

the last few stairs, limping and wincing after every other step.

"School," River and I say in unison.

"Yeah, okay. Sounds great," he says as he sits down on a stool and reaches for a fresh coffee mug. "While we're there, we should probably figure a way out of the scholarship for Raven. I refuse to let her work for Jimmy and his guys."

I raise a brow at River. I was certain Phoenix would argue some point about safety or keeping Raven here and secure within the fortress we've built. The new security will help us keep tabs on everything from an app on our phones. We don't even have to walk outside at this point.

Raven steps into the kitchen a few seconds later, wrapped in sweatpants, bright green fuzzy socks, and one of Phoenix's hoodies. She smiles at me, places a kiss on River's cheek, and grabs her hot cocoa before sitting down on the stool next to Phoenix. When she takes in the silence of the room, she lifts her hands from her mug and signs *Cat got your tongues?*

River laughs and starts to translate for me, but I hold up a hand.

"Nah, your clothes are on and your thighs aren't spread, little bird. No way a cat could have our tongues." I wink when she blushes and chug the rest of my coffee.

A knock at the door disrupts lunch a few hours later, and I get up, only for Phoenix to walk past me. He opens it up wide enough for Trip to step in, another guy following him.

"Afternoon, boys, and Ms. Hill," he tips an imaginary

hat at her, smiling when she blushes and waves at him. "Alright, so the system's all set up, and I've got the crew rotating shifts outside the gates for at least a week. If we find them before that? We'll back off."

"What about Maxwell?" I ask.

"I've told you what to do about Maxwell, Jackson." Trip narrows his eyes at me, then blows out a breath and points toward the guy behind him. "This is Lance. I'm leaving him in charge over here. I have a sick kid to get back to."

My phone buzzes, and I read off Rae's text. "Rae wants to know why she's still sick."

Trip sighs and shrugs his shoulders, meeting Raven's eyes. "No idea. Gonna take her out of town to get looked at by a better hospital. Anyway," he clears his throat and steels himself. "Lance is in charge. I sent you his contact information. He has all of yours. He knows some ASL so he may be better suited for you than me, anyways." He winks at Raven and starts to walk out of the loft.

"Wait," I call after him. I move to where he's standing near the door and fold my arms across my chest. "I'm gonna call. Want me to keep you updated?"

Trip nods and looks at Lance, before shifting his gaze back to me. "Make sure to keep us both updated. Lance is good people, too."

"Are we done talking about me like I'm not here?" Lance asks, his lips twitching as he tries to hide a grin.

"You're in good hands, Jackson. Call the guy at the FBI. Get him on the frat house if you have to. Hit Maxwell where it hurts the most first." Trip pats me on the shoulder and waves to the rest of the crew before leaving, Lance following behind him.

I turn back toward Raven and the guys and shrug. "Well, guess we're going back to school, and I'm calling in the FBI."

TO: RMHILL@MYEMAIL.COM FROM: UPINFLAMES@MYEMAIL.COM SUBJECT: RE: FOOD

I don't know what came over you yesterday, but that email was pure gold.

What would your little FBI agent say after reading all of your emails, Red?

That one in particular might throw him off the scent, though.

HURRY! How would you unalive your worst enemy?

Wait, that wouldn't work for me because my worst enemy is currently myself...

Now I'm depressed.

And hungry.

Have you decided if you're going to take that scholarship offer or not? I know the terms are a bit weird, but I think you'd be great at helping a fraternity. You have the backbone to stand up to all those fucks, and you know it.

Next time put a warning for sexual content, Red.

Nearly died.

Till next time,

Flames

CHAPTER SEVENTEEN

raven

"Holy shit, it should be illegal to be this fucking cold," River states, his teeth chattering as he pulls me to him.

Pretty sure he's holding me for his own warmth rather than to provide me with any.

My shoulders shake as I silently giggle and I bite my lip as we head toward class.

Phoenix is holding my other hand, and Pierce is walking ahead of us all, his phone still held tightly in his fist.

He called the FBI agent less than a day ago, and expects them to drop everything to help us.

"Stop complaining, for the love of God," Phoenix grits out. He reaches his free hand up and adjusts my hat back over my ears.

"But I don't love God, so can I still complain?" River snarks back, earning another stifled giggle from me, which Phoenix rewards with a pinch to my side.

"You're both fuckin' trouble," Phoenix grumbles.

"Hey, Jackson, you think I could tap your girl, too? Since the others are doin' it?" The asshat Alpha Mu guy laughs with his friends as he waits for Pierce's reply.

When he doesn't so much as respond, the group takes it as the permission needed and approaches me, River, and Phoenix. They crowd in around us and I meet Phoenix's gaze, shaking my head subtly. He's still hurt. He doesn't need to get into a fight.

"Y'know, there's a new Alpha Mu president, kitten. He told us you were free game. Said you're nice and loose, too." This douche waggles his brows at me, grinning wildly.

"Get the fuck back," Pierce growls out, pulling a few of the guys back from me. "I don't give a shit if there's a new president. Jimmy can go choke on his own tiny dick for all I care."

The first guy stumbles back and nearly falls on his ass, but rights himself at the last second and adjusts his coat with an angry glare aimed at Pierce. "You'll get yours, Jackson. All of you. Then she'll," he points toward me and I lean further into River's hold, "be ours, too. Fucking watch. C'mon boys," he yells, waving everyone on as he turns to walk away.

"I'm so fucking tired of this shit," Pierce says. He trails his eyes from my head to my toes and back again before exhaling heavily, as if seeing I'm okay helps make him okay. "Get to class. We'll head to the frat later and grab the rest of our shit. I don't like knowing Jimmy has access to a single sock I own."

Phoenix kisses my forehead before stepping away. "See you soon, sweetheart."

I grab River's hand, and we begin the short walk to our classes. *Is the danger in front of us worth going into a mountain of student debt for?*

"HOLY FUCKING SHIT," Pierce says when we enter the frat house that afternoon.

"Dude," River draws the word out before exhaling. "Shit."

"Riv, take Raven to check our old rooms, then get her the fuck out of here." Pierce grabs Phoenix's bicep and tugs him further into the house.

I barely glimpse the trashed living room before River pulls me toward the staircase.

"We've got to get whatever is left and go. C'mon."

The stairs stick to the soles of our boots, and I cringe each time I have to yank my foot up from the wood. At the top, we pause, taking in more destruction before walking to River's room first. We're unable to make it in because someone's locked it up tight, and something's jamming the doorknob, too.

"Fuckers," he grits out. "Whatever. I've got everything important to me at Junk, anyway. May be missing some funny boxers though, shit." He shakes his head and turns around, stepping down the hall toward Pierce's room.

Faint smells of pineapple still linger, and I lift my gaze right as River looks at me. We share a quiet laugh as he pushes the door open, only to hold his arm out, nearly clotheslining me before I can step inside.

"No," he orders when I try to slide under his arm. "Raven, I said n–"

I land a jab to his side. He's surprised enough to double over, eyes wide in shock. I flip him off as I step inside, his laughter echoing behind me.

What I find in the room is...a lot.

What looks like a million pictures of me and the guys line the walls. Some are innocent paparazzi style shots, but others are more intimate, taken from this very fucking house. I nearly crumble when I see a few taken from inside Junk. I stand up on my tip-toes to rip them off.

"Raven!" River shouts, grasping my shaking hands and pulling me away from the wall. "No, sweet girl. We can't touch it. This is all evidence. Let me take pictures. Stand," he looks around before picking me up and placing me right in the center of the room, "right here. Don't fucking move or touch a damn thing. Understand?"

I nod, reaching my trembling hand up to wipe away tears. A fruitless task since I keep crying. Silent sobs take me over as I look around the rest of the room. Papers ripped out of notebooks, books torn. Whoever was in here was looking for something, and they were pissed they couldn't find it by the holes punched into the uncovered walls. Nausea falls over me in waves and I cover my mouth.

"C'mon, sweet girl, let's get the fuck out of here." River pulls me to my feet, wrapping his arm around my waist as we step out of the room. "This is fucking sick," he says when we make it outside. "Jimmy must have taken that one over." He shivers and inhales the winter air deep into his lungs, then lets it out on a breath.

I rush toward the Jeep, but barely make it within a foot before I throw up everywhere, grateful the snowbank hides the evidence.

River's there in an instant, holding my hair and rubbing my back. "Shit, Rae," he grits out, "shit."

"The fuck?" Pierce calls. I hear his footsteps as he rushes toward me, but at the last second he stops in his pursuit, clenching his fists at his sides. "The hell happened in there? Did someone touch her? I'll fucking–" He stops mid-sentence when River holds a hand up.

"I'll show you pictures when we get back home. Let's fucking go before I burn this place to the ground." He cringes and shoots an apologetic look toward Phoenix. "No offense, man."

"I'm right there with you, so don't worry about it."

All three of my boys keep their eyes firmly on me as we get into the jeep and drive home. When I think they're finally going to allow themselves a moment of reprieve, they watch as I enter the loft and head straight for the bathroom.

I make them all wait outside, shutting and locking the door for good measure, even if they've shown that I can finally trust them.

Steeling my nerves, I look up into the mirror and wince when I see dried puke on the sides of my lips. I quickly grab a washcloth and clean it, brush my teeth, using far too much mouthwash, before repeating the process. I rip my clothes off, get in the shower, and turn it on scalding hot.

My body is plastered all over the walls of that room. The guys' bodies weren't zoomed in on like mine. In the throes of passion, orgasms, sucking dick like the best of them.

I feel violated, and that's saying something at this point in my life.

I curl up under the hot water and let it heat my skin far past the point of my anger.

And when it grows cold, I allow the shivers to wrack my body until all I can focus on is the rattling of my bones.

When I leave the bathroom, all three guys are sitting on the floor, staring at photos, blueprints, pages of text, and who knows what else. They all freeze when my feet cross the threshold, and I hold up a hand to stop them all from moving.

"Blue—" Pierce tries to say, but I narrow my eyes at him.

I take a deep breath and sign *What are we doing about it?*

"I, well," he clears his throat and looks between the other two, then meets my gaze, "I need a few days. I've got a meeting with this FBI agent. I have to go alone." He holds up a hand when I object with mine. "Listen, go to school this week. Phoenix is going to talk to someone to try and get you into online classes or something. Fix your scholarship. I don't know. But," he clears his throat and looks down, and I'm certain whatever he is about to say will crush me, "Maxwell called."

I wave my hand, waiting for him to elaborate.

"Rae, we couldn't talk him out of this," River says, shifting uncomfortably under my glare.

"Jimmy's requested you spend time at the frat house on Friday night." It's Phoenix who drops that bomb.

I shake my head a million and one times until I make myself dizzy, my stomach churning all over again. Rushing toward the closet, I pack my own fucking bag for my own fucking trip out of this place.

Out of the city.

The state.

Hell, out of the whole fucking country at this point.

"Hey, hey, hey," River croons as he grabs me in his arms. He grunts when my flailing limbs manage to make contact with him a few times. "Raven. Raven, please listen to us."

I shake my head back and forth, back and forth.

"Calm down now, Raven," Phoenix commands.

It's so starkly different from the sexy dominant voice or the calm requests. My body freezes and he grasps my chin in his fingers.

"You have two options, and you're going to listen to them both before you make a choice. Do you understand me?"

I meet his gaze and inhale deeply. Which one of his ribs do I kick if I want it to really hurt? Somehow, he sees through me and grips my chin tighter.

"Do you understand me, Raven?"

"Breathe," River croons in my ear, sliding his fingers along my skin where he holds me, soothing me while also keeping me captive.

I should be pissed, but I'm not. The panic is already

fading, making room for the anger to take over. After a few seconds, I meet Phoenix's gaze again and nod.

"River's going to let you down and you're going to sit on the bed and take a few more deep breaths like the one you just took. After that, you're going to listen to what we have to say." His eyes warm for a moment, and I watch his Adam's apple bob in his throat as he swallows. He squeezes my chin and I meet his gaze. "Do you understand?"

I nod and they both release me, apologies shining in their eyes from manhandling me. With my heart in my throat, I walk toward the bed and sit down, leaning my head between my knees to take in deep breaths. My head swims, but when it finally stops, I sit up straight, cross my arms over my chest, and wait for them to speak.

Pierce is the one up for this task, clearing his throat before he looks up at me from his spot on the floor. "We're gonna give you a small camera, something you can wear on jewelry, and you're gonna do whatever they ask. It'll record everything, and we can turn it into this agent when I meet with him."

I nod along as he speaks, keeping my gaze locked in his. Where the hell did we go wrong in life to deserve this shit? Obviously, an answer doesn't show itself, so I'm forced back to reality when he shifts and looks between the other two.

"Your other option," Phoenix says from behind Pierce, tapping his foot and looking uncomfortable with whatever he's about to say, "is to pack your shit and leave the country. I've got a friend in Canada who can help get you on your feet if you want."

Ice slashes down my spine at the thought of leaving everything I've known to get away from Maxwell and his plans for me. Surely, one night of sacrifice is worth it to keep hold of the men I love?

Do I really love them, though?

Through all the dumb shit they've done, they've spent the last few weeks, months even, showing me in different ways how they care.

They've spilled their secrets.

I've put them each in the doghouse, and the one still there isn't even complaining about it anymore.

I look up, meet Pierce's gaze, and sign *I'll do it.*

"WELL, HI THERE, SUGAR," Jimmy calls from the stairs in front of the Alpha Mu house. He extends a hand to help me walk up the final one.

The breath leaves me when he grabs me, spinning me around.

Pierce nearly blew the place up when the request for me to dress in a fucking *maid costume* came through his phone barely minutes after I agreed to do this. I almost backed out, too, but I really didn't want to live without my guys.

"Get that pretty ass inside. There's lots to clean up to get ready for our party tonight, and I know you love being on your knees for a man. Don't you, sugar?" He smacks my ass when I cross the threshold, and the catcalls, whistling, and loud laughter pour over me like lava.

"Ah shit," one of the guys says. I look up and regret everything when I see it's the one from campus a few days ago. "You wanna come clean my room first, darlin'?" He grins as he leans in my direction. "I've got a knob that needs polishin' all of a sudden."

I cast my eyes downward and step toward the kitchen. It's easier to start there and work my way outward. I did this enough times in the first month and a half here, so I know where everything already is. My neck is heavy with the necklace the boys made me wear, and I know the camera is working because we tested it before I left.

"Don't fucking take this shit off, do you hear me?" Pierce said as Phoenix finished clasping it into place. "This is the only reason we're sending you in there alone. The only fucking reason, Blue."

A shadow looms over me while I'm bending over to pick up a piece of trash off the floor. When I try to stand up, hands find my hips and a third joins in to hold me in place.

"Shame your boys couldn't be here to watch this. They'd have a blast watching their girl get used the way we intend to." This fucking guy.

"Manny, Jack, hands off," Jimmy snaps. "We really do need this place clean for this party. Supposed to be something for the school board. Hopefully, we get a clean slate shoved in our faces." He smacks my exposed thigh before pulling my shoulder until I stand up.

The other two grumble but step out of the room, leaving me alone with my worst nightmare.

"You're doing good, sugar. Might reward you later with a little Jimmy time if you make it spit-shining clean." His eyes darken as he looks me up and down. "Damn shame Jackson and his boys have had their hands and shit all over you, too. Might need to bathe you in some holy water. Get you all cleansed." He smacks a kiss on my cheek and walks out of the room. "You have an hour for the rest of this house, sugar. Better get moving."

I ignore the tension in my gut and clean like my ass is on fire. It might as well be with how often it gets smacked by random hands. My skin crawls with invisible touches by the time I finish cleaning the house. My hands are raw from using so many chemicals in a short amount of time, and I'm pretty sure I'm nose blind to sweaty man, too.

"You did such a good job, sugar. Wait for me, and I'll get you cleaned up before I unfortunately have to send you back to your owners." Jimmy rolls his eyes and grins as he walks toward the basement stairs, followed by his trusted few.

No one else is around right now, most of them preparing for the party upstairs, so I keep my feet light and as silent as possible as I trail behind them.

They hook a quick left and I hear a door open, but it doesn't shut.

Taking that as my cue, I lean my body against the wall at the bottom of the stairs, and pull my necklace around until the camera is facing directly at the open doorway.

Chairs scrape along the concrete floor and voices echo down the hall before it all falls quiet.

"Very good, boys," I hear Maxwell say. "Jimmy, the board will be here in twenty minutes. Make sure my daughter is nowhere to be seen in that slutty outfit, and

I'll figure out a way to let you keep her here. Maybe have a boy in blue call in domestic assault or something."

"Ah, I'd rather win her fair and square, Mr. Langston," Jimmy responds.

"Very well, then." Maxwell clears his throat, and I hear something flop onto the table, but can't make it out from this distance. "There are too many dying, boys. I need some of you to get your scientific brains moving as to why, and I need you to fix it."

"Sir, with all due respe–" someone says.

"Boy, anyone starting a sentence like that never really does mean respect, do they?" Maxwell snaps. The room is quiet. "Do they?"

"N-No sir. S-Sorry sir."

"Fix this recipe. I need people addicted, not dead. What happens if I make money, Jimmy?"

"We make money, Mr. Langston," Jimmy replies confidently.

"Good. Now, we got the cops on our side, but I've heard talks of the FBI getting involved. Keep your goddamn heads low and your dicks solidly in your filthy pants. No more dirty accusations need to hit this frat house. Do you hear me?"

A chorus of 'yes sirs' sounds and Maxwell clears his throat again.

"Jimmy, if we have to kill Jackson and his friends, I want no arguments from you. They've been tampering with shit and I know they go back and fix everything I have them break. I've got a contact with access to explosives. Take his card, give him a call."

Chairs begin to scrape against the floor again as

everyone rises, and I take that as my cue to get the fuck out of here.

I barely cross the top step before arms wrap around my waist and a hand slaps across my mouth.

"You've been a naughty fucking girl, haven't you, sugar?" Jimmy says in my ear. His tongue slides along my skin and I cringe, trying to curl my body up in a ball to avoid his touch. "I guess I'll have to teach you a lesson before my important meeting as the new Alpha Mu president."

I bite, scratch, let out silent screams, cry, kick, everything I can to escape his arms, but the rest of the frat simply allows him access to the house. One of the guys even lets him inside Pierce's old room. Tears fall in streams onto the bed, and Jimmy chuckles when my body goes slack.

The pictures are too much.

Him having Pierce's old room is the nail in the coffin of my pain.

This room is not where I'm meant to repeat horrid events over and over, is it?

"Aw, come now, sugar. You've had some fun times in here, right? Look," he says excitedly, grabbing a picture down from the wall. He twists it toward me and my stomach clenches at the sight of me, bound and helpless beneath River, Phoenix in the corner, and Pierce staring down at me as he tugs at his dick. "Now you can just add me to the next showing of your fantasies."

I thrash my body, attempting to pull out of his arms.

He's expecting it and tosses me onto the bed face first. His breath hits the back of my neck as he climbs on top of me, and I nearly gag. "I always love when you fight me, sugar, but I've got shit to do today, so I need you to stop."

I quickly grab the charm on the necklace, placing it so this can be caught on the camera. He reaches above me and yanks out a chain with handcuffs on them, clicking them in place over both of my wrists.

When his arm bands around my neck to pull me down, I bite him, hard, grinning when I draw blood. I spit it out on his white sheets, my tears falling and staining them right alongside his own vile essence.

"You fucking bitch. I do not have time for your shit." He growls as he sits back on his haunches. Cold air hits my skin when he lifts my skirt, and his hand lands heavy on my ass. "Sit still, let me get off, and you can go back to being useless after that. Damn," he snaps out.

I hear his belt buckle open, and I'm grateful he doesn't move my underwear.

He's done this routine before.

Claims it isn't rape if he doesn't enter me.

Sick asshole.

He leans over me, braces his dick between my ass cheeks on top of my cotton panties, and groans at the contact. He hardens and pulses as he grinds himself on me, and his moans in my ear are loud. He speeds up, and within seconds he's coming all over my back and under-wear. With an exaggerated exhale, he slaps my ass again and leans down to kiss my tear-stained cheek.

"I may not bathe you after all. Want you to smell like me and still feel me when you walk inside that asshole's house later." He rubs his cum all over my skin, then fixes my skirt and hops off the bed. "I'll be back later, sugar. Don't go anywhere."

His vile chuckle echoes through my head the rest of the night, until he comes back and frantically lets me free of the handcuffs and hands me to the pissed off men who've claimed me.

I don't let a single emotion or tear free until I curl up in a bath with Phoenix crooning soft lullabies in my ear.

phoenix

"I can't believe we *told her* to do that shit, Riv!" Pierce shouts, tossing a box full of bike parts at the wall. "That was barely a step above what we did to her back in September. That was fucked up entirely. She won't come back from that. She won't come back to us. She won't. She won't–" his voice cracks, and I watch from the doorway as River grabs him in his arms, pushing his head roughly into his shoulder and gripping his hair in his fist.

"She's asleep," I announce as I walk in, closing the door quietly behind me.

"Nix," Pierce croaks out. His eyes are red-rimmed with his tears and when he reaches for me, I let him pull me into an awkward group hug.

"She's strong. Stronger than we give her credit for, man." River places a rough but comforting kiss onto Pierce's skull and I back away to allow them their space.

"We knew watching the live feed would kill us all," I remind them both.

"I–" he sighs and shakes his head, pressing his forehead onto River's shoulder again. He shudders with his sobs and I watch, helpless, as one of my best friends crumbles to the ground over the woman he loves.

Silence surrounds us, and we all stare off into nothingness until Pierce's phone lights up. He nearly snaps it with how hard he presses to accept the call.

"Agent Starling, did you get it?" Silence, small chatter on the other end of the line. "Yeah. A few hours ago." More silence as Pierce nods, wiping his face with his shirt, red-rimmed eyes focused on the ground.

"Here," River whispers, handing over a box of tissues.

Pierce whispers his thanks and uses one to wipe his nose as he listens to the call. "Yeah. We'll get her in. Call ahead for us, yeah? Get us someone legitimate."

I stand and walk toward the wall where Pierce threw the bike parts and start picking them back up, tossing the ones which need to be disposed of. My entire body is shutting down after the adrenaline rush this afternoon, and I know I'm going to crash before too long. Unfortunately, there's not a second to spare.

"Okay," Pierce says after hanging up the phone. "We have to get her to a hospital. Get her checked out. Did you collect what you could, Nix?"

I nod and point toward the mini fridge. "She had spit, blood...cum." I cringe and shake my head at the last word.

"I'm gonna fuckin' kill him," Pierce says through gritted teeth. He opens the fridge and looks at the bags of evidence I'd collected off her before letting her in the tub.

Shit, was she mad about it.

She hasn't communicated with any of us.

"Does she blame us?" I ask them.

River shrugs and shakes his head. "I don't think so. We gave her the options. Maxwell is the one to blame overall, but Jimmy is his own person."

"If you can call him a person," Pierce snaps out. He shuts the fridge and types out a text before putting his phone in his pocket and sighing, the tension in his shoulders struggling to release. "I need to sleep, but I'm fairly fucking certain I'm going to have nightmares."

"Rather the nightmares in my head than the ones outside it." I shrug when he raises a brow at me and make my way into the loft. I pause on the threshold and look back at them both. "I don't want her in school anymore. We need to convince her to get out. The scholarship office has already threatened to pull her."

"I agree," River says, patting me on the back as he enters the loft.

"Let's convince her to go to the hospital first. We'll worry about the rest of it later." Pierce moves toward the stairs, but quickly thinks better of it and lays down on the couch.

River meets my worried gaze with one of his own, waving me upstairs as he makes his way to the couch as well.

I slowly walk up to the bedroom and set a chair at the end of the bed. With my ass in the chair and my ankle crossed over my knee, I struggle to stay awake as I watch Raven have nightmare after nightmare after nightmare, only to be reminded of my own.

"MR. WEST!" *the paramedic yells. I thrash more in his hold. "You need to let the firefighters do their job, son. You'll only get hurt going back in there."*

"My whole family is in there!" I scream, spit flying at the guy.

"I know, son," he says firmly, his eyes the only thing betraying his sympathy, "but you don't need to save them. Leave it to the professionals."

I twist back around and struggle to get out of the guy's hold, failing miserably. Tears fall over my cheeks as I yell out for someone, anyone to escape that fucking fire.

No one does, though.

They left me all the fuck alone and I don't know whether to join them or avenge them.

The choice is taken from my thrashing, screaming form when they inject me with a sedative after kicking the EMT again.

I don't have the fight left in me to do anything but rest on the gurney he lays me down on, the flames from my family home lighting up the night sky.

"NIXY?" River shakes my shoulders roughly.

Wonder how many times he's done it.

"I'm up," I grumble when he grabs both of my shoulders and his breath fans my face. "Get off me."

"I don't want to get off to you. Sorry to ruin your fantasies." He chuckles when my eyes snap open, and I take a swipe at him. "Rae's in the shower. I've got pancakes going."

"Pancakes won't make this conversation easier." I stand up and stretch my limbs out, regretting sleeping in the chair the moment my muscles protest any movement. "Fuck," I groan.

I walk down the stairs and sit my ass in a stool, gratefully chugging the coffee Pierce has already sitting in my spot.

He doesn't look much better than me this morning. Bags are prominent under his eyes, his face is puffy from all the crying, and his body movements are sluggish.

"Get much sleep?" I ask him.

He only glares, and I nod in return, sipping my coffee again.

"Good morning, sweet girl. Feel better?" River asks her, wrapping her up in a gentle hug. He places a kiss onto the top of her head before walking her to her normal stool next to me.

She shrugs at his question and looks down at the marble, picking at her fingernails until Pierce forces her mug of hot chocolate between her hands. Her knuckles turn white around the mug and I struggle to keep my shit together. She's going to snap at someone, and maybe I'm a pansy, but I don't want to be that person today.

"So Raven," River says, noticing Pierce and I aren't going to be the ones to break the silence. "Sweet girl. Honey bunches of oats. Sugar muffin."

Slamming her mug down on the counter, she glares

up at him, then around at the rest of us before signing, *I'm not going to the hospital.*

"The fuck you aren't," Pierce snaps out.

"RaeRae," River says softly, "we want you to get tested for any and everything he could have given you. After what we saw, and what you went through, we just want you safe."

I'm here, aren't I? she signs.

I sip at my coffee and stare at the backsplash behind Pierce, hoping it'll swallow me whole.

"Please," Pierce begs her.

"We can do whatever the fuck you want after the hospital. I don't even care if we go murder Jimmy Perkins with a butter knife slathered in vinegar." River chuckles at something, but I keep my gaze focused on the black grout between the gray stone.

It's indicative of our life right now. We're the gray stones, and the black surrounding us is our shitty circumstances.

"Yes? Awesome!" River shouts, and I finally turn my gaze back to the group. "Go get ready. We leave in five."

I watch as Raven finishes the pancake she was nibbling on and moves toward the stairs. When I can no longer see her, I keep my voice low when I speak. "Manipulating her with the chance to murder someone? You know we can't do that."

"She knows we aren't going to do it, but I have a feeling she's tired of us asking, so she's going to get it over with for our sake." Pierce shrugs when I meet his gaze. "Tell her to do something enough and she finally does it just to shut you up. Not a tactic I've used often, but one I've used when it's absolutely necessary."

"Okay then," I say before shaking my head and finishing off my coffee. I reach for a pancake and eat it while standing and walking up the stairs.

Raven is half-dressed and shoving her legs inside a pair of black jeans, her ass hanging over the top as she wiggles her way into them.

I lean against the railing and watch her, my palm covering my growing erection.

After she gets those pants buttoned, she turns around and lets out a silent scream when she sees me, but her shoulders bounce with her laughter. She shakes her head and flips me off while grabbing the cream sweater she seems to love.

"Here," I say, stepping toward her and picking up the hairbrush sitting on the end of the bed. "May I?"

She nods and I sit down on the edge of the mattress, spreading my thighs wide enough for her to sit between them. When she does, I start the soothing ritual of brushing her hair and putting it into braids.

Doing this for my sisters was the one thing that put me in a meditative state. I knew they were safe, cared for, loved. They knew I'd do a damn good job because they were the ones showing me all the video tutorials.

"I wish you'd let us care for you more, Raven. We care for you a lot. We l–" I stop that train of speech again. "We like taking care of you. Feeding you. Cherishing you." I set the hairbrush aside and trail my fingers down her arms until I'm able to grasp her hands in my own.

Her breathing picks up, and I feel her heart galloping in her throat when I kiss it.

"We don't seek to hurt you, Red. Not anymore." I lick a line from her throat to her ear and whisper, "You're ours to protect. To love." I ignore the slip and groan in her ear, grinning when she leans her head back on my shoulder. "Do this for us, and when we get back, we'll reward you. Sound good?" I remove my hands from hers and bite gently on the junction between her neck and shoulder.

Sounds good, she signs.

"Good girl," I breathe into her ear before kissing her cheek softly and patting the side of her hip. "Alright. Up now, Red. We gotta get moving."

When she stands and glares at me with her hands on her hips, my heart beats normally for the first time since I watched her latest nightmare come to fruition on a tiny screen.

She's going to be fine.

"I HATE WAITING ROOMS," Pierce mutters.

"I hate waiting," River replies, grinning when he gets the glare he was trying to incite.

"Other than when I was in the hospital, when's the last time you were in a waiting room, Pierce?" I ask, leaning back and folding my arms over my chest.

"When Rae's mom died," he whispers.

"You were there?" River whisper-yells, eyes wide and hands flailing.

"Yes, but shut it. She doesn't know." He leans his elbows on his knees and rests his face in his hands. I watch his shoulders rise and fall with a deep breath.

"I'd have crossed heaven and hell for a girl I loved if she was breaking like that," I say sternly, glaring at the back of his head.

"Yeah, well," he looks up, and I roll my eyes at the tears threatening to fall from his. "She broke my fucking heart, man. I didn't know what the hell to do. You should have seen the way she was thrashing around in the nurse's arms and knocking shit over. I've never seen her like that. I don't understand why she'd act like that."

"Her mother died, numb nuts. Are you going to look at me any different because I acted the same way when my family died?" I straighten my shoulders and clench my hands into fists, avoiding punching him square in the fucking nose.

I'll wait till we get back to Junk for that.

"No, but–"

"Shut it," River grits out before plastering a smile on his face. "Hey, RaeRae, ready to go?"

We all stand and look her over as if the doctors harmed her behind closed doors. Finding nothing amiss, my shoulders relax, and I let out a long breath.

Can I have a chocolate shake? she signs, shrugging when we all give her weird looks.

It's fucking ten degrees outside, and she wants ice cream?

"As you wish," River croons, grabbing her by the hand and escorting her out, Pierce and I tailing them.

"She's obsessed with chocolate, and it's unhealthy,"

Pierce grumbles. He smiles as he watches them walk across the lot. "So is my love for her, though, I'm sure."

"I feel the same, brother," I shrug when his head snaps in my direction and his eyes widen. "She's a dirty little thief. Stole all our hearts and doesn't even act guilty."

He barks out a laugh and pats me on the back. "She doesn't act guilty, but she sure as shit knows she's got us all wrapped around her fingers." He points toward the jeep where River is lifting her inside. "We all know damn well she can get in the damn thing herself, yet she lets him treat her like a princess."

"A queen," I correct.

He nods and shoves his hands in his pockets, grabbing the keys. "We can talk about school over ice cream. Maybe she'll be happy enough after chocolate."

I shrug.

One can only fucking hope this doesn't blow up in our faces.

"THIS. IS. SO. GOOD." River groans when he takes another bite and I watch as Raven's eyes light up with her own. She licks her lip when a drop falls and blushes when our heated stares follow the movement.

Eyes on your own food, boys, she signs, quickly moving back to take another sip of her milkshake.

"Already are, little bird," Pierce tells her.

River chuckles when she blushes.

I clear my throat and sit up straight, pushing my own milkshake toward the center of the table so I can clasp my hands together in front of me.

Raven's back straightens as she looks at me, then at the other two who assume the same positions, though River still has his fucking milkshake straw glued between his lips.

"Raven," I say as I meet her gaze, "we think you should pull yourself from school." I hold up a hand when she starts to protest, and the glare she shoots me burns. "Listen, we can't watch over you everywhere, and there's a frat guy in every class."

"If you stay in, you have to follow the rules of the scholarship, and Maxwell has already stated you have to live there again. We can't protect you, Blue. Not there." Pierce winces when she slaps the table to get us to shut up, glaring around at all of us.

She inhales deeply and reaches for her phone.

We sit silently as she types out a message, and when my phone buzzes, I instantly open it.

RAE

I don't know who the fuck you three think you are, but none of you own me. I can't just quit school. It'd be a waste of scholarship money. A waste of time. A waste of all the effort I went through to ACE every single exam I've taken. What do you propose? For me to be a housewife? Be barefoot and pregnant to appease you oafs? Fuck no. Fuck that. Fuck you!

None of us notice she's left the booth until the door chimes before slamming shut.

"Shit," Pierce grits out, sliding out of the booth to rush after her.

I toss a few extra bills down to tip the waitress for our food and her efforts to clean up the milkshake Pierce knocked over in his haste. With an apologetic smile tossed her way, I shove River out of the door and nearly slip on my ass rushing down the stairs.

"Raven, I can't fucking watch you everywhere. I can't be in the frat house. Hell, I can't even fucking hold you when you're hurt anymore! What the absolute shit am I supposed to do if you're under their thumb constantly, huh?" Pierce tosses his arms out and spins around before gripping his hair. He looks at her again. "Please tell me how to make this work for everyone."

Raven moves her gaze between the three of us. She's angry, rightfully so, but we aren't the bad guys anymore. We aren't the ones dictating her future.

"Rae," River says quietly, walking toward her with his hands up in surrender. "All we want is for you to thrive, and right now none of us are thriving. We'll work toward that, but–"

She holds her hands up, we all pause in our slow pursuit of her. Each of us crowding her, boxing her in against the jeep.

"Red," I snap out her name like a whip, "if you'd listen, we already have a solution. I want to pay for you to attend classes online."

Through CU? she signs.

I shake my head and she glares, placing her hands on

her hips as tears spill down her cheeks. "A different school. I'll make sure the credits you've already earned will transfer over." I raise my hands and sign, *I promise.*

Wind slices through the space in the middle of us all, and Raven looks torn between wanting to do as we ask and getting out of here. It didn't escape my notice that she took the keys directly from my pocket. They're clutched in her hand like she can make them choose for her.

She has to make this decision for herself, like she did about going into the frat on Friday.

My heart nearly falls to my feet the longer she thinks about it, and when she lifts her gaze to meet ours, I'm sure she's going to leave.

Her head nods a few times, and she holds her hands out in front of her. *I get to choose which school, no exceptions.*

"Whatever you want, Red. Whatever you want," I repeat. I point toward Pierce. "Can you hand him the keys now so we can go? You're trembling in this cold."

Those pretty blue eyes meet mine as she holds the keys out toward Pierce, then she meets River and Pierce's gazes before turning back to the jeep and climbing in.

"What do we tell Maxwell?" River whispers.

"Nothing," Pierce says. "Let him figure it out when Jimmy's balls shrink from neglect."

TO: UPINFLAMES@MYEMAIL.COM
FROM: RMHILL@MYEMAIL.COM
SUBJECT: CHOICES

Listen here...

I don't want to make decisions right now.

There are too many choices.

Should I go to an online school, so I don't have to face people?

Should I go to CU, be forced into working with that fraternity, but also get a free ride through my dream school?

Should I even strive for anything when I get out of here?

IF I get out of here.

Half the time, I struggle to choose what to eat in the morning, Flames.

I wish you'd tell me who you are, because I'd like to talk to you in person. We could discuss school choices. Maybe choose the same one?

If that's an option.

I don't like having this many options...

Till next time,

RM Hill

raven

Not *that one. It looks like a...* I sigh in frustration and write 'scam' down on the notepad in front of me.

Phoenix lifts his hands and shows me the proper movement for the word, and I repeat after him.

It looks like a scam I finally sign.

He grins and places a kiss on my cheek. Lifting his hands, he signs *Good girl.*

Now if only he could play my body and use sign language at the same time...

I shake my head and cover my cheeks with my hands to hide the blush.

He points toward another school on the list, and I raise my brows. "Harvard's a good choice. Your grades are good enough. Could study business while pursuing something creative."

Too much money, I sign.

"Nothing is too much money if it's something you want, Red. Nothing."

I shrug and chew on my lip.

He grabs my chin between his fingers and moves my head to meet his gaze. "I mean it. You're worth every hundred dollar bill I'll ever drop on you, and your company is just as enjoyable when I haven't spent a dime. Understand?"

I nod.

Smacking a quick kiss to my lips, he leans back and signs *Good girl* again.

I sigh and point toward Harvard on the screen, earning a smile from him. I keep my eyes on his lips while he applies for me.

He told me all about the life insurance from his family, but I never feel right when someone spends their hard-earned money on me.

"Hey, I'm gonna take Rae to this follow up appointment," River announces. "Anyone else going with?"

Phoenix waves him off. "I'm gonna sign our girl up for Harvard. You go ahead. Pierce is also working on the bikes."

"What's wrong with the bikes?" River asks, brows furrowed in confusion.

"His boredom." Phoenix looks at him, and they share a silent conversation.

I stand and put on clothes before walking downstairs to do the same with my shoes. Steeling my nerves, I quietly step inside the garage. The chill hits me hard, and I wrap my coat tighter around myself while I look for

Pierce. When I catch sight of him, I break out into a wide smile.

He's laying on the ground underneath a bike, tweaking apart for some reason. Boredom is not what I see. His chest rises and falls as he sings along to whatever song is blaring through his headphones, and I silently giggle when he uses the tools in his hands as drumsticks. His hips wiggle for a second, he pauses, then he starts grooving again.

I always loved watching him tinker with stuff, especially when he didn't know I was there. Watching Pierce enjoy a moment to himself seemed like the best sport for me, because he's unabashedly himself in these moments.

At least the version of himself he wished he got to be.

He's the kid who had loving parents.

He's the boy who got to try all the things because his mom signed him up for whatever he wanted.

He's the teen who got to take his best friend to the prom because she didn't go with an abusive dickhead.

He's the man who got to love his childhood sweetheart without pause because the world *didn't* fuck them over.

I zone out so much that when he drops the tools and scrambles to his feet, I jump and let out a silent scream. A deep blush crawls its way onto his cheeks when he asks if I'm okay. I wave him off, smiling brightly when he tries to stutter out an explanation.

You still need to work on your singing voice, I sign.

"Hey!" he yells, then lifts his grease-covered hands and concentrates hard to sign *I'm better than I used to be.*

I raise a brow, my breath caught in my throat. He's

been practicing without the rest of us? I shakily sign *You're now a two out of ten instead of a one.* I grin when he glares.

He tries to sign something else, frustration lining his brows, but River interrupts us by bounding into the room like his own personal herd of elephants.

"Alright, let's get this show on the road!" He pauses at the passenger side of the jeep and opens the door. "You comin' too, Pierce? Or is it only me and Rae?"

Pierce clears his throat and meets my gaze. "I'm staying. You two have fun." He turns around and slides back under the bike, his face no longer joyful, but pained.

"Okay then," River whispers. He grabs me by the hips when I slide up next to the jeep, helping me inside. I swear it's like he doesn't think I can put my foot on the damn rail to climb in myself.

As we drive away, I look out of the rearview mirror as Pierce sits up, watching us leave with that same pained expression on his face.

My heart aches for the boy I've hurt, who hurt me, who I'm hurting again.

Maybe it's time we took a step forward.

Together.

"WELL, MS. HILL, I," the doctor clears his throat and looks over at River.

Frustrated that he doesn't know even a little sign

language, I write the words down on the notepad he gave me.

They all know. It's completely consensual. Can we please move on?

He nods and awkwardly clears his throat again. "Very well. The implant is easy. Goes in your arm, stays there for three years. When you want it out, it comes out. Simple. No physical risk to your partners from a string, and not as much of a hormonal change like the pill has done to you in the past."

I nod and look toward River, signing *Tell him I'll do the implant, then.*

He rolls his eyes, as frustrated as I am. "She'll do the implant. Also, before you see another patient who's hard of hearing or who can't speak, learn some sign language. Not that hard."

The doctor blinks a few times, his skin growing red with embarrassment before he nods. "Okay. Let's get this over with, shall we?"

Barely twenty minutes later, I have the implant in my arm, protected against more than pregnancy. We walk out of the office and down the hall. River grins wickedly when he presses the elevator button and I roll my eyes at him, jabbing him in the shoulder.

"I didn't say anything!" he scolds me, laughing when he fails to look serious. "You were thinking about it too, little vixen. Don't lie to me now. Your face said it and your thighs clenched." He spins me and hounds me back into the elevator. "I bet you're wet for me right now, too, aren't you?"

My body heats, but a figure walks around the corner toward us, and everything goes cold. I shove him backward hard enough for him to stumble.

Painful seconds tick by until I can make them out, confirming my suspicions. Lexi Sommers isn't MIA at all, she's been here the whole fucking time. I grit my teeth, taking in her plain clothes, slumped shoulders, sad eyes.

An older couple is behind her. The man is red-faced, shaking with anger, and the woman looks terrified, but stern, as they both hold Lexi's biceps. She doesn't see us until she's practically in front of us, but our eyes connect as she passes, and my mouth drops open.

She looks like a zombie.

What the fuck did they do to her in here? Why isn't she in jail? Why do I even feel bad for her right now?

"Let's go," River says, grabbing me around the waist and pulling me inside of the elevator when the doors open back up.

I watch as Lexi is escorted out of the hallway and into the VIP elevator. They disappear before I can hear what's said. Breathing heavily, I look up and meet River's gaze. He looks angry, and I don't blame him.

That night is such a blur to me. With everything else going on, I don't think I've had time to process the fact that she made it inside Junk, up the stairs, and onto the bed without me or Phoenix knowing. He was passed out from his medication, but I was simply naively unaware.

Even after hearing all of the noises, I let myself fall asleep.

Didn't even contact the boys.

Fucking stupid, Rae. Stupid.

Pierce said the knife was aimed directly at my chest when he got upstairs.

She was going to fucking *kill me*!

I nearly bust my face in the elevator door trying to get back out of it as they close, but River bands his arms around my waist and pulls me in again. I thrash in his hold much like I did the nurse's when my mother died, and the reality of everything makes it hard to breathe. My chest heaves and the world fades in and out of my vision. My body shakes. Tears fall in streams down my cheeks.

"Hey, Rae, c'mon now," River pleads. He spins me in his arms and I wrap myself around him like a koala. He presses his face into my shoulder and tangles his fingers in my hair. "Shh, sweet girl. You're here with me. Take a deep breath with me, okay?"

I shake my head, tears now drenching his shirt.

"Yes. Let's do that. Don't argue. Deep breath in," he inhales deeply, "and out." He exhales. "C'mon sweet girl, breathe with me."

I try to shake my head again. Breathing is too hard right now. Living seems hard, too. Everything is crumbling around me constantly and–

River slams his lips against mine, tightening his grip in my hair as his other hand falls to my ass. He turns us so he can press me up against the elevator wall. Instead of pushing the emergency button, he simply presses himself into me and kisses me until I'm thoroughly fucking distracted.

Tears forgotten, breaths still heavy, I grind myself on

him, and his groan spurs me on. I scratch my nails along his skin, raking them up his abs inside of his shirt. Digging my heels into his ass, I pull him further toward me until my arms are crushed between us.

"Do you want me to fuck you in this elevator, little vixen? Would it be enough to get you to think clearly?" River bites my earlobe and tugs on it, sliding his hands down my sides and pushing them between us. He tosses my own out of the way and shoves his down the front of my pants. "Oh hell," he whispers. "You're fucking wet for it. Do you need to come to distract yourself?"

I nod, shutting my eyes tightly to ignore the rest of the world. I breathe better when one of them is touching me. Nothing but me and my men matter when they touch me like this.

"No," River says, pulling away. He cleans his finger off and glares down at me before adjusting himself. "Let's go home, deal with it there."

I gape at him as I fix my clothes, embarrassment slamming into me.

"Out," he barks. He sounds like Phoenix right now and it's both hot and confusing. "Now," he says, slapping me on the ass when I don't move fast enough.

I walk through the hospital, out into the parking garage, and climb in the jeep, eyes wide, mouth popping open and closed over and over again in utter shock.

River's supposed to be my safe zone. Cheer me up. Distract me when I need to be distracted.

The drive home is tense, and his grip on the steering wheel is hard enough his knuckles turn white.

"I DON'T KNOW why I have to be the emotionally mature one today, but I'm going to lay some shit out for all of you," River says.

We're all sitting around the living room after having eaten a quick dinner. He told us we needed to have a grown up conversation, and he was the one leading the charge. Phoenix and Pierce both laughed in his face, but when none of his joking mannerisms came to light, they sobered quickly.

"You," River points toward Phoenix, "need to report your ex-girlfriend again. Tell Pierce's FBI guy if you have to. We saw her leaving the hospital today."

"What the hell?" Pierce glares at Phoenix.

"It's not my fucking fault her father holds that much power! How she's not in prison is a shocker to me, too." Phoenix crosses his arms and looks between me and River . "What else did you see?"

"Ask Rae, because she nearly went after her," River tells him, tossing his arm in my direction.

She tried to kill us, I sign frantically, meeting Phoenix's eyes.

"Killing her in a hospital hallway isn't the best way to deal with that, is it, Raven?" Pierce snaps.

I glare at him and am about to jump his ass when River whistles.

We all stare at him like he's grown six more heads.

"Pierce," he meets Pierce's green-eyed glare like it isn't

deadly, "grow some balls. Set up the meeting with the FBI guy. Tonight."

"But–"

"Stop being an absolute dipshit. Maxwell's already watching you, what's this meeting going to do? Get the FBI on your side?" River rolls his eyes. "Oh no!" He fakes a gasp, then narrows those eyes on me.

"Raven–"

"River, whatever you're about to say to her, you better tread fucking carefully," Pierce says. His hands clench into fists in his lap, and he's vibrating with tension.

"You need to stop deflecting," River tells me. "Work *with* us. Listen to us. Let us fucking *love you* for a damn change. We're here to listen to you, hold you, fix the world or burn it down for you. Stop ignoring the possibility that you have three men at your feet. You are not alone anymore!" He throws his arms out and stares me down.

The other two are eerily silent now, watching me, hope shining in their eyes.

It always amazes me that these three personalities have meshed together so well and can agree on anything at all.

Tears threaten to fall, but I steel my nerves, straighten my spine, and take a deep breath before nodding. *I hear you,* I sign.

"Thank fuck," Pierce says, resting back in his chair.

"Oh no, Piercey Jackson. Get off that chair and make the phone call." River folds his arms over his chest and raises a brow.

Pierce gawks at him for a moment, cracks a grin, and

stands up with his phone in his hand. "Yes, daddy," he calls before the door to the garage closes.

River's nose wrinkles up in disgust. "Nope. Doesn't fit me. Cuddles?" he asks me as he flops down onto the couch next to me, his playful personality back on, like a switch flipped the second he got all that off his chest.

I jokingly roll my eyes and sidle up against him, resting my head on his shoulder.

"I don't hear you making the phone call, Nixy boy," River teases, running his hand along my side as he searches for something to watch on the TV.

"Who the fuck can we trust?" Phoenix snaps.

What about Trip or Lance? I sign, looking between both of them.

"She's got a point. Try them, see what they can do." River kisses my forehead with pride, then goes back to channel surfing.

Phoenix stands up and walks around the couch, heading back toward the kitchen. "Red?" he calls, and I turn to meet his gaze. "I'm sorry about Lexi."

"Stop apologizing for shit that isn't your fault, Phoenix," River snaps out. "Go." He waves him off and pulls me further into his side.

I meet Phoenix's gaze and shrug, smiling softly at him. *Go deal with it,* I sign.

He nods, hesitates in the doorway, but ultimately steps out, exhaling a long, frustrated breath.

pierce

"Agent Walter Starling, how can I help you?"

"Hi, yeah, it's Pierce—"

"Jackson, I've been waiting for your call back for over a week. Why haven't you called?"

I run a hand through my hair as I stare around the garage, searching for a focal point. "Honestly?"

"All I want is honesty from you, son."

"I don't trust many people, and you could be a mole for all I know."

The man chuckles on the other end of the line, and I hear the faint click of a lighter. "Fair enough. Did your girl go get the video we talked about?"

I nod, then shake my head because I'm on a phone call and he can't see me. *Dumbass.* "Yes sir, s-she did."

It's silent for a few beats, then he clears his throat. "You report what happened?"

"No, sir. Took evidence ourselves, had her seen in the hospital as a precaution for, uh, STDs." I clear my own throat, trying to hide the emotions bleeding from every one of my pores.

"I'll send a guy to get the evidence. I need you to do one more thing for me, son."

"Yeah?" I ask, sitting down on my workbench.

"Get into his office for me. Need you to get me whatever you can."

"Why the fuck can't you do that?" I grit my teeth. "Sir."

"Stop with the sir, Jackson. I know you're pissed at me. I can't get a single fucking guy in that school. Don't know who the fuck is finding us out, but the whole FBI is up in arms over bad training since we can't infiltrate a fucking *college*." He scoffs, and I hear him take a hit of whatever he's smoking.

"We do this, I need your word we won't be implicated in anything."

My heart beats erratically in my chest as I wait for his answer, and when it doesn't come immediately, I stand up again and pace around the garage. I take note of which bike parts need tuning, which ones need replaced. The back left tire on the jeep is low, so I crouch down and inspect that, too.

"Got it," he says eventually, and I blow out a breath. "You get me anything you can. Then I want you to take a vacation with your girl."

"It's the middle of the semester. We'll all fail," I tell him.

"Would you rather die?" he asks, annoyance lacing his tone. "Listen, son—"

"I'm not your fucking son!" I yell, tossing a screwdriver toward the wall and wincing when it bounces off. "I don't care about people dying. I don't care about who's mom will be without their kid at night. I care about the four of us, and that's it. In order to get ahead in this fucking life, we need those degrees. We need to get out of this fucking state, man."

"Go to a different school, Pierce. One semester off won't hurt you in the long run."

"God, you sound like an incessantly annoying old man right now." I groan, tossing my head back.

"You're young, s-" he clears his throat, "Jackson. You're all young. You have so many years ahead of you."

"If we don't die from this fucking drug next. I swear he'll end up forcing it down our throats soon so everyone is addicted and at his fucking mercy." I slap my hand on the workbench, wincing at the shock of pain shooting up my wrist.

"There may be a guy," Starling says. "He worked with Maxwell originally, then took off the moment someone died. He's been hiding out who knows where. Maxwell might have information on him."

"Think it's in his office? Plain fucking sight?" I bark out a laugh.

"Guys like Maxwell get cocky over the years, Pierce. That office has been his for so long, I'm surprised he doesn't claim it as his main residence on his taxes." He sighs. "Let me know if you find anything good in there. We'll meet up later. My guy is outside of your gates now, waiting for the shit from Friday."

"The fu–"

The line goes dead before I can finish my statement.

I'd toss my phone if I had another immediately available to me. Instead, I shove it in my pants pocket and walk toward the fridge and cabinets where Phoenix stashed the evidence from Friday.

Thank god he pays attention in his classes.

I grab my coat off the hook and pull it on while the garage door slowly rolls open. The cold air blasts into my face, and snow drifts in, but I ignore it all in favor of walking the fifty or so feet toward the front gate. "He's good," I call as I approach. Lance is standing with another guy on one side, peering through a crack in the gate.

"You sure? Looks like an angry motherfucker." Lance chuckles and shakes his head when I wave him on. "Alright then. Back up!" he calls out.

The gates open enough for him to step through, the headlights from his car shining from behind him. Lance was right, this guy is massive, bulky, ripped, and looks mad as fuck. No way Agent Starling is using him as a fucking lackey.

"Jackson?" he asks, his voice deep and gruff.

"Me," I say dumbly.

His lips twitch as he holds a bag out between us, opening it up. "Put it in here."

I carefully lay all the stuff in the bag, and lift my eyes to his. I can't tell what color they are, but I can feel them burning into my skin.

"We'll be in touch," he says before turning. He nods toward Lance and his buddy, then disappears out of the gate. Pretty sure I hear him say something along the lines of 'fucking kids' as it closes behind him.

"Well, he was fucking scary," Lance remarks after a few seconds of silence.

"Yeah, well," I clear my throat and meet his gaze. "Back to work, gentlemen."

With that strange as fuck encounter out of the way, I walk back inside and take off my coat as the garage door closes again. I hear Phoenix and River laughing when I open the door to the loft, and I kick my boots off before going to investigate.

I find my whole crew piled on top of the couch playing video games.

River's playful banter echoes through the room, and Phoenix reaches over to smack him on the back of the head. Rae's smile is bright as can be when she turns to look at River, and surprisingly only dulls a little when she sees me from the corner of her eyes.

I toss up a wave like an idiot, and she hides her giggle behind her hand, her pretty blues shining with happiness.

This.

This is what I want every single second to be like with them.

"Who's winning?" I ask as I enter the room, sitting down on the recliner.

"Phoenix," River says at the same time Rae points at the man himself.

"Typical. I swear you cheat," I say.

"Nah. You all just suck," he snarks.

"Dick," River says, comically straight-faced.

"What did you call me?" Phoenix asks, standing to his feet and glaring down at him.

"We all suck dick." River shrugs when Phoenix gapes at him. "Except you, of course."

"Hey," I interrupt, "I don't either."

"Liar," River says under his breath, and Raven's head snaps toward me.

"Yeah, keep dreaming." I lean forward and grab the fourth controller. "Keep fucking dreaming," I repeat.

Oh, I will Raven signs.

"Oh, do you dream about that, little vixen? My dick down Pierce's throat? Him gagging on it?" River groans and adjusts said dick in his jeans. His eyes meet mine and he winks.

I flip him off.

I'm sure I've gotten myself off to it a few times now she signs.

My eyes widen. "Since when do you get yourself off in a house full of horny men?"

Since two of you were put in the doghouse she signs, sticking her tongue out.

"Woof, fucking, woof," I snap out.

Her shoulders shake with her laughter.

A few rounds of games later, River stands up and holds his hand out to Raven.

I raise a brow as I watch them, putting my controller to the side and folding my arms over my chest.

These two either cuddle and game, sleep until you wonder if they've died, or they dance like they're professionals training for the next competition.

I love it all.

Raven sets her controller down and grabs River's hand, allowing him to pull her to her feet. She grins when he leans in to kiss her cheeks, and a bright pink colors her face, but she sobers considerably when he whispers in her ear.

I sit up straight and unfold my arms.

"Hey, Nixy boy?" River asks.

Phoenix sets his own controller down, keeping his eyes on Raven. "What?"

"Remember that game I said we should play a few days ago?" River waggles his brows and runs his hands up and down Raven's arms.

Color me intrigued when I see Phoenix adjust his dick. He clears his throat and his lips twitch when his eyes flit toward me for a second. "Yeah? Now?"

I'm no longer intrigued.

"I don't like the sound of this," I tell them. I refuse to have a repeat of Christmas Eve. No fucking way.

"I think Pierce has been a good boy, hasn't he, little vixen?" River croons in her ear, sliding his fingers along the waistband of her sweats. Teasing me with tiny glimpses of her flesh.

She takes a shaky breath and meets my gaze before nodding.

"Now, if it was up to me I'd have let him fuck me by now for how good of a boy he's been." River winks at me, then lifts her shirt higher until her breasts are exposed, nipples pebbling instantly in the cold air.

"But I don't think he's learned his lesson yet. I say one last test of his endurance should prove whether he has or not." Phoenix steps in front of Raven, blocking the vision of River playing with her nipples. "Now, Pierce," he grins, walking toward me with something behind his back.

"Nix, this shit is not fucking funny. Don't you dare tie me down again," I warn.

"Oh, I'm not." He pulls a pair of handcuffs and a ball gag from behind his back. "You can choose to use these, or you can show us you've learned how to keep your hands to yourself unless asked." He shrugs, tosses the items onto the couch, and moves out of the way so I can see River and Raven again. "Your choice."

I dig my fingers in my thighs as I watch her unabashedly grind her ass against River. Lust shines in both of their eyes, and my zipper digs painfully into my dick. "Fuck," I grit out.

Raven lifts her hands and points toward the kitchen, then looks back at me and signs *Barstool.*

"Blue, please," I beg.

I need *her*, nothing else.

Fuck if she'd just hold my hand right now I'd be happy.

Her hands shake as she points toward it again, and my heart falls to the floor.

How much restraint can one man fucking show?

I take a harsh breath as I stand, walk into the kitchen, and plop my ass on a barstool, folding my arms across my chest. Looking up, I meet Rae's lust-filled eyes as she leans her head against River's shoulder, and I grit my teeth.

"This should be interesting," Phoenix murmurs as he moves toward them. He places his hands on Rae's feet and slides them up the inside of her sweatpants. "Who's in control during this scene, sweetheart?"

Those pretty eyes look between all three of us, but

predictably land on him. She points at him, followed by River. She holds up a hand before either of them can speak and signs, *I am.*

"Good girl," Phoenix says, grinning when she tries to rub her thighs together. "You're always in control. You're the queen. Remember that later when you're so full of dick you can't breathe." He leans in and presses a kiss to her exposed stomach, his eyes on hers the entire time.

River lifts her shirt up, and she helps him pull it over her head. "Fuck, you're gorgeous. Isn't she gorgeous, Pierce?" He tweaks her nipples and bites her shoulder as he watches for my reaction.

I only nod, gritting my teeth hard enough my jaw's already aching.

"He wants to fuck you so bad right now, little vixen. I can practically hear the blood rushing toward his dick." River groans when she grinds her ass against him. "You want him to fuck you soon, my queen?"

She pauses for a second, then shrugs, eyes locked on mine.

"Shame. I'd love for us to fill all of your pretty holes, Red," Phoenix tells her. He bites his lip as he reaches up and tugs her pants down, removing her underwear and socks as he goes.

Standing stark naked in the loft, she practically glows between us.

"Blue, please," I beg again. I don't know what else to say. What else to do. How else to show her I'm sorry, I'm sorry, *I'm so fucking sorry.*

She shakes her head and looks down at Phoenix, burying her hand in his hair and tugging him toward where she wants him. Her eyes roll when he shoves his tongue into her, his nose pressing firmly against her clit.

He groans, and she tosses her head back until it lies on River's shoulder again.

"I want to play with your ass tonight, little vixen. That okay?" River asks her, one hand still massaging her breasts as the other descends until it has a good hold of her ass.

She lets out a shaky breath, but nods. Tilting her face toward his neck, she places soft, open-mouthed kisses on his skin.

Phoenix does something, and her entire body locks up, her thighs nearly crushing his head. He pulls back and grins, nipping at her. "Not yet, Red." He stands and kisses her long and slow, a passionate dance between lovers.

River and I lock gazes as they do, and I lick my lips. His eyes flash toward mine and I groan, palming my dick.

I'm so touch-starved, if someone breathed on me I'd come all over.

Phoenix breaks from their kiss, placing his hand on her cheek and rubbing it gently with his thumb before pulling away. "I'll be back. Put her on the couch, Riv."

"Aye, aye, captain," River calls out. He whispers something in Raven's ear that makes her blush an achingly beautiful shade of red. It crawls from her chest up to her cheeks, and her eyes glaze over when he tweaks her nipple again. "Fuck, you're responsive tonight." He lets her go, only to place a palm on her lower back and guide her to the couch.

River strips himself fully, and I stare at his bare ass as much as hers until he turns around and plops down on the leather. He grabs Raven and spins her, making her sit on his thigh. "Not sure how much longer Phoenix will be, and I want you to stay wet for us, sweet girl. Grind on me. Bring yourself to the brink but don't come until I tell you to." He grips her chin between his fingers and raises a brow. "Understand?"

She brings her hands up and signs *Got it*.

"Good girl," Riv says, his voice dropping low when she grinds on his thigh.

She's hesitant at first, but she looks up and meets my gaze when I groan, and it spurs her on. Leaning forward, she wraps her hands around the top of River's leg, and moves on him like a cat in heat.

He has a beautiful view of her ass, and he reaches out to palm it before squeezing.

"Fuck," I groan, leaning back and letting out a harsh breath. "Fuck, fuck, fuck," I whisper to myself. How am I supposed to not touch either of them right now?

"Take your dick out," River commands.

"What?" I ask him, because he sure as shit doesn't take that tone with me outside of our alone time.

"You heard me. Take your dick out like a good boy, Pierce. Show our girl how hard you are for her. For us." River's eyes spark with a challenge, knowing I struggle with this submissive shit.

I've learned quickly over the last year that River and I are switches. It's all dependent upon what we need when we share time together, but when it's only us? He's typically the one who takes control.

This would be the first time I actively showed this to Raven.

"Hesitation only asks for punishment, Pierce," River says in a low voice.

I keep my eyes on Raven's as I obey him by undoing my pants and taking my dick out. A long moan leaves me at the instant feeling of relief.

"Pants and shirt off. You know I like you better naked," River commands.

Raven stops grinding to look between us both, lust darkening her gaze.

River smacks her ass and grins when she tosses her head back on a silent moan. "Didn't tell you to stop just because I want to see his flesh, little vixen."

"Holy shit, Riv," I grit out. I shuck my pants and underwear off before tossing my shirt who the fuck knows where. Right as I move to touch my dick, though, he snaps, and I freeze, meeting his gaze.

"Hands off until she comes."

"I–"

"You can. Show her you're a good boy. I know you can." River reaches around and massages her breasts again with one hand, the other on her ass. "Keep grinding that pretty clit on my leg, sweet girl."

Raven's eyes meet mine as she grinds on him again, and within minutes, she's panting, chest heaving, nails digging into his skin.

He leisurely strokes his own dick with the hand not massaging her ass as he watches her. "Fuck yes," he says when her hips stutter, "look at him when you come, sweet girl." He grips her chin and forces her gaze to mine just as she crashes over that ledge.

It takes literal Herculean effort to not rush them both, or come on the floor in front of me.

"Good. You got her warmed up," Phoenix says as he walks down the final steps and around the corner.

"And soaking," River points out, dragging his finger through Raven's folds and bringing them to her lips. "Taste the mess you made, sweet girl." He strokes his dick a few times while she does, and groans. "Good girl," he praises, pulling his finger from her mouth.

Phoenix steps around the couch and grabs a bottle of lube from his pocket. "Since everyone else is fucking naked all of a sudden," he grumbles. He takes his shirt off slowly, making a show of it for Raven's benefit. I swallow hard when he removes his pants and underwear in the same fashion. Man should have been on one of those magic men tours. His tattoos alone are enough to draw a woman in. Make him move his hips? Fuck. "Stop staring, both of you."

"Sorry, Nix, but you're hot as hell. Our girl's already worked back up just watching you." River hides his grin in the crook of her shoulder and kisses her skin. He slides his dick along the small of her back, seeking his own relief.

"Red, do you remember when I told you about all the things my Domme made me do?" Phoenix asks as he turns back to the coffee table and grabs the lube.

She nods.

"Anything I do to you has been done to me. This is one area that could hurt you if you don't listen, so I need you to listen carefully." He looks at both me and River. "You all need to listen. Prep is extremely important. Got it?"

We all nod and watch as he coats his fingers in a generous amount of lube.

"Turn her over and shove your dick in her mouth, River."

"Fu–" I let out a heavy breath, and watch as River slides along the couch until his head is on an armrest. He pulls Raven down, putting her ass up in the air, her cunt on full fucking display.

"Don't touch it," River grits out.

Shit, he can see me perfectly from this angle.

I raise both of my hands and he snaps. Glaring, I put my arms behind my back and clasp my hands together. I'm tempted to knock him out for this, but we agreed to this dynamic, and I agreed to let him try this in front of the others.

So I'll be his good boy, knowing he'll reward me for it later.

"Pierce, move that barstool to the other side of the coffee table," Phoenix says.

I don't know why he wants me to until he moves, *his* ass now on full display as he climbs onto the couch behind Raven. I take the barstool where he said to, and resume my position with my hands clasped behind my back.

River bites his lip as he looks between me and Raven. He brushes her hair from in front of her face, letting me see clearly as her gorgeous lips part while she takes him to the back of her throat.

"Holy mother of fuck. Your mouth is the wettest of wet dreams, little vixen." River groans, tossing his head back.

"Rub it in, why don't you," I mutter.

He pops one eye open, and the glare he shoots me makes my spine stiffen.

I watch, entranced, as Phoenix rubs his lube covered fingers between Rae's ass cheeks, imagining it's me back there. I practically hump the air as I move my hips, knowing it won't get me anything but frustrated.

"I'm going to go slow. I need you to breathe for me, Red." I can't see his fingers, but I can watch her face as she blows out a breath, coating River's dick in her drool when Phoenix makes his move. He coaxes her through every single movement, and by the time he says he's finally got his finger inside, River's clenching his fists on the couch, I'm squirming, and Phoenix looks like he's about to blow.

"Good girl, Red. Good fucking girl. You ready for me to move?"

She tries to pull her head off River's dick, but Phoenix holds her down. She sticks out a thumbs up, and we all chuckle at her expense, something she doesn't miss as she glares around the room at us.

"I'm going to stretch this tight little hole until you're squirming, and after that I'm going to reward your snark with my handprint all over your pretty cheeks." He leans down until his face is right next to hers. "How's that sound, sweetheart?"

CHAPTER TWENTY-ONE

raven

My face blanches when Phoenix smacks a loud kiss to my cheek and pulls away. I look up to meet River's gaze, and he grins, lacing his fingers through my hair, tugging until he has full control of my head.

"One for green. Two for yellow. Three for red." Phoenix moves his body fully behind mine now, his dick brushing against the back of my thighs. "Color, Raven. What's your color?" he asks.

I tap once for green.

"Good. Breathe for me," he coaches again. As he stretches my previously untouched hole, my mouth falls slack.

River shoves his dick further down my throat. I move my hands between us and grab his shaft, my tongue tracing every delicious line and ridge of him.

His groans spur Phoenix on.

"Holy shit," Pierce says after Phoenix lands a hard smack to my ass. "That was–"

"Just fine. Ask her. This is part of learning consent, too, Pierce. Ask her what color she is after that." Phoenix massages where his hand hit, and I move my hips back onto him. His finger digs deeper into me, and my eyes roll to the back of my head with the feeling.

"Ask her like a good boy, Pierce," River commands.

"Shit. Okay. What's your color, Rae?" Pierce stutters out nervously.

I tap once.

Phoenix smacks my other cheek, the sound echoing through the room as the burn sets in. He chuckles when I move back on his finger again, and lift my mouth off River's dick.

"Damn," Pierce whispers.

I look over and meet his gaze as I stroke River, taking the reprieve to breathe and watch my best friend struggle with life itself in that barstool.

This is not the same man who took advantage of me back in September.

I shoot him a wink when Phoenix spanks me again, and watch as Pierce's cock bobs against his stomach, painfully untouched. Turning my head, I look up at River, then nod toward Pierce.

"Do you want him to touch himself? Do you want him to watch as we fuck you again, with only his fist for company?" River grins when Phoenix lands another smack to my ass. "Are you hot and bothered down there, sweet girl? Or do you need yet another man panting for you?"

I huff out a breath, grinding back on Phoenix when he brings his free hand down to thrust a finger into my pussy.

"River asked you a question, Red. Better answer it," Phoenix commands, stilling.

"Well, my queen, do you want him to get off to his friends taking you again?" River asks.

I nod.

"Put my dick in your mouth and suck, then," he says. When I have him eagerly down my throat, he strokes my cheek before looking back at Pierce. "Dick in your hand like a good boy, but you can't come until I tell you to."

I hear Pierce groan in relief, and glance over to see him with his dick in his hand squeezing himself hard enough his knuckles turn white.

"Yes, sir," he grits out, his cheeks growing pink with a blush.

I squirm at their exchange. It's hot as hell and not a soul could tell me otherwise.

"She loves watching you two," Phoenix says as he shoves his finger into my pussy again, moving the other one inside of my ass in a slow motion. "She's soaking."

"You like watching me tell our good boy what to do, sweet girl?" River asks, stroking my cheek as I take him down my throat again. He groans when I lick his slit, tossing his head back. "Fuck."

Phoenix slowly pulls his fingers away from me, and I squirm, seeking the fullness he promised. He chuckles and lands a soft smack onto the junction of my thigh and ass. "Condom, Red."

"Keep sucking my dick, sweet girl. No one told you to

stop." River grips my hair in his hand tighter, pulling until my head is his to control once more. He lifts his hips while pushing me down, and I swallow around him, taking him further as I squeeze him. "You're so pretty with a dick down your throat, little vixen. Isn't she?" he asks Pierce.

"Prettiest I've ever seen her," Pierce grunts. He groans after a second, and River tenses beneath me.

"Shit," River breathes, stilling us both. He calls for Phoenix, but the couch moves behind me and River relaxes. "I cannot fucking hold on."

"Got it," Phoenix says. He places a hand on my ass, rubbing it softly. "Color?"

I tap once, meeting Pierce's gaze across the room. His hand moves so furiously, I wonder if it hurts, but his groans of pleasure spur me on and I squirm.

Phoenix says nothing, only spreads me open and shoves his dick inside of my pussy when his finger breaches my ass again. He groans, and lands a smack to my cheek with a guttural 'good girl' thrown in to fuck with me, I'm sure.

"I, oh fuck," Pierce moans, and I look over to see his hips stuttering.

"Hands off," River grits out.

Pierce obliges, and my pussy clenches tight around Phoenix.

"I swear I could die like this," Phoenix mutters, gripping my ass cheek with his free hand. He slowly adds another finger to my ass, and I clench. "Breathe, Red, breathe," he coos. "You're doing so fucking good. You've got a dick filling your mouth, one in your sweet cunt. I know you can take a third, we just gotta work you up to it." He thrusts into me, dragging himself along my inner walls deliciously until I'm grinding against him again.

The pressure of the second finger hardly phases me as he thrusts his dick into me and River pushes my head down over him.

I wish I'd thought to record this, because I'm sure I'm going to pass out and forget the whole thing.

"River, please," Pierce begs, and I meet his gaze, watching as he thrusts his hips into the air, searching for the same relief we all need.

"Sweet girl, we're all dying here," River grits out, thrusting his hips up until he hits the back of my throat again.

Phoenix reaches his hand around and rubs circles on my clit, his thrusts growing more forceful, frantic. His fingers explore me in places untouched, playing me just right as his dick throbs. He leans down, growls into my ear, and pinches my clit.

I explode like a firework, and the mutual sounds Pierce and River are making, mixed with the frantically rough thrusts from Phoenix prolong my orgasm.

They laugh as they release stuttered groans, pumping into me in different places, but in sync. Aftershocks wreck me, and Phoenix pulses inside of me.

He rubs my clit, and I shake my head, pulling off River's dick.

I cannot take another second.

With or without them.

I'm stuck in the middle of pleasure and pain.

It's intoxicating.

"Ask," Phoenix says.

"Wha–" Pierce whispers, then clears his throat. "Color, Rae?"

I should absolutely triple tap here. Instead, I reach up and tap once on Phoenix's shoulder.

His grin stretches across my skin as he bites down, rubbing my clit furiously.

River sits up and sticks two fingers directly inside of me without warning, and Phoenix speeds up.

I shake my head again and again as tears fall from my eyes, but inwardly I'm floating on cloud fucking nine.

"I want you to make a fucking mess all over us, Red," Phoenix commands.

River becomes rough as he thrusts another finger inside of me, stroking my g-spot. The sounds coming from my body are so lewd, I should be embarrassed. Instead, I clench around River's fingers. "You've got another in you, I can feel it," he says, leaning forward to suck one of my nipples into his mouth.

I shake my head again and Phoenix grips my chin, biting down onto my neck. My body tightens in his arms. "Let fucking go, Raven."

My body tenses further, impossibly so.

River's dirty chuckle reaches my ear. "Listen to the sound of you, sweet girl. Fucking deliciously dirty."

I flood his fingers, but still, I can't.

"Shut your brain up and fucking come for us," Phoenix growls with one last rub to my clit before he smacks it.

"Fuck yes," River groans, still slamming his fingers into me at an impossibly rapid pace.

My entire body freezes, and both Phoenix and River

continue to rub me all over, inside and out, until I nearly pass out.

"Breathe, baby, breathe," Pierce says from his perch on the stool.

Even with his panic, he still hasn't come near us. His own sweat and cum cover him, and his eyes are latched onto the filthy scene in front of him.

Still on that stool.

Still controlled.

Phoenix chuckles from behind me and places soft kisses to my neck. "Deep breaths. Slow, steady," he coaches.

I listen, and look down when River slides a towel under me.

He winks as I gape in horror at the mess I've made.

Did I... I don't know the sign language for squirt, so I hope they fill in the blanks.

"Twice," River says. He leans forward and kisses my lower stomach before climbing off the couch. He steps over to Pierce and leans down, kissing him slow and sensually for a moment. Pulling back, he pats him on the cheek. "Good boy. Go clean up."

Pierce hesitates, but does as he's told, nearly stopping when he passes right by me. He blows out a breath and signs *I love you, Blue* before stepping inside the downstairs bathroom.

The shower starts up less than a minute later, and I relax fully into Phoenix's arms as he stands and cradles me in them.

"Bath and snacks, then bed. If you didn't drink enough, you're bound to feel dehydrated soon." He nods in thanks to River who passes him a water bottle. "That was intense. Go check on him."

"Got it. Goodnight, sweet girl," River says before placing a soft kiss on my lips. He pauses, looking like he wants to say something else, but thinks better of it and walks toward the bathroom, scratching the back of his neck.

Phoenix runs a hot bath, then provides me with snacks and water. After, he coaxes my body to a dream state until I fall into a nightmare-less sleep for the first time in what feels like forever.

WHOEVER SAID women spies had to wear tight leather and knee-high boots should die a slow death, if they aren't already dead.

This clichéd fucking outfit is riding up my ass crack, and seeing as how I've been prepping more over the last few days, I'd prefer nothing down there at the moment.

Unless it's a dick.

But Phoenix says I'm absolutely not ready for that yet.

Keyword: yet.

I grin and bite my lip to hide it as I step into the living room, waving my arms at myself when I'm in the guys' line of sight.

"Sweet baby Jesus," Pierce says.

"More like Satan," River retorts.

I shake my head as I walk toward the kitchen and grab a snack.

I don't think I'll ever fully understand whatever it was about the other night that created this confidence in me.

The guys had me at their mercy, yet I knew I was the one with all the power, anyway.

Pierce invisibly tethered himself to that barstool. He could have rushed into the scene at any point, but he didn't. He also listened when anyone told him to do anything.

I meet those green eyes across the room as I take a bite of an apple.

"What?" he asks, raising a brow.

I shrug and take another bite before walking toward the couch and sitting down.

Phoenix comes into the room with a stack of paper, and sighs while running a hand through his hair. "He's added more security." He tosses the papers onto the coffee table, then sits down on the couch and leans back, shutting his eyes.

"They won't be there at fucking midnight, though," Pierce says.

"They're twenty-four seven," Phoenix replies.

"Fuck," Pierce and River say in unison.

I lean forward and look at the blueprints of the college, noting all of the new places set up with security now. We won't get in anywhere at this rate. Not without a distraction or...

Grabbing my phone, I type out a text to Lance, asking for him to come inside.

"Who'd you text, little bird?" Pierce asks, raising a brow.

Lance, I sign.

"For what?"

Help. I shrug and sit back against the couch, resting my head on Phoenix's shoulder.

Lance doesn't bother knocking, scaring the shit out of the guys when he enters through the back door. "Maxwell has security up on every fucking street corner. He's scared. I have a plan."

"Hello to you, too, dude," River says. "Next time, knock. You never know when—oof!" He rubs at the side Pierce punched.

"What's your plan, Lance?" Phoenix sits up, wrapping his arm around my shoulders.

"I called Trip. We'll have a crew on the south side of town create a diversion big enough to warrant all of Maxwell's attention." Lance shrugs when we all gape at him. "Hey, no one said I was stupid. I'm not the FBI or CIA, so I can do what I want."

"You're not cocky at all," Pierce says sarcastically.

"I want you to take my car tonight. I'll take your jeep. Less suspicious if you guys are seen downtown at midnight than at the college." Lance holds out his keys, and Phoenix reaches up to take them in his hand.

Pierce grumbles about not getting a single scratch on the thing before passing the jeep keys to Lance. He folds his arms and narrows his eyes. "You do good tonight, I might keep you on forever."

"Ah, so I should probably do bad, then. Got it." Lance slides a hand through his hair before spinning around and walking out of the loft. He pauses, turning his head to look over his shoulder, "Be safe. No telling what he'll do if you're caught."

"Can't be any worse than the New Year's Eve party," River says. "What? I'm not lying." He shrugs and walks toward the garage. "Let's get going."

"Sure we can't convince you to stay, Red?" Phoenix asks as he helps me into my leather jacket. He sighs when I shake my head, then slides his own on.

Honestly, we all look badass in our matching jackets and all black gear. The guys lead the way to Lance's Tesla, and River waggles his brows at me when he points out the illegally tinted windows. Once inside, River pulls me into his side with an arm around my shoulders and kisses my temple.

"Alright," Pierce says the second we leave Junk, "time to infiltrate the castle."

"WHAT THE FUCK?" Pierce whispers from the front seat. He leans forward to see through the windshield. "There's half a dozen guys on the campus gates. You fucking seeing this shit, Nix?"

"Yeah," Phoenix grits out. "I'm fucking seeing it."

"How do we get–" River tries to ask, but sirens sound all around us and lights begin to brighten up the night sky. "Nevermind. Guess that's how."

"Look how many of these motherfuckers are leaving," Pierce says.

"Radios on them, too. Damn, what is Maxwell involved in? Can't be just drugs with this much security." Phoenix leans back in the seat.

"He works with my father, don't forget that," River says.

We all look at him wide-eyed and he shrugs.

What does your father do, River? I sign.

"Can I tell you later, sweet girl? I'd rather not right now." He's lucky I like him.

I nod and look back out of the windows.

It takes roughly ten minutes for every single car, aside from ours, to leave the lot. Pierce pulls up to the closest parking spot, then kills the engine. Holding up a hand, he looks back at me, gaze boring into my soul. "You stay with one of us at all fucking times, do you understand me?"

I roll my eyes, but nod.

"Anyone loses her, and I'll castrate you," he warns. "Let's go."

We climb out of the car as quietly as possible, and River instantly takes my hand in his. Our feet crush the ice and snow beneath them. I tense, because this is not quiet. Thankfully, it seems no one else is around now.

We make our way toward the gates, and Phoenix produces a key from his pocket, unlocking the security door off to the side. When I meet his gaze, he shrugs. "Maxwell didn't put me under Pierce's ass for nothing."

Pierce enters first. He looks around for a few seconds before waving the rest of us in. It's dark except for a few of the lamp posts lining the main walkways of the court-yard. The shadows are where he keeps us, though.

Hidden. Quiet. Safe.

My heart pounds in my chest when we reach the admin building, and we all stop at the side, looking at the maintenance entrance.

Phoenix produces the same key as before and walks right up the steps, unlocking it. He pushes the door open slowly, then blows out a breath when he peers inside. "C'mon," he whispers, waving us in after him.

"After you, Rae," River whispers, making me jump. He chuckles quietly as he follows me, Pierce behind him.

"Lance turned off the cameras, right?" Phoenix asks, turning back to look at Pierce.

"Yeah. About fifteen minutes ago."

Phoenix nods and meets my eyes for a second. He takes a deep breath, stands to his full height, then walks toward Maxwell's office confidently.

As if we aren't breaking and entering into a lion's den.

"Don't be scared, Rae, we got you." River tosses his arm around my shoulders and tugs me close.

I shush him.

Pierce sidles up on his other side and peers around to look at me. "No one's here. Cameras are off. We're good."

"Better safe than sorry, though," Phoenix whispers from ahead of us.

Pierce flips him off and River and I struggle to hold in our laughter.

"I felt that, Jackson," Phoenix says.

"Oh no," Pierce deadpans.

River snickers and I hide my smile behind my hand.

Maxwell's office is locked up tight, but Phoenix produces half a dozen more skeleton keys from his pockets. He manages to open each of the locks, a cocky grin on his face when we pass him.

"I want to know how you got all of those," Pierce tells him.

"Some secrets are best kept to ourselves."

"Boys," River tries to sound gruff when he snaps, "play nice." He pats them both on the back before moving further into the office.

It's...unusually dark. Not a single light shines through the window, and as I take a step toward it, I brush my fingers along the blackout curtains.

What the hell is Maxwell hiding?

"Alright," Pierce says once he closes and locks the door again, "let's get to work."

pierce

Raven gets to work scouring the unlocked file cabinets, searching for anything incriminating. Her fingers move quickly through each folder, and her eyes shine under the dim light we turned on.

Everyone is wearing black latex gloves to protect ourselves further. Keeping our fingerprints out of this office is crucial to our survival.

Maxwell used to be viewed as just another drug selling asshole, but the more I see from him, the more I find out...he's involved in things I never thought really existed.

If he's working with River's dad...

I blow out a breath before sitting down in the leather chair at Maxwell's desk. Locks are on every one of these desk drawers, and I'm about to break them when Phoenix walks up to my side, palm held out. I grab the skeleton keys from him, and he steps back up to Raven's side, helping her look through the file cabinets again. I carefully unlock the drawers, finding absolutely nothing useful.

Until I reach the final drawer on the left and see a false bottom. "Light," I snap, and River steps over, shining his flashlight inside.

"Holy...what the fuck?" River leans down next to me and peers into the drawer. "The hell is that?"

"Disgusting, that's what. Shut your mouth," I whisper, snapping pictures with my phone and sending them directly to Starling. I send them to Lance too, for good measure. I delete them off my phone, then look up to see Phoenix and Raven going through a file with my stomach in knots.

"Pierce, we should—"

Anger rises to the surface and practically burns me alive. I slap my hand over River's mouth, tugging him down until we're both hidden behind the desk. "You do not tell them of this shit, do you understand? We have to leave everything."

River's eyes are wide, and his face is turning red with his own anger.

"Do you understand me, Jacobs?" I ask again.

He nods, taking a deep breath when I release his mouth. "Fuck. What's he planning to do with those?" he whispers.

"Right now, we need to find more on him and Alpha Mu, then get the fuck out of here. The time for wondering about shit is not now." I fix the false bottom of the drawer and close it. Standing, I fold my arms across my chest, thoughts stuck in the drawer as much as the pictures are.

"Check the bookshelves?" River asks, standing and adjusting his own clothing with shaking hands.

I nod and turn toward one wall, indicating he should move to the other. Maxwell has a lot of books for someone who spends more time creating sick history than reading about it.

Hopefully, we're the reason his book ends on a cliffhanger–maybe literally.

A grin stretches my face. Yeah, that'd be a nice way to take him out.

"Found anything yet?" Phoenix asks as he walks toward me.

I shake my head. "No. You?"

He narrows his eyes, then sighs and runs his hand through his hair, cursing when it messes up the bun on his head. "No. Feel like we've walked into a black abyss with how devoid of shit this room is."

"Strange he doesn't have a computer in here, right?" I ask, turning around and leaning my back against the wall.

"Mmm, yeah. He carries his laptop bag with him everywhere, so I'm assuming that's his only computer."

"Uhh, guys," River calls. He turns, an open box in his hand. "You might want to look through these." He steps toward the desk and sets the box down carefully. Shifting his panicked eyes to meet mine, he says, "We're so incredibly fucked."

I sit back down in Maxwell's chair and begin sifting through the immense amount of files, hoping like hell the pictures we're taking for Agent Starling are clear enough.

On second thought...

"Grab the box," I tell River.

"Pierce—" Phoenix says, but I hold a hand up to stop him.

"We'll get better pictures at Junk. Make copies. Scan them. I don't care. This is too much information to get blurry pictures of." I stand and begin tidying everything else up. "Where's the bag?"

Raven holds out the messenger bag I'd told her to bring just in case, and I grab the files, putting them inside.

"We'll leave the box."

"What happens if Maxwell finds it empty?" Phoenix asks.

A valid question.

One I don't have the answer to.

I shrug and meet his gaze. "A risk we'll have to take to take him down, yeah?"

He rolls his eyes, then grabs some files in his own hands.

We make quick work of emptying the box, and River puts it back in its place right as I receive a text from Lance.

LANCE

Get out. Now. Five minutes.

"Shit," I mutter. "We gotta go. Move, move, move!" I nearly grab Raven in my haste, but hold myself back.

Her panicked eyes fill with tears, and River wraps an arm around her shoulders.

"It'll be okay, little bird," I tell her as I move past them, aching to be her comfort zone again. "Out the same way we came in. Directly into the vehicle. River?"

"Yeah?"

I meet his eyes and my heart hammers harder in my

chest. "Do not let go of her." I wait until he nods his head once before turning back toward the hall and rushing through the dark.

Our combined heavy breathing echoes louder in the pitch black as our senses fuck with us, and though I'm certain no one is here yet, I swear I see the curtains shift outside.

"The fuck was that?" Phoenix whispers when he makes it to my side after locking the door back up. His chest heaves with his heavy breaths.

"I don't know, but we need to fucking move," I tell him.

He nods, and we barely make it outside into the cold air again before footsteps sound in the hallway behind the other two. The loud clanging of the maintenance door closing signals our exit, and I cringe.

"Shit. Run," I command them, waiting until River and Raven take off before following.

We retrace our steps, and I roll my eyes at our stupidity for not covering our tracks earlier.

No wonder someone followed us; we showed them the way.

The cold winter air bites into my face, and as thick snowflakes fall, I have to squint my eyes to see anything.

The other three bolt through the open security door, and I follow before closing it. I'll have a second to think about why it was wide open later.

"In the fucking car," I yell when headlights shine from the street.

River looks back over his shoulder at me for a second, eyes wide with panic.

"Get in the fucking car," I shout again when they take too damn long.

Cars rush the parking lot when River opens the back door, practically throwing Raven in.

A voice calls out for us to stop right when Phoenix enters the passenger side.

Floodlights turn on me at the same moment I jump in the driver's seat.

Guns raise in our direction when I switch the car on.

River yells for me to duck before I floor it.

A gunshot slices through the air in front of Phoenix's face and mine, far too fucking close, just as I exit the parking lot.

My ears ring in the silence as I drive onto the highway, weaving through traffic recklessly. I don't stay in one lane for too long, taking up empty spaces between cars constantly for more than an hour. I don't dare look in the rearview mirror until I'm sure I've lost every single fucker back there.

After about two hours of driving, when the clock on the dash flips to three in the morning, I finally relax against the seat and turn us back toward Junk.

The streets are barren at this point, and the silence is so tense, so full of emotion... I crack.

A loud, boisterous laugh falls from my lips, and I toss my head back, making sure to keep my eyes firmly on the newly salted road.

Phoenix stares at me like I've lost my mind, and maybe I have.

Raven's eyes briefly meet mine in the rearview mirror, and she bursts into silent laughter, too.

"You've lost it," River says, but now he's laughing with us.

Phoenix blows out a heavy breath, glaring around at us all, but I don't miss the small twitch of his lips as the laughter echoes in the cab.

"YOU DID GOOD, KID," Agent Starling says. He pats me on the back as he passes by my perch on the stool.

"Anything useful?" I ask around a mouthful of cereal. I was craving cocoa puffs, and I may have found the box stashed behind some chocolates. With enough left for one more bowl.

Pierce–1.

Raven–...a lot more.

He nods his head a few times, twisting his mustache between his fingers. "Enough to get the frat house shut down for sure. Years of bad deeds are documented in there. As far as the blackmail goes? It'll take us a while to get through the legitimacy of the claims in there."

"Not to mention getting agents to watch the video files on those USBs," Lance supplies from my side. He takes a sip of coffee, meeting my eyes. "The frat will go down hard. We'll work on setting up a sting. Give you a date to cut and run."

Starling hums his agreement, then stands up straight and looks around at us all like a proud dad. "You kids are saving others by doing this. It may not seem worth all the trouble, but when you're old and gray and got kids of your own?" He grins. "You'll be proud as hell of yourselves."

"Need a hand with anything before you leave, Walter?" Lance asks.

"Nah. I'll give you a call when we come up with a good day to take 'em down." They shake hands before Agent Starling leaves.

"Anti-Valentine's Day," Phoenix calls out.

"Pardon?" Starling asks, pausing in the doorway.

"The Anti-Valentine's Day party. Held on the day of, goes well into the night." Phoenix meets my eyes and I nod. "Everyone gets drunk, and it ends up as a massive non-consensual orgy." He cringes and wipes a hand over his face.

"Did you boys participate?" Agent Starling asks.

All three of us shake our heads.

"No, sir," I tell him, meeting his gaze, hoping like hell he can see the truth in my eyes. "We made up some bull-shit excuse to the last president and his VPs."

"Yeah, we were sick," River says, then laughs awkwardly.

"You better be telling the truth. I know you mean the best here, boys, but I will not let you off for sexual assault. Do you hear me? Enough fuckers get by with a slap on the wrist for that shit."

I look across the room and meet Raven's gaze. *I'm sorry* I sign to her, and she nods before diving back into her book. I hope she never forgives me for it, but I also hope she lets me cherish her for the rest of our lives to fill the hole I made when I hurt her.

"Alright." Agent Starling turns back toward the door

and steps out, calling over his shoulder, "Plan a good night or two for your girl. Get the hell outta dodge, you hear me?"

"Yes, sir," River, Phoenix, and I say in unison.

"Well then," Lance says as he stands. He stretches his arms over his head as he walks toward the door. "I'll let him out and close up. Got a few guys taking my place so I can go get my car fixed." He waves at us all, and I chuckle when I hear him grumble about 'cheap-ass mechanics and their fake bullet proof glass'.

Trip must not pay enough for the good shit yet.

"Let's get some sleep." Phoenix says.

TO: UPINFLAMES@MYEMAIL.COM
FROM: RMHILL@MYEMAIL.COM
SUBJECT: FUCK

I'm convinced the world is out to fucking get me at this point, Flames.

Yeah, I'm dramatic today.

Mary took me into her office today and gave me another lecture about trying harder to speak.

Does she even have a medical degree?

I'm convinced she only has a degree in The Fucking Audacity.

Hope she's in eternal debt for that one, tbh.

If I ever get out of here, I feel like I'll be walking into a world that doesn't need/want me.

Does that make sense?

Ugh. I've made decisions I regret, Flames.

Even if I did go to CU, my ex best friend is there and I know for a fact he can come up with ruthless revenge plans.

Karma's such a bitch.

Anyway...

QOTD: What's waiting for us out there, Flames?

Till next time,

RM Hill

raven

Icy air hits my overheated skin, and I sit up, gasping at the audacity of the cold to be...cold.

I need more sleep.

I open my eyes to see all three of my men staring at me with amused expressions.

"Morning, sweet girl," River says. He's holding the blanket, a guilty look on his face.

Ah, so he's the one who froze me half to death in my sleep.

"Brought your morning goods," Pierce says, handing over my mug of hot cocoa.

I smile gratefully up at him before I take a sip, closing my eyes. The chocolate coats my tongue and the warmth soothes my throat.

"Red, we wanted to talk to you about a few things," Phoenix says, tone cautious.

Taking another sip of hot cocoa, I think about the reason these three would want to discuss important things this early in the morning. I swallow my drink and sigh before opening my eyes again. With my free hand, I wave for them to continue.

"We wanted to take you on a date," Pierce says, and my eyes snap to meet his. Red stains his cheeks, and I bite the inside of mine to keep from smiling.

"Ask," Phoenix orders.

Pierce groans and rolls his eyes, earning a smack to the head by River, who only grins in response to the glare he gets. "Raven, will you please go on a date with us tomorrow? We'll go wherever you want, but we kind of had an idea in mind already. If you're up for it, that is." He scratches the back of his neck and looks between the other two, as if seeking their approval.

"See? Her eyes are lit up, and she's blushing. Much better than her reaction to you telling her." River wraps his arm around Pierce's shoulders and smacks an obnoxious kiss to his cheek. "He can learn, ladies and gentlemen!"

"Get off me," Pierce grumbles, shrugging his shoulders until River's forced to let him go.

I take another sip of my hot cocoa, then set my mug down on the nightstand. Lifting my hands, I sign *I'd love to go on a date with you all. Does this make us boyfriends and girlfriend?* I widen my eyes, press a hand to my heart, and drop my jaw open dramatically.

"You're ridiculous," Phoenix says. When River and Pierce laugh at my antics, he points around the room. "You're all ridiculous."

"But you love us for it, Nixy boy!" River yells at his back as he descends the stairs.

Phoenix waves his hand. "The things I do for love," he calls back.

My heart lurches in my chest.

Did he mean that?

Would I mean it back?

Am I in love with all three of them?

I meet Pierce's gaze, then River's.

Maybe, just maybe, I really am.

My phone buzzes with an incoming text and I reach over to pick it up. When I see who the text is from, I look up and meet River and Pierce's gazes. *Maxwell* I sign.

They both rush to sit on the bed, Pierce on the end, River between us, as I open the text.

MR. LANGSTON

I see you've taken certain liberties in my office, Ms. Hill.

MR. LANGSTON

I'll give you until tomorrow morning to return my things.

MR. LANGSTON

This will have to be reported to the police, of course, but I won't press charges if you do as I ask.

I take a deep breath as the texts continue to come in at rapid fire. Maxwell's becoming unhinged before my eyes.

MR. LANGSTON

If you come work with me like a good daughter would.

MR. LANGSTON

Yes, I know they told you, darling.

MR. LANGSTON

Come work with me, carry my name on by marrying Jimmy. He's got my last name as of last week. He'll be good to you, I've demanded it of him.

MR. LANGSTON

Keeping things in the family will strengthen our blood going forward, too.

MR. LANGSTON

If you ditch the boys you've been dirtying yourself up with, I'll keep all charges to myself and not press a single one.

MR. LANGSTON

Make a choice soon, dear daughter.

I start hyperventilating, and River pulls me into his arms, rocking me back and forth while running a hand through my hair.

"Shh, it's going to be okay," he whispers.

"I'm going to kill him," Pierce growls as he stands to his feet. He marches toward the stairs, then turns back to meet my gaze. "We'll take the files back tonight. Get a bath or something. Bring your phone down after and we'll tell Lance about this shit." He disappears down the stairs and I sink further into River's hold.

"Breathe. Don't hold it in. Breathe," River croons. "You're here with us. We have a ton of security. You won't have to do anything you don't want to, sweet girl. We've got you, I promise."

I nod, but his words slide right over me.

As the catalyst for all of our problems, I'm beginning to wonder if I shouldn't do as Maxwell asks.

Jimmy's already had his hands on me, so it'd be nothing new, anyway.

"Do you want help with your bath, sweet girl?" River asks. He leans his head against the top of mine and breathes deep, coaxing me unconsciously to do the same.

After a moment, I nod. Numbness fills my body as I step into the bathroom. If I can do what Maxwell wants, Pierce and the guys will be safe, and that would make me happier than seeing them suffer in prison. Maybe all those years learning how to dissociate and not feel anything were lessons for the rest of my life.

Maybe I was supposed to be a tool in the end.

Not everyone has a larger purpose in life, right?

River slinks into the bathroom and shuts the door, drawing me from my thoughts as he strips. His abs are so defined lately. When the hell is he finding time to work out? The button on his jeans pops open, then he shucks his pants and underwear off. He winks at me when he catches me simply ogling him like I don't have anything better to do.

Maybe I don't.

"You gonna get naked, little vixen, or do I have to do it to you myself?"

I look up to meet his eyes, and my cheeks burn. I don't respond.

"Can I touch you?" he asks.

My hair falls in my face as I nod.

He chuckles, and the sound sends electricity through

my body. His dick hardens as he comes closer to me, and I struggle to keep from staring. He slides his finger beneath my chin and lifts my head up. Slowly moving his mouth toward mine, he whispers, "Can I kiss you?"

I should honestly tell these men they don't have to ask for simple things anymore, because I trust them and at this point they can throw me against a wall for all I care. The reality is, however, that I get an immense sense of power with every piece of consent they ask for, and I may make them seek it forever.

"Can I?" he whispers again, pulling back a few inches.

I lick my lips and nod, my eyes dropping to his mouth before he threads his fingers through my hair and crashes into me. My lips part on instinct, inviting his tongue in to tangle with my own.

He groans, tightens his hand in my hair, and squeezes my ass cheek with the other, pulling me into him. I regret still being clothed when the hard ridge of his cock grazes my center.

My hands slide up his biceps and I squeeze, bringing his tongue further into my mouth and sucking on it.

He bands his arm around my waist and pulls me up to sit on the counter, not breaking a single second of our kiss. My scalp tingles when he releases it, using both hands to take my leggings and underwear off me, tossing them to the side with his own clothes. He takes off my shirt and bra, tossing them to the floor, too. He brackets my face with his hands to tilt my head where he wants it, leans in, and fucks my mouth with his tongue, hardly breathing.

My heart hammers in my chest as I wrap my legs around his waist, pulling him closer.

The head of his dick barely breaches my entrance before he moves his hips back, and kisses me for a few more seconds. He groans in frustration when he pulls away. "Little vixen, I swear you'll be the death of us all. We need to take a bath, not fuck. Especially without a condom." He blows out a heavy breath, contradicting the smile on his face as he pokes my nose.

I gape at him, rubbing my thighs together as I watch his delectable ass when he walks away. Tossing my head back, I look up at the skylight and try to steady my breathing as I study the snow that has fallen, preventing the sun from shining into the bathroom like it usually does.

"Ready?" River asks, and I look back down to see him standing at the edge of the tub with a hand held out for me.

Hopping off the counter, I sway my hips as I walk toward him. I slide my palm along his slowly, looking up at him through my lashes.

"This is why I call you a vixen," he says. He chuckles and helps me into the steaming water, wincing at the heat. "You and Phoenix want to melt in here, don't you?"

I shrug before sliding inside of the tub, exhaling a relieved breath when the only thing I can feel or focus on is the heat encasing me. Strawberry soda scented bubbles surround me, floating along the top of the water, and when River flicks off the lights, candles cast the room in a romantic glow.

He slides in behind me, bracketing me with his legs

before pulling me into him, his dick settled against my lower back.

My favorite place to be is between the thighs of these men, knowing they're hard for me and unable to do a damn thing about it without my approval.

I smile wickedly and close my eyes, letting my body relax against River as my head rests on his shoulder.

A comfortable silence envelops us as the water caresses our bodies, coaxing us into relaxing for the first time in days. Our breathing is the only sound in the room, and I remain still. Existing. Unthinking.

My favorite place.

River breaks the silence by sliding his hands up my arms, water sloshing as he rubs my shoulders and neck. The calluses on his palms create delicious friction along my skin, drawing goosebumps to the surface.

My head rolls forward when he pushes me to sit up, and my nipples pebble when his hand caresses my spine. I clench my thighs together when his breath hits the back of my neck; dig my nails into his knee when he places a kiss on my skin.

"Does he touch you in here?" River whispers. "Phoenix. Does he get you relaxed," he pulls me back against him again, drawing one of his hands around to collar my throat, tugging my head back against his shoulder, "then touch you until you're a mess all over again?" Trailing his free hand down between my thighs, he pushes one of my legs until I'm forced to lay it over his. He runs a finger through my folds. "Answer me, little vixen."

I nod my head, because Phoenix does touch me in here sometimes. Most times.

"He's a shifty fucker." He chuckles when I tense. "It's fine, Rae. He takes care of you, and that's all I care about." He pushes my other leg over his, spreading me farther apart for him, then hums against my neck. "We all want to take care of you, however we can. Whether that's holding you," he kisses my neck, "kissing you," he plunges two fingers inside of me, "fucking you."

He stills for a second, holding my throat tighter when I try to move my head. "But," he whispers, "we also want to make sure you're safe. We're all in this for the long haul, Raven, and if you think for a second we're going to let you get away from us to take Maxwell's deal?" He laughs and bites down on my shoulder. My hips surge upward from the sweet pain I'm always searching for. "Don't entertain it. We'll follow you to the depths of hell and back, Raven. Don't think we won't. Prison doesn't scare any of us." He tightens his hold on my throat impossibly, until he's nearly cutting off my airway. "You don't get to sacrifice yourself."

Tears prick at my eyes, and I shake my head. Pulling my hands from the water, I sign *I'm not worth it.*

A frustrated growl leaves River's throat, and he thrusts his fingers into my needy cunt roughly, his palm barely brushing my clit before he pulls back again. And again. And again. "You're worth every goddamn beating we've ever taken in this life." He squeezes my throat, using his thumb to tilt my head to his. He stills his fingers inside of me, rubbing them along my g-spot until I'm squirming, making the water slosh everywhere around us. "You're worth it, Raven."

Tears fall, and I shake my head, because no, I'm not.

"Tell me you're worth it. There is no argument. You are." He thrusts his fingers into me violently again, and the tears continue to fall as he glares down at me, frustration and exhaustion lining his features. "Tell me you're worth it, Raven."

I exhale heavily, thrusting my hips into nothing when he removes his hand from me. Gasping, I grab at his wrist, but he stops me.

"No!" he shouts, startling me. "Tell me you're fucking worth it!"

"Hey!" Phoenix yells through the door. "What the fuck are you yelling at her like that for?" he asks.

River freezes, body tensing beneath me. "I think the guys deserve to weigh in on this conversation, too." His eyes track the movement of my throat as I swallow nervously, still unable to move my head with the grip he has on my jaw.

"River!" Phoenix shouts again, his voice echoing now that the room is silent.

River chuckles while sliding his hands along my body, away from where I want him. "I think it'll be the best way to show you how much you're worth it to us, little vixen."

My heart skips a beat as he speaks, and I lick my lips. Cold air slices across my skin as we get up, until we're both standing naked and dripping water.

He grabs a towel and wraps it around his waist. His movements are stiff but purposeful when he grabs another to dry me off with, not fully, though. He only pats me down until I'm no longer dripping.

With water, at least.

I'm absolutely dripping in other ways. He lifts me into

his arms, opens the door to a furious Phoenix, and shoves past him, only to deposit me onto the bed as if I'm nothing but a rag doll.

"River?" Phoenix asks sternly, but I don't miss the flash of lust in his eyes as they rake across my naked body.

"What the fu—" Pierce appears at the top of the stairs, the same angry look on his face as Phoenix. He clears his throat when he sees me laying there, then turns to walk downstairs.

"Hold up," River calls to him.

Pierce freezes, looks back over his shoulder, pain clear in his eyes. "Riv, I can't. Not right now, man."

"We're teaching Rae something right now. Need you for it." River walks over to him, turns him by the shoulders, escorting him to the end of the bed.

All I see are his green eyes, and I lose myself. I'm unable to move a muscle as I take in the lust and love and pain and longing. For me.

Every single one of these men are here for me.

But I'm not worth the trouble.

"What thought just crossed your mind, little vixen?" River says as he moves to the left side of the bed, effectively boxing me in with Pierce at the end and Phoenix on the right. "What made you curl into yourself? Hide your body from us?" He tugs the blanket out of my hands.

I didn't even notice I grabbed it.

I shake my head. I don't want to tell him.

"Red," Phoenix says, drawing my nickname out in a warning tone.

Again, I shake my head.

"She wants to toss herself to the wolves for our sake. She doesn't think she's worth the trouble we put up with for her." River scoffs, tossing the blanket onto the ground, followed by his towel. He raises a brow at me when I gawk at his erection. "Does this look like too much trouble, vixen?" His hands wrap around the head of his dick and I'm immobile.

Frozen as I watch him jerk himself with slow, smooth, forceful movements.

"Riv," Pierce whispers, his eyes shifting between me and River.

"I think she needs to know exactly who she owns. Because she sure as shit owns me." River looks up at Pierce, not stopping as he continues to stroke himself. "Boys?"

Pierce nods his head, blows out a breath, and in seconds, his dick is in his hand. He strokes it, and I squeeze my thighs together.

Phoenix traps a knee in his hand, and River does the same.

They pull my legs apart until I can't go anywhere.

"You can't escape us, Raven," Phoenix says. His eyes rake across my body, lingering between my thighs. A long groan leaves him, and it only gets me wetter. "Stay," he tells me as he pulls back. He takes his dick out, and my mouth waters.

Why is this so important? I sign.

"Because," River grits out, stroking his fingers up my thigh until he can cup me in one hand. I try to buck against him, but he pushes me into the bed. "You, our dear sweet Raven, are our queen. If a queen doesn't know how much she's worth, her kingdom is sure to crumble beneath her."

Phoenix slides his hand across my skin again, and I meet his gaze. "You're everything we need, Red. Everything." He scores his nails along the inside of my thigh and groans.

I look down to see him stroking himself like the others. I need one of them, or all three of them, to fuck me right now. Truly, I don't think I've ever been this turned on in my life. At their mercy, while also in control. An object but one so cherished they want to keep me hidden away on a shelf. Safe.

"Tell us you're worth it, Raven," River says, stilling. "Tell us you're worth it, and watch as we crumble beneath you. Because while you're worth everything, we are not worthy of you. Yet you're here with us, showing us how we're worth it."

"You've always made me feel worth a damn, little bird," Pierce says softly. I meet his gaze before looking down to see him stroking his dick in slow, measured movements. "I should have made you feel worth the world. I'm sorry I haven't."

"If you can make our ragtag little group of outliers feel worthy of you, Red," Phoenix tosses his head back and groans as he twists his hand over the end of his dick.

I try to touch myself, but Phoenix and River release their dicks and grab my wrists at the same time to hold me down. Pierce's eyes burn into me and I let out a heavy breath.

"If you can make us feel worthy of you," Pierce says,

frozen as he watches everyone touch me but him, "you have to know how worthy you are of everything."

I look around at them all, meeting their gazes and taking in the sincerity I see.

Reflections of a beautiful, albeit sexually frustrated, confident woman shine in their eyes, their words. A woman who deserves more than she's let herself have.

My heart beats hard in my chest, and I take a deep breath before nodding once, a tear trailing down the side of my face.

Phoenix shoves his thick fingers inside of me, thrusting them roughly. Stroking me faster.

River leans in and crashes his mouth to mine. He bites my lower lip, and when I gasp, he pulls my tongue inside of his mouth and sucks, hard. My eyes flare wide, and my pussy clenches.

Pierce groans, and I meet his eyes, losing myself in the dark and lust inside of them as he takes me and the guys in. He thrusts into his hand, fucking it like he used to fuck me, and the thought makes me clench around Phoenix again.

"Dirty, Red," Phoenix chastises. He releases my wrist and strokes himself in time with his fingers. "You're dirty, beautiful, filthy, fucking worthy of everything."

River pulls back and bites at my earlobe, groaning in my ear. My breath gets caught in my throat. "I want you to come for us, Raven. Not because we're telling you to, but because you fucking deserve it." He massages my breasts with his free hand, tweaking my nipples until they're hard peaks, then leans down to suck at them.

My hips buck against Phoenix's hand, but he pushes

down, thrusting his fingers so fast I can hear the wet noises my cunt is making. I toss my head back and gasp, meeting Pierce's gaze as his two friends play my body in such beautiful synchronicity.

"Come for us, little bird," Pierce groans, fucking his own fist faster, harder, hips bucking, thighs trembling as he holds himself back.

River's jacking off much the same, and he leans into my ear. "Come so hard you see stars, because you're worth the trip to space to bring you back down."

Phoenix releases himself to bring his other hand in, pinching my clit between his fingers and rolling it.

I still.

He strokes that sweet spot inside of me.

My back arches.

River sucks my nipple into his mouth and groans.

White sparks overtake my vision, and it becomes hard to catch a single breath. The euphoria these boys bring to my body makes me wonder if breathing is really necessary.

Phoenix pulls his hand from my clit, still thrusting his fingers into me, and stroking himself in earnest.

As my vision fades in and out, I watch as all three of these men, not without their faults, jack themselves off to the sight of me.

They each come, hard, the white spurts landing all over my body and coating me in warmth I never knew I'd find so hot, so beautiful, so...telling.

Pierce sits on the end of the bed, the ache to touch me so evident in his features it hurts me.

River leans in and kisses me.

Phoenix follows with the same.

After yet another bath, Pierce is downstairs on the couch and Phoenix is in the kitchen making me a post-orgasm snack. River sits behind me, my back to his chest as he rubs his hands all over my aching body, his fingers running through my newly wet hair. He whispers words of love, praise, worth.

I lift my hands and sign *I'm worth it.*

His lips tilt up against my skin, and he lets out a happy sigh. "You're worth everything to me, Raven. To Phoenix. To Pierce. You're the sun we revolve around, and without you, we'd float around in nothingness."

I let his words sink into my soul, finally believing them, if for just this moment, and slip into a deep sleep.

phoenix

After last night's debacle with Maxwell, we showed the text messages to Lance, who then conferenced Trip in from wherever in the world he was at the moment.

He told us to replace the files immediately, safely, and to stay off campus until the foreseeable future. Which, of course, Pierce argued with.

River groans and leans back on the couch, running a hand across his stomach. "Fuck, that was too much."

Pierce rolls his eyes and stands up, taking everyone's dishes with him toward the kitchen. "It was just a bowl of hash browns and veggies, chill."

Raven perks up from her book, peering over the back of the couch at Pierce before looking at me and River. *He's humble now?*

We all laugh.

Except Pierce, who's washing the dishes.

It's like the fucking twilight zone in here.

I woke up to him cleaning and making breakfast for everyone. He set it all out and said he had everything this morning. Either he's distracting himself, or trying to grovel more. Earn his way back into Raven's good graces. I'm surprised he's carned mine, but I've seen the work he's done. In and out of the bedroom.

Pierce's phone pings on the coffee table.

River shoots forward to grab it. He looks up at me, then back at Pierce. "You guys have thirty minutes. Lance and Trip have Maxwell distracted off campus again."

"Shit," I mutter. I stand, quickly place a kiss on Raven's forehead, and head toward the door to put my winter gear on.

"Wanna take the bikes?" Pierce asks from my side as he puts his own stuff on.

"Not with that ice on the ground, no. Let's just take the jeep," I say. "Maxwell knows it's us anyway."

Pierce shrugs as he grabs the keys to the jeep, then pauses in the doorway. "Hey, Blue?" She turns to see him and tilts her head in question. *I love you. Be back soon. Promise*, he signs.

River and I both look away from their moment the second tears threaten her pretty eyes.

Their connection has strengthened over the last few days, and River and I have made a bet on whether or not she allows him to touch her again by Valentine's Day or spring break. River says the former, while I say she won't let him touch her until far into our break.

He doesn't deserve shit, but she loves him despite it all.

Kinda beautiful, honestly.

Before I get in the jeep, I unlock a metal toolbox in the corner and bring out two handguns. I check them over for a second, grab a few extra rounds for each, then hop into the jeep and hand one to Pierce. When his eyes widen as he meets my gaze, I sigh. "It's not smart to keep going on this path without protection. Let's go. You promised her you'd be back."

"I–"

I hold up a hand and point forward. "Let's just go, yeah?" I lean back in the seat when he nods, thoughts of not returning circling in my brain the entire way to campus.

"It's...too quiet," Pierce says as we crest over the hill into the parking lot. "Too still."

I don't say anything. I simply nod and get out of the jeep, stuffing the gun into the back of my jeans.

"Nix?" he asks, catching up to me.

"Hmm?" I pull on black latex gloves. They know it's us, but I refuse to give them solid proof.

"You're...extra quiet and broody."

"Good observation." I unlock the security door next to the gate again, then push it open and walk through it.

Pierce grumbles something I can't hear as he moves beside me, our feet getting lost in the snow. He looks up toward the building when we make it within ten feet, sighs, and tosses his head back.

"What?" I ask, pulling the skeleton keys out of my pocket to unlock the maintenance door. I push it open slowly, checking if any lights are on. When I find none, I step inside and fist the keys tightly to keep them from clanging together.

Pierce closes the door and walks beside me. He says nothing until we're back at Maxwell's office. "Honestly, Nix, I don't know how many meetings I've had with Maxwell in this building. I listened to him go on and on about his daughter and his evil sister. Like he isn't some evil motherfucker to begin with?" He runs a hand through his hair and follows me inside when I have the door opened.

I point toward the bag on his side as I walk to the bookshelf and grab the box. "You're young, impressionable. Moldable. He used you, and it sucks."

Silence stretches and echoes around the room as we fill the box quickly.

"I also wanted revenge on the one person who only wanted the best for me," he says.

I look up to meet his gaze and raise a brow as I close the box. "Raven?" I ask.

He nods. "Yeah. I was so fucking hurt, man."

"I don't want to hear your excuses for being a shitty human, Jackson. You're doing better, so keep it that way." I put the box back up on the shelf and turn around, surveying the room to make sure we didn't touch anything.

"Nix, I–"

"The fuck is that?" I snap out, walking toward the desk.

File folder upon file folder, pictures upon pictures. All strewn across as if Maxwell was manic and in a hurry. On the top of the pile is a photo of an older man, maybe a year or two older than Maxwell. His hair is graying considerably, and his eyes look panicked.

"Who the hell is this?" Pierce asks, leaning over the desk next to me. He shuffles a few papers around, stupidly, and reads some of the information as I try to place this dude.

"Wait," I say, grabbing Pierce's wrist to stop him from moving the next paper away.

There's an address and a note scribbled hastily.

"Mark Riley?" Pierce asks, turning his head to look at me. "Who the fuck is that?"

I run a hand through my hair and stand straight up. "Take a picture. Get the address." Before I turn, something else catches my eye and I pull it up.

A Cobalt University Science Club Picture from Maxwell's junior year.

Maxwell Langston. Whitaker Sommers. Robert Jacobs. Chloe Jackson. Mark Riley.

There's a few other names, but we're running out of time, so I take a picture and place the original back down on the desk. While Pierce puts the papers away, I fold my arms and look around. What the fuck were they trying to accomplish?

"Hey, Nix," Pierce says warily. I turn my head toward him. He's holding up the note with Mark Riley's name and address on it.

I'm about to tell him to put it back again, but he turns it over to another note scrawled across it. This one more ominous.

Find him.

I meet Pierce's gaze and grit my teeth before turning

toward the door. "We need to get the living fuck out of here."

He nods, fixing the rest of the desk back up.

It's as I'm looking around the room that I find a piece of something sticking out of a crooked picture frame. I take it off the wall and remove the backing before pulling out the loose paper. When I rotate it, blueprints are drawn all over the back. I read it, and the more I see, the more my heart begins pounding in my chest.

"Pierce," I snap.

He comes to my side, and I know the second he's finished reading what's plain as day on this paper. His shoulders tense, and he fists his hand hard enough his knuckles turn white. "What the fuck?" he grits out slowly, struggling to maintain his composure.

"He's going to inject every student here with a concentrated version of Rapture," I say, voice devoid of emotion. I take as many clear pictures of this plan as I can. "He's going to get everyone addicted to his drug, to the school, to him. He'll have all the power."

"He'll also murder a ton of innocents in the process," Pierce growls. He whips his own phone out and videos the paperwork, making sure to zoom in on the parts with dates and important names and numbers.

We're silent as we place the paper inside the frame and set it back on the wall. Only the sound of our footsteps and breathing accompany us out of the admin building, thoughts louder now more than ever. We're able to step through the security gate and across the parking lot with ease.

Not a single car is in sight, not a person, not a gun.

It's solely us on a deserted campus and our panicked thoughts about Maxwell Langston, his plans, and who the fuck is Mark Riley?

SILENCE STRETCHES AROUND ME, *blood rushes loudly in my ears, and my heart thuds painfully in my chest.*

I can't see. Can't speak.

I'm immobile.

It's intoxicating and horrifying.

"Silence," Ruby says from beside me, chuckling when I flinch. "Silence can be a useful tool when you're in a scene. Take away a sense or two," she taps the gag in my mouth, before stroking the blindfold wrapped around my eyes, "and your submissive tunes in." Her hot breath fans across my ear as she leans in and whispers, "They listen closer." She wraps a hand around my cock and I toss my head back and groan, "Touch them, and their feelings are heightened. Every single touch," she squeezes the tip before releasing me, and I weep right alongside my dick, "is ten fold."

I listen as her footsteps grow quieter, disappear. Tilting my head this way and that, I try to get a gauge on where she's at, only to startle when I feel her in front of me, her hands on me again.

Her dirty chuckle makes my toes curl. I love when she fucks with me in new ways. "Deprivation of all sorts is useful. You can't speak, so your body is forced to do it for you."

I groan when she puts a ring over my shaft, sliding it to the base. She presses a button, and low vibrations travel from the base up to the head of my dick, my whole body shuddering in response.

"Your cock is begging, Phoenix," she whispers in my ear. She playfully tugs at my balls. "Your balls are heavy." She licks a long line up my neck and I moan around the gag in my mouth. "You're sweating."

I try to beg through the gag, but all I manage is to force drool down my chest.

"Deprivation can teach you many things about a person. If you allow yourself, you can take a step back and learn a lot about a person by their body language." I buck my hips into her hand when she turns the vibrations up, my dick hardening impossibly. "If you want to take care of your submissive, however, you need to know exactly when to give them reprieve." She whips the blindfold off my eyes, grips my chin, and grins wickedly. "Come for me, Phoenix," she commands, turning the vibrations up and jerking my cock so quickly I have no choice but to come all over her and her black dress.

She looks down at the mess I've made and shakes her head, clicking her tongue in the back of her throat. "Dirty boy."

She unbinds me, removes the gag from my mouth, then makes me drink a full bottle of water as I sit on the edge of the bed, recovering.

"What was that about reprieve and body language?" I ask her. She never lectures during her lessons, not really. Tonight seems different. I want to know why.

"Sometimes I wonder if you're here to learn more about the lifestyle, or if you want to learn about life. Your mother is always gone, so you're seeking some motherly advice and don't realize it."

"Don't put mother and you in the same sentence, please, or my cock might jump off and run away." I graciously take the next water bottle she offers me and groan when it hits the back of my throat.

"What I mean is," she sighs, "you're always chasing something, and one day when you find the person your heart sings for, I want you to know exactly how to please them." She shrugs when I look up at her with a brow raised. "I also want you to know that a person doesn't always use obvious communication techniques. When you go to college—"

"If," I interrupt.

She glares at me, and I look down. "When you go to college, I want you to take a class on body language. You'd be surprised what a person doesn't say, but tells clearly with their body."

"I'll think about it," I tell her honestly.

"Good boy. Now shower and go home, my husband is waiting for me and you got me all worked up tonight."

AGENT STARLING RUNS a hand through his hair as he leans back against the wall. He stares out into the yard for a moment before looking at us and blowing out a heavy breath. "My position still stands. I want you all off campus until after spring break."

"What about—" Pierce tries to argue, but with a raised brow from Starling, he shuts up.

"No. Not a smart fucking choice. Let the FBI handle it from here, son." He looks around the room and folds his arms across his chest. "You guys have stumbled across something bigger than you can imagine, I'm afraid. There's more here connected than I originally thought. Keep your noses out of it." He raises a brow and meets Pierce's gaze. "Do you understand?"

Pierce grumbles something of an agreement, before pressing his forehead into the cold countertop with a sigh.

"We take the frat down in a week. Keep your heads up. Be lazy. Be kids." He grins wryly as he passes by Raven. "You keep these boys on their toes, got it?" When she nods and her lips tilt up into a small smile, he turns and walks toward the door. "We'll take him down. Give us time." He waves as he leaves the loft, and we all let out frustrated sighs when we can no longer see him.

I look over at Pierce and note his posture. His shoulders are tense and his fists are clenched on his thighs. River sits on his other side, and I watch as he tentatively slides an arm over Pierce's back, rubbing his palm up and down his spine.

Raven leans against my side and watches them, and I wrap my arm around her shoulders, pulling her closer until her head rests on my shoulder. I kiss her temple and shut my eyes as I breathe her in.

It's silent except for the soft tapping of the light hail falling in the storm outside.

After spending so many nights playing with sensory deprivation with Ruby, I'd grown to like the silence more than I thought a guy my age would. I can tell a lot about people's emotions by listening to their breathing, whether it be steady, heavy, stuttering.

Pierce's is slow, deep, and shakes on every exhale.

He's attempting to pull himself together.

But he's too worked up to do it.

"After they take down the frat," he says, lifting his head from the counter and looking between us all, "we're going to find Mark Riley."

We all knew that was coming, so we nod, accepting yet another twist in our plans.

TO: RMHILL@MYEMAIL.COM FROM: UPINFLAMES@MYEMAIL.COM SUBJECT: ANTICIPATION

I know, I know, I changed the subject line again. Sue me. (Actually don't. Lawyers are expensive, and I'd like to keep my inheritance, thanks.)

Anyway, today's email comes to you with the thought of anticipation, both good and bad.

They told me I might be good enough to leave in two weeks. I don't like the idea, because that means I'm stuck in the outside world without my entire family, my childhood home...without you.

I know we were talking in the last email a bit about what's waiting for us out there, and while I don't have an answer for myself, I do have one for you.

The world.

You could quite literally hold the world in the palm of your hand, tell it to stop spinning, and it would.

Cheesy, I know, but I really think you have the potential to do great things, even in small doses.

As for me...well... I think I'll go to college after all. I'd like to get a business degree, maybe start up a mechanic shop, work on bikes. I like motorcycles, actually.

The way you whiz past everything on them, wild, free...near death.

Don't show anyone this email, they might think that last part is a suicide note. Shit.

Till next time,

Flames

raven

I don't know why the fuck I agreed to a date in the middle of this shit.

I stick the last earring into my lobe, watching as the hoop swings back and forth a few times before settling. Meeting my own eyes in the mirror, I assess myself.

Smoky eye shadow. Check.

Absolutely not equal wings on either side with stark black eyeliner. Check.

Blood-red lipstick. Check.

Black leather dress with a studded belt around the center. Check.

The red leather jacket Pierce had made for me. Also check.

I nod, giving myself permission to enjoy a night with the guys for a change.

Though we aren't going out as originally planned, they demanded I dress up for a night of fun.

We'll pretend for as many days as we can until the walls close in on us.

I exhale loudly, open the door and step through.

The loft is...transformed.

As if I walked in one bathroom, and am leaving another.

Twinkle lights are spread across the railing, and all the others are either dimmed or turned off. Soft music plays from downstairs, and I wonder if leather was what I should have gone for. I smell pasta and rush toward the rails, looking down to see all of my guys working together in the kitchen to prepare dinner.

A smile stretches my lips and I vow to pretend, at least for tonight, I'm a normal college girl with normal boyfriends and normal...

Wait, is having three boyfriends normal?

I shrug. It should be.

"I can feel you staring, Red," Phoenix says. "Come down here before one of us has to come up and get you."

I don't move, and he looks up, meeting my gaze with a challenge in his. I bite my lip to hide my smile.

"It won't be a fun time." He turns back toward the food, and River chuckles as he pulls garlic bread from the oven.

Deciding to be a good girl for a while, I walk to the closet and put on some black pumps. Walking slowly, I make my way down the stairs, because yes, I have fallen down stairs in and out of heels enough for one lifetime, thanks.

River is at the bottom, holding his arm out for me to take. His eyes widen as they rake over my outfit. He adjusts his suit jacket as he clears his throat. "You look stunning, Raven."

My shoulders shake with my silent giggle.

"I'm trying to be a gentleman here. Don't make fun of me for it." He rolls his eyes and escorts me around the corner toward the kitchen.

They have a fold-out table set up in the living room and I pause, taking in the tablecloth and the almost fancy set up.

The chairs are mismatched and plastic, and the dishes scream college kids use these, but the sentiment is what matters. All three of the boys came together to set up a fancy date for me, in the midst of all the turmoil. As I look up at each one of them, they're begging for my approval.

I remove my arm from River's and sign *This is stunning. I feel like I'm at an actual restaurant right now.*

"Don't lie, little bird. It's not nice." Pierce sighs as he places the last of the dishes on the table. He surprises me when he pulls out a chair. "A seat for the queen?"

He looks so eager to please, so I nod and walk over to him, slowly sitting at the head of the table they insist I take each and every time.

A point to be made to me...or to remind Pierce he's no longer the ruler around here?

I jump when a hand lands on the back of my neck, but when I look up, I see it's Phoenix, bringing a drink over for me. Disappointment travels through me, and my eyes snap to Pierce's the second I see him sit down.

"Red?" Phoenix asks, and I glance back up at him. "Wine, sweetheart. Red wine?"

I nod and look down at my lap, flustered. This is about

as awkward as my first real date with Pierce. Grateful for the wine, I grab the glass and bring it to my lips, absolutely breaking every single wine rule by chugging it. My cheeks heat when I hold it out for another pour.

"Okay then," Phoenix says. He fills the glass and sets the bottle down on the table.

"Alright, I got all the food," River announces as he walks toward the table and places a dish of spaghetti down and a pan full of garlic bread next to it.

Phoenix and River serve everyone's food to them before they sit down.

Their stares are burning into my skin, so I do what they always wait for me to do. Lifting my fork, I wrap spaghetti around it and bring it to my mouth, closing my eyes at the deliciousness that is carbs and red sauce.

The silence breaks when the guys pick up their own silverware and start eating.

We never have dinners like this, exactly. Fancy clothes. Fancy table. Fancy food.

It's awkward, and so not us.

"Okay, is anyone else feeling awkward as fuck?" Pierce asks about twenty minutes into dinner.

We're each on a second plate of pasta, and I have a piece of garlic bread held in front of my lips, fingers coated in the melted butter.

Pushing away from the table, Pierce grabs his plate and sits down on the recliner, groaning as he relaxes. "This kind of shit is not us. I can see it all over Rae's butter covered face."

I gasp, drop my garlic bread on the plate, and quickly grab a napkin to wipe at my lips and chin. Great, the lipstick is coming off, too. Fuck it. Tossing the napkin onto the table, I stand and grab my own plate, then walk to the couch and sit down, kicking my pumps off and sighing. Loudly.

River stands up from the table with his food, makes his way to my side, and sits down. "My ass feels so much better over here."

I snicker into my hand before grabbing for another piece of garlic bread and shoving half of it into my mouth. Forget the slow, ladylike eating bullshit. I crave carbs when I'm stressed. I'd say having your biological father try to set you up with your half-brother, poison your college campus, and beat the shit out of your boyfriends on the regular has me stressed.

Carbs, I love you.

"Heathens," Phoenix grits out. "It was supposed to be a nice night for Raven. Special."

"It is special," Pierce says around a mouthful of food. "You see that smile on her face? She's in heaven over there."

Phoenix taps his fingers along the table, his gaze raking over all of us in our much more comfortable positions. He sighs, rolls his eyes, and stands, grabbing his own plate. The leather couch molds to his body as he sits next to me, stuffing another forkful of food into his mouth.

"What're we watching tonight, little bird?" Pierce grabs the TV remote and holds it up, waving it.

I set my plate down on my lap and tap my chin for a few seconds before signing *World's Most Haunted Houses*.

"And she wants nightmares tonight, got it," he says.

He flips to the show for me, leans back in his chair, and when our gazes meet briefly, I smile gratefully at him.

It's not until someone is carrying me upstairs, my body limp and barely awake after hours of watching television, that I remembered I wanted to tell him... I forgive him.

"Kiss her for me, Riv," Pierce whispers.

"Always, man. She'll come around soon, I think," River tells him as he moves up the stairs.

"It doesn't matter. I'll wait for her for the rest of eternity if that's what she needs me to do. As long as I can watch that smile light up her face like it did earlier." He sighs. "All I want is for her to be happy."

"I know," River said, "and she knows, too."

Pierce hums, and I hear his footsteps retreat down the hallway.

"Sneaky," River whispers as he continues up the stairs. "I know you're awake, sweet girl."

Popping one eye open, then the other, I can't help but smile at the look on River's face. He's trying to be stern, but he's as tired as I am and looks goofy instead.

He pinches my side lightly, and I jolt enough we almost fall down the stairs. "Woah," he says, chuckling as he steadies us. Gently, he places me on the bed and wraps the blankets around me. I try to pull him down with me, but he shakes his head. "I'm gonna go cuddle the monster downstairs. Phoenix is cleaning up, but he'll be here in a few minutes, okay?"

I nod, accepting the slow, sensual kiss he leaves me with.

"Goodnight, sweet girl." He winks at me, then turns around to walk back down the stairs.

Phoenix makes his way toward me only a few minutes later, moving my tired body until my back molds to his front and our legs intertwine. He wraps his arm around me and glides his fingers between mine, squeezing softly. "Sweet dreams, Raven. I..." he sighs, and places a kiss on the back of my head before resting his on the pillow.

I love you, too, I want to tell him.

Instead, I let his warmth soothe my body into a night-mare free sleep.

river

I walk up the stairs with Raven's oatmeal and hot chocolate on a tray, my bare feet smacking against the wood loud enough to wake the dead.

Which is the plan.

Phoenix is sitting up, glaring at me, and I look to his side to see Raven.

Still fucking asleep.

I even made a shit ton of noise in the kitchen, knowing sound carries from down there.

"Morning," I say to Phoenix.

He grumbles as he accepts the tray I hand to him. "No coffee for me?"

"Nah, get your own shit." I chuckle when he takes a swipe at me. Climbing onto the bed, I slide the blanket slowly off Raven.

"I hope she kicks you in the nuts. You're gonna scare her."

I shrug. "Won't be the first or the last time my balls

get a rough treatment." Pulling the blanket down until her stomach is exposed to the cold air, goosebumps rise along her skin, she twists, reaching out for the blanket. I tug it further, and she slaps the air around her. "Feisty," I say. Laughing, I tickle her sides, and am rewarded with a rather beautiful, grumpy, playful glare from her. "Good morning, sweet girl. Time to get up!"

She flops onto the bed, star fishing and nearly smacking the tray out of Phoenix's hand. When her palm makes contact, she sits up and stares at her normal breakfast. She looks at me incredulously before signing, *You brought me breakfast?*

Of course I did, I sign back, *anything for you.*

Sign language was easy to pick up once I learned there were shorthand ways of saying things, and a lot of the different phrases followed the same movements. We've come up with new ways to say things between our group. Every time we choose to sign instead of talk to her, Raven gets this sweet little smile on her face and her cheeks light up so beautifully.

I meant it; anything for her.

Speaking of...

"Come on. We have a trip to take and a reservation to make!" I move off the bed and step toward the closet, opening it and beginning to pack all of Raven's favorite clothes. I leave underwear out, because we've got that all planned.

"Red wants to know why the hell you think it's acceptable to go through her shit right now?" Phoenix asks for her.

I turn around and grin. "We don't have much time, you need to eat, and I know where we're going."

She glares at me playfully, a spoonful of oatmeal hanging in front of her lips.

"Trust me?" I ask her, worry settling in my gut that she might say no.

Tapping her chin with her free hand, she looks up to the ceiling as if contemplating it before meeting my gaze again and nodding. She waves me away with an eye roll and I get back to work.

Barely thirty minutes after waking her up, we're all in the jeep and headed out of town for a day-or-two trip.

We may be gone a day, we may be gone two, but either way, we'll be out of the way when Starling and his crew take down Alpha Mu after nearly three decades of running drugs across campus.

"RIVER, I swear to fuck, your driving is annoying as shit and I need you to tell me where the fuck we're going so I can drive."

Pierce is so cute when he's flustered.

"Listen," I say, nearly slamming into a car on my left. "You're a raging distraction. So shut your pie hole so I don't get us killed."

"Letting me drive would be what would keep us from getting killed," Pierce grumbles, crossing his arms over his chest like a petulant child.

I meet Raven's blue eyes in the rearview mirror and wink, grinning wide when she silently giggles.

Little do they know, I planned the absolute perfect Valentine's date for us all. Phoenix and Pierce had a say so in the gifts to Raven, and one of the gifts relies entirely on Raven allowing Pierce to touch her again.

I have a contingency plan, though.

We're driving along the coast before Pierce sits up again, narrowing his eyes along the beachfront. "What did you do? This wasn't part of our plan."

"Oh, I know," I tell him, letting my grin spread wide and free.

"River," Phoenix says, drawing my name out in warning.

"Phoenix," I say back.

He huffs and yawns, adjusting Raven's head on his lap and running his fingers through her hair.

"Jesus, River," Pierce grits out, grabbing the wheel from me.

Oops, I was driving in the wrong lane.

Can't blame me for being distracted by my little vixen, right?

I drive off the main road, and follow a private one until a beach house comes into view. Pulling up in the driveway, I park, then lift a key fob and press the button. I whoop in excitement when the garage door opens. "We're here!" I sing-song.

Raven sits up, rubbing sleep from her eyes and drool from her mouth.

My cock twitches.

"Alright, kids, go explore. There's a master, and I had

them add an extra big bed." I climb out of the jeep after parking it and turning off the engine.

"This is nice," Pierce praises when we walk inside from the garage, directly into a foyer.

The house is the cheesiest of beach homes; light wood floors, sky blue walls, seashell and sand decor every-where. I didn't book this place for the inside, though. Windows line the back of the property, showing off the private beachfront view.

Raven rushes toward it, nearly smashing her face against the glass as she takes it in.

We all stand and watch her, admiring her beauty alongside the windy seascape.

Turning around, she furrows her brow adorably, signing *But it's February. It's cold. Why the beach?*

I shrug, stuffing my hands in my pockets as I lean against a wall. "A pretty view for a pretty girl. You can sit upstairs in the bay window and read, smell the salty sea air, relax."

"This is thoughtful as shit," Pierce says from beside me, wrapping an arm around my shoulders.

"Not too far from Junk to be homesick, but far enough away we won't be caught up in the raid tomorrow." Again, I shrug, looking down at my feet as my nerves take over.

"You did good," Phoenix says, patting me on the bicep a few times as he passes by me, making his way toward Raven. "We'll grab your bags, sweetheart. You explore, do what you want."

Her eyes widen in panic, and I step forward, grabbing her hands in my own. "You're safe here, Rae. Lance and some of his guys have eyes on the property. I wouldn't have brought us somewhere without protection right now."

She nods, looking between Pierce and Phoenix before taking a deep breath.

If you'd have told me a year ago I'd fall in love with my best friend's ex best friend after she broke his heart, I'd have laughed in your face and said 'No, we don't cross that slippery slope'.

But when she smiles this gorgeous smile of relief, glee, happiness, euphoria?

When her whole body lights up as she walks around, taking in all the quirkiness of the beach house?

I'll look back at you and tell you 'I know I fell for her, and I wish I could do it again, and again, and again'.

"RIVER!" Pierce shouts, throwing the beach ball back at me and glaring. "It's fucking cold as shit out here, what the fuck?"

I shrug and toss the ball back in Raven's direction, clapping when she catches it. "Our bodies are moving, we'll stay warm that way."

Raven tosses the ball at Pierce, doubling over in laughter when it smacks him in the face.

He stands there, still, with his eyes narrowed and his hands outstretched.

Their connection has only grown stronger the last month or so, since she asked him to stop touching her.

He's had to reach for her soul with his own, while also learning a shit ton from Phoenix and me.

Pierce didn't have a father to show him how to treat a woman–or in my case, how not to treat a woman–so we've taken up that role for him.

And as I watch him take a deep breath, blow it out and look up at the sky in search of patience instead of raging and rushing toward her for something playful...

I realize we've hit our mark, and our boy has learned.

Who'd have thought he could come back from his shit.

"Phoenix has some boozy hot chocolate going inside. Please," he holds his hands together in a prayer, "please, please, come inside and warm up." His eyes flit in my direction. "Both of you."

Aw, it's like he cares about me or something.

Raven shrugs and walks back up the beach toward the house, her whole frame trembling.

Maybe it is a bit too cold to be playing on the beach.

I said I'd provide her a pretty view, not pretty weather.

"You doin' okay?" I ask Pierce as I move alongside him back toward the beach house. Our shoulders brush together, and I take the opportunity to wrap my arm around his. His warmth makes me groan.

"Now I'm fucking freezing, but yeah, I'm okay." He tries to shove me off him, grinning when I pull him with me like I'm a leech. "You're insufferable," he grumbles.

I merely hold him tighter.

"I should spank both of you for being outside like that," Phoenix is saying when Pierce and I enter. He glares as he passes me the warm mug, then points to the couch. "Sit the fuck down."

"Yes, sir," I tease, laughing when he tries to smack my head. One of these days, I'm going to get a concussion from how much they hit my skull. I plop down right next to Raven and take a sip of the hot cocoa.

She meets my eyes from under the hooded blanket she's wrapped up in, and I lean forward to kiss her lips, bringing a bright smile to her face.

"Getting out of town was a good idea," Pierce says as he sits down next to me with his own mug. He takes a sip and leans his head back on the couch, closing his eyes. "I'm not worried right now."

"That's the booze talking," Phoenix says. "I'm still worried. Maxwell has too much power, and I feel his eyes everywhere still." He sits down next to Raven, wrapping his arm around her shoulders as he sips from his own mug.

"Still," I pipe up, "it's nice to be out from under his big toe for a split second. When's the last time we got to do that?"

"Never," Pierce and Phoenix say simultaneously.

"Exactly." I grin, and take another sip from my mug.

The silence is comfortable as we all sip at our hot cocoa, and the warmth seeps into my bones, as does the booze. Watching the waves crash against the sand, listening to the calm inside, and being with all of my favorite people in one room?

Life couldn't get too much better than this.

"Oh shit," I say, standing and nearly spilling my hot cocoa all over the floor. I wince and set the mug down onto the coffee table. "With tomorrow being Valentine's Day, we do have gifts for you, Rae!" I rush toward the garage where the boxes are still stored inside of the jeep.

"Do we have to do it now?" Phoenix asks.

"Yeah, some of them will be useful for her in the morning," I call over my shoulder.

The garage is fucking freezing, so I move quickly, stacking the two boxes together and bringing them inside. I place them both on the floor in the living room, then open the tops and bring out the bags of gifts.

We had decided to shower her with gifts, a nice day of pampering, and a sexy as fuck night afterward. All her choice to participate, but we can all hope she agrees.

There's also a super secret special surprise I can't wait to show her tomorrow night, too.

I smile wide as I bring gift after gift out of the boxes, placing them all on the table in front of her.

Pierce grabs my hot cocoa mug and places it on the side table so I don't spill it.

"Okay," I say, standing and rubbing my palms together. "RaeRae, this is all yours. We kind of went overboard, but internet shopping is dangerous for everyone."

"Fucking got that right," Pierce says before sipping from his mug.

She looks around the room, a blush coloring her cheeks. *Thank you* she signs, *this is a lot.* She lets out a small huff of laughter as she places her mug down on the end table. Her hands shake as she grabs the first bag, red with pink and white hearts all over it. After taking out the wrapping, she pulls out a bottle of pink champagne and a specialized glass with the same design from her jacket etched onto it. Her gaze instantly shoots to Pierce, and he sips his cocoa, shrugging like he wasn't the one who had the idea.

Shaking her head, but with this cute little smile stretching her lips, she places the items down and grabs the big red envelope. From it, she pulls out a receipt for the 'full package' at a local spa. She grins and looks at Phoenix, holding it up in question.

He smiles and nods. "A day of pampering sounds like the best thing for you, Red."

Wanting to butter me up? she signs.

"That was Thanksgiving, Rae. This is Valentine's, keep up." I laugh when all eyes land on me, and Raven's shoulders shake with her laughter. "Okay, so these," I say, shoving a box and three bags toward her, "go together. For tomorrow evening."

This is too much Rae signs, looking around at us all with wide eyes. A tear tries to fall, but she wipes it away quickly.

"It's not enough," Pierce tells her. He sets his mug of hot cocoa down and leans forward, elbows on his knees. Meeting her gaze earnestly, he says, "You're worth this and more. We want to treat you, because you're ours as much as we're yours, Blue. This is the first of many Valentine's Days where you're showered with gifts and treated the way you deserve."

Her cheeks are pink as she stares back at Pierce, and Phoenix and I look at each other before turning to watch them. Rae's hands twitch, and her body moves slightly forward, as if she wants to go to him, but at the last second she backs down and lets out a heavy breath.

The whole room gets colder as Pierce swallows and leans back, a sad look taking over his features.

"Open 'em up, Rae," I say softly.

Awkward doesn't begin to explain the atmosphere right now.

Rae practically rips through the next gifts. One bag contains two sets of sexy lingerie for her to choose from, if she wants to wear them at all. Another bag contains various pieces of jewelry; a velvet choker, black crystal earrings which will dangle close to her shoulders with their length, and a few black bangle bracelets. A box contains a set of red bottoms, and her eyes widen comically, the tension diffusing when we all chuckle at her expression.

The last and final bag is small in comparison, and contains a gift receipt for two dresses, and a note to choose whichever one she wants for tomorrow.

When all is said and done, we've laughed, she's cried, and Pierce is even cracking a smile.

I meet Phoenix's gaze after Raven gives us both hugs.

She's hesitating, wanting to go to Pierce, longing locked in her pretty blues.

Tomorrow can't come soon enough.

You do know the negative of anticipation is dread, right?

That's what I felt when I got your last email.

Dread.

I obviously haven't spent time making many friends, because I broke when I heard a rumor that a few others are leaving soon, too.

Tricia. Manny. Lucy. Phoenix.

I don't want any of them to leave, but that's for my own selfish reasons.

I might end up staying here until the end of time. Picking up sign language was great for me and Phoenix. He'd already known a bit, so he taught me some shortcuts recently that I now use frequently.

Who knows if they'll give me someone else to work with.

So I guess now I have the anticipation of...do I get to leave next?

And the dread of losing too many people in a short amount of time.

Anticipation leads to anxiety, though, and my body tries to fight me at every single fucking turn when I'm anxious.

So whether it's good or bad news, please tell me as soon as you know.

Till next time,

RM Hill.

PS: Did you see the pineapple pizza in the cafeteria

today? Absolutely disgusting, Flames. What is the world coming to?!

CHAPTER TWENTY-SEVEN

raven

I wake with the smell of cinnamon rolls and hot chocolate floating down the hall, as well as bacon. My stomach rumbles, and I hear a chuckle from my side.

Opening one eye, then the other, I smile sleepily at a shirtless River.

God, he's hot.

Rolling onto my side, I run my hand along his abs because fuck it, that's why, but he grabs my wrist and shakes his head.

I pout, and he kisses my lips in apology.

"Breakfast. We have to get you fed and to the spa in less than an hour, sweet girl." He lifts my hand to his mouth and kisses my knuckles, keeping those gray eyes locked on mine.

Pesky butterflies take flight in my stomach and I chew my lip before flopping onto my back dramatically.

"You're playful this morning," he says. "C'mon," he pats me on the thigh and stands.

With the strength of a million moons, I drag myself out of the bath and grab River's discarded hoodie from the chair in the corner. I practically drown in it, as I do most of these boys' clothes, but I don't care. They keep me warm and covered.

"If only you weren't wearing anything under that," River says, groaning when I sway my hips extra on the way out of the room. "Little vixen," he warns.

I look back over my shoulder and sign *What?* attempting to keep my expression as innocent as possible.

"Boys!" River shouts. Wrapping an arm around my shoulders, he tugs me down the hall and chuckles when I try to drag my feet. "You started it, sweet girl."

"What's going on?" Phoenix asks. He's placing the food on the island.

The cinnamon rolls are huge, and are absolutely not from a can.

"We have a tease on our hands this morning," River tells him. He pulls me in front of him, with his hands on my shoulders. "Too bad we can't do anything about it."

"We can later," Phoenix says, a small smile tilting his lips.

My face blanches.

"She knows her safe word if she wants out of it. She also knows what she's doing, Pierce," he says the last part with a pointed look at the man in question.

"What?" he asks, raising his hands. "I didn't say anything."

"No, but you were getting all defensive over your little

bird over there. We could feel the death glare." River chuckles, then slaps my ass before picking me up and placing me on one of the stools like a child.

I glare up at him, only to be met with a kiss on my lips. Sighing, I gratefully pick up a piece of bacon when Phoenix puts it on my plate and chomp down on it. Sunlight fights its way past the winter clouds, and the waves are loudly crashing against the shore.

It's beautiful.

Calming.

Peaceful.

Exactly what we all needed, even if we are technically hiding out while Starling does whatever he needs to do.

Actually...

I turn toward Pierce and sign *Any news from Starling?*

Pierce shakes his head. "No. The party won't start until later tonight, so we gotta hang on. If nothing else, we can give him a call tomorrow."

"He'll probably be busy, so let's not make plans for that yet." Phoenix places two cinnamon rolls on my plate, then leans across the island and kisses me slow, sensual, long enough to make my panties damp. When I'm close to climbing over and having something else for breakfast, he pulls away and winks at me. "Happy Valentine's Day, sweetheart. Now eat your food."

I flip them all off when they laugh at my heated cheeks and squirming thighs, then dig into my actual food.

Forty minutes later, the guys walk me into the spa they got me in for, and Pierce walks right up to the reception desk and asks for the person they specifically requested for me.

Why a specific request? I sign, looking at Phoenix.

"They know ASL," he says.

My brows shoot up to my hairline, and a wide smile spreads across my lips. Now I can be excited.

"Ms. Hill," a young woman says as she exits the side door, "We're ready for you. Ms. Emerson is in the room. If you'd just come with me?"

"Don't come with her," River retorts, earning a snort from me.

I smack his arm before kissing his and Phoenix's cheeks. I look over at Pierce and hesitate. Soon I tell myself. Awkwardly, I wave to all of them, then turn around and follow the woman through the door.

Lavender is coating this room, both the color, the flowers, and the scent. Calming and beautiful. Robes hang along a hook near a row of lockers and a small, private shower. The floors are heated and made to look like dark stone.

The young woman smiles back at me as she shows me toward the shower. "Ms. Emerson is waiting for you just past that door," she points across the room. "All you need to do is change, have a quick rinse, then put on the robe and enter the room. Strip down as far as you'd like and lay on the table, and she'll be in within a few minutes." She smiles at me, her green eyes as gorgeous as Pierce's, then tucks some of the brunette hair behind her ear. "Enjoy, Ms. Hill." She spins on her heel and walks back out the way we came.

I walk forward and quickly rinse myself in the private

shower, put on a robe, and stash my clothes in a free locker. Taking a deep breath, I step across the warm floor and enter the dark room.

She said I could strip down however I'd like, so I climb onto the table and slide the robe off my shoulders, all the way down until it only covers my ass.

A few minutes pass and the door opens.

"Good morning, Ms. Hill. My name is Steph." Her voice is erotic, and I instantly wonder what type of massage these guys paid for. "Your boyfriend told me you'd prefer someone who knew ASL, so feel free to use it here. I've been using it since I was a child, so I'm fluent. For now," she steps closer to the table, I hear a bottle click open and shut again, "relax." Her hands land on my shoulders, and I exhale loudly. She chuckles. "Don't worry. I'll get you in tip top shape. Just breathe and relax for me."

I'm going to kill these men because I did not need to be as turned on as I was by her for as long as she had her hands on me. It felt like a test of my own loyalty, or my vagina's. By the time I was done getting 'pampered' we were eating sandwiches at a local café. I was so keyed up I nearly begged one of them to fuck me on an iced over public bench.

Their grins say it all.

They want me wet and needy.

What the fuck are they going to do to me tonight?

I squeeze my thighs together, and Phoenix clamps his hand on my knee, stilling me.

Whatever the fuck I let them, I suppose.

I scarf down the rest of my food, eager for time to speed up.

"WE'RE GIVING you an hour and a half to get your pretty little self ready for dinner and dancing, Red," Phoenix says as we enter the beach house around three o'clock.

We spent the last hour playing a party game in the living room, and my cheeks hurt from smiling so damn much.

"This time," he calls as I ascend the stairs, "I expect everyone to keep their fucking shoes on and their asses at the table!"

My shoulders shake with my laughter, and I look back to him. *Yes, sir*, I sign. His nostrils flare, and I hastily enter the bedroom, closing and locking the door behind me.

It takes me forty-five minutes to shower the day off me, pick from the lingerie and dresses, plaster my face in modest but sexy make-up, style my hair, and place all of the beautiful jewelry in their rightful spots on my body. A new record for me, honestly.

I pick up the red bottoms in one hand, lift the bottom of the black sheath dress in the other–because no one needs me to trip and fall–and make my way out of the door and down the hallway.

The guys are talking animatedly about something at the bottom of the stairs, but stop immediately, the echo of their voices fading as they take me in.

My gaze immediately snaps to Pierce's, because this feels a lot like all the dances we went to together, and the one we didn't. I swallow and take a deep breath, steeling myself before taking the steps slowly.

Familiar, loving green eyes widen and darken within seconds and I watch as he stuffs his hands in his pockets, exhaling roughly.

"Stunning," River says, and I meet his smile with one of my own.

Phoenix meets me at the bottom of the stairs, holding out a hand. "Shoes?" he asks.

I pass them over, my fingers shaking with all this attention on me. The lust and tension is heavy in here, and my pulse is pounding through my body.

Phoenix drops to his knees and lifts one of my feet before sliding the shoe on much like the prince did in Cinderella. He repeats the process with my other foot and kisses my calf before standing and adjusting his suit.

All three boys dressed up in full black on black suits. Pierce's jacket is closed at the center button, River's is fully open, and Phoenix has his crisp, tight, properly done up.

I smile around at them all and take a deep breath before signing, *I'm ready.*

Phoenix holds his arm out, his brown eyes raking over my figure slowly as I descend the last step and wrap my hand around his forearm.

River and Pierce walk ahead of us, opening the door to the garage. River quickly grabs my winter coat and helps me into it before placing my hand back on Phoenix, kissing my cheek lightly as he does. All three men look nervous, and it's insane.

They've had me splayed out on a kitchen table for fuck's sake.

River opens the door for me to hop into the back of the jeep, and I climb in. I wiggle my ass for all three of their benefits when I feel their gazes burning through my black dress. I sit down, having to hide my laughter behind my hand when I see them all not-so-subtly adjusting themselves in their slacks.

Phoenix and Pierce glare while River shrugs.

Snowflakes slam into the windshield in an angry flurry as Pierce drives us to the restaurant, and I wonder how the hell he can see. Staying at the beach house would have been better. Safer.

He parks right in front of the place. River helps me out, and hands the keys off to the valet.

There's an actual red carpet.

And the boys escort me down it like a queen.

My cheeks must match the carpet at this point. I have no idea how to deal with the public and our relationship.

However, as Phoenix and River take turns escorting me places, letting my chair out, brushing my hair out of my face, I realize not a single soul is watching us with any interest.

Except for Pierce.

He's sitting in his normal spot next to River on my left side, and he keeps glancing over at me, a plea in his eyes. Anger has slowly been replaced by his longing, and my heart has shifted in much the same way.

Maybe tonight I should call a truce.

My heart skips a beat and I reach for my water, grateful for the chill it sends up my arm and down my spine.

"Good evening, folks, and happy Valentine's Day!" our waiter says as he approaches. He pulls a pen and pad out of his pocket and looks around the table before his eyes land on Phoenix, who undoubtedly gives off the air of 'in charge' at all times. "What can I get you started off with, sir?"

"Pizza," he says, and I choke on nothing, eyes wide. He raises his own brow in amusement, not looking at the waiter as he continues, "and beer."

"Okay, uhm, sure. We do have personal pizza or family size options–"

"Family sized. Two, please. Put everything on it," Phoenix tells him. He's polite, but firm, and the waiter quickly jots it down.

"I'll need to see ID for the beer," he says.

Phoenix holds up a stack of cards, showing off the fakes he managed to snag for everyone a while back. We recently got mine in, since I've only been around for a few months, and this is the first time it'll be used.

The waiter looks around the table with a questioning gaze, but seems to brush it off with a shrug, handing the cards back. "I'll go put your order in and be back with your drinks soon."

"Thanks," Phoenix says. He looks back at me. "I told you back before the party. Our guy is good."

"Don't advertise that shit too loudly, Nix," Pierce says as he leans over the table, keeping his voice low.

Phoenix shrugs and straightens his jacket before leaning back in the chair.

Our food and drinks arrive shortly after. While it's all fantastic, I find myself lost in the tension again, sneaking glances between each of my guys and hoping like hell there aren't any other plans after this, unless that plan is railing me.

A girl can dream, right?

Warmth envelops me as Phoenix wraps his hand on my knee under the table, squeezing gently. When our eyes meet, he grins this wicked grin, then looks at River, raising a brow.

"We ready?" River asks, glancing at Pierce before looking at me.

What the hell are they planning?

Those forest green eyes lock onto me, and we both get lost in each other, my heart rate picking up as I think about allowing us to touch each other again.

God do I want to touch him.

"Thank you for dining with us tonight," our waiter says. I hadn't noticed he was at the table again. "Have a great evening, folks."

My skin heats, and sweat breaks out on the back of my neck.

River stands and helps me out of my chair, then wraps his arm around my waist. "Do you think he's earned his way out of the doghouse yet, little vixen?" he whispers in my ear as we step out of the restaurant.

I bite my lip, look back over my shoulder to meet Pierce's eyes again, and sign *Yes* where only River can see.

"Don't feel pressured, Rae," he says as he helps me

into my coat. He escorts me to the jeep and waits for me to climb in.

Settled in the seat, I watch as River slides in. He slams the door closed and brackets my face. "You're in charge here. If you never want him to touch you again, he doesn't have to, but," he sighs, looks away for a second, then meets my eyes again, "you're both aching for each other right now. It's plain as day to anyone looking longer than two point five seconds."

He hurt me so bad, I sign. Tears prick at my eyes and I try to hold them back. *But I love him so much, and he's changed, I see that. Do you think I can trust him?* I meet River's gray eyes, but shut my own when a tear escapes.

He presses his lips to mine softly, giving me a tiny comfort. He pulls away slowly, as if it pains him to do so. "Do you trust me and Phoenix?" he whispers.

River earned a full tongue lashing from me in our text message thread over the last few months, and through those... I've fallen in love with him so deeply, and it all stemmed from him gaining my trust.

I take a deep breath and open my eyes to meet his again. *I trust you both with my whole heart* I sign, giving him a little insight into my feelings.

"Do you like how we treat you?" he asks, moving his hands from my face, down my arms, to clasp mine between his. "Do we do a good enough job for you?"

This vulnerability stings a little, for both of us.

I nod and look down at our hands. Bringing them up, I kiss his knuckles and watch as his nostrils flare and eyes darken. My stomach tightens.

"We've spent countless hours with him, with you. We've

shown you both how to act in a relationship. I think," River blows out a heavy breath and runs his hands through his hair in frustration, "I think neither of you had a good example, so Phoenix and I have done our best to show you both what a healthy relationship can be. As best as we could, of course."

Leaning forward, I kiss his cheek. *You've both been wonderful*, I sign.

"Let's let the guys in before their nuts freeze off, and we can get to your last Valentine's gift." He grins and opens his door, telling the guys to get their asses in the jeep.

They do, and when I meet Pierce's eyes in the rearview mirror, my body heats impossibly.

River's palm lands gently on my thigh over my dress, and I squeeze my legs together, taking in a sharp breath. He inches his hand further, further, until Phoenix spins his head around to glare at him.

I lick my lips as I watch their silent conversation, then look back to meet Pierce's gaze again.

"Take a left," River says, instructing him.

"I thought we were going to–" he tries to say, but Phoenix turns back around and shakes his head.

"Back to the beach house. Something came up." I watch as Phoenix taps out a message, and my phone buzzes a few seconds later.

PHOENIX

Are you sure he's served a long enough sentence, Red?

I shake my head and text back.

I think my body aches for him. Isn't that enough for now?

Phoenix's shoulders rise and fall with a heavy sigh before he types again.

PHOENIX

Trust me?

I look up and meet his gaze, signing *Always*.

He nods and shoves his phone into his slacks.

The rest of the ride back to the beach house is silent aside from the blood rushing through my veins.

AS WE ENTER the house through the garage, River slowly slides my jacket off, and Phoenix walks toward the living room, turning a slow, heady beat on the stereo system.

Pierce's brows furrow as he steps in, folding his arms as he looks between the three of us.

Defeat shines in his eyes before he sits down on the recliner, in for the show again.

His only option.

Or so he thinks.

I decide to fuck with him for a while longer, pulling River with me into the living room where Phoenix has now pushed the coffee table out of the way. I slide my body between both of them, wrap my arms around

River's neck, and let my head fall back on Phoenix's shoulders.

The slow, heady beat of the song draws my hips in circles between these two, and I shut my eyes to hide from Pierce's heated stare.

"You're teasing him," Phoenix whispers in my ear, and I allow my lips to stretch in a slow grin. He nips at the side of my neck and slides his hands down to my hips, grinding into me as we move together.

River leans in and kisses along my other side. A dirty chuckle leaves him when I buck my hips forward against the hard ridge in his slacks. "Need something, little vixen?" He groans when I tug at his hair, nails digging into his scalp.

I take a deep breath in and let it slowly out, raising my head from Phoenix's shoulder. My heart hammers in my chest as I pull away from my comfort zone and stand a few feet from Pierce. Our eyes meet and his widen as I take a few tentative steps toward him.

He has to know I'm in charge if this is going to work today...and in the future.

I lift my shaking hands between us and swallow hard before signing, *Who's in charge?*

He can't speak, so he raises his own hands, but instead of signing, he points at me.

What do you do if I tap three times? I sign, then grab my hands to keep them from trembling.

Raven, you don't have to do this, he signs back, a tear falling from his eyes.

What do you do, Pierce? I inhale sharply and narrow my tear-filled eyes at him.

I watch as he swallows, his Adam's apple bobbing harshly in his throat. He leans forward, as if meaning to stand, but stops himself, unsure of what happens next. *I stop everything, remove all touch, start aftercare, ask what you need*, he signs, eyes stuck on me.

And if I want you to leave the room? I sign.

He blows out a breath, his brows furrowed in confusion, frustration. *I leave, no questions asked.*

A tear falls from my lashes, sliding down my cheek. We both watch as it lands on the floor. I take one last deep breath, and prepare myself for a decision I don't know if I'll regret or not. Lifting my gaze, I meet those familiar green eyes, bring up my hand, and crook my finger, beckoning him toward me.

pierce

I'm fucking dreaming.

I never expected her to want me to touch her again in this lifetime. River and Phoenix are plenty for her to be physically satisfied, so I'm obsolete in that department.

Looking around, I find them both standing at the edge of the room, wicked little grins on their faces like they knew what was happening tonight. Is this what she and Nix were texting about earlier?

"Are you sure?" I whisper, meeting Rae's pretty blues again. I lose myself in her eyes every single time I look, and my soul sings for hers, begging, pleading, wishing this was truly happening.

Standing there with her red curls all mussed up from Phoenix's suit, her dress wrinkled at the front from River...she's like a siren as she crooks her finger at me again. She nods and straightens her spine, hands falling to her sides.

I stand and take a tentative step forward, because no fucking way is this happening. She doesn't flinch, and my heart tumbles in my chest.

Another step, my hands balling into fists at my side to stop from grabbing her prematurely. Her breasts rise and fall with her heavy breathing, and my mouth waters at the sight.

One more step, I'm right in front of her. I can see her pupils dilate, her pulse thud in her chest. She stares up at me, not moving away, not teasing.

She's fucking serious.

"Raven, I—"

She breaches the last wall between us, throwing herself at me, lips crashing against mine, a tidal wave of love, lust, and longing nearly bowling me over.

At first I don't grab her, I simply allow her to mold her body to me, her chest pressing to mine, her arms around my neck, the rest of her aligned with mine so perfectly. So deliciously.

But when she pulls back and signs *Please. Touch me.*

A man can only resist the love of his life for so goddamn long.

A primal growl leaves me and I slam my mouth back to hers and grab her by the waist, lifting her up until she has no choice but to wrap her legs around me. Heat crashes against me when she does, and I grip her ass tightly in my hands, pulling her to me until we meet.

Hard, soft, me, her.

Perfection.

My heart gallops in my chest as I move us forward, leaning her against the wall between River and Phoenix. I don't give a fuck about them watching right now, I just want to keep my lips and tongue dancing with Raven's, my body plastered to hers, and hers to mine.

I nip at her lower lip, backing away to breathe, and meet her gaze. Her lids are heavy with lust, and I lean in for a softer kiss, feeling her melt beneath me.

The benefit I've found from having to watch her with them the last few months has been getting to know every single sign her body gives. Body language was hard to learn, but it's essential in a situation like Raven's where sound is out.

Her hips twitch, and when I pull back again to look at her beautiful face, her brows pinch together as she attempts to grind against me. Pain takes me off guard for a second when she digs her nails into the back of my neck, pulling me toward her in another kiss.

I slide my hands up her hips, her sides, her spine, before anchoring them onto her shoulders and grinding, thrusting gently against her heated center.

She tosses her head back, but I catch it so she doesn't smack it into the wall. Her eyes widen, and I smile softly at her before leaning in to kiss her slowly, passionately.

Lovingly.

A hand touches my shoulder, and I pull back, looking at River. My dick twitches as I take in his flushed face and darkened eyes. Fuck.

"We're uhm, going to leave you two alone. Happy Valentine's Day, little vixen," he whispers. He leans in and kisses Raven for a few seconds, and I grip his hair, pulling him back.

Shocked, he tries to say something, but I don't care. I

crush him to me, thrusting my tongue in his mouth and kissing him as passionately as I did with Raven.

We're all an unconventional mess. The second she's free, Phoenix dives in and ravages Raven's mouth like he's fucking it.

I grind against her, and she digs her hand into my hair, using her other one to hold Phoenix to her. River twists his fingers with hers and I moan.

A tangle of limbs, lips, and hearts splayed across this wall. I wish we had a picture to save for later.

Pulling back from River's mouth, I tug at his lower lip before turning to look at Raven. I gently grip her chin and tilt her toward me, kissing her softly. Putting my forehead against hers, I meet her gaze. "What do you want, little bird? Me? Them? Yourself?"

I don't care what she tells me, as long as she gets off.

"Tell me, little bird, what do you want?" I ask her again when she doesn't reply fast enough.

Her eyes flit around the three of us before landing back on me. She slides her hands out of my hair, and I shiver as her nails scrape my skin. She grins cheekily and I shake my head. I watch attentively as she signs *All of you. Please.* She looks back up at me, cheeks red with embarrassment.

"You want us all to lay you out and make you come so hard you see stars, little bird?" I look at the other two, gripping tight to Raven's hips to still her continuous grinding. "Think we can do that, guys?"

River chuckles and looks at Raven. "I think we can do better than that." He leans in until his lips are near her ear. "Want to see a whole other galaxy, little vixen?"

Her breath hitches, and when he pulls back, she nods frantically.

"Upstairs," Phoenix orders.

I don't make a snarky retort. I simply wrap my arms back around Rae and walk with her down the hall and back up the stairs of the beach house. Goosebumps rise along my skin as she nips and sucks at my neck, my dick hardening to the point of pain.

"Close your eyes for a second," River says.

I'm assuming he's talking to Raven, but he comes up behind me and covers my eyes with his palms, the heat of him seeping into my back. "The hell?" I ask.

"Happy Valentine's Day, pup," he whispers in my ear, kissing my neck once before shuffling me forward.

Careful not to crash into the door, I step slowly inside of the room, my grip on Rae never wavering.

Footsteps cross the threshold behind us and the lock sounds after the door closes. "Open," Phoenix orders.

River frees my eyes.

The first thing I see is Raven as she turns her head to look around.

Then I see the master bedroom filled with candles and rose petals.

Raven shakes in my arms, tears falling down her cheeks.

I pull her further into me, cradling her head with one hand, rubbing her hip and holding her up with the other.

The lights are a deep red, but dim enough we aren't bathed in it. More like a sunset is setting all around us.

River rubs his palm along Raven's back, then slides it up, caressing my hand as he looks toward me. He grins, and then shrugs. "It was either you watching or participating tonight, but we wanted to set it up. Romantic. Hell," he says, laughing, "we thought she'd take you up here for herself. Which would have been fair."

"Shocked she didn't," Phoenix says. He steps forward and snatches Rae's chin in his fingers, tilting her toward him. He kisses her softly then pulls back, his warm eyes flitting between her tear-filled blues. "Who's in charge?" he asks her, with a quiet dominance lacing his tone.

She takes a shaky breath and points to herself.

"Good girl," he praises, and my dick twitches.

Rae notices, grinding against me.

I squeeze her hip in warning.

I'm going to embarrass myself the second she touches my dick, I swear.

"Put her down," Phoenix tells me, stepping back to take off his jacket and toss it onto the small bench in the corner of the room.

I slowly release Raven, letting her slide down my body, groaning when she purposefully rubs her hand along my dick. "Careful," I tell her.

She grins before spinning around the room to look at all of the little things she couldn't take in while I was holding her. A smile spreads those pretty lips as she steps forward and reaches for a chocolate covered strawberry. She stuffs it in her mouth, slow, intentionally locking her eyes on each of us in turn.

"Red," Phoenix says, a warning in his tone.

I raise a brow at him. "If she's in charge, doesn't that mean you can't punish her?"

"For now," he replies. "But there's always later."

I watch as she squeezes her thighs together at the comment, folding my arms across my chest.

River chuckles and leans into me, wrapping his arm around my waist and tugging me to him. "You're doing so good, pup."

I meet Rae's gaze across the room and as one we let out a heavy breath. My face burns from both River's praise and his blatant use of the name he gave me a few weeks after Rae banished me. It was a joke at first, but he noticed it made me hard, so he continued to call me pup when it was just us.

And it was just us a lot.

Rae finishes the strawberry in her mouth and steps toward all three of us, hips swaying, mesmerizing, enchanting us with their fluidity. She snaps her fingers and all three of us look at her in the same second. She grins, then signs, *Strip for me.*

Fuuuuck. No one told me her being in charge would get me going like this.

According to River's pained groan, no one told him either.

Phoenix arches a brow, keeping his stoic persona on as he undoes the buttons on his shirt.

Raven tries to stand still, but with how much I've watched her lately I can see the subtle shifting of her frame as she seeks the friction she needs.

Slowly, purposefully locking my eyes on hers as they drift between the three of us, I unbutton my own shirt.

One.

Two.

Three...

I grunt and impatiently rip the rest of the shirt apart, tossing it into the abyss. My pants follow, hitting the ground at the same time River's do.

We all stand there in our underwear, and Raven swallows hard, her shaky breathing the only sound for a few seconds.

Those too, she signs before pointing to our boxers. Her nostrils flare when we remove them.

When we're all standing there naked as the day we were born, she signs *Strip me, all of you*, then spins until her back faces us.

Phoenix points from me to her, indicating I go first.

Not missing an opportunity to touch her now that I can, I step forward, keeping my hips away, so my dick doesn't brush her. I might die if it does. Slowly, I lean in and place an open-mouthed kiss on her exposed shoulder. I slide my hand down her arm and feed my fingers through hers, squeezing as I take her skin between my teeth.

She shivers and tosses her head back, eyes closed tight.

I trail my free hand up her spine and push her hair off to the side before tracing my fingertips across her heated skin until I reach the zipper at the top of her dress.

River comes up on her other side and places kisses along her shoulder and neck.

Her entire body trembles between us, her free hand shooting out to tangle in River's hair, her other squeezing my fingers tightly.

"You're so fucking beautiful, Raven," Phoenix says as he steps up behind her. He moves my hand away from the zipper and places his palm against the back of her neck. Slowly, so slowly, he pulls it down until her dress parts from itself, opening to expose her body inch by delicious fucking inch. "We're all under your spell, sweetheart," he says so quietly, I wonder if she hears it.

As her dress falls to the floor, the lingerie she decided on is...sweet baby Satan...

I groan and pull back, keeping hold of her arm and stretching out to reveal more of her to us. "This is sexy as sin on you, Blue."

Her skin flushes pink as we take her in.

The lace is a deep green, almost black, and brings out the blue of her eyes. It caresses her breasts, decorating them more than supporting them. The bottom hardly covers her ass as it disappears between her thighs.

Neither piece hides a damn thing, and they look drawn on her skin.

My dick aches, and I reach down to squeeze it, relieving the smallest amount of pain her beauty puts me in.

"What do you want us to do now, little bird?" I ask her, my voice deep, husky, coated in lust.

Her eyes flash to me as she slides her hand from mine. She takes a breath and signs *I want to be full of you*, she blushes brighter, *All of you*. She looks around at us, as if she'd have scared us away.

"Are you sure?" Phoenix asks her.

She nods as she fidgets with the lace of her underwear.

I step forward and turn her by the chin, plastering my lips to hers in a scorching kiss and groaning when my dick rubs against the lace. The difference between it and her skin sends a full body shiver through me. I wrap my arms around her, pulling her close, effectively trapping my dick in the process.

She gasps, and I take advantage, thrusting my tongue into her mouth, fucking it like I want to fuck her. She slides her hands up my arms and around my neck, pulling me further into her.

River comes up to our side, his fingers trailing along both of our exposed skin. He leans toward me and feathers kisses from my shoulder to my neck, forcing a groan out of me like he always does.

Raven pulls from our kiss, her curiosity getting the better of her as she watches River play my body in the best of ways.

He meets her gaze and winks before sucking my earlobe into his mouth and tugging. He groans, and a desperate moan leaves me.

"Fuck," I breathe. "Please." I don't know why or who I'm begging, but I need to be heard.

Phoenix steps up behind Raven and tugs her hair off to one side, fisting it at the base of her skull. He leans in and places tender kisses on her neck much the same way River was doing to me.

I shift my hips, a drop of pre-cum landing on Rae's stomach, smearing between us.

She swallows hard, leaning her head back on Phoenix and meeting my gaze, her heavy-lidded eyes searing into my soul when she gasps at whatever he's doing.

"How do you want to be filled by us, Red? Do you want one of us in your ass?" He moves his hand behind her, her back arches, and I'm jealous, because he's gaining access to the last place untouched by me. "Your sweet pussy?" He shifts his hand lower, and the lace moves as he slides a finger along her slit. "Your mouth?" he asks, lifting his hand and shoving his fingers into her mouth, forcing her to lick off her own juices.

My cock weeps and River chuckles against my skin. I try to glare at him, but he grips my chin and makes me watch Raven with Phoenix, her eyes locked on me. She sucks his fingers so expertly, the phantom touch slides along my own body.

"Tell us, sweetheart. How can we fill you, fuck you, and leave you satisfied?" Phoenix asks as he pulls his hand from her mouth.

She takes a few deep breaths and backs out of our hold, undoing the lingerie as she moves. Once at the end of the bed, she lets the bra drop to the ground in front of her before pulling her underwear down.

I can't have that.

"Stop," I snap out, wincing. "Sorry," I say, meeting her gaze. "Can I take them off of you? With River?"

River removes his mouth from my skin, where I'm absolutely certain he's left a trail of hickeys. He slides his hand down my back and rubs circles above my ass, his breathing as heavy as mine as we wait for her response.

I think she's going to protest as she teases the waistband of her panties, but eventually she lets them go. Crooking a finger at us both, she nods her consent.

We walk up to either side of her and drop to our knees. I lean forward and place a kiss on her hip, chuckling when her legs shake, threatening to buckle. "Together," I whisper to River.

In a move fit for a porno, River and I lean toward her and grip the edge of her lacy underwear with our teeth. We slowly pull them down, our fingers feathering across her heated flesh.

Goosebumps line her skin, and I shoot a cocky grin at River when she practically flings the piece off her feet. She grips our hair, tugging until our faces are tilting up, gazes forced to the ceiling, but we only see her. She looks down on us like the queen she is, and I watch her as she frees River to beckon Phoenix into our party.

River grunts when she grabs our hair again, and I chance a look at his dick, mouth watering when he wraps his hand around it, squeezing much the same way I did a few minutes ago.

Body shaking, sweat forming on her skin, Raven sits down on the bed, releases our hair and slides herself up on the mattress. Her eyes betray how nervous she is.

What exactly is she thinking?

Phoenix brings a box of condoms and a bottle of lube with him, his own hand already working himself over as he stares down at Raven, splayed out and ready for us. His eyes flash to meet mine, then River's, before looking back at her. "Trust me, Red?" he asks her.

She swallows nervously and nods.

"River, on your back on the bed," Phoenix orders.

He does as he's told, quickly making himself comfortable. Phoenix tosses him a condom and he puts it on, eager to please anyone at this point so long as he gets his.

I chuckle as I watch him, and he shoots me a glare which quickly shuts me up.

Phoenix hands the bottle of lube to him. "You're the nicest dick for her to take in the back first, so be fucking gentle. You could ruin it for everyone with a single misstep. Got me?"

River's eyes flare wide and he looks at Raven, swallowing nervously. "You okay with this?"

She nods, then signs *Phoenix has been prepping me for this.* Her cheeks glow a brilliant mix of red and pink, and she looks down to avoid our gazes.

Phoenix moves to her side of the bed and grips her chin in his fingers, tilting her head up. "Don't be shy, Red. We're all here for you and your gorgeous body. What you desire is what we desire. Don't ever doubt that."

She nods as best she can in his grip, and when he releases her, she moves toward River tentatively at first, growing with confidence when he runs his hands up her sides.

He pulls her to him, capturing her mouth in a searing kiss. It's indecent the way he has his dick in a condom, ready for her, and she's sliding along his shaft, coating him in her own wetness. He uncaps the lube and practically pours it onto her ass before trailing his hands down and sticking a finger into her.

"Fuck," I groan, squeezing the head of my dick to keep myself from blowing all over the bed.

After a few minutes, River turns Raven around and sits her up. He hesitates before pulling her legs to rest on top of his, spreading her thighs wide. Slowly, as if scared he might break her, he enters the more forbidden spot inside of her.

I'm struggling to keep up, my attention split between the blissful pleasure pain on her face and the way River's dick disappears into her ass. Imagining it's me, but unsure which one of them I really want to be.

Everyone hears the second River's fully seated, because he blows out this shaky breath groaning loud enough I'm convinced he came. His face contorts in pain, and when Phoenix taps his leg and tells him to lay sideways on the bed, he growls in an un-River-like way. He still obliges, twisting until his and Raven's heads are at the edge of one side, and his feet are at the other.

I can't help but laugh, catching a glare I'm not scared of for the moment.

He's too occupied.

Raven's heavy pants fill the room as River slowly moves inside of her, checking on her constantly as they both adjust. Her hips eventually twitch, and she grinds on him. She looks up and meets my gaze, crooking that finger like the temptress she wants to be tonight.

"Condom," Phoenix says, tossing one in my direction.

"We're really fucking doing this, then?" I ask. My jaw drops when Raven nods, and I shake my head as I slide the latex over myself. I've watched enough porn to have an idea of how this works, but being a part of it? Seeing her lithe body stretch and mold to River's so obscenely? Watching as his dick thrusts in and out of her ass in such shallow movements, and her expecting me to fill the other hole?

I'm fucking dreaming.

Remembering the key to introducing something new to a scene–thanks Phoenix–I crawl along the bed and meet Raven's gaze as I hover over her. "What's your safeword, Rae?"

She drags her hands up my arms, leaves one on my bicep, and brings the other to my cheek. She taps three times, firm enough to catch my attention, then tugs me toward her.

"Color?" I grit out, struggling not to thrust inside of her when my dick accidentally rubs the outside of her, the heat forcing a groan from me.

She taps once.

I meet her gaze. "Green?" I ask, wanting to verify. To be sure. I have a feeling none of us will be the same after tonight. I don't know if I'm asking her for the green light for putting my dick inside of her, or if I'm asking her for permission for more.

She taps once, and tugs me down again, crashing her lips to mine.

I thrust into her in one push, slowly, carefully, until my balls slap against River's shaft and I can feel him through the thin veil inside of Raven.

"Oh, shiiit," River moans out. He trails one of his hands to my ass and digs his nails in, encouraging me to thrust.

I break from Rae's mouth and stare in awe at both of them, slowly thrusting in when River pulls out.

We spend a few minutes trading kisses, thrusts, loving touches and scratches.

Phoenix steps toward the bed and tilts Rae's head until it's hanging off the bed. He leans down and kisses her slowly, sensually, taking her gasps and heavy breaths for himself.

My hips stutter when her pussy squeezes me, and I grip at River's side with one hand, Rae's hip with the other. "This is…"

"Insanely hot?" River asks.

We both chuckle when I nod, unable to form proper words when he trails a hand down and rolls my balls between his fingers.

Shit.

"Open up for me, beautiful," Phoenix says to Raven. He uses one hand to help her open her mouth and the other to guide his dick down her throat.

"Oh," River says, tilting his head away.

I meet his gaze, and notice how close his face just was to Phoenix's balls.

We both laugh, but Raven clenches around us when he collars her throat, and our laughter turns into twin groans.

She reaches up to clutch at my hair, and moves her other arm to do the same to River. We look at her then, all of us. She's ethereal, twisted up and full of dick, the dim red lighting glowing across the flush of her body.

A sight to remember.

"Fuck, you're so gorgeous like this, little bird," I tell her, placing a kiss to a nipple, sucking it into my mouth when she clenches around me.

"Think you could get used to this, little vixen?" River asks, reaching between our bodies to caress her other breast.

She tries to nod, but it forces Phoenix's dick further

down her throat, and his groan has her clenching her cunt like a vise.

"You're such a beautiful little fuck toy, Red. I hope you know we plan to share you, break you, then put you back together afterward." He thrusts his dick into her mouth, rough enough to push her down onto me and River.

We both groan, our gazes clashing at the feel of the other sliding inside our girl.

It's hot as hell, and my balls are drawing up tight, threatening to send me over the edge too soon.

River shuts his eyes when Rae clenches around us again, and I rest my forehead on her breastbone, looking down at the sight of me entering her. I twist my hips, dragging against that sweet spot inside of her, and her entire body seizes. I repeat the process, and watch as River brings his hand between us, rubbing her clit in slow, firm circles.

Her back tries to arch, but he wraps an arm around her stomach, holding her to him.

Phoenix groans, and I look up in time to see him grab Raven's face. Her eyes water, and I can't help but collar her throat with my hand, feeling the way he slides in and out.

Fuck.

We're a sight to see, I'm sure.

Rae, so full of dick she's struggling to breathe.

River, dying with the tension in his body from holding back his release.

Phoenix, face-fucking Rae like he hates her.

Me, watching each piece of this convoluted puzzle

and forgetting my own part in it long enough for Rae's body to rock onto me.

We move in unison, fucking her, filling her, loving her.

We hold ourselves back until Rae's tears are streaming down her cheeks, mascara staining her pretty face, and lipstick is smearing around Phoenix's dick. She's struggling, holding her own release back.

"Come for us, sweet girl," River whispers, his own voice strained as he rubs furiously over her clit.

I drag my dick along that spot again and pinch her nipple between my teeth, heart pounding in my chest as Phoenix pushes as far as he can inside of her when she detonates.

We ride her through the waves of her orgasm, as her body twitches, writhes, freezes, but as she melts beneath us, we slam into her furiously.

Like Phoenix said, she's our little fuck toy, and as we ride her from one orgasm to the next, not letting her come down, she spasms again, squirting all over me and River.

That alone sends us careening past the edge.

I growl through the pain mixed with pleasure of my release, and lose my goddamn mind when River's dick twitches as he finishes. We both still and grind ourselves into Rae like animals until we can't move anymore.

Phoenix is last, tossing his head back as he comes down her throat, stroking her cheeks lovingly, smearing the mascara across her skin in the process.

The sound of our combined heavy breathing fills the room, and I plaster my body gently over Rae's, careful not to squish her. Sweat sticks our skin together as I rest my forehead between her breasts, but I ignore it as I place soft little kisses all across her chest up to her collarbone. When she's free of Phoenix, I plaster my lips to hers, devouring her until we're both extra breathless and have to pull away.

"Sit her up so she can have some water," Phoenix says as he moves back to the side of the bed and sits down near our cuddle session. "Easy," he says to River, warning in his tone.

"Got it," River says.

I ease out of Rae first, kissing her softly until I'm free of her. I sit up and hold my hand out for her, which she takes and squeezes.

"Slowly, Red," Phoenix tells her.

She nods, and I help her lift off River. When a look of pure anguish slams into her, I glare at him.

"She's fine," Phoenix says. "We should have waited to fill her like that until she'd had the other experience at least once. Drink up, sweetheart," he says, handing over a cold bottle.

She leans forward into my arms, her cheek resting against my chest as she chugs the water greedily.

I brush my fingers through her hair and hold her to me, placing kisses periodically to her skull, breathing her in. I'm still not sure if I'm dreaming or not.

Phoenix walks toward the en suite bathroom and River offers to take my condom with him as he follows.

"I love you, Blue," I whisper into her hair.

Her breath hitches, and she sits up slowly, tilting her head until our eyes meet. She doesn't have to say it, but when she signs *I love you, too, Green*, my heart finally settles back in my chest, a little beat up, but no worse for wear.

I kiss her languidly, massaging my fingers through her hair, until Phoenix comes back and demands to get Rae clean, River at his side with a warm towel.

An hour later, after we've all drank enough water to appease Phoenix the Dom, we comfortably splay out on the bed. Rae lays in the center with me on one side and Phoenix on the other. River slides in behind me, wrapping his arm over my waist, his hand resting on Rae's stomach.

It's blissful, warm, and we all easily drift off, satiated physically and emotionally.

TO: RMHILL@MYEMAIL.COM FROM: UPINFLAMES@MYEMAIL.COM SUBJECT: GOODBYES SUCK...

I'm not gonna lie, I can already feel how tense you are through the screen, Red.

I'm sorry.

I'm deleting this email before I leave today.

I should be excited about getting out of here, but because I'm effectively losing you in the process?

Sucks ass, and it's tempting to do something to keep myself in here.

I want you to do a few things for me, Red. I won't be able to get a response, so I won't even know if you do, but you will know whether or not you do, so here's the list. Take it or leave it.

- Get out of here. Do your best to do it sooner than later. For your own good.

- Go to CU. You mentioned it was your dream school with your ex best friend. Why not go anyway? Dreams aren't always dependent on the other people in them.

- Keep up learning sign language. Others might not know it, but it will help you in the long run.

- Grow. Run. Breathe. Fight. Whatever you have to do to get through this dark spot in your life, I want you to exist in the emotions, then kick their ass and just be you.

The you I've got to know is so special, and whoever gets to get to know you next is lucky.

One final goodbye,
Flames

raven

The bed shifts, and cold attacks my frame.

I shiver, but warmth covers me again when arms wrap around me from behind. Another body leans against the opposite side. Sighing, I nuzzle my face in the neck of the guy in front of me, inhaling the smells of the beach, and drift back into a deep sleep.

"PIERCE, I don't know where the fuck you are, but the only reason I'm not more mad right now is because you had the decency to leave us the fucking jeep. Call me right the fuck back, text us, something. Not fucking cool to leave in the middle of the night, man." River pushes hard on the button on his cell like it'll satisfy him, then slams it onto the counter.

I wince when it cracks, and nervously nibble on my sandwich.

"He'll be fine, River," Phoenix says, patting him on the back a few times as he passes. "We'll get cleaned up, and if he's not heard from by checkout, we'll call some of our guys to look for him on our way home."

River grunts before bending down and pressing his forehead onto the cold countertop. His shoulders rise and fall with deep breaths, and I lean over, running a hand through his hair.

I don't know where Pierce would go in the middle of the night like that, especially after the things we did. The way they worshipped my body while simultaneously treating me like a fuck toy? Yeah, we need to repeat it.

Phoenix sighs as he sits next to me. He slides my stool toward his, close enough our thighs touch, and leans down. I meet him halfway for a soft and sweet kiss. His fingers brush across my face, pushing back a strand of stray hair. "You okay?"

I nod, chew my lip, then shrug. Dropping my sandwich back on my plate, I lift my hands and sign *I'm worried. What would he have to do in the middle of the night? What if Maxwell called? What if–*

Phoenix grabs my hands, halting my movements. "I called Lance. He said he had no idea where Pierce went. We kinda...gave the guys the night off."

"Stupid fucking idea now," River says, standing. "Good fucking job, River. Give the bodyguards the night off and hope for the best. Ha!" He throws his hands up and storms out of the beach house, the glass door rattling as it slams shut.

My whole body radiates pain as I shift to move off the stool, and Phoenix pulls me back into my seat. I watch, helpless, as River rages to himself in the middle of the beach.

"He'll be okay," Phoenix whispers, though the concern in his voice settles nothing in me.

I don't know if he means River or Pierce, but after trying to contact the latter all morning, and only having an hour left until checkout?

A sick feeling settles in my stomach that he, in fact, is not going to be okay.

I turn back to my sandwich, taking a small bite as I scroll through my phone.

Hey. Where are you?

Sent at 9am

Unread.

Is something wrong? Is this not working for you anymore?

Sent at 10am

Nothing.

Pierce, please at least talk to me about it. Don't ditch like this.

Sent at 10:30am

The last text, sent but unseen, hurts the most.

I don't know why you left, where you are, or what's happened...but I want you to know that I love you. I love you so much it constantly hurts. If it's something with the guys, or how this relationship has taken this turn to include us all...can we talk it out? I don't know if I could give them up...but I know for you? For you, I think I could. You're the love of my life, Pierce Jackson. You don't get to ditch out after ten years. Please...come back. To us. To me.

Phoenix's phone rings, and he swallows his own bite of food before picking it up. "Phoenix West."

I can't make out the words on the other end, so I dig back into my sandwich, shifting my eyes to River outside, hoping he comes inside soon.

A storm is raging, and my gut is yelling at me. Something is terribly wrong.

"Uh, I'm sorry, let me put you on speaker so our girlfriend can hear this, too. That okay?" Phoenix asks, resting his arm on the top rail of my stool. He brushes his fingers along my back in soothing circles.

When I look up and meet his gaze, the tension on his face scares me.

He sets the phone down on the counter, turning on the speakerphone.

The door to the patio opens and River steps inside, looking confused when the voice comes through.

"Okay, yeah," a man says, his voice deep. "Hi there. Again, my name is Drake Thompson. I'm with the Cobalt City Morgue. This is the number I was told to call with any concerns, and well," he clears his throat, sounding uncomfortable. We all sit a little taller. "I have a body you need to see."

My world tilts on its axis again.

The boys are shouting something, but their voices are fuzzy.

I never noticed how beautiful the ocean looks. I wanted to spend more time watching it while we were here. The winter storm is finally rolling in, bringing the tide with it, only to push it away.

Someone grabs me, and I let them.

A smile stretches my lips when snowflakes land on the window. I think I like snow now. Used to hate it. Too cold.

I tilt sideways, but River catches me before I can crash to the floor. He kisses my forehead as he carries me to the couch, cradling me in his arms as he sits down.

His eyes really are a gray storm, matching the winter clouds outside. I raise a hand and brush my fingers across his cheeks.

They're wet.

Is he crying?

"It's okay," he whispers, "it's going to be okay," he repeats.

Over and over.

I can't help but think he's trying to reassure himself more than me.

"We'll be there in three hours," Phoenix says after a brief pause. "Yeah. Okay. Storm shouldn't pose a problem. Yep. See you soon." He hangs up with a loud curse.

River tenses beneath me, his hands digging into my skin. "You should try–"

"Already on it," Phoenix grits out. He taps something on his screen before holding it back up to his ear.

Time stands still.

"FUCK!" he shouts, stuffing his phone into his pocket. He runs his fingers roughly through his hair, then marches up the stairs.

"Where are you going?" River asks, his voice shaking.

Phoenix stops in the middle of the staircase and looks back at us, worry and anger contorting his face. "I'm going to clean up. Get our shit together. You, uh, you take care of Rae. Make sure she doesn't pass out. Hydrate. Get dressed. Then we're headed back."

"You think it's him?" River asks, his voice cracking at the last second.

Phoenix meets his eyes, then mine, his face crumbling. A rare tear slides from his lashes. If I was in any better shape, I'd rush forward and console him, but I'm not, so I don't. He doesn't deny our own suspicions, simply shrugging before turning to walk up the stairs.

AWKWARD and tense silence fills the jeep, only made worse by the frigid air invading the car in the last half hour.

"It's too motherfucking cold in here," River snaps. "Turn on the heat."

"Grab a blanket or something," Phoenix says, gripping the steering wheel until it creaks.

River unbuckles his seatbelt and climbs between the seats. He leans forward and switches on the heater, turning the fans all the way up.

Uncomfortably hot air blasts me and Phoenix in the face and I cough. He looks over his shoulder to glare at River, swerving to the left, threatening to smack into another car. "Get the fuck back in your seat and stop being a fucking pansy."

I reach for the steering wheel and hold it in place, ensuring we don't swerve again, glaring at the side of Phoenix's head, needing him to pay attention to the road. He finally does, narrowing his eyes at me until I remove my hands. I sit back in the seat and check my phone for messages from Pierce again.

> Please tell me you're okay at least. Even if you've left...just tell me you're okay. Breathing. Alive...

Nothing.

Still. Fucking. Nothing.

My heart aches with worry, and I curl up into a ball, wrapping the winter coat he left behind around my body and inhaling his scent.

He has to be okay.

I just got him back.

A tear trails its way down my cheek, landing on his coat and creating a dark spot, much like the one growing in my heart.

"THIS PLACE ISN'T CREEPY AT ALL," River remarks as we walk up the steps to the funeral home.

"It's a place where dead people go to get prettied up, and living people go to pay for it," Phoenix tells him. "Of course it's fucking creepy. Death is a scam for the living."

"That's such a depressing thought. Why are we so depressed, Nixy boy?" River grins, big and fake, as we enter the building. "It's not like one of our best fucking friends is possibly in here, dead as a fucking doorknob."

After trying to call Pierce one last time, I shove my phone back into my coat pocket. I stomp my way ahead of Phoenix and River, folding my arms around my middle. I try to keep myself together. It's become harder and harder to breathe the closer we've come to this fucking place, and I'm about to knock them both out for their constant bickering.

"Nice, now she's mad," Phoenix grumbles from behind me.

I spin around. *You're acting like toddlers*, I sign. *Grow up. Everything changes if Pierce is on that table, do you understand? My soul wouldn't be able to handle it.*

I've dissociated much of this trip, but right now, when I'm barely minutes away from finding one of the loves of my life on a cold table in a morgue?

Reality slams into me, hard.

A sob works its way up my throat, and I nearly crumble to the ground.

"Shit," River says. His footsteps pound against the tile

until he reaches me, gathering me in his arms. He plasters kiss after kiss to my temple, my forehead, my hair. "I'm sorry. I'm so sorry."

Phoenix kisses my cheek, before caressing it with his palm. "Let's go down there and find out, yeah? We've got you either way, Rae. I promise."

"I promise, too," River says, looking between us both.

I take a deep breath, allowing the sharp bite of cold winter air to slice into my lungs, then nod.

We all walk to the desk. A young woman is sitting with her biker boots propped up, headphones on. She's bobbing her head, and her bright blue hair is falling in front of her heavy shadowed eyes.

She doesn't see us at first, consumed in something on her phone, but Phoenix pushes at her boots, and they fall, slamming hard onto the floor. "What the fu–" she shouts, but when she sees us, she sits up and fixes herself as best she can. "Welcome to Cobalt City Morgue. How can I help you?"

"We got a call from Drake Thompson a few hours ago. Came as fast as we could," Phoenix tells her.

She nods her head and pulls her phone up in front of her face. At first I think she's ignoring us, but she sets it down and smiles. "He'll be right with you." She puts her headphones on and kicks her boots back up on the desk, effectively dismissing us.

A few minutes go by while I lean against River, my future without Pierce passing in front of my eyes.

A future I don't want to entertain, but very well might have to.

"Mr. West?" a deep voice calls.

We all straighten up and turn toward him.

"That's me," Phoenix says, extending a hand.

The guy introduces himself as Drake, and they shake. His blonde hair is in disarray, falling over his forehead and into his hazel eyes. He takes in our group, then waves us after him. "I was told to call you when someone of interest hit my table. Had a list of names to keep tabs on. Unfortunately," he says, escorting us down to the basement, "I had a familiar face and name come up today."

The cold which seeps into my body has nothing to do with the temperature.

We enter through another door at the bottom of the staircase, and my stomach tries to revolt. I hold a hand to my mouth, my heart pounding hard enough I can't hear anything else. A new chill hits me first, and when a body covered in a sheet appears in my vision my knees buckle.

River catches me, pulling me to stand and taking hold of my hand. Phoenix grabs on from my other side.

They both walk with me behind Drake.

He looks apologetic as he puts gloves on and moves around to the other side of the table. "This, well, it might be jarring. Prepare yourselves."

I meet his gaze as I squeeze both River's and Phoenix's hands to the point of pain, then I nod.

Drake lifts the sheet off the table, revealing the body to us. When I finally muster the courage to take a look...all of the air whooshes from my lungs.

**To be continued in A Conspiracy of Ravens book 3
coming early 2023!**

acknowledgments

To my husband, thank you for all of your support in the last six months. It has been a whirlwind, and we have had plenty of downs while I was writing this one. Here's to moving up.

To my kids, while you shouldn't be reading this unless I've handed it to you just to show you this paragraph, I hope that one day you'll pick it up and enjoy it. Who knows. Your excitement for me and all of your help (even just packaging swag packs) is what fuels me daily. Thanks for being so awesome!

MiMi, Kennedy, Poppy, Rebecca, you guys are some of the most influential to my author career. I will always tell you four how thankful I am for your friendships.

Drea, I was not expecting you. You have been a catalyst to some of my hardest moments the last few weeks. Thank you for being my Emotional Support Drea!

Kendall, you're still a pain in my butt, but you've been immensely helpful. Thank you.

To the Book Witch, Raeleen, you jumped right the hell in and did the thing at the last second even though I told you not to (lol I can't tell you not to do anything). Thank you and I look forward to working with you forever, and ever, and ever, and ever...Wait, where are you going?!

To my BETA Readers, holy heck you guys did amazing. Thanks for loving on my books the way you do. You make everything that much better.

To my ARC and Street Teams, thank you for always shouting to the rest of the world about me. It means a hell of a lot.

And to you, dear reader, thank you. Thank you for reading Phoenix Flames. I hope you had a wild and intense ride and that you're okay after that cliffhanger. Just by reading this book, you've done a lot to help me continue on this life path.

Thank you. Thank you. Thank you.

Sincerely, Shelby Lee <3

also by shelby lee

A Conspiracy of Ravens

Pierce Me

Phoenix Flames

ACoR 3 (Early 2023)

ACoR 4 (Mid 2023)

Novellas

Overnight: An ACoR Spin-off Novella

Shelby Lee is a dark romance author specializing in the act of trauma dumping into her own stories in the hopes of eventually healing herself, and possibly others, along the way. She resides in a semi-small town in Nebraska with her husband, two kids, and guinea pigs.

When she's not writing, she's mentoring youth in the community on the off chance she just might leave the world a better place than she found it.

Other than that, you can probably find her on TikTok.

Find me on linktr.ee/authorshelbylee

facebook.com/authorshelbylee

instagram.com/@authorshelbylee

tiktok.com/@authorshelbylee

patreon.com/AuthorShelbyLee